"If you've been wa
futuristic romanc
Robin D. Owens
—Ja

Praise for the futuristic fantasy of Robin D. Owens

Heart Choice

"The romance is passionate, the characters engaging, and the society and setting exquisitely crafted." —*Booklist*

"Character-driven story, brilliant dialogue . . . terrific writing with a very realistic and sensual romance, make *Heart Choice* a fantastic read." —*Romance Reviews Today*

"Maintaining the 'world-building' for science fiction and character-driven plot for romance is near impossible. Owens does it brilliantly." —*The Romance Reader*

"[A] well-written, humor-laced, intellectually and emotionally involving story, which explores the true meaning of family and love." —*Library Journal*

"*Heart Choice* is a wonderful book to lose yourself in for a while! I'll be anxiously awaiting the next book in this wonderfully imaginative series." —*Romance Junkies*

Heart Duel

"[A] sexy story . . . Readers will enjoy revisiting this fantasy-like world filled with paranormal talents." —*Booklist*

"An exhilarating love story . . . The delightful story line is cleverly executed . . . Owens proves once again that she is among the top rung of fantasy romance authors with this fantastic tale." —Harriet Klausner

"With engaging characters, Robin D. Owens takes readers back to the magical world of Celta . . . The characters are engaging, drawing the reader into the story and into their lives. They are multilayered and complex and grow into exceptional people." —*Romance Reviews Today*

continued . . .

Heart Thief

"I loved *Heart Thief*! This is what futuristic romance is all about. Robin D. Owens writes the kind of futuristic romance we've all been waiting to read; certainly the kind that I've been waiting for. She provides a wonderful, gripping mix of passion, exotic futuristic settings, and edgy suspense. If you've been waiting for someone to do futuristic romance right, you're in luck; Robin D. Owens is the author for you."
—Jayne Castle

"The complex plot and rich characterizations, not to mention the sexy passion . . . make this a must-read . . . I just wish Robin D. Owens wrote faster. I hope she's got a huge pile of ideas for future Celtan stories, and I for one can't wait to go back."
—*The Romance Reader*

"Owens spins an entrancing tale . . . Although the setting is fresh and totally captivating, it is the well-developed characters, both human and animal, that make this story memorable. Crafty villains, honorable, resourceful protagonists, and sentient pets drive the plot of this fast-paced, often suspenseful romantic adventure. As have others before her (e.g., Anne McCaffrey, Marion Zimmer Bradley), Owens has penned a stunning futuristic tale that reads like fantasy and is sure to have crossover appeal to both SF and fantasy fans."
—*Library Journal*

"Owens has crafted a fine romance that is also a successful science fantasy yarn with terrific world-building."
—*Booklist*

"A tremendous science fiction romance that affirms what many fans thought after reading the prequel (*HeartMate*): that Robin D. Owens is one of the sub-genre's giant stars. The story line is faster than the speed of light, but more important is this world's society seems so real that psychic powers feel genuine . . . [a] richly textured other-planetary romance."
—*BookBrowser*

Praise for

HeartMate

Winner of the 2002 RITA Award
for Best Paranormal Romance
by the Romance Writers of America

"Engaging characters, effortless world-building, and a sizzling romance make this a novel that's almost impossible to put down."
—*The Romance Reader*

"Fantasy romance with a touch of mystery . . . Readers from the different genres will want Ms. Owens to return to Celta for more tales of HeartMates."
—*Midwest Book Review*

"*HeartMate* is a dazzling debut novel. Robin D. Owens paints a world filled with characters who sweep readers into an unforgettable adventure with every delicious word, every breath, every beat of their hearts. Brava!"
—Deb Stover, award-winning author of *A Moment in Time*

"A gem of a story . . . sure to tickle your fancy."
—Anne Avery, author of *All's Fair*

"It shines and fans will soon clamor for more . . . A definite keeper!"
—*The Bookdragon Review*

"This story is magical . . . doubly delicious as it will appeal to both lovers of fantasy and futuristic romance. Much room has been left for sequels."
—*Paranormal Romance Reviews*

Titles by Robin D. Owens

HEARTMATE
HEART THIEF
HEART DUEL
HEART CHOICE
HEART QUEST

Heart Quest

Robin D. Owens

BERKLEY SENSATION, NEW YORK

THE BERKLEY PUBLISHING GROUP
Published by the Penguin Group
Penguin Group (USA) Inc.
375 Hudson Street, New York, New York 10014, USA
Penguin Group (Canada), 90 Eglinton Avenue East, Suite 700, Toronto, Ontario M4P 2Y3, Canada
(a division of Pearson Penguin Canada Inc.)
Penguin Books Ltd., 80 Strand, London WC2R 0RL, England
Penguin Group Ireland, 25 St. Stephen's Green, Dublin 2, Ireland (a division of Penguin Books Ltd.)
Penguin Group (Australia), 250 Camberwell Road, Camberwell, Victoria 3124, Australia
(a division of Pearson Australia Group Pty. Ltd.)
Penguin Books India Pvt. Ltd., 11 Community Centre, Panchsheel Park, New Delhi—110 017, India
Penguin Group (NZ), Cnr. Airborne and Rosedale Roads, Albany, Auckland 1310, New Zealand
(a division of Pearson New Zealand Ltd.)
Pengin Books (South Africa) (Pty.) Ltd., 24 Sturdee Avenue, Rosebank, Johannesburg 2196,
South Africa

Penguin Books Ltd., Registered Offices: 80 Strand, London WC2R 0RL, England

HEART QUEST

A Berkley Sensation Book / published by arrangement with the author

PRINTING HISTORY
Berkley Sensation mass-market edition / September 2006

Cover art by Voth / Barrall.
Cover design by George Long.
Interior text design by Kristin del Rosario.

For information, address: The Berkley Publishing Group,
a division of Penguin Group (USA) Inc.,
375 Hudson Street, New York, New York 10014.

ISBN: 0-425-21084-7

BERKLEY SENSATION®
Berkley Sensation Books are published by The Berkley Publishing Group,
a division of Penguin Group (USA) Inc.,
375 Hudson Street, New York, New York 10014.
BERKLEY SENSATION is a registered trademark of Penguin Group (USA) Inc.
The "B" design is a trademark belonging to Penguin Group (USA) Inc.

PRINTED IN THE UNITED STATES OF AMERICA

10 9 8 7 6 5 4 3 2 1

To my editor, Cindy Hwang.
There are not enough words to express my thanks.

Acknowledgments

My Critique Buddy, Anne Tupler, whose idea it was, lo those many years ago . . .

My first-draft readers, critique buddies, and proofreaders: Kay Bergstrom (Cassie Miles), Maureen Kiely, Peggy Waide, Janet Lane, Steven Moores, Denee Cody, Sue Hornick, Alice Kober, Diana Rowe, and Rose Beetem.

My agent, Deidre Knight.

Burton Silver and Heather Busch, authors of the book *Why Paint Cats*: www.whypaintcats.com.

Those who made the labyrinth in the carousel house of the old Elitch Gardens.

Excerpts and other fun information about Celta and *Heart Quest* at: www.robindowens.com or www.robinowens.com.

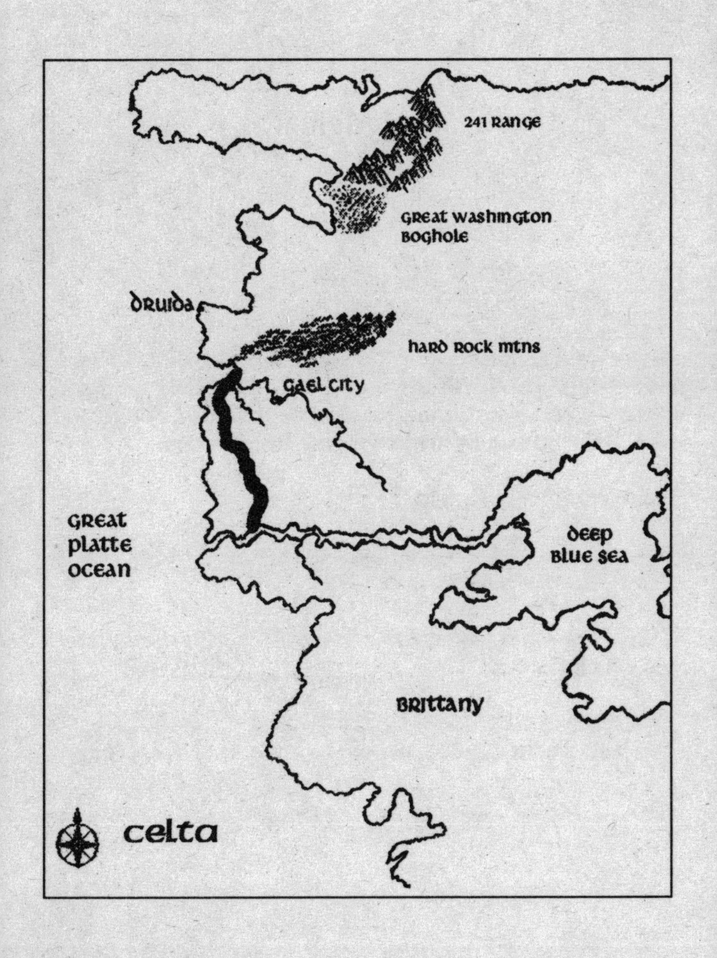
241 Range
Great Washington
Boghole
Druida
hard rock mtns
Gael City
Great
platte
ocean
deep
blue sea
Brittany
celta

One

Druida City, Celta,
405 years after Colonization, late autumn

Black Ilex Winterberry watched his HeartMate from the shadows. He shouldn't approach her, but knew that he would.

Trif Clover was irresistible to him. Even from here he could see her deep green eyes fixed in concentration. She yanked a strand of dark brown hair behind her ear and drew in an audible breath. He would have treated her hair with respect, smoothed it between his fingers. . . .

She wore a tunic trous suit of deep green that matched her eyes. Since the tunic was just above her knees and the trous legs weren't outrageously bloused, the clothing marked her as a middle-class woman who worked for her living.

His mouth tightened when Trif performed her little ritual as she hunted for her mate. She held the charmkey she'd fashioned against the door of GrandLord Ginger's mansion and intoned, "HeartMate." It was common knowledge that a HeartMate could fashion a key and open his or her love's door, and Trif was obviously on a quest to find him.

He wished he could end her search.

They'd connected emotionally three years before, during her last Passage—the fever fugues that freed her Flair psi power. Her Flair was unstable, and they'd linked a few times since in dreams. Each instance left Ilex aroused and wanting, and yearning for more than her body. But he hadn't known whether she'd believed the connection was anything other than an erotic dream with an unknown lover.

He had made it a point to find her—and now she was trying to do the same. But he was an experienced hunter.

He'd kept his distance from her. He was far too old, more than double her age. Worse, he had a touch of prophetic talent and had experienced a brief vision a long time ago that his life would be relatively short, nothing near the two centuries of the most aged Celtans.

Furthermore, he sensed he had only a couple more years left, and he refused to have this lovely, vibrant *young* woman die within a year of his own death, as always occurred with HeartMates who'd wed. He couldn't bear to cut her life short.

Her face fell when the door refused to open; then she sighed, looked at the key in her hand, shrugged, and straightened her shoulders. "No HeartMate here. Too bad. Perhaps the next house. Stay optimistic," she murmured.

"What are you doing, Trif Clover?" he asked.

She jumped and flushed. Her gaze went first to his guardsman's insignia instead of his face, causing him a twinge of emotional pain that she didn't think of him as a man first.

"Oh, I, uh . . ." She whipped her hand holding the key behind her back and increased the charm of her smile.

Ilex shook his head.

Her shoulders slumped a little. "You know."

"Is it worth your and my time for me to tell you it can be dangerous wandering the streets of Druida alone?"

She looked startled. "Druida's safe, especially Noble Country."

Noble Country was the portion of Druida where the highest nobles, including the FirstFamilies—the descendants of the colonists who'd funded the trip from Earth to a new home—lived. Here the estates were huge, hidden behind greeniron gates. The streets were wide and tree-lined.

It didn't help his ego that she hoped her HeartMate was

noble. But that wasn't the real problem. The true difficulty was that there had been two murders—of young, extremely Flaired people whose psi powers were unstable. Murders that Ilex's superiors wanted kept quiet for the moment.

"No one's safe all the time. Come with me, Trif." He took her arm and let the touch of her shoot through him, heat his blood. The scent of her came too, the light fragrance of spring flowers.

When she smiled up at him and followed willingly, he suppressed the urge to kiss her.

"Please don't continue testing your charmkey," he said neutrally, leading her down the drive to the walled entrance into the mansion grounds and the wide-open gates.

Ilex frowned. Most of the Nobles he knew were paranoid about security and their gates would be locked and spell-shielded. His recent "cases" had included the crème de la crème of Celtan society, the FirstFamilies. Those people were obsessive about most things.

Trif stopped and looked over her shoulder wistfully. "GrandLord Ginger is a widower and he has *three* sons, not to mention all the other unattached male Gingers working in the household."

"Ah. A good source of men."

She shrugged. "I suppose you think my quest is stupid, like everyone else. But it's *my* business."

"Not when you trespass on Noble land."

"Has anyone reported me?"

"Well, the Gingers and their neighbors won't this afternoon," he said dryly. "Most nobles are attending a ritual at GreatCircle Temple."

"Will you report me?"

"No. Not yet." He glanced at his wrist timer. "I'm off duty now. Let me take you home."

"Must you?"

"I think so. It's a *neighborly* thing to do."

He'd moved into her apartment building, MidClass Lodge, a couple of months ago, *after* he'd heard she'd gone door to door there, beginning her search for her HeartMate. And after the first murder.

They had reached the entrance pillars when the wind

changed—and brought the smell of death. His Flair surged. He sensed *wrongness* indicating a crime. His psi sharpened all his other senses until he knew the death was human, and murdered, and the body lay a few meters away.

Ilex tightened his grip on Trif and urged her out of the estate and onto the sidewalk. He shot a glance up and down the street. Nothing.

T'Blackthorn, Ilex shouted mentally to the tracker. They were distant relatives. Ilex had hoped there wouldn't be another death, but had decided to contact Blackthorn if the unspeakable occurred. The guards would need powerfully Flaired people to help.

Trif looked up at Ilex, frowning. "You shouted to T'Blackthorn?"

He dropped her arm. They were connected and he didn't want her to sense all that was happening.

Guardsman Winterberry? a strained whisper said into Ilex's mind.

Who speaks?

The T'Blackthorn Residence. T'Blackthorn is out of Druida on a rescue mission.

Ilex was surprised that he'd been able to mentally reach Blackthorn's sentient home. Something to think on later. *Thank you.*

Should I inform Lady D'Blackthorn of your call?

No. This is guard business. He hesitated. *Could you send a glider to pick up Lady Blackthorn's cuz at GrandLord Ginger's?*

If this is urgent, Lady D'Ash visits. She can teleport there.

Fine. Actually, it was a barely acceptable solution, since three women's curiosity would be stirred, but Ilex wanted Trif out of here *now* so he could investigate.

Lady Danith D'Ash has been informed of your request. Blessings, Guardsman.

And to you, he replied.

Trif studied him narrowly, arms crossed over her breasts. "What's going on?"

"Danith D'Ash is coming to teleport you to another location."

Incredulity flashed in Trif's eyes. "Why?"

"It's best you leave immediately."

"Something is going on—isn't it?" She tipped her head. "There's been a—a peculiar atmosphere in the city." Her brow furrowed as she considered. Then she shook her head. "I don't have such Flair that I can determine the cause. But you do, don't you." She reached out and touched his arm. "You're a hunter."

"And I must hunt. Now." He had to get her away from the scene. She had nothing to do with the death, and he had to start procedure on another murder.

"Will you tell me—"

"I'll tell you to be careful. Very careful. Abandon your quest for the moment, Trif."

Her lips thinned. "I think we should discuss this."

At that moment, a faint pop announced that Lady D'Ash had arrived. "Trif!"

Trif grasped Ilex's hand, squeezed. "Meet me in the caff-house in the basement shops of MidClass Lodge at Mid-Evening Bell." Then she turned to D'Ash.

"Greetyou, Danith."

The petite GreatLady's gaze went first to Ilex, caution in her eyes, though she smiled. She dipped a head to him. "Greetyou, Winterberry."

"Merry meet," he said—not words of greeting, but cutting off all comment by impatiently starting the ritual farewell ceremony.

"Come along, Trif, I have a present for you," Danith D'Ash said, taking Trif 's hand. "It's waiting at T'Ash Residence."

"Really? Zow," Trif said.

"And merry part," Trif and Danith said in unison to Ilex.

"And merry meet again," Ilex murmured.

"Tonight!" Trif shouted, then winked out of sight as Danith D'Ash teleported her away.

Thank the Lady and Lord they were gone and safe! Ilex stepped back into GrandLord Ginger's estate. He touched the gate. "By order of Guardsman Black Ilex Winterberry, I seal you to all."

The greeniron gates clanged shut.

He lifted his hands and sent his Flair searching for the body. His psi flowed around plant life and found a large corpse, probably male. Evanescent traces told him that three live people had been there briefly, less than three minutes—probably to drop the body. This had occurred not more than a septhour and a half ago.

The body was several meters to his left—and someone else was there.

Halt! His spell would immobilize the person. He ran toward the essence of death, his Flair deluging him with information that he'd later recall and sort out.

He burst into a tiny clearing. As he'd feared, the body of a young man lay sprawled faceup. Hunched over the body, his face set with fury, was Tinne Holly.

"A fighting Holly standing over a dead body," Ilex murmured. With a snap of his fingers, Ilex mitigated a portion of the spell and said, "You may speak."

Tinne dragged in a breath. "What are you doing here?" he spit out.

Raising his brows, Ilex said, "Investigating. And you?"

"I was looking for him!"

"Time passes and trace evidence can vanish quickly. Let me do my job." First, observation. Ilex looked down at the naked body of the young ginger-haired male victim. Not a mark on him. His skin was pale, his light blue eyes glassy. The scent of death was recent. And it hadn't occurred here; none of the plant life sent out psi terror-trembles of recent violence.

"Step back, Tinne. Leave the area as undisturbed as possible. Don't touch him." Waving a hand, Ilex freed him from the rest of the spell.

"Don't touch him! Gib Ginger is—was—one of my best friends."

"I'm sorry. Please retrace your steps so I can use my Flair to record everything possible. Every instant, information is lost."

Muttering, Tinne glided back a few steps. "This is where I 'ported."

"Thank you." Ignoring his distant relative, Ilex took a personal sensorball, a clear crystal orb he could curl his fingers around, from his guard belt-bag.

He settled into a light trance, extending all his senses, pushing his Flair for the best record he could make. He didn't think, didn't evaluate, merely used all his senses to compile everything around him. This included the fading recent muscle-memories of the body, the infinitesimal pressure of others' fingers upon the skin—how the body hair lay, whether any follicle had been disturbed and how.

Ilex distanced himself from the last echo of emotions of the body, the last sensory impressions. The last thoughts of the brain were already gone.

His sensorball noted the strange scent surrounding the corpse—a mixture Ilex could not identify, but which was recorded now for further analysis.

He scanned the scene, the area, drew in as much data as possible about the three people who'd dumped the body. He wished he could see tracks, like T'Blackthorn, but the killers had spent little time here, at least one of them had enough Flair to teleport. So tracking Flair wouldn't have been much use in this instance. Too bad.

When he reached the limit of his Flair—and when he knew the trace clues had disappeared, Ilex stopped and rose from the light trance. His sensorball was black with the load of information.

A white-faced Tinne was grimly recording the scene himself with an image sphere.

"I'll take that for the investigation," Ilex said, walking past the body and sweeping the sphere from Tinne's hands, stowing it in a pocket.

Tinne frowned, but said nothing.

"And now you can tell me why you are here." Ilex stepped close so he blocked Tinne's view of the corpse.

"I was worried." Tinne let out a shaky breath and speared his fingers through his silver-gilt hair. "Gib was supposed to have lunch with my wife and me at T'Holly Residence. He didn't show. I got worried."

"How did you know to look for Gib here instead of along the main gliderway?"

Tinne's face tightened in arrogant lines proclaiming that he hailed from the highest class. He looked down his straight nose. "You know better than that, Black Ilex. I'm a Holly, I can sense death as well as you can." His shoulders shifted.

"The recent demise was human. I looked. I found Gib." He swallowed. "This isn't the first of my friends who has died under odd circumstances lately. There's another."

Ilex stilled, then wrapped a hand around Tinne's elbow, ready to move him on so Ilex could shield the body and signal his Chief.

Tinne jerked his arm away and settled into his balance, and Ilex knew nothing short of brute force would move him.

"How many more, Winterberry? And why hasn't the guard notified the FirstFamilies of these killings?"

Staring at him coolly, Ilex said, "Currently, you haven't been cleared to received any information. Furthermore, you could be a suspect in this killing."

Complete shock crossed Tinne's face and he straightened. "No."

"We're going to my office," Ilex said.

"I had nothing to do with Gib's death!"

"I'm inclined to believe you, but it would be best if you were cleared by a truth-sensor."

Tinne looked briefly interested, then shook his head. "I should be with the Gingers. My word of honor that I'll drop by in a couple of hours." His mouth flattened. "And we are all too aware what happens to a Holly who breaks their word of honor."

Ilex said, "You don't seem to realize that you're in trouble."

With a shrug, Tinne said, "A truth-sensor will clear me." Face hardening, he continued. "I want to know what's going on, and the FirstFamilies will definitely hear about this from me."

"As you please. You may direct them to my Chief, Sawyr, who is in charge of this matter."

Grimacing, closing his eyes and opening them, Tinne said, "Oh, man. That guy believes silence is a religion. He might give a few of the highest FirstFamily Heads like my father and GrandLady D'Grove some facts, but I won't hear a word. *And it's my generation that is being murdered, isn't it? It's murder and it's men my age.*"

They locked stares. Tinne could be useful, and no dark taint of recent death clung to him. Finally, Ilex inclined his head. "Yes, another man your age was killed."

"What's going on?" asked Tinne softly. His hand rested on

his blazer gun—not a threat to *him,* Ilex thought, but a willingness to fight to discover the killers. An eagerness to destroy those who'd murdered his friends.

There would be no keeping this quiet. At the very least, the FirstFamilies Council would have to be told. Right now, reports had only gone to the Captain, T'Hawthorn, the previous Captain, D'Grove, and Tinne's father, T'Holly. Soon all twenty-five of the great nobles would be sent reports, and probably their spouses too.

Ilex only hoped the Chief could keep them from interfering in his investigation. Ilex himself would have to take a strong line against them, not easy when they were the most powerful people on Celta. But one or two of them might be able to help. Like T'Blackthorn. Like Tinne, who now had a personal stake in the case.

Ilex nodded toward Gib Ginger. "He's the third." Ilex lowered his voice too, made it coaxing. "Think, Tinne, what did Tern Sedum, Anetha Dill, and Gib Ginger have in common?"

Blood drained from Tinne's face again. "Anetha? No one told me of Anetha. Her Family said it was . . . was fluctuations in her Flair during another Passage echo. That's one thing they have in common. Unstable Flair, suffering through Passages that linger, or return."

"Yes."

Tinne licked his lips; his fingers switched from blazer to sword and caressed the pommel. "They're young. Gib is my age—twenty-two. Tern was younger—twenty." His face set. "And Anetha was just eighteen." He raised stormy eyes to Ilex's. "Tell me what I can do to help. *Tell me.*"

"What else, Tinne?" Ilex hoped his voice calmed Tinne. "You knew them better than anyone I've spoken with. What else?"

A frown line etched Tinne's forehead. "Tern and Anetha belonged to Families who have been feuding in the last year."

"Yes."

"But not Gib Ginger. The Gingers have tempers, but they prefer fistfight duels. Gib hasn't been in one of those for—oh—six months."

"Ah."

Tinne tried to look around Ilex at his lost friend. Ilex

shifted so Tinne still couldn't see. His gaze filled with sorrow. "He was a good friend," he said thickly.

Banging came from the front gate, along with T'Ginger's furious voice. "By the Cave of the Dark Goddess, what is going on here! Winterberry, you grychomp-treat, are you still here?"

Ilex winched. Insults. He'd had an unfortunate incident with a grychomp beast in the wilds last year. T'Ginger was angry now, but Ilex preferred that to the heart-blow he'd deal the man. His youngest son, dead. This was going to be hard.

Tinne straightened his shoulders, squared his jaw. "I'm a close friend. I'll tell them."

"No, I'll do it."

Tinne just shook his head. "I'll 'port to the house." He blinked several times. When he spoke again, his voice was thick. "They all had animal Familiars—Anetha, Tern, and Gib."

Ilex hadn't known that, and it reassured him. He'd believed that Trif might fit the profile of the victims. But she couldn't be a target. She didn't have an expensive and rare telepathic animal companion. Thank the Lady and Lord.

"Go on ahead. I'll be right with you," Ilex said. He had to examine the body more closely.

Nodding, Tinne vanished.

Ilex walked over to the body, placed his hand on the young chest—not fully developed into the heavy musculature of an adult man. Closing his eyes, he sent his senses into the body, confirming what he already knew.

The body had no heart.

Two

Trif and Danith D'Ash teleported to a comfortable sitting room in T'Ash Residence.

"What do you think happened back at the Ginger estate?" asked Trif.

"I don't know," Danith said. She rang for tea. "Sit. I do know that it would be best for you to stop this . . . ill-advised . . . quest for your HeartMate. I would never have thought you'd be someone who'd wander alone in Noble Country. And being caught going door to door." Danith blushed. "Not only is it personally humiliating, it reflects badly on your Family."

Trif sank into a plush chair. "Actually, Guardsman Winterberry was very decent about finding me using my charmkey." She was glad he was a friend—well, a neighbor, and she was on good terms with everyone in MidClass Lodge. She'd talk to him tonight and persuade him her Heart Quest was no problem for him.

When he'd said her name, she'd thought she might be in real trouble, but she'd seen the resigned humor lurking in his eyes and relaxed. He hadn't been the authoritarian guardsman then, but an attractive man she often discreetly watched.

Then something had changed and his whole bearing had exuded guardsman. His body had looked big and tough beneath his light brown uniform of simple shirt and trous. His face had become stern, his blue-gray eyes piercing. He'd moved like a guardsman, a hunter. Which, unfortunately for her, made him even more attractive.

"Trif! I'm speaking to you," Danith said.

Trif eyed Danith warily. She was the most powerful of all Trif's friends, the highest in status. If Danith wanted to stop Trif in her quest, the GreatLady could do it. Trif wasn't sure how, but figured Danith could probably think of several impressive and creative ways that would work.

Licking her lips, Trif said, "I'll consider revising my plan."

Danith's narrowed gaze pierced her. "Oh?"

"I'll avoid lonely places—try my charmkey in busy residential sections of town, not Noble Country—mid-class and Commoner blocks. And I've stayed away from FirstFamily estates. I know those folks are weird." She smiled guilelessly. Danith was D'Ash, now a FirstFamily GreatLady. And no one could call Danith's husband-HeartMate, T'Ash, normal.

Before Danith could reply, the door opened and the butler brought in a tea tray with a teapot and two mugs. Trif sighed. She didn't like tea, but always drank what Danith served out of politeness.

Zanth, T'Ash's scruffy tomcat Familiar, and a tiny white kitten followed the butler. With a grunt, Zanth flopped onto Danith's feet. The kitten climbed over him, snagged claws in Danith's dark blue trous, and climbed up to sit in her lap. As an animal Healer, Danith always housed a menagerie.

Danith studied Trif over her cup, and Trif attempted to be the picture of innocence. "How's Nuin?" Nuin was Danith's son, a toddler.

Though Danith's face softened, she just raised her eyebrows. "He's with his father today at the ritual. I had other plans." She eyed Trif; then, instead of issuing a gentle scold, Danith touched the small white kitten, and the little cat aimed big blue eyes at Trif. "Do you want a free Fam?" Danith asked.

Delight surged through Trif. "Yes!" She hadn't thought she'd be able to afford one for years.

"She won't be totally free," Danith warned. "She has expensive tastes."

Since the cat sat like a queen, Trif was sure Danith was right. Still, a Fam of her own! A little friend, a companion she could speak *telepathically* to, who would live with her. Oh, yes.

"She's about eight weeks old. Zanth brought her home a week ago," Danith said between her teeth. "She's his daughter, of course, but we can't get a word out of him as to her dam. Since most of the people on my waiting list want an impeccable bloodline—or at least a *known* bloodline"—Danith glared at Zanth snoozing on her feet—"I don't feel right giving her to them."

"Me?" Trif clapped her hands together. "Me! *I* get a Fam! A teeny kitten Fam?"

Danith sighed. "I'll warn you right now that she will be a pai—challenge. Teeny kitten or not, she has very stubborn ideas in her head." Danith put down her teacup and held up the kitten to scowl into serene blue eyes. The Fam smiled seraphically. "Unlike some kittens, I believe this one will remain pure white."

The kitten mewed, then pouted.

Trif stared in fascination. She'd never seen a kitten pout before, but knew the look. Or maybe it was the tip of the minuscule tail twitching in annoyance.

"This one." Danith angled the little cat so Trif could see her better. "Gets around, and as I said, she has ideas."

Danith cleared her throat, and pinkened. "She visited Samba FamCat on the spaceship *Nuada's Sword* and viewed *The History of Cats*. Apparently, she got some incredible idea that cats were once *tinted* on ancient Earth. 'Cat painting,' she said."

The little cat grinned, showing small pointed teeth. "Yessss," she said.

Danith slid her gaze to Trif, then away. "Do you know anything about this?"

A wave of Flair flooded Trif—her psi power consisted of being able to *see* past events—even as far back as ancient Earth. The teacup trembled in her fingers, and she set it aside to grip both arms of the chair, steadying herself. She breathed through the onslaught as a parade of strangely decorated cats flashed through her mind. Centuries worth of tinted cats. How odd.

Her always erratic Flair evened out, and her mind and body did the same. She wished, as ever, that she could control her Flair better. She wanted her Third and last Passage over, when she'd have command of her magic, but it was years away. She let out a slow breath and met Danith's wide and sympathetic gaze. Trif smiled weakly. Danith too had had unruly Passages, had not progressed easily and evenly into her Flair.

"If you ever want to talk, I'm here," said Danith.

"I know," said Trif. She wished to return home, stand under a waterfall, and clean away the film of sweat that coated her skin.

The kitten mewed imperiously. When Trif glanced at the small cat, the Fam slitted her eyes.

Danith's lips tightened. "She says you saw the truth of her words."

Trif said, "Yes, cats were painted for centuries. It was considered an art form—animal aesthetics."

Danith rolled her eyes. "Incredible." Her jaw went tight again. "I think she wants something outrageous—at least it looks that way—very odd—when she's tried to mentally send me the idea. Her image telepathy isn't totally developed yet."

Trif stared at the kitten and wanted her. "She really is mine?"

"She's yours, though where you'll find a cat tinter, I don't know. I'll send you home in a glider. *Don't* teleport."

Trif flushed. Her teleporting lessons had not been going at all well. Instead of a smooth process from one place to another, she arrived somewhere between the locations, and fell down.

Danith smiled, and it was warm and gentle and comforting. "The kitten's name is Greyku."

The little cat preened and mewed in agreement. She hopped off Danith's lap onto Zanth, who grunted, but kept his eyes closed. Then Greyku trotted over to Trif. Sitting at her feet, the kitten gazed up at her, exuding innocence. Just the same look Trif had tried before. The kitten was better at it than she.

Greyku revved up her purr, and Trif lifted her into her lap, stroking the softest fur she'd ever felt. A mind-to-mind connection formed between Trif and Greyku—inherently stabilizing Trif 's Flair.

"I knew Greyku was right for you." Danith looked smug.

Tenderness bloomed inside Trif. Greyku was a Clover name. The kitten was proud to be Trif 's.

Danith was watching her closely, so Trif tried a smile. Greyku's purr rumbled louder.

Zanth's tail twitched. He didn't open his eyes, but mentally sent, *Trif makes pretty music.*

Chuckling, Danith said, "That she does. Would you play something for us, Trif? I think it would soothe us all."

"I only have my tin whistle, not my flute," she said as she pulled a small pipe from the large bag she carried that could hold her biggest instrument case. She wet her lips, and began to play. She let her feelings spill into the music, spoke of longing, of yearning for love. As that tune wound around, then faded when her spirits began to lift just from the act of playing, another twiddle came into her head and she began a lively dance. Greyku jumped from her lap and zoomed over to pounce on her sire. Zanth grunted, and they began a mock battle. Zanth growled fiercely and Greyku went for his tattered ears. Danith laughed, and it was contagious, taking Trif 's breath. She stopped on a high note. The cats continued to tumble.

"Oh, that was wonderful, Trif." Danith beamed, then her expression turned considering. "Have you thought of studying with the composer D'Holly?"

Choking at the idea of imposing on *the* musical genius of their time, Trif hastily drew her tin whistle from her lips. "Me? No!"

"Your tunes are wonderful."

Packing the whistle back in her bag, Trif said, "Thank you, but my music is—ephemeral, of the moment. It should be made and appreciated in the moment, not saved. It's enough to play and to *feel.*"

"Hmm," Danith said. At that moment, a door slammed open.

T'Ash comes, Zanth said, then swatted Greyku so she rolled from him, and the tom stalked to the door and through the cat exit.

Danith's face had lit, love glowing in her eyes.

"You were going to send us home in your glider?" prompted Trif, scooping up her cat.

"Yes. It's at the door."

Heavy footsteps accompanied by Zanth-murmurings passed their door. Danith glanced toward Trif.

She waved a hand. "We'll see ourselves out."

Smiling, Danith said, "Thank you for taking Greyku."

"You're welcome." Trif grinned. Getting a Fam was the best thing that happened to her in a long while. "But I should be thanking you. So I'll do it—a three-thanks to draw blessings to you. Thank you. Thank you. Thank you."

In his office that afternoon, Ilex stared down at his poppets in frustration. They were small peoplelike figures made of soft commoncloth cotton about seven centimeters tall. Two were dressed in little trous, like men, and one in a tunic trous suit like a woman. They all had a tiny bit of golden thread belted around their middles—showing Nobility. And that was all the slight knowledge he had about the three who had dumped Gib Ginger's body. He didn't know who had killed and who had been accessories to the deed.

He was strong in poppet magic, but there were few crimes where the perpetrator was unknown and he didn't use that Flair much. The more information he had, the more he could form the poppet like the criminals, and the more the poppet would reflect a real person and act as a magnet to draw guards to that person. If a poppet was strong enough and a guard carried it, the doll could even indicate where the person had been, and then tracking was easier.

Of course, that was when the premiere tracker, the First-Family GreatLord Straif T'Blackthorn, was out of town. As he was now.

But since Ilex's data was slight, so were the poppets' properties, and they were nearly useless.

Still, he had something to build on.

Tinne Holly had been as good as his word, and had arrived at Hazel Quadrant Guardhouse for a Flair scan and Truth Sensing. He cleared the tests for violence easily, and continued to show interest in what was going on. Ilex had no doubt that Tinne's father, the powerful T'Holly, would grace the guardhouse within a day or two. From Chief Sawyr's irritated manner, Winterberry deduced that his superior understood that too.

Unable to pursue the investigation further, Ilex returned home to find the grandfather clock in MidClass Lodge lobby chiming Mid-Evening Bell, and he thought of Trif 's invitation.

He strode through the hallways and took the stairs down to the caffhouse in the basement, which was small, cozy, and filled with his neighbors winding down the weekend. The glass front showed Trif sitting at a small round table, vivid in a simple dark red dress. A couple of people stood talking to her. Then she caught sight of him, smiled, and waved. The others moved on, nodding to him as he entered and they left.

He stepped into the room, and all the other scents diminished until he smelled only her fragrance. The sound of discussions around him faded and he heard her slow, steady breathing. Felt the cheerful aura of her in the air.

Folly. Worse, his doom, hers. Too late to retreat.

Ilex saw the tiny kitten sitting atop the round glass table and froze. His pulse thudded loudly in his ears. The kitten looked like a Fam. He tore his gaze away from it to Trif. Her expression was dreamy and she petted the little cat with a lovely hand.

Then the cat stared at him from sharp, blue eyes. *I am Greyku.*

His stomach knotted. His HeartMate had a Fam. His beautiful Trif of the volatile Flair had just become a target for murder.

He didn't know how he managed a calm manner or an easy

smile when all he saw in his mind's eye was the heartless body of Gib Ginger.

"Greetyou, GentleLady Clover," he said, and seated himself.

She glanced up and smiled. Greetyou." Her brows dipped. "We're neighbors. I can't keep calling you Winterberry, though I haven't ever heard you called anything else."

"Call me Ilex, please." He ran an index finger down the tiny head of the kitten. "Greetyou, Greyku."

Greetyou.

"How lucky you are to have a Fam," he said.

"Yes, I hadn't anticipated having one for a long time, but D'Ash gave Greyku to me today." Her brows lowered. "Though Danith D'Ash was too subtle to say anything, I think that Greyku was meant as a bribe to . . ." She stopped.

"We can talk about your quest shortly. Have you eaten?"

Yes, said Greyku.

Trif chuckled. "Yes."

"Would you like a drink?"

Nodding, Trif said, "I wanted to hold a table. It's busy tonight and I didn't know how the counterman would react to Greyku if I took her up there."

"I'll get a caff," he said. He wanted whiskey.

"I'll have a cinnamoncaff."

I'll have a bowl of fluffcream, said Greyku.

"I'll get you a small saucer, Fam. You aren't large enough to eat a bowl of fluffcream." With a finger that seemed too rough and clumsy, he stroked her head. The kitten purred.

Ilex nodded and went to the counter, where he ordered the drinks and waited while they were being made. He unfocused his eyes and stretched his senses, sifting through emotions. Some people felt mild irritation due to personal problems, but there was no violence. In fact, the strongest emotion was pure fascination as the patrons darted glances at Greyku.

He paid for the drinks and returned to the table. The saucer had a small dollop of fluffcream. Greyku looked at it and wrinkled her nose. *More!*

"It's enough," Ilex said.

She eyed him, but stalked over to the saucer and began to lick daintily at the treat.

Ilex kept his gaze from the sweet cream on Trif's lips as

she played with her foaming drink. He burnt his mouth on his strong, black caff.

Trif shot him a serious gaze from under her thick lashes. "So, are you going to lecture me?"

Ilex winced inwardly. That's what she thought of him—an older, neighbor guardsman, ready to lecture. "Why do you attempt this quest?"

She tilted her head. "I know I have a HeartMate and I want him." Her hand dipped into a pocket and pulled out an intricate key.

Everything in Ilex tensed at the sight of the key. It was a pretty gold key with loops and colored crystal jewels—and hearts. Fanciful and exuberant like Trif.

At least the object didn't have the powerful lusty Flair of a HeartGift. Just his luck that Trif wanted to find her mate, knew enough and had Flair enough to make the key to hunt him.

She wouldn't make a HeartGift until her Third Passage at twenty-seven, seven years from now.

He was sure from his vision that he'd be dead by then. He probably had a couple of years left—and the most he could allow himself was to see her. Though HeartMate attraction and love being what they were, she might develop feelings for him if she ever saw him as a man instead of an authority figure.

Ilex was more concerned with not giving himself away and not making a fool of himself. He'd move out of MidClass Lodge, or arrange that she return to her large and loving Family at the Clover Compound as soon as this danger to her was gone.

Right now he wanted to keep an eye on her.

Her head tilted, she was studying him. He'd been wrapped in his thoughts too long. He nodded to the key. "Nice bit of work." His voice was harsher than he expected.

She flushed a little, her chin lifted. "More often than not my Flair is under control." She fiddled with the key, dropped it back into her pursenal. "I want to find my HeartMate," she repeated. "I'm tired of being alone."

Ilex went motionless as anger rose. *She* was tired of being alone—Lady and Lord, he'd been solitary for years and now dared not claim her. Ruthlessly, he banished all emotion from his tones. "You're very young."

She shrugged. "Clovers marry young. Several of my cuzes around my age are already wed. My HeartMate's out there. I connected with him during my Second Passage. A lifetime of love. Why wait?"

"So impatient," he murmured.

Laughing, Trif stirred her drink again. "Just assertive."

"But your Family and friends don't agree with your—adventure?"

"My quest. My HeartQuest. No, one approves. Not my family, nor my friend Lark Apple, nor my cuz, Mitchella D'Blackthorn. I tried to keep my—quest—quiet, but word spread." She colored, then her face set in determined lines. "I won't quit. The charmkey will work, why not use it?"

"Because it could get you in trouble?"

"Catshit."

"*Cat*shit?"

Greyku lifted a cream-covered muzzle and growled.

Trif grinned. "I started saying that when my friend Lark got her cat Familiar, Phyl. It irritated the kitten." Again, a wistful expression crossed her face. "I miss Lark, all the way south in Gael City." Trif shook her head, reached out, and petted Greyku.

"Couldn't you concentrate on bonding with your Fam instead of searching for your HeartMate?"

"It's not the same."

"Of course not, but Greyku should keep you busy. Fams do." Ilex leaned back, propping his elbow on the back of his chair. "Everyone wants Fams. But sentient animal companions are rare."

"Yes, but at least I got a cat instead of a dog. Cats aren't so uncommon."

He thought of his Fam, and she must have caught the shadow of expression on his face—or a pulse of emotion in the tiny thread spinning between them. Her eyes narrowed, and she pounced, like a cat. "*You* have a Fam, don't you?"

Before he could answer, she said quickly, "That's it!" She chuckled. "I knew you had a secret. But I've seen the shadow in the large inner courtyard at night. That's why you wanted a room facing the courtyard when you moved in, right?" She leaned forward. "Is it a feral tomcat?"

Heat crept up his neck. "A fox."

"A fox!"

"Quiet. We aren't the only residents here. I don't want him trapped or harmed." He smiled wryly. "And I doubt our landlord would understand."

"I know who's here, nobody who'd care whether you had a fox Fam." She glanced around. She'd greeted all the neighbors by name as they'd dropped by or as they left. Since she'd lived in MidClass Lodge longer than he and had a naturally curious bent, Ilex suspected she knew exactly who could be trusted with a secret. But he was uncomfortable that she'd sensed he was hiding something from her. What would she do when she finally figured out that his Fam was just one of Ilex's secrets?

"A fox Fam," she whispered in awe. "Wild, and rarer than dogs."

"I've planted additional brush near my windows." And had opened a small door in the outer wall of his apartment, in case Vertic wanted to spend time inside.

She nodded. "I noticed. You didn't strike me as a gardening type, but people are wonderfully complex. That's what makes everyone so interesting." She grinned.

"About your quest."

Her smile flickered out.

Steeling himself, he leaned forward to curl his hand around her wrist. Warm, soft woman-skin. He ignored the heat spreading through his veins, the escalating beat of his heart. "Your days of prowling Noble Country are over. 'Adventure' close to MidClass Lodge."

"I did the Lodge months ago."

He knew. He wouldn't have moved in otherwise. "Do your questing on busy streets. Not isolated estates in Noble Country."

She snorted.

Ilex squeezed her wrist, released it. "You must be careful and take care of yourself, or I'll ensure your safety. I don't think you'd appreciate my methods."

Expression darkening, she met his eyes. After a moment, she dropped her gaze. "I was wrong to trespass on Noble estates." The tips of her ears turned pink.

"It's best all around if you limit your wanderings."

She stared at him. "You have more than one secret."

More than two.

"What's going on in the city? Like I said earlier, I feel a change in the . . ." She opened and closed her hands, grasping thin air. "Atmosphere."

"I can't tell you." He still didn't know her character as well as he liked, didn't know if she'd break a confidence. A HeartMate made for him *shouldn't* be able to do that, but who knows? He hadn't thought his fated woman would be so young. He'd paid little attention to HeartMates until that first staggering dream when she'd reached out to him.

As they watched each other, he could *feel* his face take on the stony lines of his profession, knew she'd draw away from him.

She leaned forward instead. Something inside him crumbled, and the word *folly* echoed in his mind and he knew he'd be foolish. He'd spend time with her.

Her head tilted again as if she was listening inwardly. How much of a connection was building between them? How much could she sense it? Finally, she said, "Is whatever you're working on why you want me to be careful on my quest?"

"You make sure you're safe." He glanced at Greyku. "How loud can you screech, kitten?" From what he'd heard and seen, Fams always made themselves known.

The little cat opened her mouth, showing pointed white teeth and a pink tongue. *I can screech VERY loud.* She lifted her nose.

Ilex nodded. "Good." Looking back at Trif, he said, "I won't report you and I won't curtail your activities if you keep in busy areas and *always* take Greyku with you."

"What if I want to do a couple of blocks of houses after my work at Clover Fine Furnishings and Greyku isn't—"

"Those are my terms," Ilex said. He'd like her to continue the search because it would distract her from him, from his work, would keep her busy. There were other ways—Flair ways—to protect her, and he'd arrange those too. He leaned back in his chair.

She frowned. "Or else you'll report me."

"That's right."

Pulling her hand from his, she stood. "I'll be careful."

He didn't think she knew what the word *careful* meant. He

kept his feet flat on the floor as she left. She only had to go through the corridor and up the stairs to the lobby, then to her small apartment. Sipping his caff, he used the small bond between them to sense her, and knew when she slammed the door to her rooms.

Three

Of course he dreamt of her. For the first time, he'd spent more than five minutes in his HeartMate's company, and the meeting and emotions involved stirred his deep need for her.

So she played in his dreams—they played love games together—in his bed and in hers, which he could only imagine. In his mainspace. His large hands stroked and molded her high breasts, his tongue circled pink nipples, suckled, and her sweet moans drove him to higher and higher levels of aching passion. He awoke, tight with arousal, on fire for her, then spent some long moments under a cold waterfall. When he looked in a mirror, his face was tight, strained, showing dark stubble. And old.

If he'd been a precocious youngster, she could have been the age of his child's child. He shuddered, and his eyes went black with disgust at himself. Compared to hers, his skin was rough and weathered, and old. Compared to hers, his ideas were unimaginative, and old.

Compared to hers, his sexual experience was long and varied and . . . stodgy? Maybe not. Lady and Lord knew, his dreams of her, and more, the linked sexuality they'd shared, had been inventive and fresh, orgasms roaring through him like he'd never known.

He still wanted her, despite everything. His hands fisted at his sides as he gazed at the tumbled coverings of his bedsponge. He wanted her there. Now. Forever.

In the two years since they'd connected, he'd stopped having love affairs, even stopped having much sex—only when his body was desperate would he visit a friendly barmaid. Now that he'd spent some time with Trif, he couldn't think of sex with anyone else. He rubbed his face. How was he going to survive? How was he going to follow an honorable road and keep his hands off her?

By concentrating on his job. Unfortunately, his current case was all too horrific. So it demanded his best. He would *not* allow himself to be distracted. Going to his desk, he pulled out the sensorball from the first murder to study it again.

Trif awoke, unusually happy for a Mor morning after the weekend. She'd had wonderful, sweaty dreams of her HeartMate again last night. For the first time, she'd sensed emotions beyond the lust they'd shared—tenderness, perhaps even affection, or the edge of love.

Also, she had a Fam of her own. The small white kitten was curled sleeping on the pillow beside her. Trif eyed Greyku. The little Fam was right; she'd be much more striking if she was tinted.

Trif had dressed and eaten her own meal before Greyku strolled into the kitchen. *Breakfast time.*

"Yes." She turned to the no-time food storage and pulled out a bowl of warm furrabeast-and-greens mixture that D'Ash had advised. Trif now had ten recipes of kitten food, and had made up a week's worth of meals and put them in the no-time, where they'd stay as fresh as when she'd cooked them. Placing the food on the floor, she watched Greyku take dainty bites.

"You are the most beautiful kitten."

Yes. Greyku swiped a bit of meat from her muzzle and grinned up at Trif. *And you are all Mine.*

That was one way of looking at it. Trif chuckled and tidied the apartment. It was small, but relatively expensive. Still, it was away from the Clover family Compound and she enjoyed living on her own. She wasn't impatient for her father, uncles, sisters, and brothers to finish up the construction of her own house within the Compound. She had the idea that by the time her townhome was done, she'd be ready to be surrounded by family again, though with her new Fam, the floor plan might need a bit of altering. Again.

They'd hate that, since she'd already changed the blueprint five times . . . and had wanted to change it five more, but if they'd built it as quickly as they'd promised, she'd have been living there for a year. Yes, Greyku would be an excellent excuse to revise the plans, incorporating all the other little touches that she'd thought of lately, but hadn't had the nerve to ask for.

She'd take Greyku to work with her to the family furniture business, and they'd eat dinner with the Clovers. As the only Fam, Greyku would be cooed over and spoilt by the rest of the family. Trif knew enough about FamCats to understand that the kitten would adore the attention and petting.

What do We do now? asked Greyku.

"I don't work here. I work for Clover Fine Furnishings—in the business office." She was trapped in the job, her Flair of past-visions led to no useful career. She'd been expected to take a place with the family firm and she had.

Greyku stopped licking a forepaw to look at her with wide, curious blue eyes. *Interesting.*

Trif grimaced. "Not really, but I'd like you to come with me." She picked up a quilted basket that she'd previously thought Greyku would sleep in. "You can explore the offices and sleep near my desk when you tire."

Will there be play?

Thinking of the other family members who worked in the office, most of them female, Trif said, "I see papyrus wads and string in your future."

Good. Do We 'port there?

"Uh, no. We are middle-class people. I'm the one with the most Flair in the family." She shifted. "There isn't a teleport pad area set up." She had no idea when she'd be able to master that particular set of skills. It sure would be convenient, though.

Yet, Greyku said, between licks at her paw and swiping her head.

"Yet," Trif agreed. Who knew a kitten would be so amusing?

I will survey the office to make sure it is Fam-friendly.

"Ah." Trif choked on a giggle. "Good idea."

The kitten sat up straight, lifted her chin. *I am ready. Call the glider.*

Eyebrows raised, Trif smiled. "We are middle class. The business only has freight-gliders."

Greyku frowned. *How do We get to work?*

Trif was pretty sure that Greyku would be doing no work. "We ride the public carrier."

Greyku's eyes widened. *Very interesting to watch people. They will admire Me.*

"I think you've been spending too much time with T'Blackthorn's Fam."

I only say what's true. You said I was beautiful.

Laughing, Trif swooped down on Greyku and snatched her up, putting the kitten on her shoulder. The little cat dug in. "Ouch!"

You will need shoulder pads.

"I guess so." She glanced at the wall timer. "We don't want to miss the carrier."

Will We see Ilex and Vertic this morning?

Trif's pulse jumped at Ilex's name. She'd been irritated at him last night, but was feeling more charitable this morning. He wasn't going to report that she'd been trespassing on Noble property. That hadn't been a good idea anyway, just an impulse.

She picked up the charmkey and turned it over in her hand. It hummed with Flair. Only her Flair, not her HeartMate's, despite the dreams. But the emotions she'd experienced last night made her all the more determined to find him. Slipping the key into her pursenal, she slipped the pursenal on her belt and snicked it shut.

I want to meet the FamFox. I am not sure what a fox looks like.

"I don't know whether we'll see Ilex or his Fam this morning. I believe foxes are nocturnal."

So are feral cats.

"*You* aren't feral. If you want a good life with me, you'll be a day cat."

Greyku sniffed.

Trif left her rooms. At the far end of the hallway she saw Ilex, and hurried to catch up. He was dressed in his uniform—pristine brown shirt and creased, narrow-legged trous—and appeared grim and focused. Definitely a guardsman on a mission, and a dangerous man.

"Ilex," she called, and his shoulders seemed to hunch; then he stopped and turned, meeting her gaze. His eyes were more blue than gray this morning.

He sighed at the sight of her. She looked radiant. Satisfied, and bubbling with energy and optimism—and Ilex knew he'd unconsciously lingered in his rooms just long enough so he'd meet her in the hall. He knew her morning schedule, had seen her catching the public carrier often enough.

He blocked all the hot images of her in his bed, and nodded. "Greetyou, Trif and Greyku."

"Greetyou," she said breathlessly as she closed the distance between them. "I wanted to apologize for being abrupt with you last night and to thank you for your restraint."

He hadn't been restrained in their dreamtime loving. Heat crept up the back of his neck. She hadn't wanted him to be. He cleared his throat. "You received Fam Greyku from D'Ash yesterday, and your cuz is GrandLady D'Blackthorn, which means that she is wealthy, and also close to the Ashes. I advise that if you want to continue your quest, you have T'Ash make you a protection amulet."

She frowned. "More conditions for your silence?"

"I don't want you hurt," he said quietly, and he didn't have the Flair to protect her.

Her mouth twitched in a wry smile. "Thank you, but do you know how much an amulet from T'Ash would cost?"

"How important is your quest to you?"

That seemed to surprise her. She took a step back, glanced at her timer. "I have to hurry to make the next public carrier."

We cannot teleport yet, said Greyku. *There is no pad at My new day place, and We have not linked to try to 'port. I can teleport well.*

He didn't like that he'd drained Trif 's enthusiasm from the day, though worry for her bit at him.

Before he realized what he was saying, he offered, "I had a

nephew who had problems 'porting. I still remember the spell learning-program he used to establish the proper mental pathways. I worked with him, since I teleport around the city often in the course of my duties. I could help you." The moment the words were out of his mouth, he regretted them. It would mean a lot of physical contact, which was what had popped into his head when he'd thought of the offer. But he hated the older/younger, authority figure/citizen image—and he was wrong there too. He *shouldn't* want her to look at him as a man instead of a guardsman or instructor.

She blinked. "You'd help me? The only learning program I know of is T'Bean's Teleportation Teacher."

"That's the one. As I said, I went through it with my nephew."

"Oh, I'd love to teleport better."

It was for her own safety, Ilex assured himself. She might need it someday. "You know that teleporting takes a certain level of Flair, and can be quite draining."

Her spine straightened. "You saw with my charm key that I can do good work. I *really* want to teleport well."

Ilex thought she was in that stage of life where everything she wanted, she wanted with a passion. What was he doing, spending more time with this woman, his HeartMate, when he'd determined to avoid her? She was smart. She'd find out sooner or later that they were mates. Later would be better. "I'm busy tonight." He'd spend time shoring up his control. "We could start tomorrow evening," he found himself saying.

"Great!"

The little cat mewed. *I will help too. You will learn fast. Now I want to see the strange Fam the FamMan had in his thoughts.*

That was disconcerting, having a kitten read his thoughts. "I don't know," Ilex said, glancing at Trif. "Foxes have been known to eat cats."

Trif drew back, horrified, curved her hand around Greyku protectively. Then she lifted her chin. "I can't believe any sentient Fam animal would eat another."

"I think there are a lot of things you can't believe," Ilex replied softly.

Again they locked stares, and he felt old when he saw the

vitality in hers. "I didn't see Vertic come in yet," Ilex said. "He may be sleeping in the bushes. He doesn't always come when he is called."

Of course not, Greyku said smugly. *No self-respecting Fam comes when called. Only lesser Fams like dogs do.*

Ilex laughed.

Tilting her head, Trif said, "Laughing is good for you, you should do it more often."

Stiffening, Ilex glanced at his wrist timer. "Doesn't the public carrier come in two minutes?"

With a horrified gasp and a quick word of good-bye, Trif took off at a run.

Ilex waited for GreatLady Danith D'Ash, the animal Healer who placed all Fam animals, to authorize opening the greeniron gates outside the T'Ash estate. He contemplated his next move. The Fams of the victims were the only witnesses to their companions' deaths.

This had to be the strangest thing he'd ever done in his career—interviewing Familiars. But ever since he'd been assigned to the FirstFamilies six years ago, his life had been one strange experience after another. The worst had been the grychomp incident a year past. Not only had he been petrified, but he wouldn't live down the humiliation of literally being caught with his pants down in this lifetime.

"Winterberry?" D'Ash's voice echoing from the scrystone set in the gate pillar sounded breathless, harassed.

"Yes, GreatLady," he said soothingly.

"Come in, come in." She drummed her fingernails on the stone. The greeniron gates opened wide enough for a large man to enter.

He strode up the gliderway and to the great front door of the modern Residence. As he reached the entrance, this door too swung open.

Zanth, T'Ash's tom FamCat, as disreputable as ever, met him. *Come.*

Lifting his brows, Ilex followed the tom through the house to a series of rooms dedicated to D'Ash's profession as an animal Healer. *The* animal Healer.

He found her sitting cross-legged on a carpet that had once been beautiful and now appeared stained and ragged. An orange tomcat coughed in her lap. She stroked and praised it, and waited until it was done before looking at Ilex with tear-filled eyes. "Gib Ginger's cat, Rhyz."

Pampered, cowardly, useless Cat, Zanth grumbled. *Should live feral Downwind a year or two.* He stalked back the way they'd come, tail high and stiff with disdain.

The cat started coughing again. Winterberry eyed it dubiously, wondering if it would retch on his newly shined boots.

"Shhh." D'Ash curved herself over her charge. "You are a very strong Cat, a wonderful Kitty, excellent . . ."

Again they waited for the cat to finish coughing; then D'Ash rose to her feet and offered the limp Fam to Ilex. Bracing himself, he took the orange tom who looked at him with sad green eyes.

"Reassure him," D'Ash told Ilex. "And I'll get the other two you want."

The cat was heavier than he looked. Opening his Flair shields, Ilex sensed deep depression from the cat—more, swirling sensations of an experience that had terrorized it. Anger. Helplessness.

"Shhh," he found himself saying. "You are a valuable per—uh—Cat." Ilex was good with upset people, and he sent the same calming Flair to the cat. It started coughing again. Wincing, Ilex found a battered and scratched chair and sat, murmuring to the Fam, "You are—wonderful." Not as wonderful as Vertic. "You *are* strong. And you will be very helpful to me." The cat looked at him, stopped coughing.

At that moment D'Ash returned carrying a small housefluff—a genetic hybrid of an Earth rabbit and a Celtan mochyn. She was accompanied by a drooping puppy trudging beside her. She waved a hand and the walls throbbed with waves of lulling color, music lilted in quiet rhythms.

"This is Anetha's housefluff and Tern's's dog."

"Greetyou," he said. "I didn't know that housefluffs had become sentient enough to be good Fams."

Pink tinged D'Ash's cheeks. "Only one generation. I've, uh, been breeding them for intelligence, empathy, and Flair."

Much as the FirstFamilies had bred themselves. But D'Ash

had been born a commoner. Ilex nodded. He rubbed the cat he held under the chin as he considered the other Fams. "Still, I have a feeling that this guy will be the most useful to me." The cat rumbled a rusty purr, barely audible. "Is there somewhere I can . . . speak . . . to him privately?"

D'Ash's lips compressed. "If you insist."

"I think it would be best. Your emotions . . ."

She gave a watery sniff. "You're right. But Rhyz lost his FamMan just before dawn yesterday, hardly time to grieve—"

"He knows the time Gib died?" Ilex's mind went on alert, though he kept his voice mellow.

"Well, of course, they were bonded." She cuddled the housefluff in her hands, chose another large chair, and sat, lifting the puppy up beside her thigh. It settled with a small sigh. Nibbling on her lip, she angled her head toward her right. "A couple of rooms down is my informal parlor for clients. Rhyz might be comfortable there."

Yessss, Rhyz said mentally.

D'Ash nodded. "Very well then. You can communicate there." Her brows lowered. "Be very careful of him, guardsman. He's had a terrible shock. His coughing is not a physical, but emotional, illness, due to stress."

Ilex dipped his head. "I understand."

"You should speak with the dog here next. None of the Fams wanted to stay with their lost companions' families, so I am finding them new homes. I have a prospective new FamPerson for the housefluff coming in a septhour."

Clearing his throat, Ilex said, "One question. Has Rhyz been bathed—"

Rhyz hissed and struggled in Ilex's arms. D'Ash murmured, "Bathe a *cat*?"

"My apologies. *Groomed.* Have you spoken to him about Gi—his experience?"

"No," she replied stiffly. "I have done no emotional Healing with him yet."

"Thank you." Ilex turned the cat in his arms so he could meet its gaze. "I believe we could help each other, Rhyz."

The cat lashed his tail and looked aside, but didn't protest as Ilex carried him to D'Ash's sitting room.

When the door to that room was closed and locked and Ilex

and the cat had settled into a plush armchair, he set the cat on his thighs facing him and spoke to it as he would a human. *It would be best if I could share the memory of the experience with you, Master Rhyz.*

Four

"*The new furniture line you designed for the family is selling well,*" Trif said to her cuz Mitchella D'Blackthorn during mid-morning break in the office lounge. She was glad her cuz had dropped by; the morning had stretched long with boring, repetitive tasks, as usual.

"Thank you. The family finally appreciates me." Mitchella grinned, then turned serious and sent a narrowed look at Trif. "But you are *not* going to distract me. I've made an appointment with T'Willow for you."

"The matchmaker?" Trif squeaked. Her hot caff slopped over the rim of her cup and fell on her leg, staining her light blue trous, just missing a snoozing Greyku. Mitchella rose from her chair, hurried over, and recited a cleansing spell, and the cloth dried without staining.

A few minutes before, Mitchella had swept down on the office, every inch a FirstFamily GrandLady, and whisked Trif and Greyku into the small break room.

Trif continued. "But T'Willow is a GreatLord, his services must cost . . ." Her mind boggled at what they'd cost—probably a decade of her salary.

"It's not a consultation, but an informal meeting, to talk to you about HeartMates and all." Mitchella patted Trif 's shoulder.

"He just ascended to his title, and that means most of the First-Families will present him with welcoming gifts." She smiled coolly. "And see what sort of man he is and whether he'll be a good ally. You can take him a small table fountain I bespelled for him."

"There must be some other payment for this 'informal meeting.' And what do you mean, talk to me about Heart-Mates? You're trying another way to dissuade me from going door to door."

Mitchella sighed. "I don't think that's wise and it's not—" She waved a hand.

"Proper? Have you gone all formal on me?" Trif asked.

"No. It's not—elegant."

Trif put her cup down with a clink. "I think it shows self-confidence and initiative."

"Your mother worries—no, I won't use manipulative guilt on you."

Making a face, Trif said, "Then you're the only one. If I lived at home in the Clover Compound, they'd lock me in my room."

"No, they wouldn't."

"Maybe not, but one of the uncles would insist on going with me."

Mitchella wrinkled her nose. "Not good."

"No."

"But maybe one of the cuzes . . ."

"No! I don't need anyone tagging around with me."

Greyku opened one blue eye. *I will go with my Fam-Woman,* she sent loudly.

"I heard that!" Mitchella exclaimed. "My Flair has increased slightly since marrying Straif and living in a Grand-House." She tickled Greyku on her stomach. "But you aren't much protection for Trif."

Greyku sat up and lifted her nose. *I can scream very loud.*

"She can too. I've already had complaints from the neighbors. Speaking of which, one of them is going to help me with teleporting."

"Who?" asked Mitchella sharply.

"Ilex Winterberry."

Mitchella relaxed. "I like Winterberry. I'd forgotten he was living in MidClass Lodge now." She nibbled on her lip. "I think he's the younger son of a GrandLady. Estranged. Though I don't know how powerful Winterberry's Flair is. Very, I think. He could probably Test and become a GrandLord in his own right—just as you could Test and rise to GraceLady status."

"Why would I want to?"

"A title has its uses. My shop is so busy I have employees running it now, and I'm booked all next year for decorating projects."

Trif set Greyku on the floor, stood, and kissed her cuz on the cheek. "Your career is skyrocketing because you're a good decorator." She looked around the room, which Mitchella had recently refurbished, pale seafoam green walls, comfortable chairs, pretty carpet bespelled against traffic and stains, a small dining table of the Clovers' new line. The lounge was now a place where people liked to eat and gather.

Trif said, "This room is lovely and your house is gorgeous. Everyone wants the designer who renovated T'Blackthorn Residence and restored its glory."

Mitchella hugged Trif hard. "Thank you." She held Trif at arm's length and looked at her. "You know I love you and just want you to be safe."

"Yes."

"So go see T'Willow. I asked him if anyone's done what you are doing. He didn't know of any instances, and he sounded intrigued. He said that he'd speak with you for a favor from you."

"A favor! What kind of favor?"

"I don't know. You can deliver the fountain and ask him. I've set the appointment for tomorrow afternoon, a septhour after WorkEnd Bell. Come by my place first, and I'll give you the fountain. The T'Blackthorn glider will transport you and wait to pick you up."

"The clunky old glider or one of those new models Straif commissioned?"

Mitchella chuckled. "One of the new ones, but not Straif's two-seater. It was just delivered and he hasn't driven it yet." She crossed to the window and smoothed a curtain.

"Have you heard when he'll be returning?"

"No." A shadow passed over her face. She shifted her

shoulder. "Our bond is strong, so I know he's not hurt or worse. But that assignment from the Noble Council to track the lost last-of-the-Family Lord Ginseng took him to the eastern wilderness. Straif 's weary and tired."

Trif curled Greyku on her shoulder and went over and kissed her cuz on the cheek. "You'll be fine."

After a watery swallow, Mitchella said, "Of course I will. This is just the longest he's been away and the farthest he's gone." In a lighter tone, she added, "Though that snotty Fam of his might drive me crazy in the meantime."

With a chuckle, Trif said, "You took the man, you had to take his Fam."

"If only he'd met me first," Mitchella murmured, then shrugged, calling attention to the drape of the stylish gown she wore.

Trif stepped back. "Oooh, what a robe!" She reached out and touched the material, silkeen, then shook her head. "Admit it. You like living as a FirstFamilies GrandLady."

"I love it. Most of all, I love Straif." Mitchella glowed.

"Then you should understand why I want to find my HeartMate."

Huffing a breath, Mitchella said, "Touché."

Ilex slowly pulled his Flair from deep-examination of the Fam's sensory impressions of the dawn before. He found himself rocking the cat. He'd been using Flair to calm the young tom and gently massaged him. Blinking, Ilex realized that touch was the best technique when "interrogating" FamCats. He slid his fingers down one of Rhyz's forepaw pads, and the cat hissed and yanked it away, but not before new images flooded Ilex, more detailed than before.

FamMan gone. Dead. Abandoned Me here in this bad place. Dead! Feel full, full, full. So big with Flair—a giant Cat, ten times bigger than Zanth, than hunting Cats. Bigger than the biggest human.

Dimness around Me except for bright spots of flickering light held in human hands. They dip and move and make seeing hard. Lying on a rough cloth that smells like musky-nasty-bad-humans-death. Hair rising, but only a low growl in the throat instead of the loud warning yowl. Light slips down silver coming toward Me. Heart jump! A blade. Bad, bad, bad. The blade stabs forward, slices paw. Whimper in pain. Emptying.

Fear at sound of howling like vicious dogs. Dipping and swaying of the bobbing lights. Horrible man-woman scent. Sweat. Triumph. Bad happiness throbbing from humans. Mean humans laughing not-real-laughter.

Heavy cloth drops over head. Terror! Can't see. Too much smell. Smoke. Spices. Dark comes.

Danith calls, holds out hands, commands. Go to her. Yes. She will care. Yes. Danith. Human-mother. She cradles, sings, comforts. Bad things gone. Bond with Gib gone. Sad.

With a light stroking between Rhyz's ears, Ilex said, "Forget, it is over. Live through the moment and find past memories to cherish. Your loved one circles on the Wheel of Stars, awaiting rebirth." A standard guardsman patter for those who have lost, but almost wasted on the Fam, since cats were the best creatures at living in the moment that Ilex had ever known. He'd already learned that much from little Greyku. He touched the cat's pad again, and Rhyz hissed and swatted his hand, claws slightly extended.

"That was well done," Danith D'Ash said, and Ilex looked up to see her watching him from the threshold of the door. "You've effected some emotional Healing for Rhyz. My thanks."

Ilex lifted and dropped a shoulder. "It was nothing."

"But you look as if you do it often."

Raising an eyebrow, Ilex said, "When I first met your HeartMate, he was in a killing rage at having his HeartGift stolen. I assure you, being able to summon calming Flair is necessary in my work."

D'Ash nodded.

"Did you notice this cut on his paw?"

Frowning, D'Ash came over and crouched down, taking Rhyz's foreleg and extending it so she could examine the paw. Rhyz purred. With fear in her eyes, she said, "I Healed this slice. Yesterday after I got him back, and again last night, when I thought I'd been mistaken that I'd taken care of it." Her fingers brushed the paw and blue light flowed into it, mending the slash.

"Third time's a charm," Ilex offered, hoping it was true.

D'Ash scowled and took Rhyz. "You can examine the housefluff and puppy now."

As Ilex rose, he nodded. "Now that I know what I'm looking for, it should be easier on the other Fams. Did they have knife wounds too?"

"Knife wounds!" She looked horrified.

"T'Ash didn't see the Fam's injury, did he?" That man would have recognized knifework when he saw it.

"No." She swallowed, petted Rhyz. "The housefluff had a long scratch in her ear. I only Healed it once. The puppy had a puncture in one of his paws. I Healed that one twice." She shook her head. "Punctures often pick up infection."

"May I see the housefluff and pup?"

She brought them in and he soothed the Fams, then examined them under D'Ash's watchful eyes. Again, he scented the heavy incense that had lingered on the murder victims. He received impressions of darkness and fear and bad-laughing-howling, nothing more. But he had discovered additional information. There was more than one murderer, not just a killer and accessories, and the incense was unusual. He'd never smelled the combination before, and though he could identify frankincense and myrrh, there was a third elusive scent that could be key to finding the murderers.

When he looked for the knife scars on the puppy and housefluff, he saw no trace. He grunted. "You do good work."

"Thank you."

Clearing his throat, he said, "You know I have a fox Fam—"

Her eyes lit, but before she could speak, the door opened and one adult and two children walked in.

GreatLady D'Hazel, the adult, wore a closed expression and stood a little away from GreatLord Vinni T'Vine, who held her youngest child's hand—Avellana, who was five years old. D'Hazel made a half bow, one GreatLady to another. "Please forgive us the *inexcusable* breach of your privacy. *He*"—she exhaled audibly, gestured to the eleven-year-old Vinni—"insisted we enter."

Vinni grinned audaciously. "And hardly anyone ever disagrees with me when I insist."

Of course not. He was a prophet. Uncanny.

He looked down at the small Hazel, and his eyes, which

Ilex would have sworn to be green-brown, appeared deep blue. They were an odd trio.

"Time to choose your Fam, Avellana," Vinni said.

Danith squatted and held out the housefluff. "Would you like this soft lady housefluff Fam?"

The housefluff's pink nose wrinkled, her long ears twitched.

"Pretty," Avellana declared. She giggled as the puppy raced over and gamboled around her; then her gaze focused on the young tomcat and her eyes lit up. She hurried over to where he'd curled onto a chair, watching them. He rotated his ears. "Mine!" she squealed, stroking him gently.

Vinni T'Vine frowned.

"My FamCat," Avellana said, grabbing him and letting him dangle down her body. Vinni joined her and put his palms under the Fam's back paws, supporting them. "You hold him like this." Vinni cupped her hands under Rhyz's paws.

"Are you sure you want Rhyz?" Danith said, nibbling her lip, casting a glance at Ilex.

Rhyz butted his head under Avellana's chin, his purr loud.

D'Hazel joined the children. "Avellana is sure."

The little girl turned. "Vinni can have the housefluff."

Vinni's eyes widened. "N—"

"A good idea." Danith chuckled.

Ilex got the impression that the boy hadn't anticipated Avellana's action—interesting. Hesitantly, Vinni took the housefluff from Danith, grinning when the Fam snuggled into his arms. "Her name is Flora."

Ilex eyed Vinni. A prophet. It wasn't often Ilex was in a prophet's company. His own occasional foreseeing gift was minuscule compared to this lad's.

Cuddling his new Fam, Vinni stared at Ilex as Danith spoke with the Hazels. "I can guess what you're thinking," Vinni said. "Yes, we can talk, but I'll demand a price. Personal, from you."

Raising a brow, Ilex said, "I don't think—"

Vinni jerked his head. "We'll talk." Glancing back at the group of females, he said, "I'll be right outside." He walked into the corridor and down to the reception area. Ilex followed. "I won't give you a reading about your case." He sounded more serious than any young boy should.

"Why not?"

His fingers trembled as he stroked the housefluff 's fur and he shook his head. "I can't see it well. It's ever shifting, as if there are too many variables in the future, too many options." This time, his smile was unamused. "And there's a darkness around the crimes." He looked up at Ilex with fear in his eyes. "I don't want to look into the darkness."

Ilex curved his fingers around the boy's shoulder. "Then don't. No one would ask you to, especially since the future is in flux."

The shoulder under Ilex's hand relaxed. "Thank you." With a sidelong look: "Now, my price for that information. You listen to my advice."

"And that is?"

Vinni's lips curved; his green-brown eyes once again met Ilex's steadily. "Don't believe everything you *see.*"

Ilex spent the rest of that and the next day visiting the best incense makers and shops, but didn't get a whiff of the unknown herb he'd scented while interviewing the Fams. He reported to his Chief and handed off the investigation to his night-shift colleague who'd been equally unsuccessful. His sense of smell was ruined for the day.

He entered MidClass Lodge, anticipation at giving Trif a teleportation lesson fizzing in his blood. He heard her piercing scream and felt her pulse of horror all the way down the corridor. He sped down the hallway and was at her threshold, blazer drawn, just in time to hear her gasp.

"What's wrong?" he demanded.

Huge tears rolled from her eyes. Her breath choked and she only pointed.

His FamFox, Vertic, sat at the threshold of her bedroom, a tiny limp kitten in his mouth, his eyes dancing with satisfaction.

Ilex's blood ran cold. He didn't know whether to holster his blazer or kill his own Fam.

The kitten twitched.

"Lady and Lord!" Trif screeched, then rushed into her apartment and dropped to her knees, shaking hands outstretched for her kitten.

Greyku hissed.

Vertic dropped the little cat into Trif's hands and panted, tongue lolling. *Bad kit. I caught her running around the garden, about to slip under the gate to the road.*

Trif held Greyku up by the scruff of her neck. "Is that true?"

Slowly blinking huge, innocent eyes, Greyku said, *Garden bo-ring.*

Ilex holstered his blazer and propped a shoulder against the doorjamb, crossing his arms. Vertic loped over and Ilex bent down to rub his head.

"What about the apartment?" asked Trif. "You were the one who wanted to stay here."

Home bo-ring.

Trif's lips quivered, but she continued to scold the kitten. "You promised to *stay inside.*"

The window looked good, then the garden looked good, then the road beyond the gate looked good, and the beach beyond the road. With her thought, Greyku projected overwhelming temptation.

Trif sighed and rubbed the kitten against her face. "I know what you mean." She glanced at Vertic. "Thank you, Master Fox."

Vertic dipped his head at her. *Blessings.* He glanced at the late afternoon light filtering through the window. *Time for me to nap. Then I will hunt and eat and visit my old den.*

Ilex pushed off the door jamb. "I thank you for not hunting and eating the kitten."

She Family. The fox shook his head. *Too adventurous by herself.* He lifted a forepaw in good-bye, then trotted back into the bedroom. There was a slight *thump* as he jumped to the windowsill, then silence.

"I guess she is too bold," said Trif, stroking her little cat.

The garden looked good, Greyku repeated.

Ilex shook his head too. Both Greyku and Trif were young enough to succumb to overwhelming temptation.

Good thing he wasn't. "Well, as long as the current crises is over, I'll—"

"We had an appointment for teleportation lessons."

"Yes. I thought you might reconsider." He had. He was torn; he wanted to be with her, knew he shouldn't.

Her mouth set. "I want to learn how to teleport well. It will allay my family's fears when I search for a HeartMate."

It would allay his fears too. "Did you commission a protective amulet from T'Ash?"

Her mouth turned down. "He'll make the jewelry at cost, but then I need a retrieval spell from D'Alder to automatically teleport me to a HealingHall. I can't afford it, not even if I worked twice my normal hours for the next three months."

Ilex knew where he could get a good spell to return her. His gut tightened. He'd have to see his mother.

Five

Two hopeful faces lifted to Ilex. He gave in. "Shall we practice your teleporting?"

Her face lit. "Yes!"

Me too! I will help.

Ilex studied the kitten. "Perhaps you're right, for now. But Trif will need to know how to teleport without you—"

The kitten sniffed in disdain.

"—in case you want a treat from somewhere across town, say D'Ash's, and don't want to face Zanth when you go beg it."

Frowning, Trif said, "Thank you for letting the kitten think she can make a servant of me."

"All cats think people are servants."

I am not afraid of Zanth. And I don't beg. Greyku extended a forepaw and flexed her claws.

He'd offended both of them. "My apologies, ladies. But the point stands. Eventually, Trif must practice alone, to know in her bones that she's capable of mastering teleporting by herself."

But I get to 'port now. Where are we 'porting to? asked Greyku.

"You must teleport *from* somewhere very familiar *to* somewhere very familiar," Ilex said.

Let's go to the Ship, Nuada's Sword. *The Ship can be seen everywhere in Druida. I can show off my new FamWoman to Ship's Cat Samba.*

"A major consideration," Ilex murmured.

Trif smiled. "But it's impossible to teleport into the Ship because it dampens Flair. And I don't know the coordinates of Landing Park very well. So *not* the Ship." She waved to a yellowed, cracked learning sphere on her dining room table. Ilex recognized it as *T'Bean's Teleportation Teacher*. Trif made a face. "It said the same thing, practice with well-known places I can easily visualize. That means the teleportation pad in Clover Compound and here."

Ilex glanced around, committed the room's furnishings and placement to memory. Part of his Flair was an excellent recollection of settings. Extending his senses to examine his surroundings was his greatest Flair. "I don't know the teleportation pad at Clover Compound. I do know the park across from the main entrance." Over the last several years, he'd spent a lot of time lingering in that park, after he'd tracked his HeartMate down, then discovered it was Trif. He'd watched the Family he wanted to call his own, but had never approached them, had seen Trif grow from a pretty teenager into a lovely young woman.

"The park across from Clover Compound?" She glanced at him. "The family owns that park, another to the south of our Compound, and a grove to the north."

"I helped Straif Blackthorn plant trees and bushes from his estate in that park." The words were out of Ilex's mouth, demonstrating his need of her approval, before he could stop them.

She beamed and warmth uncurled inside him. He said, "I'll hold your hand and we can practice teleporting to the park."

"The learning sphere says that for best results, we should be close as possible." She looked away and flushed. "My Flair is so temperamental, I don't think just holding hands will work."

His pulse leapt, but his mind cursed. Trying to keep his reaction to her hidden would be tough. Why hadn't he remembered that he'd hugged his nephew close during their sessions—their short three sessions? Ilam had learned quickly after being tutored. Ilex had the impression that Trif, with her uneven Flair, would need more lessons. The notion was both an anticipated pleasure and delightful ache.

"Of course," he said steadily.

"Good!" She set herself directly in front of him and he wondered how to hold her to give them a close enough connection, but not be too aroused. Impossible. "Let's try this." Keeping his lower body from hers, he loosely clasped his arms around her waist, aware of the warm curve of her hips.

"That's fine." She shifted a little.

"Tell me when you're linked mentally with Greyku."

"When," Trif said.

Done, Greyku sent at the same time.

Ilex loosened his shoulders. "Just preparing."

Trif made a sound of agreement.

"I'll be brushing your mind now." This was the worst idea he'd ever had in his life. Connecting with her mind would be so intimate, so much what he shouldn't do if he didn't want to be haunted by her forever. He closed his eyes and was enveloped by her—her vibrant aura, the whisper of her breathing felt through his hands, up his arms, and into his lungs, the scent of her, young woman. He sent out a questing thought, *Trif*.

Ilex. The mental lilt of his name—the respect and affection that came with it—staggered him as they slid easily into harmony.

I am here too! said Greyku, her thought wriggling in his mind impatiently. *Let's go.*

"I'll set the visualization. Clover Park. Late autumn. Evening." He drew up the images, projected them to Trif. She joined him, showing her own vision, but it wavered. She tensed inside the circle of his arms.

"Easy," he said. "I'll hold the image and sharpen it. Take my visualization."

She relaxed as she accepted his vision, solidifying the scene. "It's very good! A better visualization than I've ever had before. I can see the bare branches of the trees as they shift in the wind, dark against the sky."

"That's my Flair. We have an emotional connection to the park, you because you've lived and played and worked there, and both of us have planted growing things. Can't you *sense* the park, the reality of it as you've known it, as well as a present link to the actual location?"

"I don't know. . . ."

"Relax, try, don't worry about teleporting, just *be* in the park. Breathe slow, deep breaths. No hurry."

But—cried Greyku.

"No hurry, kitten. Think of resting in the park."

Greyku shifted around on Trif 's shoulder, then settled.

Ilex found that he stood easier himself. This was right, holding Trif, helping her. His breathing synchronized with hers—or hers matched his, he didn't know which, and it didn't matter. For one special moment, they were together, living in the moment. He wasn't worried about the future—hers, his, or theirs.

He savored the balance between them—and the kitten—one last instant, made sure her focus on their shared image of the park was solid, then spoke softly. "We will go on three."

She tensed.

"I'll wait until you relax again, then we will go on three. There is no hurry."

A few breaths later—a few more seconds of enjoying her in his arms—and he began the count. "One, Trif Clover. Two, Greyku cat. *Three*."

They arrived in the park. No hesitation, no unbalanced landing.

"We *did* it!" Trif pulled from his arms, whirled around with Greyku shrieking in glee, small tail straight out for balance.

His heart squeezed at the youth of them. When was the last time he'd spun around in happiness? Maybe when he was ten. Before his father had died and his mother had become the woman she was—or revealed the woman she'd always been.

Trif ran up to him and grabbed his hand. "Let's go! We'll head for the landing pad that the family has put up in the corner of the Compound courtyard. Then we can teleport back. I'm *sure* I can hold the image of my mainspace in my head and guide you this time."

"You are certainly more familiar with that than I." He lengthened his stride to keep up with her running steps. They crossed the empty street; then Trif opened the door to a hallway leading to another, open, door and the courtyard. Ilex frowned. Neither of the doors had been locked. He'd have to speak to the Clover Family elders.

They were through the hall and into the open space before he could ask Trif who was the head of the Clover household.

She cried in rage, dropping Ilex's hand and shooting toward the far left corner of the yard where a tangle of children bounced up and down on a huge red pad that looked like an oversized bedsponge. The teleportation pad.

Pure horror scrambled his wits. If he'd known the location of the pad and they'd tried to teleport . . . they could have killed themselves by entangling their solidifying molecules with others—and taken a couple of children with them. *Stop!* He sent a mental command that could be heard throughout the Compound.

All activity in the rectangle stilled. Adults looked to him as he followed Trif to the pad. The children tried to scramble away. "Hold!" With a sweeping gesture, Ilex froze the lot of them. This too was part of his Flair and demanded a certain level—Noble level—and energy to use. But the energy to power it was easily found—fear at what might have resulted, and anger that the Clovers had not been more careful.

Now even the murmuring of the adults ended.

"What were you thinking!" demanded Trif of her younger family members.

"Let me handle this, Trif," Ilex said, nudging Trif aside so he could confront the bespelled children. It looked as if the oldest was about ten, a girl. The youngest sat in a diaper on the pad, staring up at him all wide eyes and round mouth, eyes terrified that it couldn't move. "Get that one," Ilex said, releasing the toddler from his "still" spell. A wail rose and echoed off the walls of the surrounding houses.

Trif scooped up the baby and cuddled it. It hid its face into her neck, hiccupping cries until it spotted Greyku; then a chubby hand lifted. A woman came and took the babe.

Ilex snapped fingers under the oldest girl's nose. "You may speak." He angled his chin at the pad. "What is that?"

The girl gulped, swallowed again, but met his gaze. Brave child. "It's a teleportation landing pad." Her eyes slid to Trif. "For cuz Trif. She's the only one of us who has enough Flair to 'port and she don't often get it right."

Reddening, Trif said, "*Doesn't* often get it right."

"Do you know the penalty for occupying a lit teleportation pad?" He nodded to a post next to the pad that held a bright light—signifying the pad was empty and it was available for use. He flicked it off.

All the adults had gathered behind him. He could feel their auras pressing against his.

"The penalty is all their allowances for the next month, *and* a favor-debt from each for you, guardsman," boomed a voice.

Ilex's eyes widened. There must be twelve children caught in his spell. Debts from twelve young Clovers. This would tie him to the Family for some time to come.

A big man with a fat belly bowed to Ilex. "Greetyou, Guardsman Winterberry."

Ilex bowed back. "Greetyou, gentlesir."

"I'm Pink Clover, Trif's father." He scanned the children, looked back at Ilex. "What is the penalty for occupying a lit teleportation pad?"

"For a Family landing place, it is yours to decide, as you did. For a public place, it is a year outcast from Druida."

Gasps came around him. Ilex met each child's stare in turn. "Realistically, it is death." He shrugged. "Or could be death, in the worst-case scenario." Ilex was used to thinking of worst-case outcomes.

Pink nodded. "I believe you've made your point. If you would release the children, please?"

Lifting his fingers, Ilex ended the spell. The children tumbled back onto the pad.

"You twelve will await us in the common room," Pink said.

"Uh-oh," breathed Trif beside Ilex.

The children ran to one of the doors as fast as their trembling legs could take them. Ilex turned fully to Pink.

The man's expression was grim. "Though it's our fault too." He studied the rest of the adults, who all nodded. "We aren't used to having someone with Flair and were negligent in thinking of the consequences of an occupied landing place." He bowed again. "Trif told us last night that you would be helping her with her 'porting." He grimaced and tapped his temple with his finger. "Didn't sink in. I promise you, this will not happen again."

"I appreciate that. I've never seriously harmed anyone in all my career, and I don't want to start with a Clover child now," Ilex said.

"We all agree," said a woman, throwing her arms around Trif and hugging her tightly. Ilex had met Trif's mother, Pratty, before. "Greetyou, Gentlelady Clover."

"Oh, don't call me that. There are too many of us. Call me Pratty. And my thanks for helping my girl."

"We *'ported* here," Trif said proudly. "I mean, to Clover Park across the street. Ilex didn't have a good image of the teleportation pad . . . good thing too."

A teenaged boy came up. "The kitten's here too! Can I hold her?"

With that, the strain eased.

The kitten leapt into the outstretched hands and purred loud enough to attract chuckles and a group of teenagers.

"We *are* practicing teleporting, so we'll be returning to MidClass Lodge shortly," Trif said.

Ilex stared at Pink. "Do you consider yourself in my debt?"

Wariness entered the man's expression. "Yes."

"Then I want you to be more security-conscious. Lock your doors. Spellbind them." Ilex glanced over the courtyard and saw several sturdy young men and women. "Send one of your youngsters to Tab Holly's Green Knight Fencing and Fighting Salon for training."

Pink stepped back. "What?"

"At least one of your Family should have experience in fighting and security."

Looking bewildered, Pink spread his hands and said, "But we are Commoners, no more than middle-class, and only Trif has extraordinary Flair."

Narrowing his eyes, Ilex gestured around him. "You Clovers are a byword in Druida, in all of Celta—the most prolific Family in the world. Your adopted daughter Danith Mallow is now Danith D'Ash, and your daughter D'Blackthorn. They move in the highest circles. Don't tell me that T'Ash and T'Blackthorn don't listen to you. You have *numbers* and for that you are the envy of every Family, high or low, in the world. That makes you unique, the members of your Family unique, and individuals to be prized. Your influence is beginning to be felt in other circles, your status raised. Recognize that. Send someone to train with the Hollys."

Several of the oldest generation looked stunned at Ilex's words.

"He's right," Pratty Clover, Trif's mother, remaked.

"I want to learn to fight!" said a gangling girl.

"No, me!" A bigger youth shouldered her aside.

"Me!"

"Me!"

"Me!"

Three boys shouted at once.

Pink rubbed his forehead, sent a sour smile to Ilex. "We're Commoners, and we have minor Flair, but nobody called us cowardly or noncompetitive." He raised his voice to the courtyard seething with young people excited at the new opportunity. "We'll have a family meeting!"

The idea of fitting everyone around a small table like most Families boggled Ilex's mind.

Pink turned to Trif. "I suppose *you* don't want to train with Tab Holly."

She gave a delicate shudder. "No." Then she lifted her chin. "I want to learn to 'port."

He grunted, nodded at Ilex. "You listen to the guardsman." Then Pink raised a fat finger and pointed it directly at her nose. "Having a Heart Mate is a wonderful blessing, but looking for him. . . . Watch yourself carefully when you go on that damn fool quest of yours."

Trif flushed, snatched her kitten back, set Greyku back on her shoulder, and stalked off to the empty landing pad. She pressed the button lighting the signal on the post—sending notice to anyone who stretched their senses before teleporting to the pad that it was ready for use.

With a sigh, Pink clapped Ilex on the shoulder. "Thank you for taking care of our girl." He studied the younger generation, who'd arranged dining benches around the rectangular courtyard and watched him impatiently. "Thank you for your good advice." He shook his head. "We'll have to let more than one go. Perhaps even as many as three. It's going to be expensive."

"Tab Holly might be—intrigued—with teaching Clovers, imparting the knowledge of a proper duello to the middle class."

Pink winced. "We're more used to scuffles and fistfights."

"I'd wager you're a keen negotiator. You might have an interesting session with GentleSir Holly."

Pink perked up. "Really?"

"Yes."

Rubbing his hands, Pink grinned, then bowed. "Merry meet."

"And merry part," Ilex said, the standard reply.

"And merry meet again," Pink said, and went to a large bell and pulled the rope.

Clanging filled the courtyard and people spilled from the house doors. Ilex blinked at the sight of them all. Shook his head. He'd underestimated the size of the clan. A little dazed, he joined Trif, wrapping his arms loose around her supple waist.

"Let's go quickly, while people aren't watching." She formed an image of her mainspace and he and Greyku shared the vision. Shifting a little, she distracted Ilex so he had to focus hard to keep the image from wavering. "On three," she whispered. "One, my mainspace; two, my mainspace. *Three!*"

They stumbled a bit when they landed, but Trif whooped with victory and once again danced out of his grasp. "We did it, and you *let* me take the lead, and I *brought us here*! Thank you, thank you, thank you, Ilex." She swept up to him and grazed his cheek with a light kiss. The brush of her lips ignited a firestorm in him. He reached for her, but she'd already spun away, lifting Greyku from her shoulder and holding the kitten high, looking at her Fam and not him. "I think this calls for a drink! I have some brithe brandy." She glided into the minuscule kitchen, and the sound of an opening no-time door came.

Ilex couldn't speak. His physical reaction at the mere touch of her lips on his skin in a friendly kiss fried all his logic. All the rationalizations he'd used to stay in her company were lies.

All the warnings he'd given himself were true.

He was in trouble.

Trif danced out of the kitchen with two small brandy snifters, Greyku trotting beside her. She handed one to him, then clinked it in a toast. "To teleporting!"

Ilex wished he was anywhere but here.

Trif went to a small twoseat, settled, sipped, and said, "Do you have a HeartMate, Ilex?"

His head began to ache. What to say? He'd never lie to her. "I never felt one in my own Passages." The Third and last one had been when he was twenty-seven, a little more than two decades ago, as was usual. She'd been two years old.

The incredible lust and joy at touching a HeartMate had come from her during the heat of her Second Passage at seventeen, and the fluctuating echoes of that had continued over the last three years.

Her mouth softened. "I'm sorry."

He shrugged. "It's rare enough to have HeartMates."

"Yes. We don't have any in the family now except Mitchella D'Blackthorn and Straif." Her brow wrinkled. "Though I think there was a pair of Clovers a few generations back. What of your Family?"

"My mother is a widow. My father died when I was a boy." He smiled humorlessly. "My aunt and uncle on my father's side were HeartMates. Childless, but HeartMates. Their line died out, like so many."

Trif squirmed a little on the sofa. "My main Flair is to see the past. The cities on old Earth were *huge*. So were the Families. The entire population."

"Four hundred years after colonization and we're still taming the planet," Ilex murmured.

"That's sad." She stared at the liquid in her cup, lifted her chin. "But HeartMate marriages produce more and stronger children. Offspring better suited to Celta, and with more Flair."

Ilex sat in a chair across from her, drank some brandy, and smiled. "So you're hunting for your HeartMate as a duty for your Family. I think your Family would disagree on that."

"That won't stop me from searching for him." Her smile lit her eyes. "Everyone in the family older than I am has lectured me. Danith D'Ash has spoken to me. Cuz Mitchella has arranged a meeting with T'Willow for me tomorrow afternoon."

He strove to keep his expression placid. T'Willow, the matchmaker, could very well have the ability to divine Trif's HeartMate by just looking at her. Especially since Ilex had made the mistake of meeting her. To Ilex's Flair sight, the thread that bound them together was small, spiderweb-thin. Trif hadn't noticed it at all. T'Willow would.

Overwhelming temptation had done him in.

Six

That night Trif once again had erotic dreams of her HeartMate—this time seeing the outline of broad shoulders, feeling strong muscles under her hands as she stroked him, the weight of him pressing on her as they moved in love together. It was a mature man's body, not a young man of her own age still filling out his frame.

She awoke sexually fulfilled but mentally and emotionally frustrated. Why wouldn't he claim her in anything except dreams?

Though it was just after dawn, there was no way she could sleep, so she dressed and set out breakfast for herself and Greyku. "We're going heart questing," she said to the sleepy kitten.

Fun!

It wasn't fun for Trif. It had started that way, a lighthearted undertaking, but had become a serious quest. If she could find her HeartMate this morning, then she could beg off visiting T'Willow. She'd briefly touched her lover's mind and knew he wasn't of the FirstFamilies—all the men of that highest class had a different perspective. Her HeartMate hadn't echoed with the fierce desire to carry on his line, to rule. That was *something* she'd learned. He could still be a Noble, but not of the highest. Which meant he wasn't the new T'Willow, since T'Willow was of the greatest rank.

Probably.

And the man was in Druida. She'd sensed that too.

She didn't want to visit T'Willow. He'd only give her another lecture, and there was that unnamed favor she would owe him.

As Greyku ate her breakfast and Trif nibbled on nut cereal, she unfolded her map. She liked the two-dimensional aid instead of a three-dimensional orb. She hesitated marking her route as a thought occurred to her. Was that why teleporting was more difficult for her, because she thought more in two dimensions than in three? At work, and for her home, she'd always used blueprints. With a nod of decision, she decided to force herself to become accustomed to the three-dimensional decorating spheres at work. Mitchella had one of the home the Clovers were building for Trif. Trif would ask for it and make a copy herself.

She frowned. That would cut into her free time and teleporting with Ilex, and she didn't want that. The lessons had become important.

Trif looked at her map, crossed off the Ginger Residence in Noble Country, and shivered. The newsheets had announced Gib Ginger's death and that Ilex had found him. That was why he'd sent her away. Her friends and Family were right about Noble Country. She didn't belong there and wouldn't go back until she'd exhausted every other section of Druida.

Greyku gave a discreet burp. *I am ready. Do We 'port?*

"No." Trif lifted the kitten to the table and pointed on the map. "This is where I'm going; it's a street of shops and homes near CityCenter. Very safe. The shops won't be open yet, but there will be people stirring, early risers, and I don't know the area well enough to teleport to."

With a little growl, Greyku pawed at the papyrus map, crumpling it. *I don't see.*

"Stop that!" Trif lifted the kitten and looked into her wide, blue eyes.

"You're not that innocent."

Why can't We look at homes around the Ship?

Glancing at the map to confirm her own memory, Trif said slowly, "That may be a good idea, to work around Landing Park. The lower Nobility have estates there. It seems safe enough."

And We can teleport back here or run to the Ship if We need to, Greyku said.

"Information Library," Trif addressed her personal unit. "Give me the next scheduled time for the public carrier to Landing Park and CityCenter."

"A carrier leaves for Landing Park in six minutes and to CityCenter in thirty seconds. The next carrier for CityCenter is in ten minutes."

Landing Park is closer to Clover Fine Furnishings than CityCenter, Greyku observed.

"All right. We have to hurry, though." She grabbed her pursenal, checked it for fare, gilt, and her charmkey, then put it on her belt and whipped it around her waist. "It's going to be a long day."

We are going on an adventure! The little cat's enthusiasm lit her own.

"Yes!"

*Ilex awoke just after dawn sexually satisfied and grim. Be*ing with Trif outside dreams made it all too possible she'd discover who he was. He stripped the sheets off his bedsponge, threw them in the cleanser, remade the bed, then stood under a cold waterfall. He'd promised Trif he would help her learn to teleport, and even though he knew he should back out of that stupidity, he feared for her safety. She'd been proud of the 'porting she'd done the night before, but if he hadn't steadied her, they'd have fallen a few feet to the floor of her apartment. He couldn't trust her—and Greyku's—skills in the matter. Which meant he had to ensure she had a retrieval amulet that would send her to a HealingHall if she was hurt. Which meant he must visit his mother and request the spell from her, and pay whatever outrageous fee—monetary or emotional or both—that she demanded.

He hadn't seen his mother in two years.

Though he wasn't expected at the guardhouse for two

septhours, on such a case as this, he usually would have gone in early and stayed late, taking only time for sleep.

But there was Trif, and his promise to her. Most of all, his need to protect her. And his thoughts circled back to his mother.

Carefully he dressed in his best daily uniform and checked his appearance. *D'Winterberry GrandHouse,* he sent mentally to the place he'd grown up in.

Greetyou, son of D'Winterberry, Black Ilex, the House replied in lugubrious tones.

Please request a consultation with D'Winterberry as soon as possible, Ilex said. His mother would know that he wanted to ask for something. Her greed and curiosity would prompt her to answer him quickly. She might already be up. Addicts to the potent yar-duan liquor slept at odd intervals.

A consultation as soon as possible? Even the House sounded interested.

"Yes."

GrandLady D'Winterberry welcomes her son if he wishes to consult now.

Ilex adjusted his cuffs. His sleeves and trous were not bloused for efficiency and thrift reasons. *I will arrive shortly.* He sent a questing thought to his home, receiving the information that the light of the teleportation pad glowed, ready for his use. He darkened it and 'ported.

Dust rose as he landed on the pad in the corner of the large entryway. No serving member of the Family was there to greet him, which was new, but unsurprising. The room itself appeared more barren than it had been the last he'd seen it, the squares of dark green tiles dull and unpolished, the last of the art gone. A cheerless room. The house itself seemed shrouded in the silence of near-emptiness.

Ilex's brother had left as soon as he'd reached his majority and moved south to Gael City. The last time Ilex had heard from his brother, he was considering moving farther south still—across the Plano Straight into the southern continent of Brittany.

Something in Ilex flinched from the idea, even as his brain reminded him that if Celtans weren't people with wanderlust, they wouldn't have been on the planet at all.

As he walked to his mother's suite, a fine tension imbued his muscles, but he could do little to mitigate it, except breathe deeply and shut out the past. He knocked on the door to his mother's suite, and it was opened by an aged woman dressed in faded red robes. He bowed to her. "Greetyou, Auntie."

She did a little head dip, then stepped back, holding the door open. Ilex stepped into the sitting room. Heavy drapes blocked the morning sunlight and the room was lit by faint glowballs. His mother sat in a heavily carved wooden chair—that was the same at least—and held out an imperious hand to be kissed. Her fingers trembled slightly.

Shock rattled through him as he saw the papery texture of her pallid skin, the prominent blue veins in her hands. "Greetyou, guardsman," she said.

Yes, he'd pay dearly for what he'd ask.

The strong scent of yar-duan ladened the air, though she was meticulously groomed and dressed in robes only a few months out of fashion.

He brushed a kiss over her bony knuckles and released her fingers. A wispy thought probed at his mind from her. He kept his mental shields up and it slid away. Only blood linked them, they shared no mental or emotional ties.

She swept a hand to a hassock near her. He sat stiffly. "What can I do for you, Black Ilex?"

Her voice was cool, her words slightly slurred, and the lack of any antagonism from her surprised him.

"I would like you to set a strong retrieval spell on an amulet."

A faint line creased her forehead. "A retrieval spell. If a person is injured wearing a retrieval amulet, they are sent to a HealingHall," she recited.

"That's right. It should be within your Flair abilities." She had strong teleportation and relocation Flair, some of which she'd passed on to him, though his foresight came from some other unknown Familial source. The Winterberrys had intermarried with so many Families that no extremely strong line of Flair flowed from one generation to the next. A detriment in a Celtan Family, especially a Noble one.

With a rustle, she took out some worry beads and flicked them along their chain, a nervous habit that was new to Ilex.

Her gaze was fixed in the distance. After a moment, she nodded. "I can do that. The amulet must contain an item carrying the lifeforce of the person and a piece of a HealingHall." Her gaze swung back to him, dark and piercing. "Primary HealingHall?" She named the highest-class one.

"MidClass HealingHall," he said.

She sniffed, and it reminded him enough of the kitten that he nearly smiled. "I must have a good amulet to work with."

"T'Ash will craft it."

"T'Ash? Perhaps you'll be useful after all." Her aura brightened and he saw a strong thread leading from her to . . . someone else not in the suite. All his instincts rose.

"Two years of your Noblegilt as the price."

Ilex clamped his teeth shut on a protest and replied mildly. "My Noblegilt as a younger son of a lower GrandLady isn't much," he said.

The lines around her lips creased deeply as she pursed them. "You have strong Flair and that increases the gilt, and any gilt we can get is better than nothing. We have plans to reestablish the Family status."

She'd always had.

"I know you haven't been accepting your Noblegilt from the Council, but living on your salary," she said.

"I don't provide any free Flair services to the public," he replied steadily.

"You are a *guardsman*." Spittle dampened her bottom lip. She'd never accepted his "lower-class job" and made it sound as if he were a waste transmuter. "You work *every day* as a servant of the Council guardsmen. I also know that the Council has praised your work and offered you Noblegilt as well as your salary to you for your duties. Accept the Noblegilt and send it to me. That is my price." She crossed stick-thin arms over a flat chest.

He studied her, extended a faint brush of his Flair. She was not alone in this plan. He turned his head to look at his aunt. She wasn't the new force behind his mother. There was another. Female . . .

"I'm waiting, Black Ilex."

There was no give of negotiation in her. She'd set the price and was adamant. "Agreed," he said reluctantly. "I'll send the request to the Noble Council clerk today."

"You'll request it *now.*" She pointed to an elaborate bronze scrybowl on its own table.

Ilex stood. Before he reached the bowl, the door opened. A middle-aged, heavy woman about fifteen years older than himself bustled into the room, dressed in deep green velvet with light green piping around the hem of her tunic, sleeve, and trous cuffs—which indicated she was WinterberryHeir. Another shock. His brother was the strongest Flaired Winterberry. Everyone knew that.

"You remember your cuz, Dringal," his mother said drily.

He'd been obvious in his disbelief and his lack of recognition.

The woman lifted a fleshy chin. "I married GrandLord Thyme." She sniffed and glared at his mother. "I believed him when he said he had great plans to revitalize his fortune. At least when he died I took over the title. I am D'Thyme, equal in rank to you, D'Winterberry."

Ilex gave Dringal a bow of exquisite precision due to her rank, and not a hair more. She didn't offer her hand to be kissed, and he was grateful. "It's been a long time," he murmured.

"Black Ilex has requested a retrieval spell on an amulet," his mother said. "I've set a price of two years of his Noblegilt."

"Good," D'Thyme said briskly. "With that gilt, we can convince my daughter to quit her job so we can enter the new year's social season and she can make a good match." The woman eyed Ilex. "I hear you've reacquainted yourself with our distant relatives, the Hollys." She rubbed her hands. "Good, good. Dear Passiflora D'Holly would surely grant a small request to house us during the season and introduce us to all the FirstFamilies. Too bad her sons are already wed, and Tinne to that Furze slut."

Anger seared him. This time he kept his emotions under rigid control and from showing. "Genista Furze Holly has always been kind to me. Such discourtesy to her is not appropriate."

D'Thyme narrowed her eyes at him. "Bedded you too, did she? Then you might have some influence with her."

"No," he said. "As for your daughter—surely you wouldn't want her living in a cursed Residence."

D'Thyme looked startled. "Cursed? What are you talking about?"

"The senior Hollys broke a Vow of Honor. It wears on the inhabitants of the household and the Residence itself."

Snorting, D'Thyme said, "Balderdash." Then she waved her plump hand again. "A minor inconvenience."

No one in Druida believed that. Certainly no one who'd seen any of the Hollys.

His mother shifted uneasily. "We wouldn't want your daughter to bring any illness to our House. And she must be at the peak of her meager beauty to snare a fine Lord. Perhaps we should rethink the part where she stays with the Hollys."

To his disgust, Ilex realized he'd walked into a waiting spiderweb. "I'll send my Noblegilt for the last *three* years to you, as well as my next guardsman bonus. I will not speak to the Hollys on your behalf."

"Ilex's a man, and low-class," muttered his mother. "He'd only bungle that part anyway. It will be best if I send a request to Passiflora D'Holly." She straightened bony shoulders.

"For the amount I'm paying you, I expect the amulet to be your greatest priority and quickly done," Ilex said coolly, though he was sure his mother had no other commissions.

"I don't have the strength to work around the clock," she said, her voice close to a whine.

"How long will it take you?" He walked to the door. "I'll notify T'Ash to make the amulet."

"Three days," she snapped, gestured again to the scrybowl. "And I want my payment up front."

Ilex inclined his head and went to the bowl. "Noble Council Clerk's Office," he said as he tapped the water in the bowl. It held a nasty film that coated his finger and he banished it with a Word.

The image of a box appeared in the scrybowl. "Noble Council Clerk's Office Message Cache."

"Black Ilex Winterberry requests his last three years worth of Noblegilt transferred to the Lady of his GrandHouse, D'Winterberry." He wondered if his brother had withdrawn his loyalty from their mother and Tested to become a Lord on his own. Surely his brother would have told him. It shamed Ilex that he'd been so wrapped up in his work that he hadn't spoken with his brother, let alone visited, for over a year. They hadn't been a close Family. Perhaps he could try and change that.

He turned to the whispering women, not caring to use his Flair to overhear them. The sooner he was done with this bargain, the better—leave them all to their pitiful, greedy, social-climbing household. Clearing his throat, he caught their attention. "D'Winterberry's spells are not always known for their efficacy."

Spots of color appeared on his mother's cheeks like circles of rouge. "Lies."

"I expect this spell to be potent, long-lasting, and *effective*. For that result, I advise you to cleanse yourself spiritually and purge yourself of any problems your yar-duan addiction causes."

She flung her hand out. "Go!"

He met D'Thyme's eyes. "Ensure she is capable of casting the spell. If it fails *in any way*, I will challenge her authority and see you both on the streets."

D'Thyme wet her lips. "We can't be held responsible for a faulty amulet."

"You think T'Ash does poor work? And if you try to blame any defect on him, I'll let *him* tear the House apart."

Both women paled. T'Ash had a certain reputation for violence.

Ilex jerked his head at his mother. "Take her to the HouseHeart and get her on a purge and a fast."

"I'll do that," D'Thyme said, then gave him a tight-lipped smile. "Though you were no help when *I* had my troubles."

Ilex's mind went completely blank.

"Couldn't even bother to look at my husband's burnt laboratory when I asked."

He recalled now. Her husband had blown up their home. "I was out of town."

"Getting your bare ass bitten by a grychomp. But you could have investigated."

"I was involved in another inquiry at the time, and everyone knows that experimenting with time is beyond dangerous."

Her face mottled. "You could have at least stopped D'Willow's rumors that my husband was an incompetent madman."

Ilex figured anyone who fiddled with time and destroyed a house was by definition an incompetent madman. He agreed with the new laws banning time experimentation.

But he merely said, "As my mother said, I am but a low-class man. I have no credibility in social circles."

D'Thyme's chin came up. "I suppose so. All you are good for is giving us gilt that is our due."

He replied in his softest tones. "I commissioned a spell from my mother. I warn you again, if you want to keep any more scandal from attaching to your name, you'd best ensure the spell works."

He opened the door and left. The stink of stale liquor clung to his uniform.

At the front door, he bumped into a tall, thin, stoop-shouldered woman of about twenty-seven. Her hair was unfashionably long, but clean. She wore a shabby commoncloth trous suit that proclaimed she was middle-class, not of the Nobility. Still, he thought she must be Dringal's daughter. Who else would live with the two women if they could help it? He steadied her and found sheer, huge Flair tingling his palms. There was also a Family connection. "You must be Dufleur Thyme."

She flushed and raised her gaze, meeting his eyes with those that were luminous and smoky blue. He was nearly stunned speechless by the beauty of those eyes, widely spaced and heavily fringed with dark brown lashes.

He bowed at the same time she curtsied. "I am, cuz Black Ilex." Her voice was soft and husky; a man might think of it as seductive.

"Just Ilex."

She smiled and revealed another feminine weapon—dimples at the corners of her mouth and white, even teeth. Her smile made her completely beautiful. How could the two old women think finding a man to wed her would be difficult?

Wrinkling her nose, she said, "If I were called Black, I'd drop it too."

Ilex chuckled.

She glanced at her wrist timer and flung open the front door. "I must hurry to catch the CityCenter carrier."

He let the door fall and slam behind them and lengthened

his stride to match hers. Narrowing his eyes, thinking of murder, he asked "Have you endured your Third Passage yet?"

A slightly shocked glance came from those staggering eyes and she flushed unattractively again at the personal question. But they were kin, and she must have sensed it as he had, so she answered. "Just last month." A frown knit between her brows. "I had to take off work for two weeks." She picked up pace. "It put me behind."

"Any aftershocks—flashbacks to Passage since?"

"No." They'd reached the corner and she stopped at a public carrier plinth and looked up at him.

"Good. There's a murderer out there targeting those with irregular Flair." He scanned the street, still shrouded with night shadows, and something tickled his senses. Trif? Was Trif around?

Dufleur shivered and he brought his attention back to her. "No," she said and smiled again. "My Flair isn't unstable."

"You don't have a Fam?"

She rolled her eyes. "I wish, but of course not, cuz Ilex."

He patted her shoulder. "Be careful."

The public carrier glider drew up. She glanced back at him as she mounted the steps. "I will."

"And Dufleur"—he couldn't stop the words; they came from him with the force of one of his prophetic visions—"Test your Flair, establish a GrandHouse of your own."

Her face tightened. "No. I loved my father. I don't care that scandal has blackened his name and reputation. I'll be Thyme."

"Test and take the title from your mother." He'd raised his voice as the public carrier closed its doors. Through the glass, he saw her shaking her head.

Trif had tried her charmkey on the gates of the six estates directly south of Landing Park with no result. The morning was quiet and a few lights were just coming on in the windows. She'd moved one street down from the park and these houses were noticeably less grand. Instead of a long front drive and grassyard that generally hid the entrance of the house, these had waist-high greeniron fences and short sidewalks up to a small set of steps and a covered porch.

She was at the second house when her spine tingled and she turned her head to see a man about her own age staring at her with not-quite-nice amusement on his face.

He strolled toward her, his gaze sliding down her body and back up. She tucked her charmkey in her pocket and thought of her mainspace and how she'd teleport there. If she could recall where the wretched low table was. Was it angled, or had that been last week?

The man stopped just inside the sphere of her personal space and made a short bow. "Trif Clover, I believe? Your *fame* precedes you."

She cringed inwardly, looked around for Greyku. "Is this your home?" If it was, she was glad it hadn't opened to her key.

His glance went past her, dismissed the house. "Of course not. I'm Cyperus Sedge. My Residence is east of the park." The most prized location. He turned his hand in a casual gesture that caught the gold embroidery on his cuffs. Heir to the Sedges. She bobbed a small curtsey. "Greetyou."

"Merry meet," he said, slightly inclining his torso.

"Merry meet!" she rushed out on a breath.

Yowl. Greyku raced from investigating the gate of the next house back toward Trif, stopping and sitting on her feet, glaring up at Cyperus with hot blue eyes. *Snot*, she said mentally to Trif, and since Cyperus only looked down at her, blinking, Trif thought he hadn't heard the kitten.

"*You* have a Fam? Danith D'Ash is particular to whom she graces the company of Fams."

Trif picked up Greyku and cuddled her. "Yes, my Fam."

A glider door whirred open and shut down the street. Bootsteps sounded. Cyperus's sneer was back. "If I were you, I'd teleport home." He glanced ostentatiously at his gold wrist timer. "It's only half a septhour before WorkBell." His voice made it clear that he *didn't* work. He might accept commissions from others of his class for goods or services from his Flair, and Trif sensed it was great, but he didn't work at a regular job.

"Really, Cyperus, must you be so snobbish?" A young woman stylishly dressed in evening wear joined him, tucking her arm inside his. Unused to gliders parked on the street, Trif hadn't considered that behind the tinted windows one of them had apparently been occupied. "I'm Piana Juniper," the woman said. "What an adorable Fam!" She lifted her hand.

Greyku preened a little and let the lady stroke her head. When the woman was done, Trif took the opportunity to circle around them. "Merrily met," she called as she summoned a bit of dignity and hurried along to the carrier plinth on the far corner. She'd hoped to finish the entire block. She glanced back to see the couple staring after her. Piana waved, then smiled.

And Trif ran into Ilex.

Seven

He steadied her with strong, warm hands on her shoulders. Trif wished she could melt into the pavement. Better, teleport away. That she had been *able* to teleport away. Her face went hot.

Merry meet! Greyku chirruped a greeting.

"Merry meet, Greyku." Ilex dropped his hands. His eyes had gone a flat gray. "As for you, Trif Clover, I don't consider this a good meeting. In fact, I believe it was very unwise on your part." His gaze looked beyond her to where the man and woman had been. The soft click of glider stands retracting came, and the whir as it sped away.

"What are you doing here?" she blurted.

"I don't think that's important to this conversation," he said. For an instant, Trif wondered if he'd stayed overnight somewhere other than his home, just as the couple she'd met had, and her spirits drooped. "I had an early appointment," he said. "What were you doing here?"

She set her shoulders. "You know I was searching for my HeartMate."

"I had hoped you would do that in a safer fashion. In a more populated area."

"It's not Noble Country," she protested.

"It's not safe."

Samba watched! Greyku sent indignantly.

"Samba?" Ilex said at the same time Trif did.

Greyku flicked a paw to the sky. They looked up. There, hovering high, was the flying saucer of Samba, the Ship cat.

"Samba watched," Trif said.

He dropped his hands from her arms and she missed his touch. Ilex lifted a brow. "Did you know that?"

She sighed. "No."

He stared at her, and she felt like a young child about to be punished.

He winced.

"What?" she asked.

"Nothing," he said. "I've arranged for a retrieval spell to be put on an amulet. Contact T'Ash about making one. He'll let you know what he needs for it. Now I must go to Mid-Class HealingHall." He nodded to the public carrier pulling up. "That's your glider to work, isn't it?"

"Yes."

"Better go," he told her and before she could reply, he teleported away, leaving her feeling small and wishing he'd offered to 'port her to work.

She spent the whole morning unhappy that she'd disappointed him and trying to convince herself that his feelings didn't matter. But they did. Somehow, in the space of a couple of days, he'd become a friend. That happened to her often, so it wasn't too unique—except he was a handsome, sophisticated, much older man.

Trif put away the two-dimensional worksheets she used, and set out several spheres that everyone else in the office employed to image the furniture and place it in various surroundings. "About time," said one of her cuzes.

"I thought this might help me learn to 'port. I haven't been thinking in three dimensions."

The woman held the ball, made a small change, and the desk looked better situated in the model den. She handed the globe back to Trif. "Couldn't hurt." She tapped the sphere. "The orb has inbuilt Flair, and I only use what's there. You have considerable Flair of your own. Maybe it clashes. And if it does, you'd better learn to use it."

"Yes," Trif said, and called up a bedroom, envisioning the new Clover Fine Furnishings suite inside it. The activity made her head hurt. A small mew preceded a tiny nip at her finger. "Greyku?"

Are you getting a tinter for me? I am all white. She stared at the model bedroom in the globe, bold with primary colors. *White is SO bo-ring.*

"You're sure you don't want to be white?"

I'm sure. I think I might want to be magenta. Or sapphire. Or emerald. Or golden. Or magenta and sapphire and emerald and golden, with silver whiskers. "Yesssss!"

Something else Trif couldn't imagine. "Very well."

During lunch, Trif nerved herself to scry the only artist she knew—Citrula, who lived in an artist colony on Mona Island. They had been adversaries, but the last time they'd met, they'd parted on relatively civil terms.

To Trif's surprise, Citrula looked relaxed and fulfilled. "What can I do for you?"

Trif held Greyku above the large office scrybowl. "This is my Fam, Greyku. She wants to be tinted."

At Citrula's surprise, Trif gave a little cough. "The Ship states that ancient Earth cats were tinted for centuries."

Citrula appeared intrigued. "I think one of our community is experimenting with nano-art and in contact with the Ship. I'll ask it for vizes."

Greyku scowled down at the close water and issued a series of meows. Trif translated. "She likes the idea of jewel tones, being a—ahem—multicolored kitty."

Citrula raised her brows. "A challenge." She eyed the kitten, who was stiff and with claws extended over the large watery scrybowl. "Will she sit still for the work?"

"Yessssss," hissed Greyku. *Put Me aside now. The artist has seen enough.*

Trif did as she was told.

"I think we'll do her in layers," Citrula said.

"Layers?"

"A cat has many-layered fur. We might be able to accommodate her taste and my vision."

They'd better. Trif coughed, struggling with amusement again. "My primary concern is that Greyku is happy."

"If you want this done for a reasonable rate, you'll let me have my way." That was a issue too. Especially since Trif was paying T'Ash for an amulet. Even at cost, the jewelry was going to stretch her budget.

Laughing, Citrula said, "Let the kitten pay me."

How? Trif stared at Greyku. "Can you pay the artist?"

Greyku lifted her nose. *She should be honored to tint Me.*

Uh—huh. *If you can't pay her, you will have to abide by Citrula's decision as to how you will be tinted.*

The kitten lashed her tail and subvocalized a growl that sounded like cat swears. Trif held firm. She'd heard that cats demanded payment for *their* services.

Very well. Greyku hunkered down, ears flattened.

Citrula said, "Where can we do this? I don't think it should take more than an afternoon."

D'Ash will let us do it in her office suite, Greyku said. *She is curious. As are Samba and Drina and Zanth. I will charge them to watch and pay the artist!* she rumbled in triumph.

"A good idea," Trif said to Greyku, then spoke to Citrula in the scrybowl. "Some Fams and people will be paying Greyku to observe the process. So I think you should consider a few options. Including jewel tones. Why don't we say Midday Bell at T'Ash Residence."

"Very well, but not today, perhaps in a couple of days. I'll scry." Citrula shook her head. "Tinting a kitten jewel tones." She laughed.

Greyku smacked the water with her paw, rudely ending the call.

Mitchella wisely sent one of her elegant gliders to ferry Trif from Clover Fine Furnishings to T'Willow's Residence. An ugly stone fountain sat carefully protected at one end of the back glider bench. Greyku inspected it, then crawled into the basin and curled up for a nap.

During the trip, Trif fretted whether Ilex had told her powerful cuz about finding her questing that morning. She sensed he was worried for her safety, but if he'd reported her to Mitchella, he was no friend. She'd rather he officially charge her with trespassing than inform her Family and her friends of her faults.

No, Ilex wouldn't tell on her. Not without alerting her first. She knew it. And that kindled warmth inside her.

They drew up to T'Willow's and a man in bright red livery lifted open the door and helped her out. Since the only two Nobles Trif knew had more casual servants, this made Trif extremely self-conscious.

She pulled the small stone table fountain along behind her. The thing had a floating spell, but was still ungainly. It was also hideous. Trif couldn't imagine why Mitchella, the queen of good taste, was giving it to someone she wanted to impress.

Furthermore, Greyku sat like a queen in the bottom. Trif thought cat hair couldn't be good for the pump, but maybe the waterspell took care of that too.

The T'Willow GreatHouse looked a little like Clover Compound. As the most prolific family on Celta, the Clovers had purchased a whole block and begun ringing it with homes, with the courtyard in the middle. The T'Willow Residence wasn't much like the fancy Earth castles or the towering fortresses most of the FirstFamilies had built.

There was a nice-sized grassyard around the front of the building, but the walls were a pale cream-colored featureless armourcrete showing square windows and an inset door. Trif was sure all the loveliness of a Residence would be inside. She didn't think the courtyard would have anything like a dusty playground, though.

The server opened the door with a flourish and an older woman also in red, awaited them. She glanced at the fountain and beamed. "Oh, Saille will be so *pleased*! Come this way, GentleLady Clover." She bustled into the house and Trif followed with the fountain.

Greyku preened. *Everyone is pleased when I visit.*

Trif hit back a grin and touched her small Fam on the head. "I think the lady meant T'Willow will be pleased to see the fountain."

Sniffing, Greyku glanced around at the basin. *It is not very pretty.*

"No."

The woman led Trif to a corner room and knocked on the door. "GentleLady Trif Clover is here, and she has a *surprise* from GrandLady D'Blackthorn!"

Trif eyed the door. She'd been testing a lot of doors, lately. She wondered. . . .

The door opened and a man in his late twenties, clad in shirtsleeves and trous, stood before her. He was taller than she, had patrician features, dark chestnut hair, and bright blue eyes. He smiled down at her. "No, you don't need to try your charmkey on this door. I am not your HeartMate."

A wash of heat warmed her face. This was a man great in matchmaking Flair. "Sorry."

"No, I am the one who is sorry," he said, smoothly bowing her into the sitting room.

"Saille, look what T'Blackthorn and D'Blackthorn have given us! How *kind* of them."

T'Willow looked past Trif at the floating fountain and his expression lightened. "What an excellent gift. I'll pen a note to them personally." He nodded to Greyku. "Greetyou, Fam."

I am Greyku.

"Greetyou, Greyku, may I place you on this pillow?" He indicated a twoseat stacked with boldly colored pillows.

I would like the sapphire one, please.

He arranged the pillow, carefully lifted the kitten from the fountain basin, and laid her on the pillow. She purred and rubbed her head against his hand. He looked at Trif. "You're lucky to have a Fam. My name is on D'Ash's list, but . . ."

I have a brother. Zanth brought him to D'Ash this dawn, Greyku projected.

T'Willow nodded.

"Zanth is T'Ash's Fam," Trif said.

"Everyone knows Zanth." T'Willow looked amused.

Trif cleared her throat. "Neither Greyku nor her brother have known bloodlines."

Shrugging, T'Willow gestured for her to sit down on the twoseat, and took charge of the fountain. "I don't care about bloodlines."

Trif didn't believe that. Every member of a FirstFamily thought of nothing *but* bloodlines.

He said a Word and the floatspell vanished. Setting the fountain on a pedestal that looked made for it, he glanced back at her. "I'm in the matchmaking business. I care more about the *heart* of a person than the *blood*. Wouldn't you say that is true?"

His careful expression alerted her. She caught her breath, her pulse skipped, then quickened. She wet her lips. "You know who he is."

T'Willow lifted a shoulder. "It only took one glance at you."

She narrowed her eyes. "How is that?"

Laughing, he shook his head. "Ah, now that would mean a three-septhour lecture on my Flair."

"I suppose you won't tell me."

He frowned and turned away, tapped the fountain, and water surged from the top of the ugly mound to roll a clear crystal ball at the top, then rush down a groove. The crystal glowed as it spun, shooting out iridescent sparks. "You must thank your cuz and T'Blackthorn for returning this T'Willow meditation tool."

Trif stared at him and the fountain. "It was yours? How did it come to be T'Blackthorn's?"

"Let's walk and talk."

Glancing at the glass-paned door opening on the garden outside, Trif frowned. Clouds had rolled in and the wind had picked up.

But T'Willow followed her gaze, then crossed to a door in the end of the room. "Come into my ResidenceDen."

She hesitated. Entering a GreatLord's ResidenceDen was too much like a very, very expensive consultation.

Putting his hands in his pockets, he tilted his head at Trif. She studied him, handsome and noble, and secretive. But she sensed he might not have refused to answer her questions, just wasn't ready yet. She'd have to work on him. She smiled with all her charm.

T'Willow laughed. "Ah, you canny young woman. The door to the conservatory is through the ResidenceDen."

Trif tickled Greyku's belly. The little cat stretched but didn't open her eyes. "I'm going to talk with T'Willow in the conservatory."

Greyku rolled over and presented her back to Trif. She

took that as rejection of any exercise. Shrugging, Trif went into the ResidenceDen. One wall was nothing but glass, showing verdant plants beyond. The furnishings were carefully kept antiques of dark wood. A slight smell of green wood, incense, and laquer drifted through the room. Trif saw thin sticks spread out on a heavy blotter atop the massive desk.

He glanced at the desk. "My MotherDam had her own matchmaking divination sticks which she destroyed before I became the head of the Family. They'd been passed down through generations." He shrugged. "I'd made my own, as Heir, but now I have the title, I need new ones—more Flaired." One side of his mouth twisted. "GreatLady D'Willow's sticks would never have fit my hands anyway." Still, he considered the sticks, then a sudden, charming smile curved his lips and lit his eyes. "I think I'll make two sets. One for my personal use, and one to replace those lost . . . Start a generational set of my own."

"Good idea."

"Yes, and you prompted it. Thank you." He opened the door to the conservatory, and humid air rich with the scent of earth and flowers flowed out to her. The thought of a walk in a space that was still green pulled at her. She hurried through the door he held.

They strolled along a path banked with flowers. T'Willow spoke first. "You know, my Family is matriarchal."

With a frown, Trif thought back to her grove study days. "Yes."

Not looking at her, T'Willow said, "My MotherDam, old D'Willow, was very displeased when the oracle at my birth announced that I was the strongest in Flair of all the generations present and should be designated as Heir." He asked permission of a maroon and gold iris bloom, and the spear fell into his hand. "Irises were her favorite flowers." He inhaled the fragrance, then gave it to Trif. "My compliments. The iris represents friendship. Also faith, hope, wisdom, and valor."

Trif sniffed, admiring the flower. "A lot to live up to."

"Yes. My MotherDam didn't believe that men should have matchmaking Flair. She banished me to our country estate for most of my life, then did all she could to circumvent me as her Heir. That included sending Family treasures away as gifts." He turned down another path that ended in a bench under a secluded arbor, and Trif followed. "But I had faith and hope that I'd assume my rightful place—use my Flair as I'd been destined to." He smiled, but it was more wry than amused. "I had the wisdom to stay out of D'Willow's sight."

"And?" There must be some meaning to this story.

"When my MotherDam . . . left, the Family—most of them women—designated me as T'Willow and called me back to Druida City to lead the Family and practice our craft. I did not push, I cultivated patience. That which was out of my grasp eventually came to me. Many of my Family Flair tools and possessions have returned too." He sat on the bench.

"You don't think I should go knocking on doors for my HeartMate with my charmkey."

"I think," he said carefully, slowly, "that your HeartMate doesn't want you to find him."

Trif stood, stupefied. "Why ever not?"

"His reasons," T'Willow said, and Trif didn't know if that meant the GreatLord knew the reasons and wasn't telling, or hadn't sensed them. She *did* get the idea that T'Willow was more on her HeartMate's side than her own.

"He knows who I am?"

T'Willow inclined his head.

Stomping up and down the path, Trif muttered to herself, then came back and asked another question. "It seems to me that most men know their HeartMates before the women do, like me."

"Passages to free our Flair are when most people connect with their HeartMates. With many couples, the man is older than the woman. Therefore, he has experienced Passage before her, and has the time to search for her—if he is lucky enough to recognize her when they connect."

Mouth set, Trif paced up and back again. "My best friend is Lark Hawthorn Apple. I saw Holm woo her. He *knew* she was his HeartMate. He used a charmkey on her apartment."

T'Willow grinned, white teeth gleaming. "My MotherDam was consulted by Holm Holly, now Holm Apple, in that instance. She kept detailed records of the matter. Holm was not a HeartMate to Lark until he suffered through and overcame some difficult experiences. He *grew* and so became her HeartMate. Lark had weathered her Passages without connecting with a HeartMate and was not expecting one in this lifetime. Holm was focused on marriage and HeartMates when he met her. And often when HeartBonding Flair occurs, it has more impact upon men."

"Oh. So if I were older than my HeartMate, I might have connected with him earlier and figured out who he was."

"Correct."

"But I'm at a disadvantage because I might not experience the HeartMate Flair as strongly as he does."

"Correct again."

"I don't like the rules."

T'Willow tipped back his head in a hearty laugh. When he was done, he said, "I wouldn't worry. I don't think he'll be able to resist you, Trif Clover."

She kicked a little stone on the path into a flower bed. "That doesn't help me now."

"Patience."

She wasn't acceptable to her HeartMate. A sour taste coated her mouth. She didn't think she'd tell anyone that, it was too demoralizing. And she needed to consider this information carefully.

"Your Flair is for matchmaking. How come you can't find this woman?"

His jaw set. "I don't know what spells my MotherDam used, but she hid my HeartMate from me. She bound the rest of the Family to silence. I. Can't. Find. Her. I can't even sense her."

Trif set her hands on her hips. "So what are you going to do about it? Sit and wait and practice patience?"

"No, I am going to give you this." He reached into his pocket and pulled out something. Opened his palm. Trif squinted, but saw nothing—except a slight haze of a round aura. "What?"

"My HeartGift. Only my HeartMate and I can truly see it. Or, in this case, since it is a perfume ball I made, smell it." He took a pouch from his other trous pocket and dropped the HeartGift into it and pulled the red strings tight, then held it out to Trif.

She took it gingerly. The pouch had weight, and bulged, the only indication that something was inside. Lifting the bag to her nose, she sniffed, sure that the strong scent of a perfume ball would be evident. All she smelled was the furrabeast leather of the container.

When she glanced at T'Willow, he was standing and gestured for her to walk back toward the den. She turned and started down the path weighing the pouch in her hand. "What do you want me to do with this?"

"Ah, that's my price for this little talk, the information you squeezed from me."

Trif didn't think he'd told her anything he hadn't intended. "And?"

"Take the HeartGift. I *think* my lady is middle-class like you or lower Nobility and here in Druida. I did link with her during my Passages, after all. My MotherDam couldn't prevent that." His tone was light but his mouth grim.

"Go to the busiest place you know, and leave the HeartGift."

Sheer shock stopped her. Her mouth dropped open as she fumbled for words. "You're sending your *HeartGift*, an intimate piece of yourself, out into the *world*?" She'd stopped emphasizing her words a year ago, but now and then fell back into the habit.

T'Willow kept walking, but his shoulders hunched slightly. "I can think of nothing else to do. Eventually, she should find it." He stopped and glance at Trif with a sardonic smile. "Or it will come to her. She will want it, be drawn to it, naturally."

"And she'll accept it and in accepting it, accept you as her HeartMate."

"Those are the rules—the law."

"But to have your HeartGift out in the world. Being kicked around, fumbled with grubby fingers, maybe eaten by an animal, then eliminated or vomited up—"

"*Please.*" He lifted a hand to halt her words.

"Sorry." She shook her head, and walked past him into his

ResidenceDen once more. "As one of my uncles would say, you got balls."

"Yes," he replied politely. "I do. And so does your HeartMate. Don't think him cowardly."

She snorted. "He has to be, not to claim me."

But T'Willow had moved to the fountain, where the crystal had turned scarlet, the Willow House color, and shot off silver sparks. He stared at it, inhaled and exhaled a few times, and the sphere became a calm aqua blue. Smiling, he looked at her. "Truly hideous thing, isn't it?"

"Uh, yes."

He held out his hand. "Friends, Trif Clover?"

She put hers in his. It was warm and strong, and there was no sizzle of attraction. He kissed her fingers, then went over to the sleeping Greyku, gently lifted the kitten, and gave her to Trif. "Yes," said T'Willow. "I want one of these for my own." As his gaze met hers, his deep green eyes were clear of the previous storms. "My creative Flair is perfumery, something that also runs in our Family, thus the perfume ball HeartGift. I have a small book of perfume recipes written by T'Ash's mother, Jasmine D'Ash. Do you think that will be an acceptable trade to D'Ash for a kitten of no pedigree?"

"Oh, *yes*. That would get you a kitten of the highest rank, and probably placed at the top of her list too. T'Ash has so little of his Family treasures, probably nothing of his mother's. The fire, you know."

"Yes. I know." He looked around the room. "Sometimes when I think my lot was hard, it's best to consider others' fates. I have great Flair, a beautiful home, a FirstFamily title." He bowed. "Merry meet."

"And merry part," she replied automatically.

"And merry meet again." He ushered her to the door, glancing down at the pouch hanging by its strings over her wrist.

"I won't forget to send it on its journey, T'Willow," Trif said quietly.

"Thank you." His smile was dazzling, and his gratitude warmed her as she left. Too bad that they weren't attracted to each other, that they weren't HeartMates. A handsome, sexy,

Nobleman, and for a FirstFamilies GreatLord he didn't seem too weird.

But he wasn't hers. As she slipped back into the T'Blackthorn glider, she looked at the pouch again, sensing nothing. He was someone's, but not hers.

She wanted her own HeartMate. She needed something more than the charmkey. She had to revise her strategy.

Eight

For Ilex, the morning had continued badly. His night counterpart had reviewed the sensorballs, but had not been able to distinguish the same scent of incense that Ilex had, so had been unable to follow up on that. So Ilex had continued making the rounds of incense shops. Mid-morning, Ilex's superior, Chief Sawyr, had stiffly informed him that Tinne Holly and his father, T'Holly, had visited the guardhouse and demanded to see Winterberry, who hadn't been scheduled for duty yet. The GreatLord had requested all the files of the cases, and Sawyr had provided him with a large memory sphere containing much of their information. They still wanted to see Ilex.

Grumbling, Ilex teleported to T'Holly Residence. Since he was part of a distant branch of the Family and had made a courtesy visit or two before, the shields let him through. The butler informed Ilex that the two Hollys were practicing their fighting craft in Sparring Room Two and directed Ilex there.

When he entered, neither of the men looked at him, but in the next minute, each turned or took a fall to glance at him.

Tinne flashed a wicked grin. "Come join us, Ilex."

He was tempted. His inner embarrassment at being caught

near his childhood home had mixed with anger at Trif for continuing her quest. Also, he'd felt a spear of anxiety that his old House might betray him to her if she used her charmkey. He didn't think so, he'd been gone from it a long time, but he didn't know.

Chief Sawyr's bad mood had rubbed at him too. Sawyr was solidly middle-class and he didn't like mixing with Nobles. He didn't like them nosing into his cases, and most of all, he didn't like them in his guardhouse. A few years ago, he'd convinced the rest of the guards that a special position should be created for dealing with the Nobles, and that Ilex should fill it.

Ilex had grudgingly agreed at the time, and the last few cases had been sufficiently interesting—except for that humiliating incident with the fliggering grychomp.

Before the murders. Before his HeartMate was at risk. And now he was wasting time pandering to Nobles instead of working on solving the case.

Grunts from the Hollys brought his mind to Tinne's offer. "I'll watch," he said.

Sweat beading on his brow, T'Holly bit off a chuckle. "Black Ilex the pretty boy."

No one had called him that in decades, but the insult still worked. A red tide washed over his vision and his patience snapped. With a Word, he skinned down to his loinwrap and his uniform folded itself on a chest.

He gauged the fight and when the other two men drew slightly apart, he pounced, hitting them both and rolling away, taking only light taps from jabbing hands and feet.

The three of them wrestled with renewed vigor. Blood pumped fast and hard through his veins and his energy surged. It was *good* to fight. To release the tension of anger and fear and *act,* not think. To feel his hands sting as he hit flesh, accept the ache of landed blows.

Tinne grunted, ducked Ilex's fist, pivoted on a foot, and kicked out with a leg that grazed T'Holly's ribs. "Never. Knew. You. Were. Called. Pretty. Boy. Or. Black Ilex," Tinne sucked in breaths between words, than dived at Ilex and took him down.

His body slick with sweat, Ilex twisted from Tinne's hold.

"Nobody calls me that." He swept out a foot T'Holly couldn't dodge and brought the older man down.

They all escaped each other's grasp and sprang to their feet, grinning—teeth showing, fierce with battle.

Tinne's head snapped back at a blow from his father, and he returned the favor, then shook his head, his eyes meeting Ilex's. "He's in a snide mood. Called me a snotty toddler."

Ilex was too busy fighting T'Holly, then Tinne himself, to answer. It was time to end this. He had business. Gathering his strength and focus, he sent Tinne rolling off the mat—the younger man was now out of the match.

A few minutes later, Ilex pinned T'Holly, then rose and stepped back, panting.

The older man looked aghast as if he'd never lost a fight. Ilex's anger cooled and he felt the impassive mask he often wore settle over his face. He didn't offer to help T'Holly up.

Tinne stared at his father, then looked aside and grabbed a towel. He swiped it around his neck, down his chest. He was growing into his stature and musculature, Ilex noted. Tinne grinned. "If I didn't know better, I'd say that the demon 'love' was riding you."

Ilex hesitated an instant in drying off, and Tinne caught his stillness and swore. "Oh, zow, not you too!" He shook his head in mock disappointment. "Another bachelor gone to marriage."

He should talk, he'd wed a couple of years ago. "I won't be marrying," Ilex said.

Tinne glanced at his face and his own expression sobered. "I don't think I'll ask."

"Good." The young man wouldn't press, Ilex knew. Tinne's HeartMate was wed to another man.

T'Holly rolled to his feet and stood, shaking out his limbs, face dour. His heavy brows lowered as he stared at Ilex. "That should not have happened. I am the premiere fighter of Celta. I request a rematch. Now."

Ilex didn't have time for this. His jaw flexed, but he kept hasty words inside his mouth, though they tasted bitter. "I would be honored with another bout, but not now. My time is not my own." He made a half bow.

T'Holly scowled. "I must insist." Another smile with teeth, but this wasn't in the joy of fighting.

Reciting a Couplet, Ilex pulled water and air from the atmosphere to whisk around and cleanse himself and his underwear. He picked up his shirt and snapped it to remove wrinkles, locking gazes with T'Holly. "Holm Senior," he said deliberately. "I won because this Residence, your Family, and you yourself are suffering under your broken Vows of Honor."

T'Holly stiffened, paled. "No."

Tinne had gone motionless, watching from hooded eyes.

Ilex dressed. "Yes. Your broken vow is costing you. And if it's affecting you this much, what of your lady? She hasn't debuted a new orchestral piece for several months." He exhaled slowly; this was a dangerous man in a dangerous mood. "You Hollys pride yourselves on protecting your women, yet your own stubbornness keeps her health poorly. You cannot cherish her very much if you can't bend your pride to keep her safe."

T'Holly flushed, fury emanating from him.

Ilex turned his back on the man and walked to Tinne. "But I didn't come to talk to you about that. I know you and the other FirstFamily Lords and Ladies must have discussed the murders. Does anyone have any information? Do any of you have children at risk? Those with shaky Flair and Fams?"

Tinne handed Ilex a mug of cold water. "The victims haven't been of the greatest Nobility, no one of greater status than a third son of a GrandLord." He too sounded angry.

Slanting a glance at him, Ilex saw fire in his eyes. "What of you and your wife?"

His mouth tightened, then he spoke. "Genista passed her Third Passage well. Her Flair isn't strong and her Passages were easy. I'm fine. My two previous Passages went well enough, with clearly defined beginnings and ends." Tinne hunched a shoulder. "I won't experience my Third Passage for a few years."

"And your HeartMate?" Ilex asked softly. Everyone close to the Hollys knew Tinne's HeartMate was wed to another. Tinne knew who she was, if no one else.

The color drained from Tinne's face. He drew in a shuddering breath. "Her Second Passage won't be for a while. Her Flair is . . . powerful and consistent. She should not have any trouble or be a target for this murderer."

"Good."

"Besides . . ." Now pain showed in every line of Tinne's face. "Those who have died have been unmarried. The lady you speak of is wed."

"Yes," Ilex said, and dazzling temptation rushed through him. He could eliminate Trif as prey if he wed her . . . only to lead her to another early death. He suppressed a shudder himself.

"Another thing that wasn't in your report," Tinne said. "Gib complained about losing a favorite belt that he'd worn for years. The other victims had also lost some small, old possession just before they died."

Ilex stared at him, nodded. "Good work."

"Thank you."

T'Holly joined them, looking every centimeter the GreatLord. "Naturally, the FirstFamilies discussed this in a closed council session. We agree with your superior, Chief Sawyr. We want this to be kept quiet."

"Always conscious of the status of the FirstFamilies," Tinne muttered. "I think you FirstFamilies should loan the services of your private guards to patrol." His smile was more grimace than amusement. "I'd call in Holly relatives, but we've been delaying any training. I don't want any more people stuck in this cursed household than there already are."

"Don't you speak to me that way!" T'Holly thundered.

Tinne pivoted to face his father. "Then be the man I thought you were! Strong and honorable. Someone I respected." He gave an ugly laugh. "What will you do, disown me? I'm the only Heir you have now."

"The miasma works on you both," Ilex said calmly, but his heart squeezed at the conflict between the two. At Tinne's words, T'Holly's head had jerked back as if with a blow. He looked worse than when Ilex had overcome him.

With a flourishing bow, Tinne said, "My apologies for my

rude manners. Come, I'll walk you out." He turned his back on his father, strode to the door, and flung it open. Ilex followed.

They walked down halls decorated with weapons arranged in geometric patterns. It always chilled Ilex to think that anyone in the Residence could pick up a weapon at any time from the walls. Soon, they were outside the fortress. Tinne's shoulders shifted as if a burden had eased, but the estate grounds too showed the effect of the GreatLord's and Lady's broken Vows of Honor. The plantings appeared dry and brittle, as if winter had already touched the land.

"I want to offer you all my expertise in this matter," Tinne said. "Anything I can do to help, let me know."

"I will."

Turning on his heel, Tinne looked back at the looming stone fortress of the T'Holly Residence scowling. "I hate living there. Mamá is not well, never recovered from her injury as she should have. I want to leave, but Gen—" He stopped, flashed a glance at Ilex.

Ilex gripped his shoulder, squeezed. "I'm Family, distant, but Family all the same. I won't speak of anything if you ever want to . . . go drinking."

A laugh tore from Tinne. "I can't think of the last time I glided the bars. I'm an old married man." He shook his head. "I've never heard that you dally in bars either."

Shrugging, Ilex said, "I go incognito." He lifted his eyebrows. "I have an alternate identity, someone that Commoners—even Downwinders, might talk to."

"Really?" Tinne sounded fascinated.

"Yes."

"This matter *could* get me out of the house," Tinne murmured. "T'Holly insists I handle 'Heir matters' that my brother Holm always did. I hate it."

Opening all his senses, Ilex probed the emotions from the Residence, the grounds. A layer of grime seemed to coat him. He coughed, then said, "The breaking point is coming soon. I don't know what it will be, but the strain on the household is too great."

"My father will have to admit he was wrong to disown Holm, that he truly *did* break his solemn Vows of Honor.

Sometimes, I think he's softening, then—" His mouth twisted. "You beating him in sparring, my angry words—they only made things worse for the moment."

"I'm sorry."

Tinne sighed. "He's not been the same man since Mamá was injured, but by the Cave of the Dark Goddess, he needs to accept the changes in our lives and move on!"

"I don't know what to say to help you."

Tinne shrugged, mouth flattened, then said, "There is no help. All rests with T'Holly. He's had it so easy all his life! And except for the time Mamá was wounded, even the last few years haven't been difficult." He sent a brooding gaze around the grounds and finished softly. "This disarray grows on you, so you don't even see it. You hardly notice that you've been sick more often in the past months than you were the year before, and the year before more than all the rest of your life."

Ilex laid a hand on his shoulder and squeezed. "I can't help, I don't have the resources you need." Sweeping a bow, Ilex looked Tinne in the eyes. "Merry meet."

"Merry part." His face had relaxed into his usual easy lines.

"And merry meet again." Ilex straightened and teleported away from the sad estate.

That evening, Ilex returned to his apartment bone-tired. He'd interviewed—again—the victims' Families, and though most were more coherent, he'd learned nothing new. His head ached from all the Flair he'd spent and the soothing he'd done and the emotions that had battered at him. He was glad he hadn't made plans with Trif for teleportation lessons since his temper was so frayed.

He stripped off his uniform and dressed in new white bloused trous and shirt, then sank into a comfort chair. For a while, he sipped lager and watched the last leaves of the tree outside his window whisk around as the wind tugged its branches. Then sound twined subtly into the quiet—a few rippling of notes now and then, weaving into a simple melody. The odd tune teased his ears; he caught himself straining to hear more. Underlying the music was a beat that sounded a little like footsteps. "Come to me." "Come to me."

"Come to me."

His curiosity roused, he stood and crossed to the doorway, opened the hall door, and cocked his head to listen.

The notes were pure, liquid.

Trif was playing them, calling to her HeartMate, calling him. He'd heard her play before—her tin whistle, her panpipes, her recorder, but this was a flute. He'd bet good money that it was expensive, fine, and Flaired.

More overwhelming temptation. But the music reached down in him, soothing the jagged edges of his bad day, tugging at him.

He shouldn't go to her.

But he wouldn't snap at her now; the music had made that impossible. He leaned against the corridor and found he wasn't the only one listening. Doors had opened all along the hallway and people stood outside. No men seemed drawn in a bespelled trance to her apartment and for that, Ilex was thankful.

He looked toward the lobby entrance, and found doors open in the opposite hall and clusters of folk in the lobby. He smiled. She certainly had a talent here. What was she doing wasting it in her Family furniture factory?

Pretty music, said Vertic, joining him, seeming nothing more than a shadow just inside Ilex's apartment door. *A heart song*. He nudged Ilex's calf with his head. *It calls to you.*

It was damn near too hard to resist. Ilex's body stirred. He clamped his hands around the doorjamb until his knuckles whitened.

Then Trif stopped and the cold wind of loneliness, of being in autumn, settled in his soul.

Quietly, other doors closed. Sending a tendril of Flair in both directions, Ilex learned that she'd soothed this whole front block of the lodge. Incredible.

While he was bemused, Vertic trotted across to Trif's door and scratched on it. Ilex's eyes widened—he was careful to keep Vertic out of sight of his fellow residents.

Trif opened the door, a silver flute in her hand, a dreamy

expression on her face, and smiled affectionately down at Vertic. She stooped to pet his thick red fur, then looked straight into Ilex's eyes. "Come talk to me," she said.

He was lost.

Nine

He walked to her and she stepped back so Vertic and he could enter her home. "It seemed like a night for the flute." She made a rueful face. "It's been an odd day." Sliding a glance toward him, she said quietly, "I'm sorry I went off on my quest this morning." She shrugged. "It seemed the right thing to do at the time."

"The area near Landing Park is not thriving with people on the streets at dawn. Those Nobles usually participate in Druida's social season and sleep late. None of the Family members that serve them would be outside either." His voice was deeper than he liked, resonant with emotions she could read if she dared. "Can you *please* promise me to quest in populated neighborhoods?"

Pink rose to her checks. "It's a little embarrassing going door to door when there are a lot of people around."

"I didn't think that bothered you."

"Some."

At that moment, the kitten Greyku zoomed into the room. *Ah, here is Vertic. Here is Ilex. We can go to the beach now. Fresh fish. Yum.*

Trif looked down at her kitten. "You had your dinner."

You didn't and you must eat so you can play lots of beautiful tunes that everyone loves, Greyku said virtuously, then spoiled it by adding, *And I want More.* She angled an ear at Vertic. *Vertic Fox kept Me in the garden today. He said I could not go for fish by Myself and that the fish man sells the food.* She looked thoughtful an instant. *Though I think the fish man would give Me free food I am so beautiful.*

Ilex laughed and Trif laughed with him. It felt good. She raised her brows at him. "Have you eaten?"

"No."

She licked her lips. "When was the last time you ate fish from a foodcart on the beach?"

He smiled. "The beach across the road from the garden gate . . ."

Trif grinned and shrugged. "May as well let Greyku see the beach."

The fish smelled goo-OOD all day, Greyku pleaded, watching them with huge blue eyes.

"That means for the last septhour and a half we've been home," Trif informed Ilex.

Vertic swished his tail. *I would like fish too.* His tongue darted out to whisk around his muzzle.

Greyku pranced to the door.

"Can't we teleport? I'd like to practice," Trif said.

He frowned and looked at windows painted with the weakening rays of the sun. "Evening and dawn are the *worst* times to teleport. Visualizing the light can be difficult. Don't you know that?"

Her smile was quick and charming. "Yes, but I'd like to spend time with you."

Words he shouldn't have been pleased to hear, but was. "I'll buy everyone fish at the vendor's cart. Greyku can see the beach and Vertic can play in the waves."

"Yesss," Greyku said, the tip of her tail twitching with excitement. "I have never seen the ocean."

Fish are good to eat, Vertic said.

Trif stared down at him thoughtfully. "I can hear you too."

Greyku smiled a little cat smile. *That is because he is clever as a fox.*

They laughed again. Trif scooped Greyku up and arranged her on her shoulder. Ilex offered his elbow to her and she curled her hand around his arm, tingling every nerve in his body. Vertic slunk out the door and donned his shadow illusion.

Pleased at the sheer happiness of the moment, Ilex said, "We'll eat and walk and talk until full dark, then teleport back."

"Yesss," Trif said, in perfect imitation of her kitten, and did a little dance step as well, and the moment became burnished with gold.

Trif finished eating before Ilex and they stood on the small stretch of beach and watched the sun go down.

Greyku looked up at him and twitched her whiskers. *I am sleepy and your shoulder is bigger than Trif's. I will nap on you.*

"Running up and down the beach, teasing the waves, and screeching defiance to the ocean takes a lot out of a cat," Ilex commiserated, finishing up the last bite of flaky fish wrapped in seaweed.

Yes.

So he arranged her on his shoulder and kept her cradled there with an "encompass" spell. She blinked sleepy blue eyes at him a couple of times, then stretched out and slept.

"I want to show you something," Ilex said to Trif. He started off to his favorite place in Druida.

"What?"

"Wait and see."

They walked for some minutes on the firm sand of the beach until they reached the rocky outcropping that defined the northern limits of the beach. The tide was out, and Ilex led Trif along the narrow slice of sand into a small cove no more than two meters across. He picked her up and sat her on an extruding ledge, then joined her.

With a gesture, he motioned to the cove. "Look. Just look. See how the waves have made patterns on the sand, how the seaweed and shells lie, arranged perfectly by nature."

He wondered if she'd appreciate this place as he did, and waited. Would she be bored by this place? All his nerve endings prickled in anticipation of rejection.

One minute. Two.

"It's ever changing, isn't it?" She pointed a finger. "See how the foam is sometimes wide, sometimes narrow? And the empty shells roll as the waves pull them back into the ocean."

"Yes. And though it is always changing, the ocean and the sand and the rock remain the same over the days, transforming in small increments."

"It's lovely. Peaceful."

"I think of it as a garden."

"A garden!"

"A sea garden designed by the Lady and Lord."

She tilted her head. "I suppose. Ah! There's the last flash of Bel as it sinks beyond the ocean."

Once again they lapsed into silence, and their breathing matched the swish of the waves. The whole world seemed to pulse inside Ilex, the sea his blood, the rock his bones . . . waiting for Trif—her touch or her words or her music.

Finally, he noted the tide turning and jumped back onto the beach. Before he could lift her down, Trif was beside him. She laughed. "We'll have to hurry or we'll get wet." She grabbed his hand and sped back down the beach.

When they reached the place where they'd started, Trif stopped, whirled around, then heaved out a breath. "My friend Lark Apple loves Maroon Beach to the south but I just don't have the time to go down there." She shrugged. "Too impatient for the carrier ride down and back."

Ilex glanced up and down the beach. "Not much of a beach here in the city . . . the docks are just around a curve to the south."

"Yes, whatever prime beach land Druida has was settled by the FirstFamilies. Maroon Beach is the closest nice one, and glider can get you there faster than the public carrier. Do *you* have a glider? You're a Noble, aren't you?"

Heat crept up his cheeks. "I'm the second son of a GrandLady, a distant relative of the Hollys. I won't ever inherit the title. No, I don't have a glider." As far as he knew, his mother had sold it. He smiled slightly. "I am a Druida Guardsman, and I rarely leave the city. And in the city, I can *teleport.*"

"I'm working on that," Trif said.

Greyku, sat up on his shoulder. *I want FamWoman now*.

Ilex transferred her to Trif 's shoulder. As soon as the kitten was settled, she revved up her purr. *We are helping you learn to 'port.*

"Speaking of which," Trif said, "I understand why 'porting during dusk or dawn is hazardous, but you said you could teleport back home." She looked around. "There isn't anyone here, not that it would matter. Vertic is gone on foxy business, and I'm getting cool. Can we try 'porting back?" An uncertain expression flashed in her eyes. "I haven't ever tried it at night."

"We'll be fine," Ilex said.

She shook her head. "You are so certain sure, it's amazing. So solid. I feel so safe with you."

Ilex winced inwardly. "You are completely safe with me."

He wrapped his arms around her loosely. "Stretch your mind and your Flair toward the landing pad in MidClass Lodge lobby. Envision it. Can you sense whether the light is on or off?"

With an automatic flick of his Flair, he knew it was on.

"Yes!" She quivered in his arms, her voice lilting with joy. "Yes, I can see the light. It's on." She looked up at him, lips curved and eyes bright, and it took all his willpower not to tighten his grip, turn her, and kiss her.

Her smile faded. "What's wrong? You look . . . hurt."

Gas pain, Greyku said, making Ilex choke.

Trif turned her gaze to her kitten. "I didn't think you knew what a gas pain is."

It is a belly pain, My sire Zanth says. He gets them a lot when I am around.

Ilex chuckled. "Perhaps he gets them because he eats sewer rats. Even Vertic doesn't eat sewer rats." He squeezed Trif lightly around the waist. "I think you've lost the image of MidClass Lodge. Check the light again, and visualize it once more. Greyku, if you're going to help, you think of it too."

An instant later the odd image of the enormous lobby from a kitten's point of view melded with Ilex's, then Trif 's vision. Ilex studied it. "I think you could fine-tune your perspective." It was skewed, flattened, and not because of the difference in their heights.

"Practice your breathing and sharpen your focus, see if you can actually connect with the place in the here and now."

For a moment Trif 's picture sharpened; then Ilex felt her Flair whip out of control and a different vision came.

It was daylight and the ground was roughly the same as where MidClass Lodge stood, but it and all the buildings of the city were gone. A group of oddly dressed people tramped over the land, the beach was visible, and so was only one other structure, the Ship, *Nuada's Sword*. It seemed a few centuries newer, but not as . . . whole . . . as it was now. It had just landed, Ilex realized with shock as his ears were assaulted by a language only vaguely Celtan. They were looking more than four centuries into the past!

"Incredible. Fascinating," he said, wanting to see more, but any link with his HeartMate would strengthen the bond between them.

Trif gasped and trembled in his arms. No use for it. He linked with her, took control of her unruly Flair, shaped it into the image of MidClass Lodge lobby, and held it without faltering.

Her Flair went straight to his loins, hardening him until he ached with need. One step would bring his yearning flesh against the sweet softness of her bottom. She would turn and welcome him, they would fall on the beach. . . .

No!

He clenched his teeth against the hot rush of passion. Concentrated on the rock-solid visualization that he could make appear in a hologram, the Flair cycling between them was so great, instead of the iron readiness of his sex. But he couldn't fight lusty desire, the sweetness of her scent, hold the image and speak at the same time. So he spoke to her mentally, with forced calm. *Don't just look. SEE. Observe all the details. Calm your breathing into the proper pattern.*

I don't think I can—

No! Stop that thought. Most of all, you must BELIEVE you can do this. I know you can. She'd said he was certain sure and he was, of himself and his abilities. Of her Flair and that she could tame it, force it to do her will. *Belief is EVERYTHING.* He sent her his own certainty.

The next breath she took was steadier. Her confidence rose with the solidity of the link between them, the knowledge that she wouldn't, couldn't, fail while he was here—and that he was waiting for *her* to teleport them home. That he was confident she could do so.

Trif 's vision of the past had overwhelmed Greyku too, and she had lost her own unique perspective of the landing pad in the lobby. "Greyku, give us your visualization again, please, so Trif can integrate it."

The kitten obeyed, and Trif grabbed onto the mental picture with near-desperation, and suddenly all three ideas merged and snapped into one firm focus—Trif 's.

Ilex waited patiently as she went through another round of the breathing cycle, and Greyku held very still too.

"The landing pad light says it's clear. On three," Trif said evenly, though her muscles held the fine tension of rising Flair. "One, Guardsman Ilex; two, cat Greyku, three!"

Instantaneously they 'ported to MidClass Lodge's lobby. Only a few people were there and didn't goggle. Trif relaxed and Ilex dropped his arms from around her.

She bounced up and down on the resilient pad, joy radiating from her. "I *did* it! *I* 'ported us, and it was clean and right!"

Smiling back at her, Ilex stepped off the pad. Greyku had jumped from Trif 's shoulder and raced around the room like a mad thing. Trif exited the pad area and the landing light, which had blinked out as they teleported, flicked on again.

"Congratulations." Ilex bowed deeply. "You have executed one fully successful teleportation, so now your Flair and your mind and your instinct know the path. It will be easier to duplicate in the future."

"You are the *best* teacher! So patient and understanding."

He kept his smile on his face. She'd described him many times in the last hours: solid, safe, patient, understanding. She'd used his title, Guardsman, in her countdown as if that was what she primarily saw him as. And that was good, he assured himself as the lover inside took blow after blow harder than Holly fists, and fell defeated.

She swept Greyku up in her arms and pirouetted, then danced down the hallway to her apartment. Halfway there, she looked back over her shoulder. "Come *on,* Ilex."

"More brandy?"

"Oh, yes!" she caroled. "Or ale. That would be good too." Cradling Greyku, she nuzzled the kitten.

"I think I'll pass."

She pouted. "Please?"

He just shook his head. "Play a jig or two with your whistle. I'll hear it and it will please me." Torture him.

"Yes, it's a night for music. One of the best nights of my life."

She should have been naked on the beach with him, saying those words. He smiled with what he hoped looked like indulgence and not "gas pain" and waved her on.

Trif nodded and began to hum a tune, her mind obviously already on music. Then she put her hand on her door latch and a puzzled expression crossed her face.

Ilex was at her side in an instant, his hand covering hers, and he felt it too. Strong, masculine energy—in a strange form.

"I'll check out your apartment."

She frowned. "No, it might be my HeartMate, he might be waiting inside. . . ."

Ilex was already nudging her aside. "Guardsman Winterberry, overriding shieldspell," he announced in his official tones. The door opened under his fingers, and he sent it wide and hard and it banged against the wall protector. He was in, wishing for his blazer, when the odd Flair washed over him.

Trif followed him in and shut the door. "You feel the unusual Flair, don't you." She moved her shoulders as if trying to shrug off an uneasy feeling. "I think I know what it is. Something T'Willow gave me."

The fact that she'd had an appointment with GreatLord T'Willow had gone quite out of Ilex's mind. He swallowed. What had the man said to her? Obviously, the matchmaker hadn't told her Ilex was her HeartMate or she'd have had him on the bedsponge now.

Thank the Lady and Lord. Maybe.

"I'll have that drink after all," he said.

As she went into the kitchen, he casually sent his Flair questing.

And found a HeartGift. He was stunned. It *couldn't* be for her, not from T'Willow.

Fisting his hands, he regulated his ragged breathing and stopped the tumble of despairing thoughts. Slowly, he walked over to a box. He opened it cautiously to see a leather pouch rounded with an item inside. T'Willow's HeartGift.

Trif walked in, sans Greyku. Ilex smelled hot, fresh meat and heard slurping sounds. The kitten must be eating again. Well, it *was* a baby.

"I see you found it," she said, offering him a bottle of ale.

"Thank you." He placed it on the table. As soon as his fingers brushed the pouch, he set his teeth. He didn't like the feel of it at all. His flesh crept.

He picked it up anyway, weighed it in his palm, felt sweat bead along his hairline, forced his jaw open enough to say, "It's a HeartGift."

She settled herself on her sofa. "Yes, he gave it to me to send out into the world, can you believe that!" She shook her head.

Ilex dropped the thing in surprise. It lit in the box.

"I put it in the box just in case Greyku thought it might be a toy and play with it." She shivered a little, then glanced around. "I've learned that Greyku thinks everything in the apartment is her toy."

Deliberately, he shut the lid and took up his lager. Drinking deeply, he was beyond savoring the liquor. He took a chair opposite Trif. "So tell me of your meeting with T'Willow."

"He's a nice enough man, but wasn't very helpful to me." She told him the rest, ending with: "And I promised him that I'd leave his HeartGift in some very public place." Tapping a fingernail on her glass, she asked, "Isn't a HeartGift supposed to be invisible to everyone except the HeartMates?"

"Nearly invisible," he corrected. He glanced at the box again. "I haven't had much experience with HeartGifts." The one he'd made so many years before was safely tucked away. In a bank, where he wouldn't be tempted to do something terminally foolish like give it to her in a weak moment of overwhelming temptation. "I would guess we could barely see what's in the pouch, and of course the case gives it some protection. Not nearly enough in my estimation."

Her mouth turned down. "I wouldn't want my HeartGift roaming the world either. I wonder if I'll have to wait way until my Third Passage to make one, so long away. Years."

He didn't want to get on that topic. "T'Willow must have used some elaborate Flair on the thing. It would naturally attract his mate. He'd want it to repulse others, but not be so distressing that they'd throw it away."

She nibbled her bottom lip. "I suppose. I think I'll take it to the club, the Maypole, tomorrow night. The moons are waxing and it will be a good time. It will be full twinmoons on Samhain, then the new year in a few days. I hope he finds her soon. Or she finds and accepts the HeartGift. It's law that if you accept a HeartGift, you accept the HeartMate, right?"

"Yes. That's the law, though I haven't ever heard of anyone enforcing it."

"More like an instinctive thing too, I guess. And the Heart Mate who makes the gift isn't allowed to tell his love they're HeartMates, it's against the law."

"Taking free will away."

She switched her nibbling to her thumbnail, then stopped. "I'm hunting for my HeartMate, but I don't think I could force him to do anything, and I wouldn't be telling him he's my HeartMate, just introducing myself to him," she said, rationalizing her actions.

"You think so?"

"I really wouldn't want to take his free will away." Her expression turned stubborn. "I just want to know who he is to—to court him. T'Willow said he knew who I was."

"What?"

"My HeartMate knows who I am and has his own reasons for not claiming me." She crunched a sofa pillow to her, threw it aside, then stood and paced. "Why wouldn't he want me?" She flung out her arms. "What's wrong with me?"

"Stop that line of thinking now. Nothing is wrong with you. You're a young, beautiful, intelligent, and talented young woman."

She sent him a smile, but flushed a little. "I think so too."

"Good. Accept the fact that something is wrong with him."

Her expression turned into a scowl. "There's nothing wrong with him that I couldn't accept. *Nothing.*"

Greyku strolled in, tiny tongue curling a bit of food from whisker to mouth. She slid a slyly innocent look at Ilex. *Maybe he's old and gray.*

"I don't care if he's old and gray!" Trif shook her head. "No, he can't be too old or too gray or we wouldn't suit and HeartMates always suit." She looked at him. "Don't they?"

This whole conversation was too uncomfortable. He stood. "I'm not the one to ask."

"I've thought of a thousand more questions I should have asked T'Willow," she grumbled. "Isn't that always the case?"

"Thank you for the drink," Ilex said. "I'll see you later."

She smiled, then shook a finger at him. "Don't think this is the end of our teleporting lessons." Vulnerability was in her eyes, in her voice as she ended, "I want to make sure I have it right."

"Then I'll help you practice."

And Me too. Greyku had explored the mainspace and sat next to Trif 's feet.

"No one could forget you, Fam Greyku," he said.

At that moment a knock came on Trif 's door. "Special Delivery," a man's voice called.

Ten

*Ilex tensed, moved quickly to the door, looking out the one-*way security peephole. The man was uniformed as a professional courier. "Isn't it late for a delivery?"

The guy outside the door looked at where the glass should be, though it was bespelled for invisibility. He snorted. "From T'Ash. Everyone knows those FirstFamilies are weird. And no one refuses T'Ash."

Ilex opened the door. "I'd heard that."

"It's my amulet." Trif reached past Ilex to snatch the gold box labeled T'ASH'S PHOENIX from the courier.

"You'll seal my delivery orb?" The man offered a small glass sphere to Ilex.

He pressed his thumb to it, and the deep green sigil of his personal seal floated into the ball.

"Fare well," said the delivery man.

"And may you do the same," Ilex said, and watched the man walk down the hallway. "Trif, the desk guard should have scried you that the delivery man was here. Better, he should have taken the delivery for you, determined its safety, and then handed it over to you."

Trif was busy dispelling the box. "The guard knew you

were here with me. Besides, T'Ash said personal delivery, and no one refuses T'Ash."

"I'd heard that."

"Oh, it's incredible, it's fantastic, and it's mine, mine, mine!" Trif had gotten the box open and was dancing around with a necklace in her hand.

Greyku watched the dangling silver chain and the pale pink and white stone with utter fascination. Ilex was sure the kitten wanted to claim Trif's new treasure as a toy.

"What's the stone?" Ilex asked.

"A bit of calcite from my house Dad and my uncles are building for me in Clover Compound. They've done some built-in tables."

"Pink calcite is good for grounding." Ilex nodded. The stone was a simple ovoid shape, highly polished.

T'Ash was also the best man on Celta with stones.

The gift was fabulous. Two FirstFamily GreatLords had given Trif incredible gifts today. He'd given her nothing. Ever. It was enough to depress a man.

She slipped the chain over her neck and the stone fell between her breasts. Something about the pinkness and the curve of the stone lying in her cleavage sent hot fire racing in his blood, hardening him. "The man is a genius," he said.

Trif admired her new necklace in a mirror. "T'Ash? He is, isn't he?"

Ilex cleared his throat. "If you will give me the amulet, I will take it to my—source and have a retrieval spell imbued into the stone." He held out a hand. His fingers trembled. He steadied them with effort and Flair.

She made a moue. "I suppose I must." Then she blinked. "You'd go now?"

"Yes. T'Ash isn't the only one who is rarely refused."

Her eyes widened. "Why, Ilex, you look—" She stopped.

He raised a brow. "Yes?"

"Ah, quite, ah, dangerous."

He laughed and shook his head. "It's only my guardsman's manner."

She looked doubtful. Reluctantly, her hand went to the necklace; then she pulled it off and handed it to him. His fingers closed convulsively over the stone. It was warm from her body, her energy, her Flair. Definitely radiated essence of Trif.

So sexy he could whimper.

"The spell should be ready in three days. Or two nights and a day. I'll bring the amulet to you when it's charged. Now will you promise me not to go questing?"

"I won't go questing alone. I promise."

"You won't go questing only with Greyku." He put steel in his voice.

"I won't go questing without a human companion," she clarified.

"Very well. Don't break your promise to me."

She appeared insulted.

He left.

The next morning, Trif woke up and stretched, just knowing it would be a good day. She'd teleported by herself! Ilex and Greyku had been with her, but she had taken them along, not the other way around.

She wanted to do it again. She bounced off the bedsponge. Greyku grunted and curled into a tighter ball. As soon as Trif finished her morning ablutions and had a bite of breakfast, she scried Ilex.

"Here." His shaven face surrounded by wet hair and strong bare shoulders appeared in the scrybowl. Her mouth fell open at the virile image and she had to snap her mouth shut. "I was wondering if you'd accompany me on my questing this morn—"

"No."

Giving a heavy sigh, she put a plaintive note in her voice and widened her eyes. "Then could we have another teleportation lesson? I *really* want to—"

"In case you don't recall, I was out late last night." He muttered a Word and a shirt clothed him. It was too bad. She kept her mind on her mission.

"Oh, Ilex, you're not an old man! And I bet you teleported wherever and back too. I want to be able to do that, and I feel I'm *so close* to getting my 'porting skill right."

"Where did you have in mind?" He shifted and she guessed his trous were on now.

She gulped and persevered, though he and her imagination were distracting. "Um, could we try a few places? Like to the beach and back here and to Clover Compound and then to my work?"

There was silence.

"*Please,* Ilex? Don't you—do you need any furniture at all? I promise I'll give you something top-of-the-pyramid from Clover's Fine Furnishings? Or maybe I could have Mitchella do a look around your apartment and give you tips—" He stared and a little shudder went through him. She rushed into speech. "Maybe not. Uh—could we do a trade or something?"

"Another boon?"

"Yes."

"You shouldn't agree so quickly." Now his eyes crinkled and he was less the sexy man she'd awakened and more her good friend, looking amused.

"Whatever you like."

He laughed, and she had to take a step back from the scrybowl it was so potent: flashing white teeth in a pirate's grin, a crease beside his mouth, his eyes pure blue with no hint of gray. Zow. All these new thoughts about Ilex!

"All right." His gaze grew speculative. "Or rather, let's try a little something. See if you can teleport to the lobby landing pad. I'll meet you there shortly. Fare well." Her scrybowl went blank.

Trif curled her toes in anxiety as all her doubts zoomed back. She didn't want to make a fool of herself before Ilex. But she wanted to be able to 'port anywhere. And this was her first test. Such a short hop. Were short hops supposed to be easier or harder? She couldn't recall and there wasn't time to look it up in the instruction sphere.

I believe I can teleport to the lobby, she mumbled, and began the breathing pattern that would raise and focus her Flair. She sent her mind reaching to the landing pad to see if the safety light was on. It was. She formed a mental image of the room, added sunlight, thought how it smelled in the morning—lavender-fresh from the housekeeping spells, recalled the atmosphere—people rushing to work. "On three," she said. "One, Trif Clover; two, I can do. Three!"

Just as she said the last word, Greyku wandered in from the bedroom and Trif 's concentration broke.

She 'ported to the pad and landed unevenly.

A couple of people clapped, and she flushed deep red as she stepped off the pad, flicking on the light. As she met her neighbors' eyes, she realized they were genuine in their appreciation. There were very few middle-class people who could teleport. She sent them a wavery smile. They nodded and hurried out the front door. She glanced around for Ilex, but didn't see him.

Greyku's yowl echoed down the hallway. Trif didn't know if she heard the scratching on her door in her ears or her mind. *Stop that!* she scolded the kitten.

You left without Me. I want breakfast and want to come with you too.

Trif saw a shadow in the hall—Ilex. Had he seen her wobbly landing? He tilted his head, then turned and walked back, past his own door and on to hers. She heard whispering in her mind—Greyku and Ilex? She thought so, didn't hear the whole conversation, but did get a sense that Greyku was trotting into the kitchen to get her own breakfast, purring.

Ilex came down the hall with a loose-hipped stride she hadn't noticed before. He moved with utter confidence and command. He was a guardsman, a hunter, a fighter, and she was just realizing how powerful he was—not just his Flair, but his aura of authority.

She tried to look casual and smiled. He smiled back and her insides did a funny twinge thing.

When he came up to her, she said, "Merry meet." She didn't often use the greeting, but somehow this new view of Ilex demanded it. He was a Noble, after all, even if he was a second son.

He bowed. "Merry meet." He went to the light and turned it off, stepped on the landing pad, and held out his hand. "Ready?"

Her breath was a little fast. "For anything!" she said, and he blinked.

"The beach first?" he asked.

She stepped onto the teleportation pad and cleared her throat. "Yes."

He linked his arms around her and she became overwhelmingly aware of his masculinity, the spicy scent she associated with him. She hadn't felt like this before, noticing his maleness and her own femininity.

"Give me the image of the beach," he said.

It was the same tone he always used, but she could barely think. Focus! She thought of the beach, where they'd been last night. How it would look in the morning light. More, as she breathed, she considered the scent of the ocean, a whiff of the docks around the bend. Then she layered on the *atmosphere,* how it felt. Not crowded. Some people walking. Couples. Like her and Ilex. She formed the image using all her senses for detail, not just sight. The wash of the surf.

"Excellent," Ilex murmured, and the warmth of his breath teased her ear and was another diversion. She tensed.

"Easy," he said.

"Yes," she breathed out. Gathered her Flair, her courage. "On three. One, Ilex neighbor; two I can do; *three*!"

The force of their leaving pushed her back into him for an instant—just enough for her to feel a *very* aroused man against her backside.

She lost the image, grabbed at it, failed. Darkness spun around Trif, an eerie black whistling *nowhere*.

A quick image from Ilex flicked into her mind, and they materialized with a whoosh into the center of the Great Labyrinth, miles north of Druida City. A beautiful, mystical place.

Anger emanated from the man behind her, showed in the white knuckles of his fists.

"Ooops," she said, but didn't turn to face him. Her heart raced and hot blood pumped through her—from revelation and excitement. Ilex found *her* sexy? Visions of them frantically exploring each other on a bedsponge filled her mind.

His hands dropped from her and he stepped far back, out of her immediate aura. She stifled a sigh.

"Do you know how dangerous losing focus is?" he asked in repressed tones.

Of course she did. It wouldn't stem a lecture, though.

"If any portion of you, one neutron, materialized into a solid object, you'd be trapped. If more than a small amount of you 'ported into—say, that wall over there . . ." He gestured to a pretty, quite solid stone wall about ten feet from them. "You'd die. Haven't you ever heard of Four-Fingered Pete?"

"Everyone has heard of Four-Fingered Pete," she said lightly, cocking her head to listen to Ilex, still not turning around. He cared for her. He'd been worried about her safety. But she couldn't get the feel of him out of her mind.

She tingled at the memory of his long, solid erection settling into her bottom. She wished she dared to reach back. . . .

His hands clamped on her shoulders and spun her around.

Yes, his brows were lowered, his mouth thin. Drawing on all her control, she kept her gaze from wandering down to the front of his trous.

"Do you think this is a joking matter?" he asked.

"No," she said, unobtrusively bunching her tunic in her fists to keep from stroking his face. She could allow herself to admire him now since she knew he found her attractive too. She forced her expression into solemnity. "I was distracted and lost the image. I'm sorry." She thought she heard him grind his teeth. To test herself—and him, she said, "Perhaps you are reconsidering your generous offer to teach me to 'port."

"No," he bit out. "I promised you."

And he'd always fulfill a promise.

Since she couldn't touch him, she ran her fingers through her own hair, ruffling it. There was sweat at the roots and a breeze had picked up that would dry it. His glance followed her hand, lingered on her hair.

"Trif, you *can't* be distracted."

What could she say to that? She firmed her lips. "I under stand."

He exhaled slowly, his wide chest barely moving under his brown shirt. Her glance wanted to drift downward. She yanked it back to his impassive face. Clearing her throat, she said, "At least my Flair wasn't fluctuating. It was solid." Along with a certain man. "I think I've found the channel to keep it in during 'porting."

"That's progress."

She looked around the Great Labyrinth. She hadn't been here since her best friend's wedding. "So why are we here?"

"The Great Labyrinth is an excellent tool."

Her turn to frown. "For grounding yourself. I don't have that problem. I ground fine."

He waved to the winding path. "*Look* at it. Think about it."

Her frown deepened and her tongue darted out to moisten her lips. She let her eyes unfocus, but not enough to trigger her Flair and see the past. The Great Labyrinth was in the middle of a crater and the path out rose steadily, circling around until it reached the rim, which was the horizon here at the middle. It was a beautiful place, both naturally and because NobleHouses had raised small shrines showcasing their Families to decorate it. The Vines had erected a grape arbor, stone benches, and bottles of rare vintages. The Birches had planted a lovely, swaying grove of their name trees. In the grove was a small altar and on it were small curls of birch bark for prayers. A few feet away was a pond where the birch spells could float—only three did.

Since her family, the Clovers, weren't Noble, they had contributed nothing. If they had . . . she could imagine a green of nothing but clover rising to the rim, a beautiful green bowl. She smiled.

"Trif?"

"Why don't you just tell me what you want me to figure out?"

"Because then you won't come to the conclusions on your own."

"I've never been one to think that what you work for is more valued than what you get free," she said, knowing he believed that implicitly.

"But my telling you something instead of you deducing it is a lesson easier for you to forget."

Now he was wrong there. Looking back, she'd always paid attention to whatever he'd said. She probably could repeat word for word every conversation they'd had. Too few conversations, too few meetings for neighbors living within a few doors of each other, she now realized. She eyed him more closely. "Have you been avoiding me?"

For the blink of an eye he looked startled, and she knew she was right. "Why?" she asked.

"We don't have many things in common."

She didn't like that response. She'd have to think about it, and his physical reaction to her, but later, when she was alone. She studied the labyrinth again, nibbling on her bottom lip. "When I was in grove study, I think I remember that some of the simpler labyrinths look like an apple."

Ilex nodded, and his face subtly relaxed.

"But this one is more convoluted." She cudgeled her memory. "Like a—a brain."

"Rather like. More circular. But all labyrinths have been made to affect the brain. Or Flair."

"Or Flair," she repeated on a breath, looking at the long path to the top again. "You think that if I walk this, I might be able to channel my 'porting Flair better if I concentrate on it?"

"You might even be able to master your Flair, steady it into mental pathways as you tread the physical path."

"Hmmm. Good idea." A spurt of happiness at his caring fluttered her blood. She smiled at him and offered her hand. "I've heard that no matter what your mastery of Flair, how much Flair you have, walking the labyrinth is good for you."

He didn't take her hand, and rapidly moved from the center clearing under the tall ash tree to the beginning of the path out. "It's not as if you can do anything else," he said. "The spells on this place only let you teleport in, never out. Come along. Let's see what results it might have on you. When we reach the rim, you can teleport us to the pad in MidClass Lodge."

A thought struck her. What was Ilex doing in MidClass Lodge? She narrowed her eyes as he took a few steps along the short straightaway leading out of the labyrinth. "Why do you live in the Lodge and not your Family Residence?"

His shoulders tensed. But when he answered, his voice was casual. "I don't get along with D'Winterberry."

She crossed to the beginning of the path with long strides, and decided to press the matter. "What's her relation to you?"

"My mother." He didn't even glance back at her. "No more talking now. Think about your Flair, how to regulate it, channel it, carving a deep path for it to flow through your mind."

Trif really didn't like that particular image, but she began a breathing cycle and as she walked the curving path she let her mind drift, her Flair rise. She fell into a rhythm. And around the sixth curve, she lost it. Her aura spiked, she saw it blaze in front of her.

When it receded, she saw the past. The morning sky was the same. Everything else was different. Even the scent—a harsh acridity came to her nostrils and her nose twitched the odor away. Instead of a well-worn trail winding gently up a slope, bedecked with little Family shrines, she saw the rough soil of a newly made crater. Layers of sediment showed raw in the sunlight. The rim wasn't smooth and worked, but ragged with sharp edges.

Trif couldn't see the path, couldn't feel it under her feet. She lost her way. There was nothing but bare ground. She turned in place and noticed a huge piece of seared metal in the center of the space. Movement caught her eye. Two figures walked to the rim and stared down. A man and a woman. Waves of strong emotion smacked her, whirled her under. She crumpled with a cry.

Eleven

Feeling came back to her first—she was being held in a comforting embrace, her bottom on a warm lap, her legs stretched out, her back cradled by a strong arm.

A damp, herb scented, smooth cloth—silkeen?—caressed her face.

"Come on, Trif. Open your eyes. It's safe." Ilex's voice was quiet, soothing. As steady as the man himself.

Trif made a little sound and tried to burrow deeper. His supporting arm tightened around her, then released. "Come on, Trif, we still need to get out of the labyrinth." This time his voice was cooler, with a note of command. Oh, yes, he was a minor Noble. And a guardsman.

Sighing, she opened her eyes and met his. They immediately went from soft to sharp and darkened into blue-tinged steel. He slid her from his lap onto a cool stone bench.

She looked around. There was a table inlaid with gleaming strips of wood and atop it some cut cheese and fancy crackers. "What's this?"

"The Caraways' contribution. It was the closest. What happened?"

Lifting one shoulder, Trif reached for a slice of cheese, put it on the cracker—it fit perfectly, Ilex being efficient as always—and popped it in her mouth. She handed another treat to Ilex.

After she swallowed and drank from a cylinder of spring-water, she said, "My Flair spiraled out." She grimaced. "I couldn't control it, and I had a vision." At least it hadn't been violent.

He stilled beside her and again his eyes met hers. "Like we had last night?"

She grimaced. "Yes."

"A very interesting experience."

Heat crept up her neck, fired her cheeks. "I should have apologized before now."

His eyebrows rose. "Not necessary. So," he said a trace too casually, "you have some *sight*. Do you foresee?"

She shook her head. "No, I don't see the future, I see the past." She scanned the portion of the labyrinth she could see. Before her, the path was set with crushed rock the color of charcoal. Dotting the landscape were about ten Family shrines; a tangle of plant life in various hues banded the slope of the crater up to the smooth rim. "It didn't look like this long ago."

"How long ago?" His voice was even, mild, but she felt a throb of intense curiosity from him.

"I don't know." She put together more cheese and crackers, dividing the amount evenly between herself and Ilex and handing him his. "But there were people, so it was after the colonists' ships landed." She screwed up her face, reaching for impressions. "Perhaps just after Landing."

"That was over four centuries ago."

She glanced aside. "I can sometimes see all the way back to ancient Earth."

"Lady and Lord."

Trif waved a hand. "This was new then, the crater." She frowned. "Very new. Do you think it had something to do with the colonists?"

He shook his head. "I don't know."

"Maybe I'll research it."

His face lightened. "A good idea." *It will keep you out of trouble.*

She barely heard the thought, but the muscles of his face shifted and she knew what he was thinking. "Humph." She stood and tossed her head, stepped back out onto the labyrinth, glanced back at him. "And maybe I won't."

With a gesture, he sent the cheese and crackers back where they'd come from, probably the wooden cabinet at the other side of the bench that had a no-time food storage. Knowing Ilex, he'd inform the Caraways of their meal and offer to replace the amount they ate. A thoroughly honorable man, Ilex.

Sometimes that grated on her nerves. He seemed too perfect. "I don't think I'll be raising my Flair again on this walk out."

Nodding, he said. "I agree."

Yes, too damn perfect.

Ilex watched Trif closely as she marched along the path. She wasn't letting the labyrinth do its work, but he was in no mood to reprimand her. She'd scared him to the bone.

He'd been acutely aware of her walking behind him, and when the path doubled back, he watched her intently. Her Flair had fluctuated wildly and his gut had tightened as he'd sensed the uncontrolled power. He had the idea that she thought she'd been managing it. Far from the truth. It was obvious her psi power still mastered her. And she still wasn't proficient in teleportation. When he thought of those instants where they spun in nowhere, what might have happened if she'd been alone, his very bones chilled with fear for her and he shivered in the sunlight.

They were on the last stretch of the path when Ilex was enveloped by the scent of heliotrope, and was struck by a vision of his own. He stopped in his tracks, the familiar rippling rainbow haze alerting him that his weak foresight Flair was starting. He'd have tried to press on, but he didn't want Trif to notice anything was wrong, and his small visions usually didn't last more than a moment—of outside time. Internally, they might stretch hours. Cave of the Dark Goddess, why now? They were so close to being able to teleport out. Had his HeartMate's spiky Flair triggered his own?

Then he was frozen in it, a reluctant observer, lost to outside reality.

As always, details were foggy. There was a gleaming curve of brass he couldn't interpret. Then he saw a reddish tiled floor, wet with water and blood.

His prone body.

The side of his head looked—bad. Blood covered his still face, coating it like a red death mask, turning the light brown of his uniform rusty. It didn't look as if he was still bleeding.

That meant he was dead.

A creak came, a pair of huge red eyes stared at him, then undulated through the room in a terrifying manner.

Trif's scream in the *future* mixed with her shout in the *present* and he snapped back.

She'd reached the end of the labyrinth and was dancing ahead of him; then she waved her hand in the air and her tin whistle appeared in it. She began a merry tune.

Teleportation of objects—an excellent sign. He ached to know that she'd be safe when he was . . . gone, that he'd helped her in one way, at least—teaching her to 'port.

He fixed a smile on his face and forced his feet to move to the end of the labyrinth where they could teleport away from this place and the vision that had wrecked his fragile hope of love once more.

As soon as he finished the path, she pulled her lips from the whistle and leapt at him.

His arms curved around her reflexively. Her lips still pulsed with music as she pressed her mouth to his.

And he was lost. Again.

He opened his lips to her probing tongue, desire pouring through him as her sweet taste slipped forever into his being. His hands went to her hips, pulling her tight against him, delighting in the feel of her against his rigid shaft. The length of her fit him, her scent—fresh with a hint of arousal—sank into him. His own tongue thrust into her mouth, mimicking the love act. A fog of passion numbed his mind and only his body mattered—and how she felt. Her soft body, humming with vitality, her round breasts, full hips, slightly curved stomach against him, holding him.

She broke the kiss and looked up at him with emerald eyes. Her lips were red, marked with his hard kiss. "Ilex," she said on a ragged breath, blinking. "You *are* attracted to me. You don't have a lover, a HeartMate?"

Nettle lashes of pain stung him. He flinched. He'd just seen his own death. What was he thinking to endanger her so?

"I told you I didn't connect with one during my Passages, and linking with someone then is the only sure sign. Leave it be, Trif. Our kiss was a sudden impulse, is all." It hurt to say the words, to deceive her.

Not to be able to claim her.

The more he was with her, the more it hurt. Reckless, he pulled an image of her work place from her mind and 'ported them there, then left her. He teleported to his own office, shut the door, and leaned against it. His head ached, his body throbbed with vicious need. At the same time his very soul felt shattered beyond mending.

He couldn't have her. He'd been a fool to think he could.

If he loved her, took her, bound her to him, she would die soon after he. And a solidity to his vision meant it would be shortly in the future.

He couldn't allow that to happen.

Trif managed to get through the day, head buzzing with questions about Ilex. He wasn't a man who showed his emotions, yet there'd been a flash of excruciating pain after she'd asked her stupid question.

Obviously, the matter of HeartMates was a sensitive one with him. Why hadn't she realized sooner? Something had gone wrong with his life in that direction, she sensed it deep inside. Something about his HeartMate had wounded him. Had he found her, but she'd died before the HeartBond was in place? Was she married to another as Trif had heard was the case with Tinne Holly's HeartMate?

There were a few reasons why HeartMates stayed apart, but not many, and she'd messed up her chances of asking him casually. She'd just caused him pain, and for that she ached too.

She'd done everything all wrong with him, and now it would be difficult to find an easy manner with him again. The kiss had been exciting, ravishing even. And she'd forfeited any more of those feelings too.

When she reached home that evening, she wanted to play something on her silver flute that would soothe Ilex, but her own emotions were too raw. They'd spill out into her music and hurt him even more with melancholy tones. Besides, she'd promised T'Willow that she would leave his HeartGift in a very public place, and had decided the Maypole dance club would be perfect. Maybe the place and people and the live music would lift her spirits.

She eyed the small wooden box she'd placed T'Willow's pouch in. Though she didn't feel the waves of heavy sexuality a HeartMate would from the gift, waves of *something*—T'Willow's intense desire to find her—emanated from it enough to make her uncomfortable. She wanted it out of her home.

So she dressed up in fancy underpinnings and a filmy chiff gown that floated around her. Instead of braiding her hair—this year's fashion—she left it loose around her shoulders, and used discreet makeup.

Greyku watched the whole process with fascination, now and then licking a paw to groom herself. *Where are We going?*

Trif lifted her eyebrows at the little cat. "I am going to a dance club, the Maypole."

I can dance! Greyku jumped and did a pirouette.

Trif 's mouth fell open. She shut it and cleared her throat. "Yes. Well. I think cats' natural movements are dance."

Greyku sat smugly, nose lifted in the air. *Of course.*

"But the music may be very loud, and there will be a lot of people." Trif looked at her kitten doubtfully. "I'd hate for you to get lost or, or *stolen.*"

With a huff, Greyku said, *I will not let Myself get stolen. I can yowl.* She opened her mouth.

"No, don't demonstrate. I've heard you yowl." Trif frowned. "If you're sure you want to come . . ."

The kitten looked around the apartment. *You will be gone and without you this place is bo-ring. I want More.*

"I think you always do," Trif murmured.

Nothing wrong with wanting More, Greyku assured her.

"I suppose not." She wanted more of Ilex's kisses, but put that stray thought out of her head. It wouldn't happen . . . until she figured out what had gone wrong with his HeartMate. Could a man ever really love a woman if he had lost a Heart-Mate? So many difficult matters that she'd never considered.

How much did Tinne Holly love his wife? Now that was something she'd never learn. Still, from the times she'd seen the couple together, they were attracted to each other and caring.

Clovers didn't often have HeartMates, yet she knew her parents loved each other deeply. For an instant, Trif thought she could settle—perhaps with someone like Ilex—then brushed the thought aside. Ever since she'd felt her HeartMate in her Passage, she'd wanted him, and the erotic dreams she experienced made her yearning something that wouldn't vanish soon.

She wondered if he shared those dreams.

The idea was revitalizing. She cast one last look at herself in a mirror, put T'Willow's box in her pursenal, then picked up Greyku and held her to meet her eyes. "You must be careful."

And how had she become the lecturer? She smiled. "Let's go."

Greyku purred. *Go get more fun.*

"Yesss," they said together, and Trif laughed and left.

Ilex had spent the day listing everything he sensed about the individual killers. Right now, three seemed to be the correct number. Two men and a woman.

He'd gone over the sensorballs again and again, assigning deep laughter and taller height to one, a hitch in breathing and heavier perspiration to another . . . and on and on, trying to sort out distinguishing features. If he had enough, he could make poppets, and if the poppets were identical enough to the person, they might serve as compasses to the real human. It was a near-futile effort, since the best poppets needed something directly from the person and all Ilex had were a few skin cells left on Gib Ginger.

Again, he'd canvassed the incense shops, but for that too he didn't have enough information. He dreaded getting more, because that would mean another murder.

So he sat in the gloom of his apartment and brooded. He heard Trif laugh as she walked down the hall, murmuring to Greyku. The sound stabbed him as he recalled she was off to the Maypole to dance and mingle with youngsters her own age.

A cat's demanding growl near his feet surprised him. "Lights!" he ordered and looked down.

Vertic sat looking up, mouth open in a silent laugh. Beside him was a small, short-legged cat. One glance told Ilex it was feral.

This is Fairyfoot, Vertic said. *She is an intelligent cat, of Fam quality.*

"She's feral."

She only needs to bond with a person. I told her you would find an acceptable human.

Ilex grunted.

The cat had big, round green eyes she used to great effect, making Ilex feel like she deserved a better life than being a feral. She stood and stropped his ankles, no doubt leaving cat hair on his trous. He shrugged. They were black.

Her pretty eyes, tufted ears, and slightly scruffy appearance reminded him of someone. Eyes narrowed as he considered her, he realized it was his cuz, Dufleur. He chuckled, then studied the cat. No doubt Dufleur hated living with his mother and hers. Narrowing his eyes, he visualized the cat and Dufleur together, using a smidgeon of Flair. They fit well.

Dufleur could do with a companion, and a Fam was a status symbol. If it came from Danith D'Ash.

"I'm picking you up," he informed the cat.

He did so, and the scent of her had him tensing. He was sensitive to fragrances, and this was one he'd never forget. He'd smelled it on other cat fur.

A flash of the other experience rose to his brain. Incense. Scary-laughing adults with odd swooping lights—candles, and they were dancing, laughing, drunk on smoke? liquor? *Flair?*

Trif had distracted him. Any fool, scenting the odor of incense, recalling the testimony of the Fams, would have come to the conclusion that there was ritual magic going on—ritual murder for *negative* magic. Black magic.

The fact no one had seen it before now—maybe no one wanted to understand the ramifications—didn't lessen his guilt.

Ilex knew his history. There had been some cases of black magic before—but not since he'd joined the guards. The fact was, most of the real misfits of Celtan society ended up leaving the cities and forging out into the interior of the planet. There was plenty of frontier on Celta.

But this wasn't mere alienation from society, or pursuit of other cultural beliefs than the mainstream.

This was evil.

He didn't know enough about ritual black magic—what these people wanted, why they were killing—to understand them and find them. He was sure the *why* was the biggest part of the puzzle that needed to be solved. So he needed to talk to someone who did. He had to get his clues in order: young people with uncontrolled Flair and Fams, altars, a special incense, the taking of the heart—*through* the body somehow—the cutting of the Fam. And that might not be the correct order of importance.

Should he go to the leaders of the Temple, priest and priestess? Or a mystic? Or a scholar?

The priests and priestesses would want to deny what was happening, or interfere more. Mystics tended to keep to themselves and their ideas might not be associated in any way with regular Celtan spirituality or black magic.

Who was the greatest mystical scholar on Celta? Were there any in Druida? He didn't know, but suspected they had to be a GrandLord, of the High Nobility—perhaps even a FirstFamily son or daughter.

Which meant he should scry Tinne Holly, who might know the name of such a person.

At that moment, his own scrybowl pinged. From across the room he could see the deep green with sparkles of white. His gut clenched. His mother.

Twelve

He held the cat, stroking her as he crossed to the bowl. "Here," he answered.

The water stopped spinning and the hard, heavy face of D'Thyme looked out. She snorted as she saw him, then her glittering gaze fastened on the cat. "You have a Fam?"

"Yes."

"We're on D'Ash's waiting list."

Ilex shrugged. "What do you want?"

Her expression tightened. "The retrieval spell is placed on the amulet."

"But is it done well?"

Frown lines etched deep and gray around her mouth. "You didn't tell us the amulet and spell were for your HeartMate. Your mother performed the spell in the HouseHeart and the HouseHeart possessed her—flooding her with energy and Flair—using her to craft the spell. She's a fragile woman. It nearly killed her. She's resting now. Come and get the thing. We want it out of the Residence." The bowl flickered dark as she ended the call; then the water became clear and serene again.

Yowl! The cat wiggled in his arms and he opened them to let her drop. She sent him an irritated look.

You squeezed her too hard, Vertic said, cocking his head. *A night full of adventures. Where do we go first?*

Ilex stared down at the cat, who stared right back up at him. Something bit his arm. He slapped his sleeves, then muttered a spell vanishing fleas. "I'm taking her to D'Ash. She can evaluate Fairyfoot and get rid of the livestock. Are you sure she's Fam?"

Fairyfoot turned her back on him and flicked her tail. *You are rude. And snide. But the Fox has confidence in you. Take Me where I must go to fulfill My destiny.*

That was interesting.

"Where were you that you smell of incense?"

The cat shrugged. *Don't know. I go to many empty places.*

No help there.

I would like to teleport, said Vertic. *We have not often teleported.*

"You haven't wanted to."

Because I am a fox and run fast and fine.

Ilex sighed. "We go to D'Ash, then to my mother's house."

Vertic's ears pricked. *To your kit den?*

"My childhood home, yes."

Interesting.

Ilex didn't think so. "I believe *that* cat would do well with my cuz, Dufleur."

The cat looked over her shoulder, sniffed. *You do?*

"I used my Flair," Ilex said stiffly.

Lashing her tail, the cat turned back to stare at the door. *The fox trusts you. I will see your cuz.*

With a half bow in the Fams' direction, Ilex said, "Good of you."

Yes.

"I'm picking you up again so I can scry D'Ash. Try not to infest me with any more of your fleas." Gingerly, he picked the cat up. She didn't wriggle or scratch.

"T'Ash Residence, Danith D'Ash, please," he ordered the scrybowl.

The bowl played an echoing melody, then D'Ash said, "Greetyou, Winterberry." She was flushed and laughing. She held a bundle, a solid toddler with the black hair and dark blue eyes of her HeartMate. Just seeing the child made Ilex's spirit lighten. T'Ash had had a hard road, and cherished his son. The little boy clapped fat hands. "Win-ter-bee!" he said, then beamed up at his mother.

"He remembers you," she said proudly, then brushed a kiss atop her son's head. "He's precocious."

"I wouldn't have expected anything else of T'Ash," Winterberry said.

D'Ash flung back her head and laughed.

Beautiful woman, Fairyfoot breathed, almost in awe.

D'Ash had a way with animals, and her Flair got stronger every year.

Her stare fixed on the cat. "Who do you have there?"

A corner of his mouth lifted. "My Fam brought her to me. They both say that she's a Fam."

"She's feral."

"Yes."

"Hmmmm." D'Ash studied the cat. "Zanth was a feral Fam. It doesn't happen often, but . . . Yes, bring her to me." The scrybowl water rippled.

"One moment. I used my Flair and think she'll be right for my cuz."

D'Ash looked out at him once more. "Very well."

"I'll be 'porting, and bringing my Fam, Vertic."

Eyes bright, D'Ash said, "The fox? I get to see the fox? Yes!"

"The fox gets to see you."

D'Ash laughed. "Come now. I'll hand this one"—she jiggled the boy on her hip—"off to his father. You may end the scry, Nuin."

A plump little hand slapped the water.

Trif felt the throbbing vibration of the music before she opened the Maypole's rose-colored door. Bespelled instruments, for sure. She grinned, impatient to see the band.

She wasn't known to the Maypole management—it was a far too expensive and high-class place for that—but her name was recognized by a few musicians. Maybe she'd be lucky and she could play. On that off chance, she'd packed her silver flute—also bespelled with her own Flair.

There was *nothing* better than playing for a room packed

with people enjoying themselves, who sent off bits of Flair in happiness and flirtation with the opposite sex. A charged room, oh, yes.

"Are you ready?" she asked Greyku, whose little rump was stuck to Trif 's shoulder with a spell.

Oh, yes.

The door was taken from her hand by a doorman inside dressed in rose and pale green. He nodded to her, a touch of disdain in his eyes. "GentleLady."

Greyku hissed. The doorman started, then narrowed his eyes, bowed. "And Fam."

Trif walked to the counter, where she paid an entrance fee, then went to the glowing door in the translucent shieldspell that would let her through into the low-lit club. She hadn't often been to the Maypole, but it was *the* place to dance. A place where Nobles mixed with Commoners, a place where many single people gathered to play—or connect. A perfect place to leave T'Willow's HeartGift. She was glad that he'd given her an excuse to indulge herself in a treat, even though she'd be eating meals she'd saved in no-time storage for emergencies.

As she wound her way around the huge dance floor to a small, empty table for two she'd spotted, a man swung her into a dance, yelped as Greyku scratched his hand, and hastily let Trif go. He melted quickly into the crowd. The embroidery on his cuffs had proclaimed him the Heir to a GrandHouse.

Rude man, Greyku said, licking a drop of blood from her claws.

I like to dance. And like to listen to the music even more. We'd better put you somewhere safe.

The small table was still empty. Trif rushed to it and claimed it, banishing Greyku's stick-spell so the kitten could hop from shoulder to the table. Trif glanced around. No one was paying her any attention. Not many people were even looking at Greyku. Trif hung her bag from one of the spelled security hooks on the underside of the table, then slipped her hand in it. Her fingers touched her silver flute first, caressed it; then she reached for the box. She set her thumbnail under the latch and opened it. The furrabeast leather pouch fell into her hand, nearly searing the skin of her palm, the heat was so intense. She jerked it out and dropped it on the edge of the table.

Greyku pranced over and settled near it, bracketing the pouch between her outstretched forelegs, claws evident. *I will guard.*

Trif slid the kitten across the table back to the wall. *No, you will not. I must send the gift out.*

The kitten stretched out a paw, but couldn't reach the pouch. *I like the toy.*

It is NOT your toy.

At that moment a Maypole serving woman addressed Trif. "Do you want anything to drink?" Her gaze wandered to Greyku. "We have milk too."

I would like cinnamon mousse, Greyku said.

Trif winced. She couldn't imagine the price for that delicacy here. "I'll have Crimson Nut lager, and my Fam will have warm milk with a sprinkling of cinnamon."

"Will do." The woman shook her head. "This is the first Fam I've seen in here." She looked around. "It doesn't seem the place for a kitten."

"She's adventurous."

"I guess so." The woman smiled and left.

Leaning back in her chair, Trif looked toward the small stage and saw the man playing a lively jig on the tin whistle wiggle his eyebrows at her.

It was a friend—GrandSir RedMelon. He tapped his whistle with a free hand, gaze questioning. She dipped her hand in her bag, showed him her flute. His eyes widened. He gestured with his head for her to come up on stage. She shook her head, waving at the crowd on the dance floor. She wanted to dance and listen first. He nodded, then added a flourish and returned his gaze to the dancers.

The waitress arrived, carrying a tray. "Your lager." She placed a glass beaded with condensation before Trif, then put her tray down and set her hands around a huge bowl twice the size of Greyku. Milk liberally spiced with cinnamon sloshed gently as she slid the bowl to the Fam.

Thank you! Greyku shouted mentally, and had several people looking at the table.

Flushing, the woman nodded her head. "You're welcome."

"How much do I owe you?" asked Trif.

The woman shook her head. "Drinks compliments of the chef."

Trif slipped a gilt coin on the table. "For you then."

"My thanks!" She whisked away, and as she did so, the pouch containing the HeartGift fell into her apron pocket.

Flair at work. Fascinated, Trif watched the woman check another table, clear one, and fumble with coins in her pocket, pull the pouch out of her apron, and set it with an absent-minded expression on an empty table.

A man blocked Trif 's view as he came to her table. Young, like her, Noble, unlike her. He bowed. "May I have the next dance?"

"Yes."

Ilex, Fairyfoot, and Vertic met D'Ash in her office. She was full of efficiency as she banished the fleas from Fairyfoot and examined the cat physically, mentally, and psychically. Fairyfoot watched the woman with open adoration in her big round eyes. D'Ash certified the small cat as a Fam and sent the notice of record on to the proper bureaucratic clerk, along with the information that Fairyfoot was the Fam of Dufleur Thyme.

Then D'Ash and Vertic had a mutual-admiration session. She ran her hands over him, murmuring pet names, and did another certification. "My first for a fox!" She grinned. "He's beautiful." Then she spoke to Vertic. "You can bring any fox kits with Fam qualities here to me." She raised a hand, palm outward. "I vow to protect and raise them." A frown line appeared between her brows. "You foxes are very rare. I don't want you dying out."

We won't. Vertic sat on her examination table. He raised a paw.

D'Ash shook it. "Done. You beautiful thing, you."

Vertic opened his mouth in a foxy laugh. *T'Ash Residence is a good hunting place, and I have several food caches here.*

D'Ash laughed again.

"Who is making my HeartMate too amused for my liking?" rumbled T'Ash from the threshold, a mock scowl on his swarthy face. His son rode his shoulders, small fingers clamped in T'Ash's hair.

"Greetyou, Winterberry."

Ilex bowed. "Greetyou, T'Ash."

T'Ash's gaze went straight to Vertic. He stalked over with a fighter's grace. "May I study you, Master Fox?"

I am Vertic, the Fam projected mentally.

"I've heard Straif Blackthorn speak of you." T'Ash circled the animal, eyes piercing. "Would you stand, please?"

Vertic did.

When T'Ash returned to his starting point next to Ilex, he was smiling and rubbing his hands. "I can predict a fad in fox jewelry this season." He took his son, kissed the boy on his lips. "Will you take him, Danith? Inspiration has struck." He handed the boy to his wife.

Nuin squirmed opening and clenching his fingers, reaching out for Vertic. "Foxy, foxy, foxy! Me touch!"

" 'I want to touch,' " corrected D'Ash.

"I want to touch *now.*"

T'Ash snorted and strode from the room, passing his Fam, Zanth, as the tomcat prowled in.

"If you ask Vertic nicely to touch him, and he says yes, you may *pet,* not grab."

Vertic inclined his head. *Nuin may pet.*

With careful pats, the toddler stroked Vertic, his eyes blazing glee. "Me want foxy!"

Zanth snorted, sounding like his FamMan, or T'Ash had sounded like his cat.

"The fox is his own, but is *my* Fam," said Ilex.

Nuin pouted, turned big eyes on his mother. "I want a fox!"

She cuddled him. "You're a bit too small, I think. Perhaps next spring." She glanced at Vertic, who had cocked his head and was staring at Nuin. "Will you keep a nose out for a good fox kit Fam for my Nuin?"

Vertic nodded. *Yes.*

Growls came from the corner. Zanth sat big and hulking before Fairyfoot.

"Zanth!" D'Ash warned.

Don't want no more Cats here, Zanth said.

"She's on her way to D'Winterberry's," D'Ash said.

Zanth nodded and trotted over to look up at Vertic. *Greetyou, Vertic.*

Greetyou, Zanth.

Got two sewer rats by smithy.

Thank you, no, Any mice? asked Vertic.

Three fat mice by back door.

Vertic jumped from the table and ran out the door, *See you later, FamMan*, he said to Ilex. Zanth followed.

"Time to go," Ilex said. He walked over to Fairyfoot. "I'm picking you up now."

She shrugged and allowed him to take her. She smelled good—the effect of the de-fleaing smell. When he held her, she leaned against him and purred in a low tone. "May I use your scry?" he asked D'Ash.

"Of course," she said, and led him to the office scry, rubbing her hand over her son's back. After Vertic left, Nuin had fallen asleep against her shoulder with the suddenness of youth. "I need to put this one to bed. Can you show yourself out?"

"Yes," Ilex said, envying T'Ash his home life.

D'Ash nodded and left.

For a moment Ilex just stood and soaked up the atmosphere around him. The whole Residence was suffused with love—love for their careers, their animals, for their Fams. More—HeartMate love and the couple's love for their son. He longed for that, especially when he recalled the first time he'd met T'Ash—an angry, rough man who'd had the HeartGift with which he'd hoped to snare his mate stolen. Now T'Ash had everything any man could wish for. And if T'Ash could have it all, anyone should be able to.

Except Ilex Winterberry. Ilex snorted. Self-pity. He was truly small of character.

Fairyfoot relaxed in his grip, and purred. A little contentment would through him. Enough for now.

He tapped the scrybowl with his forefinger nail. "D'Winterberry Residence, Dufleur Thyme, please."

"Here," came the startled voice; then her expression eased when she recognized him and smiled. "I never get calls from FirstFamily Residences, and T'Ash is . . ." She shook her head.

"I heard that," Ilex said.

"What?"

"Whatever you were going to say about T'Ash. It's true."

They both laughed. Ilex turned his head to whisper in Fairyfoot's ear. "Look appealing." He didn't think she could look beautiful, but she could be very appealing. A lot like Dufleur. He angled Fairyfoot over the large bowl of water. She went rigid.

"Trust me. I won't drop you. The fox trusts me," he said soothingly.

That didn't work this time.

"What's that?" asked Dufleur.

"Want a newly certified Fam?" Ilex asked, trying not to show pain when Fairyfoot dug her not-so-fairylike back claws into his gut.

"A Fam?" Dufleur breathed the words out.

"This is Fairyfoot." He nearly grunted at renewed scratching. "I think you'd do well together."

"For *me?*"

"Yes. I'll be right over to pick up an item from my mother. I'm bringing the cat and you can see if you suit. Meet you in the entry hall." He ended the scry, stepped back from the bowl, and detached claws from his skin.

Don't like water, Fairyfoot said.

It was the worst semi-apology he'd ever heard in his life. "You're damn lucky that I didn't drop you in it."

She stared away from him.

"Ready to teleport to your new FamWoman and home?"

"Yesss!" She wriggled.

A moment later, they were in the dark entryway of D'Winterberry Residence. A darker shadow in the far corner separated from the rest. Dufleur walked toward them, searching his face. "Really a Fam for me?"

"Yes."

"Why?"

"Because you both need someone to love."

She blinked up at him. "I don't think I like your perception, cuz Ilex."

He shrugged.

Sighing, she said, "My rooms are this way."

To his shock she used the worst, tiniest suite in the house, situated at garden level. She opened the door to show stark white walls and minimal furnishings that were all much-mended. This was a woman who could benefit from a visit to Clover Fine Furnishings. He walked in, boot heels ringing on stone until he reached a small ragged rug, where he set Fairyfoot down.

"Is it so surprising that I chose the rooms farthest from the old women?" Then she flushed as if hearing her own bitter words and remembering one of the old women was his mother.

"No, cuz Dufleur. Not at all."

"They have their plans for me. They want me to make a Noble marriage, as if that would right everything in all our lives!" She paced back and forth the breadth of the small mainspace. "I hate this—this need for wealth, this obsession with status." Her chin shot up. "As if it's dishonorable to work for someone else!"

"What do you do?"

She picked up a pillow and tossed it to him. "Embroidery."

He glanced down at the lovely stitches, traced a finger over them. "Very fine work." Then he met her eyes. "And I completely understand working for someone else, and how a mother can consider her child's job low-class."

Dufleur flushed again. "Sorry."

There was a little cat cough. *I am here.*

Fairyfoot and Dufleur stared at each other.

I like the looks of you, said Fairyfoot. *And you have honor and drive and passion.*

"I like the looks of you too," said Dufleur.

The little cat launched herself at the woman and Dufleur caught her.

Their auras spiked and mingled. Fairyfoot's purr filled the room. She turned a happy face to Ilex, round eyes nearly glowing with pleasure. Her whiskers twitched. *Thank you, Black Ilex.*

"You're welcome." He left his cuz's spartan chambers and trudged up the stairs, where he met D'Thyme hands on hips, tapping her foot.

"Took you long enough to get here."

"I had other business to see to."

She grunted, extracted a box from her pocket, and looked down at it sourly, frustrated greed in her eyes. "The House-Heart encased the amulet in this." Reluctantly she handed the small round box of beaten gold to him, obviously a Family treasure she didn't want to relinquish.

"Thank you." He bowed. Then he addressed the Residence. "Thank you, Residence."

You are most welcome, Son of the House, Guardsman. The reply was barely a whisper in his mind. That more than anything clogged his throat. His fingers tightened over the box. What had happened to the strong Residential presence he'd known as a boy? His mother had not been a good guardian.

It was not his place to remedy this. His mother was D'Winterberry. The distasteful woman before him was her Heir. His brother, the former Heir, was gone from Druida. Ilex was only the despised second son with a "lowly" profession. It was not his place.

Thirteen

As the box warmed in his fingers and the essence of Trif radiated through the gold to his skin, tingling, tantalizing, he left the regretful path of the past and faced the present threats to his HeartMate. Clearing his throat, he repeated, "Thank you."

D'Thyme's lips tightened into pursed disapproval. Had she hoped he'd take the amulet from the box and give the treasure to her? With a whisk of heavy skirts that stirred up a trace of dust, she stalked away.

Still depressed by the gloom and disrepair of his former home, Ilex slipped down the hallway and the stairs and into a small back parlor that had been a quiet sanctuary in his youth. He had one more call to make.

This chamber had not fared well under his mother either. He'd have called up a housekeeping spell to clean it, but was unsure of the Residence's energy. Yet he found a scrybowl and when he summoned water for it from the kitchens, the instrument hummed with renewed Flair.

"T'Holly Residence, please. Tinne Holly."

It wasn't Tinne who answered the scry, but the T'Holly butler. "I'm sorry, Black Ilex, but Tinne and Genista are out this evening—at the Maypole."

"Thank you," Ilex said hoarsely.

He'd debated taking the amulet to Trif that night, and had decided against it. Now it appeared as if he should. The Lady and Lord had a way of pushing you toward your fate, whether you wanted to go or not.

Trif was traipsing down the line of dancers when her hand was caught and squeezed and she looked up to see Tinne Holly.

"Hey, Trif Clover," he said, and she read his lips more than she heard him above the music and dancing footsteps.

"Hey," she said faintly, then louder, "Genista?"

Tinne smiled and waved to a woman far down the line, his wife flushed with enjoyment. They both looked happy. Trif knew from her cuz, Mitchella, that T'Holly Residence was a difficult place to live in at the moment.

Then the dance took him away and she whirled herself, smiling, until she clasped hands with the next man. She recognized him at once. Cyperus Sedge, the man she'd met when she'd been going door to door near Landing Park. He arched a thin eyebrow. "Trif Clover," he murmured, and she *heard* it. The words seemed to slide along her skin up to the nape of her neck, ruffling the hair there. Luckily, her time with him was as short as with every man until she returned to her partner and they ended the set together. He returned her to his seat, thanked her, and drifted away. So much for her many charms.

Greyku lay on the table, little round belly up, forepaws curled, sleeping. Cinnamon and flecks of dried milk dotted her whiskers.

Trif scanned the room and saw Cyperus Sedge with the woman she'd met before too. Unreasoning or not, she didn't like them.

Tinne and Genista Holly strolled up. Tinne seated his wife in the chair opposite Trif, hooked an empty chair from the next table with his foot, and dragged it to sit at right angles to them. "Greetyou, Trif Clover."

"Greetyou, HollyHeir." She bobbed her head, then realized it was the wrong thing to say as his expression saddened.

"Pleased to meet you, Trif Clover," said Genista Holly. She

rubbed Greyku's belly with a couple of fingers and smiled. "So soft. Who's this?" Greyku snuffled and opened one eye, looked at Genista and Tinne, and went back to sleep.

"My Fam, Greyku. Zanth's her sire, but the rest of her bloodline is unknown."

"Bloodline is very important," Genista said. "But beauty is a good quality too, and this one is extraordinarily beautiful."

"Kindness and generosity are to be prized also." Tinne picked up Genista's right hand and kissed her fingers.

She blushed and withdrew her hand. "Tease," she said to her husband. "You know you only married me for my dowry."

Tinne leered at his wife's low-cut neckline, showing full breasts and a great deal of cleavage. "Oh, yes, just for your dowry."

"Excuse me," a man said. It was GrandSir RedMelon. He made quick, unimpressive bows to Tinne and Genista. "Trif, will you play in the next set?"

The Hollys looked surprised. "You play?" Tinne asked.

RedMelon's smile was dazzling. "She's wonderful." He slipped his thumbs into the waistband of his trous and rocked back on his heels. "And I know she brought her flute, *and* I know she likes to play for crowds." He glanced over the busy tables. "This place is charged with Flair. Gives the musicians a real buzz."

The Hollys laughed. "I never thought of that," Genista said. She narrowed her eyes slightly, and Trif realized she was observing the room with her Flair. "There *is* a great deal of sparking Flair." Raising her arms, she stretched. "No wonder I feel so good."

A few twiddles came from the stage. "Trif?" prompted RedMelon.

She indicated Greyku. "I've kept an eye on her while I was dancing, and she was awake. But—"

"We'll watch her for you," Tinne offered. He looked at Genista. "You aren't ready to go home yet, are you?"

"No."

Tinne flapped his hands at Trif. "Go!"

"Greyku's had a lot of milk, she may need—"

"Trif, we raise hunting cats. I can take her outside, if need be," Tinne said.

That was all Trif waited to hear. She dug out her silver flute and went up to the stage. This was going to be fun!

The fiddler stuck his instrument under chin and raised his bow, looking at her. RedMelon had told her the tunes they'd be playing, and let her know she'd have time for a little improvisation at the end of the first dance set and before the next. Zow!

Energy filled the room, swirling around her. She could almost see streams of Flair emanating from the Nobles who had great gifts. The fiddler drew his bow, and they were playing!

The Maypole specialized in ancient country line dances, along with an occasional slow one, dances everyone learned as young children. Trif swirled into the music, letting her flute sing, send Flair out, and receive it. Fabulous.

During the middle of the dance, her eyes half-shut to appreciate the flows of Flair, she noticed a bright golden glow around a small object. T'Willow's HeartGift. Even from the stage, she saw the pouch had gathered a few stains and the strings no longer looked like pristine scarlet braid. She watched it as it was casually, almost abstractedly, picked up and moved from table to table until it landed where Cyperus Sedge and Piana Juniper sat along with four others, now and again including a couple of women at the next table in their conversation.

As Trif took the lead in a reel, she noticed Cyperus poke the pouch with a finger, jerk his hand back, then wipe his finger on a softleaf from his pocket, sneering something. Piana picked it up, turned it over in her hand, her nostrils flared. Then she shuddered and passed it to the next table.

The striking brunette weighed it in her hand, frowning. Her beautiful friend leaned forward and was given it. That lady grimaced and tossed it aside. The pouch landed on a server's tray and was carried to the bar.

Interesting. Not the way she'd want to find her HeartMate—sending an intimate part of herself out into the world. She much preferred using her charmkey.

Then the dancers came to a laughing halt, bowed and curtsied to their partners, and the other instruments stopped.

RedMelon stepped forward to claim the crowd's attention

and introduce her, but Trif shook her head. She was ready to play solo, but not to be singled out as a musician.

She held a long note and thought rapidly. The dancers were hot, tired; perhaps a dreamy improvisation would suit them, something with a special rhythm. Something yearning, something hopeful—like the rounds of Saille T'Willow's HeartGift, calling, calling.

Trif played, and gradually the room fell silent. Every note she sent out echoing into the large room, laden with Flair, returned to her along with a bit of buzz until she felt full of light, of energy.

Then Ilex Winterberry walked in.

He stopped, stunned at the power of her music. His heart wrenched from him and flew to her. Hers forever.

He couldn't move, struck still by the sight of her—dreamy expression on her face, nearly vibrating with energy and Flair. All the emotions she churned up inside him, she expressed with her music. The yearning, the passion, the love.

He wanted her more than he'd ever wanted anything in his life.

A flash of the vision he'd had only that morning shrouded his eyesight. Himself dead. He couldn't do that to her.

Gathering all his courage, all his strength, he moved into the room. His eyes met her widened ones only for a second. Her breath and music faltered, then wound down.

Furious clapping shook the room. Trif flushed.

The fiddler struck up another fast dance and all the musicians, including Trif, picked up the tune. Dancers swung onto the floor.

Ilex tore his hungry stare from Trif and shifted his shoulders, settling into a more professional manner. He scanned the room for Tinne Holly, and found him and his wife sitting at a table. Genista was idly amusing Greyku. Tinne studied Trif with a considering look.

Striding through the crowd, Ilex reached the table, but the words that came from his mouth weren't about his investigation. "She's phenomenal, isn't she? Do you think your mother would consider taking her on as an Apprentice?"

Tinne turned to Ilex. "More like a Journeywoman, but I think it would be very, very likely that my mother would be interested in her. And it would be good for Mamá too."

"I have some casual recordings of her music," Ilex said.

"Oh?" Tinne's eyebrows raised.

Ilex shrugged. "I'm her neighbor. Most everyone on the first floor of MidClass Lodge opens their doors to listen when she plays."

"I'd imagine so." Tinne shook his head. "Trif Clover, the next great Celtan composer. Who'd have guessed? Life is a wonderful thing."

The statement reminded Ilex why he was there—on a matter of death. "Lady Genista, can I take your husband aside for a moment, please?"

She looked up and graced him with a smile. "Of course."

Tinne rose, accompanying Ilex to a corner near the bar. Then Ilex was distracted an instant again—T'Willow's HeartGift, looking the worse for wear, lay on the bar's surface. He shuddered at the thought of what the man might be going through tonight. His own HeartGift would stay safely in the bank.

"Winterberry?" prompted Tinne.

Ilex lowered his voice. "Your Vow of Honor that you will repeat nothing of what I tell you to anyone—without my leave."

Paling, Tinne jerked a nod.

"It looks as if the killings are ritual murders. For black magic."

Tinne just stared unblinking at him for a moment. "Cave of the Dark Goddess," he breathed.

"I don't think She'd be pleased."

With a hard swallow, Tinne said, "What do you want of me?"

"I'd like you to find out the name of the best scholar of the occult in Druida, and hopefully in Celta."

Eyes widening, Tinne said, "Funny you should ask that. Sedwy Grove just came to Druida from her dam's country estate."

"How long ago?"

"Ask her yourself, she's right over there." He angled his chin.

Ilex followed his glance, muttered under his breath.

"What?" asked Tinne.

"When the Lady and Lord take a hand, you find your destiny whether you want to or not."

Tinne's smile was unamused. "Isn't that the truth."

Trif watched Ilex walk over to the table where Cyperus and Piana had been sitting. They'd left shortly after her solo piece. Ilex looked good, more virile than most of the men in the room. He asked one of the remaining women at the table something and she gestured to the other table of two women—the striking, flirtatious one and the quiet beauty. He nodded his thanks and went over to the two women. Trif blew a sour note, and when RedMelon looked startled, she sent him an apologetic expression.

Ilex's face had been expressionless when he'd met her eyes. She was right, it would be very difficult to get back onto a good footing with him. And she wanted him in her life, wanted his respect.

Ilex bowed to the two women sitting at the table. One was laughing and vivacious, with golden brown wavy hair and green-blue eyes. The other had a creamy complexion, dark hair and eyes, and was simply beautiful. Both of the ladies' auras showed great Flair. Since Sedwy Grove was a daughter of GreatLady D'Grove, her Flair would be great.

He addressed the dark one. "Merry meet. I'm Ilex Winterberry and I'd like to speak to GreatMistrys Grove about her studies."

She said nothing, but sent him a shy smile. The woman beside her laughed and tapped the table with pretty fingernails. "That would be me, GrandSir Winterberry."

Since she seemed pleased instead of insulted at his mistake, Ilex allowed his surprise to show.

The band's music increased a notch, led by a silver flute. Sedwy leaned forward, and Ilex appreciated the view of ripe breasts. "I don't think this is the time to speak of ritual magic," she said in a raised voice, gesturing to a chair near her.

He sat and hitched it closer. "You're right. May I call on you tomorrow morning?"

Her teeth gleamed white in a wicked smile. "I would be honored."

"May I buy you and your friend a drink?"

"Yes indeed." She tossed her head in the direction of the other woman, who smiled slightly. "My friend is Zinga Turmeric."

"Merry meet," Zinga said, her voice low and pleasant.

Sedwy gave him a sly glance. "I'll have black frankincense wine. Appropriate, don't you think?"

*The women were flirting with Ilex. Trif was so aggra-*vated she nearly steamed—her flute did, as she gathered Flair from the mass of dancers, transformed it into loud, fast music. The band had circled around her, letting her lead.

Ilex and the women talked and the pretty one sparkled at Ilex. The other sent him long glances from under lowered lashes, seeming to draw him with her beauty and graceful gestures. Both were Flaired, Noble, older. Fashionable, rich, sophisticated. They made Trif feel like a little girl and sweaty Commoner.

She began toning down her music, noticing the louder the band played, the more Ilex bent his head to speak with them. He ordered drinks and the waiter fulfilled his request quickly, even more quickly than others, more obviously Noble. But command sat on Ilex's shoulders.

Trif didn't like the women. If they were friends of Cyperus and Piana, they couldn't be good.

She liked them even less when they made Ilex laugh! Now his body had relaxed in his chair. The bit of profile she could see showed crinkles around his eyes where he was smiling. She had to do something.

A flash of memory came. Ilex's favorite tune. She knew when doors opened to listen to her play at MidClass Lodge—and knew who liked what. Meeting RedMelon's eyes, she quieted her flute and let him finish the melody with his whistle. As soon as he was done, she asked. "Do you all play any of D'Holly's compositions?"

The fiddler grinned. "We do 'Tinne's Traipsing.' And since the man himself is in the audience. . . ." He gestured to where Tinne sat. "It would be fun."

The rest of the band hooted. The tune was very old, written by Tinne's mother when Tinne was two. Fast and complicated, and only the best dancers could keep up.

"Right then," said the fiddler. "Ready?"

"On three," agreed RedMelon.

At the opening notes, Tinne winced and the crowd roared, most standing, then flooding onto the huge dance floor. The lively lady grabbed Ilex's hand and pulled him up and into the dance. His feet were nimble and he moved with confident ease, but the lady faltered and her breasts heaved as she laughed and fanned herself with her hand, then led him back to the table.

And Ilex looked at Trif, toe tapping. She got the idea that he somehow knew that she'd engineered the situation. She used the tune to improvise, and let her notes soar above and twine between the melody. Ilex's lids lowered as he just appreciated the music.

The bright aura of T'Willow's HeartGift sparked. Flair soaked into Trif, into her flute. She wondered if she could add a little spell to T'Willow's pouch. Something that might rush it to the right woman.

Measuring the beat, she gathered her own Flair, formed the spelltune, sent it along with all her will.

Feet dance.
Ladies prance.
Men bow.
And vow.
Love forever.
Forsaking never.
T'Willow's gift
Needs a lift.
To HeartMate right.
Tonight! Tonight!

She saw a man drop the grubby pouch in his pocket and stroll out of the Maypole. The gift was now out circulating in the world. Who would it bring T'Willow? Had she helped the spell at all? She certainly felt aglow—with Flair and perspiration.

Then the tune was over.

* * *

Finally having himself well in hand and braced for the emotions that would inundate him from a meeting with Trif, Ilex stood and bowed over the ladies' hands in turn. Raising his voice, he said, "I thank you."

Sedwy's eyes twinkled at him. "I look forward to seeing you tomorrow at my mother's Residence. . . ."

The serene beauty said nothing, but inclined her head. "A pleasure meeting you. I hope to see you in the future."

He nodded to Zinga. "Perhaps."

Then he wound his way to Trif's table, and Tinne stopped playing with Greyku and greeted him.

"Where's Genista?" asked Ilex.

Tinne waved to the dance floor. A huge circle dance had started, which would break into two circles, then become smaller and smaller, until only couples rounded the floor in pinwheels. Ilex caught sight of Genista, laughing. "She looks happy."

"She is, for now," Tinne said in a repressive tone, and Ilex left the topic alone.

Without looking at Trif, Ilex made a show of taking the round gold box from his pocket and placing it on the table, where Greyku immediately pounced on it, rolled onto her side, and clutched it to her with her forepaws. *Something good inside!* she purred. *Smells-tastes-feels like FamWoman.*

Tinne gave a low whistle. "Nice box. Family heirloom. What's in it?"

As an answer, Ilex reached under Tinne's collar and flicked out the amulet he wore, also made by T'Ash, an Earth hematite.

"Oh." Tinne frowned. "For Trif? I got mine because the Hollys were dueling and I was missing a kidney. The Clovers are solid, upstanding middle-class people. They don't duel. So why the amulet?"

Leaning down to speak in his ear, Ilex said, "Trif Clover is single, has a Fam, and her Flair is unstable." He straightened.

Tinne's eyes had widened. "She's not of the Nobility as the others were."

"I'd rather not take a chance."

"I don't blame you."

Genista joined them. She tickled Greyku's stomach and touched the box.

Mine, mine, mine, mine, mine, mine! Greyku sent telepathically, and everyone around them laughed, looking at the kitten curled around her prize.

"I'm afraid not, Greyku." Ilex brushed a thumb over her head.

Mine!

"It's Trif 's."

"Not the box," Trif said on a ragged breath.

Ilex had known when she'd stopped playing, of course, but hadn't looked up. He didn't need to. With every step closer, he felt the link between them thicken as the distance between them diminished. The bond that he hadn't wanted to make, but that grew every time they spent time together, and had doubled during their brief kiss.

Trif laid her silver flute on the table and scooped up the kitten, turning her so their eyes locked. "The box is not yours. Not mine either. It belongs to . . . someone."

"D'Winterberry," Tinne said helpfully, picking up the box and handing it to Ilex.

He really didn't want to touch it since the necklace inside still radiated of Trif. But he took it and flipped the latch open with his thumbnail, revealing the gold chain necklace. The pink calcite glowed, along with a tiny polished white bead of stone from MidClass HealingHall. The necklace rested on a bed of plush dark green velvet. "Trif 's retrieval amulet," he said.

"Ooooh!" Trif placed Greyku on her shoulder. "Stay!" she said to the kitten, and since the word was a spell too, Greyku grumbled but subsided. "How beautiful!"

"T'Ash does fabulous work," Genista said with a sigh.

Tinne took his wife's hand. "Does that mean I need to buy you another trinket?"

She looked at him from under lowered lashes. "Only if you want to. But you're always well rewarded when I get something from T'Ash, aren't you?" Her purr was almost as good as a cat's.

Chuckling, Tinne squeezed her hand, then let it go.

"Put it on!" said Genista.

Trif touched the chain, then uncurled it from its nest and brought it over her head to dangle between her breasts, a shining pink stone against filmy chiff. Ilex glanced away, then flinched when her fingers covered his, sending sexual energy through every nerve as she offered the box. "It's a beautiful case."

He wanted to give it to her. Knew it was too valuable and special a gift to offer publicly without comment, so he pocketed it. Damned if he'd give it back to his mother. He had no right to visit the Winterberry HouseHeart without permission, so he couldn't return it there. He'd send it to his brother.

Genista's brows knit. "It's a retrieval amulet?" She glanced at Trif.

Trif sighed, fingering the stone. "Yes, I promised to wear it when . . . uh . . . when I went out by myself."

"Good idea." Genista nodded. "So, does it work?"

Dropping the necklace she'd been studying, Trif said, "I don't know."

"T'Ash made the amulet, so that would be solid. Who did the spell? D'Alder?"

"D'Winterberry," Ilex said.

"That unreliable old hag?" Genista said, shot a look at Ilex, and winced. "Sorry." She lifted her chin. "But the amulet should be tested."

Trif pulled a bag from under the table, encased her flute in a shieldspell, and put it inside. She straightened to her full height. "I agree. We should test the amulet. Greyku, you should—"

I will go with you.

"Ha! Really—" Trif winced as Greyku curled her claws into her dress.

Tinne folded his arms. "Don't look at me to hit her."

"Of course not," Genista said. She tipped her head toward Ilex.

He shook his head. "Not me."

Genista rolled her eyes and sent a grimace to Trif. "You men—" She swung a fist at Trif's jaw, taking her by surprise. The blow connected audibly.

Trif crumpled.

Then vanished.

Fourteen

Genista dusted her hands and looked at Tinne, whose mouth had fallen open in shock. "It had to be done," she said.

"I didn't think—" Tinne began.

"I've lived in Holly Residence for two years and a season, Tinne. During that amount of time, even *I* learned a thing or two about fighting."

"You certainly did," Ilex said, sending a telepathic probe down his link with Trif. She was already being revived by a Healer.

"Where do you think she went?" asked Genista.

"The amulet is bespelled to take her to Intake at MidClass HealingHall first, then any other close HealingHall." He knew she was at MidClass HealingHall through their bond.

"Let's find out," Genista said cheerfully. She walked over to the small teleportation pad, waited until some Noble newcomers departed, and flicked the safety light off. The three of them stepped onto the pad and Genista held out her hands. "I don't 'port well, so why don't you take us, Tinne?"

"One, Genista. Two, Tinne Holly. *Three!*" Tinne whisked them away and they arrived at MidClass HealingHall Intake.

"I've never been here," Genista said, looking around at the

pale pink walls and pastel art. She shrugged. "Not much to see. Bland decorating."

"Greetyou," Trif said, rubbing her jaw as if in remembered pain.

Greyku mewed a greeting. Then Trif smiled at a hovering FourthLevel Healer. "As I said before, you can charge Genista Holly for the fee."

Genista looked surprised. Tinne laughed.

Trif walked up to Ilex and linked her arm in his. "Now, I will 'port us home to MidClass Lodge."

"Trif—"

Her eyes flashed up at him. "Ilex. I have something to prove to myself and *you.* I won't fail this time."

Behind the determination, he saw just the hint of anxiety, and something more—hurt, as if his abrupt departure that morning had injured her feelings. Her lips trembled, then firmed. "You promised to teach me teleporting. And we're not done yet."

I will help, Greyku said.

He found his hand grasping hers, and the bond between them grew from thread to braid. "Very well." In the back of his mind, he'd had strategies to implement to mask himself from her if she got too close to finding him. She was *far* too close.

They crossed to an area designated for teleportation. Trif turned off the light and they stepped inside black lines. Before he could say anything, she sent an image to him of MidClass Lodge—with additional senses, the faint odor of dinners that drifted through the halls the quiet of the shadowy lobby at this time of night.

"One, silver flute. Two, Greyku kit. *Three.*"

Her Flair took them fast and strong and correctly. They materialized on the landing pad of MidClass Lodge Lobby.

Trif smiled triumphantly. "I did it!"

I helped, Greyku added, though she hadn't.

Ilex could do no less than acknowledge her feat. "Well done."

She looked away. "The program says that for some people there is one last fumble just before the teleportation skill is learned."

"You're right. I'd forgotten."

She brushed his mouth with hers, and once again fire flooded his veins. He fisted his hands and hid them from her.

"Thank you, Ilex. I'm glad we're friends again."

She walked down the hall, her hips swaying under the fluttery dress.

The kiss must have meant nothing to her. Just as well.

Still, Ilex was glad he didn't have to pass her room to reach his own.

The next morning, Ilex stared at the recording spheres of Trif 's music on his home desk. There were more than twenty. He had no idea he'd made so many. He'd promised Tinne Holly a few to give to his mother, D'Holly, the composer who might be interested in teaching Trif. Part of Ilex's plan to distract Trif from her questing.

So he sorted his spheres, and realized he didn't want to give up a one. Muttering under his breath, he chose the three he liked the least—more renderings of Earthen tunes than Trif 's own—and sent them to the T'Holly collection box.

Then he walked into the hallway and used all his disguising spells on his apartment door. It *would* open to Trif 's charmkey if she tried, but he hoped that his threshold resonated of impressions of others he'd layered on it, as well as an avoid spell. In the past, he'd been grateful that his space had been closer to the lobby than Trif 's and he wouldn't have to pass her apartment door all the time. Now he wondered at that strategy.

His wrist timer vibrated, notifying him of his imminent appointment with Sedwy Grove. Vertic trotted up. Ilex had never actually seen the fox teleport, but there was no way his Fam could be in some places unless he used Flair. Maybe he walked through walls—a talent no one had ever mastered. Ilex frowned, making a note to ask a Healer about how a heart could be removed from a body with no trace . . . lifted through chest walls? The thought made him shudder.

"Greetyou, Vertic."

I wish to accompany you.

"Oh?"

Last night I saw this woman you visit. She had an interesting smell.

Ilex raised his brows. "What sort of interesting smell?"

She walked through grass full of insects and mice and voles.

"Ah."

Where she lives would be an excellent hunting ground for my kind.

"I see." He held out his arms and Vertic sprang into them. Vertic's fur wasn't nearly as soft as little Greyku's, but his presence was much more comforting to Ilex than the kitten's. He and his Fam understood and respected each other—something he wasn't sure was possible with a small, vain, female kitten.

"Since you're with me, let's 'port from the apartment." With a Word, Ilex opened the much-bespelled door, entered, and kicked it closed. He sent a mental questing to D'Grove's estate and found it secured against teleporting inside, with only a spot by the front gates accessible. "Ready?" he asked Vertic.

Yes. Vertic hummed a little in his throat. *It is always a pleasure traveling with you.*

"I'll return the compliment." His Fam felt warm and vital in his arms.

A moment later, he was addressing the scrystone outside D'Grove's greeniron gates, and Vertic had melted between the bars and into the estate, already lost to view, even in the bright sunlit grassyard. Ilex tapped the scry a second time, deepened his voice, and added an authoritative note. "Guardsman Ilex Winterberry to see GentleMistrys Sedwy Grove."

The scry projected a holo inside its crystal planes, and cool blue eyes in a haughty face studied him. "I believe GreatMistrys Sedwy is under the impression that this meeting is a social appointment." The butler enunciated each word precisely. "By T'Winterberry, or WinterberryHeir. She wasn't sure of your exact title."

Or lack thereof. "You know me," Ilex said steadily. "I consulted with D'Grove fairly often when she was Captain of the FirstFamilies Council."

The butler's nose lifted. "You may teleport to the atrium of the round tower. No one is there at this time."

"My thanks." Once more, he glanced around for a hint of red fur or plush tail. Nothing. Vertic was on his own business.

The butler met him in the round tower's small entryway. "Lady Sedwy is in the top dormer room. I'll lead you."

Ilex had never been in that room, but was sure the man was taking him there to keep an eye on him instead of showing him the way. They wound up two flights of stairs spiraling around the tower wall. When they came to a large, old oak door with leather straps, the butler rapped sharply, then opened the door and strode in. Ilex followed.

It was a small room, tucked under the conical roof of the tower, lit by two small dormer windows opposite each other. The furnishings were cherished antiques, with a few scars that showed family living—the chairs were of deep brown wood and pale green velvet; the carpet was thickly woven with a background of beige to a deep green grove of leafy trees. Sedwy Grove sat on a twoseat.

"Guardsman Black Ilex Winterberry," pronounced the butler. Then he withdrew, more rapidly than Ilex expected.

"A guardsman, how interesting," she said, and her considering gaze made Ilex think that this interview could tip one of two ways, chilly and polite and uninformative, or flirtatious and social and very informative.

He swept a flourishing bow and caught her lips twitching. "I'm afraid the music at the Maypole last night wasn't conducive to good conversation." With as much grace as he could muster, he walked to her and waited for her to offer her hand. When she did, he took it, pressed her fingers and lightly brushed his lips across the back, then released it with a lingering squeeze.

Her flirtatious smile was back. Since she seemed to expect it, Ilex took the seat next to her. "And last night I *had* asked Tinne Holly about you." Ilex smiled and shook his head. "He said you were a scholar of the occult, and that piqued my interest. Hard to believe."

She threw back her head and laughed, spread her arms wide. "You don't think of me as a scholar?"

He was a man, and appreciated her lush breasts and hips, and let her see his interest. "I am sure no man would look at you and think 'scholar.' "

Eyes twinkling, she said, "Thank you." She gestured to a nearby table. "Caff?"

"My mouth is watering." He gazed at her.

Chuckling, she opened the cabinet, and Ilex realized it was a no-time storage. She pulled out a silver tray with caff pitcher and cups.

As they drank, they spoke of Druida, and Ilex scraped his memory for stories of the social scene of her class. It wasn't his class, but he was assigned to the FirstFamilies, so he tried to stay informed. Of course, the biggest news was the killing, but he couldn't bring that up without violating his orders from the FirstFamilies Council to keep the murders confidential.

After his last swallow of caff, he cast her a puzzled glance. "You really are a scholar."

She smiled. "I really am."

"And of the . . . occult."

Placing her cup in the saucer, she leaned back and said, "Yes. The dark side of our religion has always drawn me. It's so forbidden." She slanted him a look. "And being a guardsman, you wouldn't know much of it?"

"Not much. I attend ritual circles." He gestured. "Healing circles, Sabbats. Full and New Moons celebrations. But those are all . . . open, sanctioned. And being a guardsman, I'm curious about everything." He smiled slowly, wondering if she'd take the bait.

She leaned forward, face animated. "Yes. Every child is taken to Celtan rituals, taught our culture, but we don't talk about what could be done with Flair outside our ceremonies. Black magic."

"Why?"

"Why don't we talk about it, or why participate in black magic?" She smiled. "As I said, it's forbidden. As for practicing black magic—inverting our psi power of Flair into a purely negative force—simply, Power." She flicked her fingers. "The use of Flair always demands a price, physical or mental exhaustion, and from my experience it's difficult to form a great ritual with all minds in harmony for the same purpose."

"Straif T'Blackthorn had a Residence Renewal ceremony last year."

She cocked an eyebrow. "And how many favors and alliances did he have to promise?"

Ilex shrugged. "I don't know."

"When it comes to doing something major, few agree on all the particulars . . . like cleaning up the slums Downwind. That's what we all think of rituals . . . for the common good of a Family or our society."

Her smile turned a little cruel. "But with black magic, it calls to the basest emotions in all of us. We can agree that we want, oh, a boost in Flair, more energy, more vitality."

"And . . . sacrifice?" asked Ilex.

"In our societal GreatRituals, we all sacrifice a bit of ourselves—our energy, our Flair, to power the changes we want. In black magic, it could be animal sacrifices."

Or human. "The greater the sacrifice, the more the benefit."

"Of course."

So whatever the participants of this particular group were doing, they were worse than the triad gangs that had preyed Downwind.

She looked at him from under lowered eyelashes. "Sex would most certainly be a part of the rite."

Ilex lifted a pastry. "And food."

Laughing, she said, "Probably."

"Drink?"

Now she frowned. "Difficult to say if alcohol or the more potent herbs would be used. Not if you wanted the greatest outcome. But then, once you tap into the black part of our souls, it's hard to deny other lusts of drink and drug."

No doubt the cult figured that human sacrifice gave them great power, even if they indulged in herbs and alcohol. "And the trappings would be rather the same as our ceremonies, only . . . inverted? Incense? Altars?"

She nodded. "Oh, yes. The symbols on the altar would be different. Instead of a circle, the participants might try and make a more angular pattern—a square or rectangle."

"Interesting," Ilex said truthfully. He frowned. "What sort of incense—"

The door opened and D'Grove streamed into the room, tall and matronly, surrounded by great Flair. As former Captain of the FirstFamilies Council, she'd been one of the first people to be informed of the murders.

Though her hair and eyes were the same color as Sedwy's, their features were different. D'Grove nodded abruptly to Ilex. "Guardsman Winterberry, I think it is time you leave. I will not have my daughter bothered with this matter." She was every inch a mother defending her young. His heart twinged. He couldn't imagine either of the women living in D'Winterberry Residence bestirring themselves on behalf of their children.

"What's wrong, Mother?" Sedwy's lovely brow wrinkled. "We were just talking. . . ." Her eyes sharpened, her face set, and she suddenly resembled her mother very much. She turned to Ilex. "It wasn't just idle conversation or flirtation. You pulled the information you wanted from me quite easily. Very persuasive." Her voice was brittle now.

He inclined his torso, kept his own face serious. "I am under orders from the highest authority"—he glanced at her mother—"not to speak of this matter. Thus my methods are not as pristine as I would like, especially when speaking with such a fascinating lady as yourself."

"What did you question her about?" demanded D'Grove, fear shadowing her eyes.

Ilex stood, bowed. "GreatLady, your daughter is an expert on the occult. Isn't that why you called her back? When did she arrive from your estate?"

D'Grove paled to her lips. "She came to consult with me. She arrived after . . . much later than certain events."

"What is going on?" Sedwy rose.

"I am still under orders for silence," Ilex said.

"Mother?" asked Sedwy.

D'Grove made a cutting motion with her hand. "We'll talk about this later."

"If it involves my studies, we certainly will," Sedwy said coolly. "I think I'll go on that outing Zinga asked me to." Sedwy nodded to Ilex. "Merry meet."

"And merry part. It was a real pleasure sharing your company, under any circumstances."

"And merry meet again." She left.

After a hard look, D'Grove offered her hand to Ilex. As he

bowed over it, he banished irritation, thought of something more pleasing, and allowed himself a smile. "My Fam is a fox. Currently, the only den is located on T'Blackthorn's land. I believe more foxes might like to establish one here. Would that be agreeable to you?"

She looked startled, blinked, then the first genuine smile crossed her face. She dipped a tiny curtsy. "My household would be honored."

There was a bark and Vertic sat by the door, mouth open in a half laugh, bushy tail waving languidly.

D'Grove stiffened, then tilted her head. "How did he do that?"

Ilex smiled his most charming smile. "He's my Fam, and I don't know. But I believe that everyone is entitled to a few secrets, right?" he asked rhetorically, and stood as Vertic leapt into his arms. Then he let his smile sharpen. "As long as they harm none." He 'ported to the guardhouse.

A note from Tinne Holly lay on his desk. That young Lord had had several casual conversations with people his own age. As far as he could determine, Sedwy Grove had returned to Druida a couple of days before the first murder had occurred.

Greyku jumped up and down on Trif's back as she tried to get in one more minute of snuggling in the warm bed before she had to prepare for work.

The kitten screeched and Trif shuddered, reached for a pillow. It wasn't there.

Come, come, come! shouted Greyku mentally. *There is a message for Us! From Citrula about tinting ME! Today! Come.* The kitten nipped at Trif's bare shoulder.

"Why did I ever want a Fam?" Trif mumbled.

You wouldn't know what to do without Me. Greyku walked down Trif's spine, and she had to admit it felt good.

She grunted. "Getting up. Waterfall. Breakfast. Work."

Listen to the scry! More jumping up and down. Lucky it wasn't on her kidneys.

"All ri', all right," Trif replied in a husky morning voice. She rolled over, tossed back the covers, and slid from the bedsponge, straightening her nightgown, pushing one of the straps back up her shoulder.

Scrybowl first!

Trif stumbled into the mainspace. Her dreams had been a noisy confusion of the Maypole, with Ilex dancing with every woman, then disappearing into the shadows with them, while Trif played her fingers bloody. She shuddered. She much preferred erotic dreams of her HeartMate.

Finally, she reached her scrybowl and found the water rippling in a rainbow pattern. She snorted. Artists. She tapped the rim of the bowl to access the cache.

"This is Citrula. I will be in Druida tomorrow, Qwert."

Today, squealed Greyku, who'd jumped onto the small rectangular scry table and was circling the scrybowl.

"I've arranged a room to tint the kitten at D'Ash's office. I have a preliminary concept that I think will be appropriate. Pastels. See you and the kitten Mid-Afternoon Bell. The cost will be eighty gilt." Citrula cut the spell with no farewell.

"Eighty gilt!"

Sire Zanth will pay. And Samba, Ship's Cat, and Drina, T'Blackthorn Fam, and Mitchella.

Completely awake, Trif stared down at her kitten. "You had the nerve to charge *my cuz* to see you tinted!"

Greyku lifted her nose, set her muzzle. *Mitchella is a decorator. I am being decorated. She will learn much.*

Trif's laugh became a cough. She shook her head. "Cats."

Other Cats fascinated with My tinting. I may start a fashion.

"Like being tinted instead of having jeweled collars."

Greyku's eyes went wide with shock and horror. *I MUST have a jeweled collar TOO.*

At least Trif knew the "rules" with regard to this Fam custom. "When you're full grown, we'll talk about it."

Hopping aggitatedly, Greyku said, *Zanth has emerald collar, Samba has old Earthen stuff. Drina has blue diamonds. Even Princess, who is not a Fam but only a Cat, has much jewelry. I need too!*

Trif's alarm rang loudly. "When you're an adult cat," she said, and headed for the waterfall room.

* * *

*It was later in the morning, when Trif was sipping an ex-*cellent cup of caff during her morning break, that she realized she hadn't tested Ilex's door with her charmkey. The man kept haunting her thoughts since yesterday morning. Could he possibly be her HeartMate?

How did she feel about that?

Her toes curled and a warmth spread from low in her body. He was strong, emotionally, physically, morally. In Flair too, she supposed, but that was secondary to her own values—those instilled in her by her family.

She frowned, wondering how large the Winterberry Family was, how many siblings or cuzes Ilex might have. It was a given that it wouldn't be as many as she did—so far the Clover family was the only one on Celta that had a birthrate like that of ancient Earth. And the Clover genes seemed to dominate in two thirds of the marriages they made—the new families generally had more children. But it was a consideration when choosing a mate, how large their family was. Until lately, the Clovers had intermarried only within their class, or lower, and beloved children had been numerous. But they all watched what happened every generation, and sooner or later they would probably marry into the lower Nobility. What would be the trade-off in Flair or family size?

Ilex. His name whispered in her mind, bringing images of him—authoritative in his guardsman's uniform, silver hair gleaming, expression serious. Or even better—dressed casually, sophisticatedly, dancing with that innate grace of his, eyelids heavy. She gave a little shiver.

Could she compare the friend she knew with the erotic man, her HeartMate, who moved over her and in her when she dreamed? She closed her eyes and tried to *see* the man, but feelings swamped her. Desire. Yearning. Fulfillment.

Her man's shoulders were broad. As broad as Ilex's? Maybe.

She couldn't visualize her HeartMate's face or his hands or even his hair. How his lips feathered over her body, how his hands stroked, soft and tender or fast and arousing, but not the shape of them or his fingers. She made a frustrated noise and opened her eyes to see her father, Pink, staring at her over the rim of his own cup.

He cleared his voice. "You haven't been going questing lately, have you?"

Heat burned on her cheeks. "No, I've been concentrating on learning to teleport." She tossed her head and grinned. "I'll be Testing for the skill tomorrow."

He frowned. "You're taking off early today to tint that Fam of yours." He shook his head. "Crazy business."

Trif hunched a shoulder. "I know, but I couldn't deny her."

Pink chuckled. "You're learning what it's like to be a caretaker."

"As if I haven't watched the little cuzes often enough."

Shaking his head, he said, "Not the same."

"Probably not." She leaned forward. "You know, she's *charging* others to watch her be tinted!"

His eyes widened and he laughed. "Good business. Clever kitten you have there."

"Yes. She's lounging at home today to save her strength for the beauty treatment."

"She's always welcome here, though it's a bit boring for young ones."

Trif stood, washed her cup out, and upended it on the drying rack. "I'm doing fine."

"So you are. But we thought you might want to Test with T'Ash's stones again and find out the strength and what sort of Flair you have—besides those useless visions—now that you've mastered teleporting and all."

"Every time I've messed with those stones, my Flair has gone wild and given no indication at any Flaired profession. I think I'd rather stay here."

"Hard to believe. You never really liked working here."

He was right, but now she liked the sheer familiarity. "It's different now." She didn't want to explain that lately she'd been feeling as if her personal atmosphere had altered, bringing change into her life with her search, and the Fam, and the talk with T'Willow—and Ilex. She'd even experienced an atavistic feeling of being *watched* a time or two. The shelter of the family business was comforting.

"Pink!" one of her aunts called from the outer office.

Her father grunted and sauntered out. "We'll talk later."

Not if she played least-in-sight. She didn't think she could sit under T'Ash's frowning study as her uneven Flair once more wreaked havoc on his highly calibrated Testing Stones.

Fifteen

That afternoon, Ilex interviewed T'Heather, the best Healer of Celta. Like D'Grove and T'Holly, T'Heather was a FirstFamily GreatLord, part of the Council that held the ultimate authority over the Druida Guardsmen. Everyone on that Council—all fifty members—would have received copies of Ilex's reports.

The Healer was appalled at Ilex's questions regarding lifting a living heart from a person's body. After sitting stunned for a moment, T'Heather had agreed that such a thing could be done. For what reason, he didn't know and didn't want to conjecture. He did hypothesize that it would take at least three people at FirstLevel Healer status to accomplish such a feat—but that was if they wanted to keep the victim alive and the heart in good shape. Otherwise, he believed it could be done by at least two people of lower Noble status, like Winterberry, to handle the matter and leave the outer chest tissue unmarked, but it would cost them in energy and Flair for several days.

He postulated that for the results Winterberry gave him, and for the murderers to have a regular amount of energy—to look normal to others—there would need to be at least four or more people.

That was something Ilex had not wanted to hear. So many people corrupted.

T'Heather was furious that none of the victims had been seen by a Healer after their deaths and before their Families had transported them to Death Groves.

Nor had T'Heather been pleased that the priests and priestesses of the Death Groves failed to scan the bodies and send him reports of anything unusual, as was procedure. He'd obviously paid no attention to any reports, meetings, or rumors within the FirstFamilies Council on the case. He insisted on seeing the next victim, if there was a next victim, himself, and was stern and scrying the Captain of the Councils when Ilex left.

Ilex was summarizing the interview when a brief tapping came at his guardhouse office door.

"Come."

A smiling and flushed Trif threw open the door and entered, accompanied by a prancing Greyku.

"I've been teleporting all day and just went to the GuildHall and took my Test and passed. Thank you, thank you, thank you!"

A muttered Word masked his work from her, not that she glanced down at his desk. Greyku, though, appeared in the middle of his desk. *I passed my teleporting Test too!*

"Congratulations. A three-thanks, eh?"

Trif nodded decidedly. "Yes, you deserve more than just a magical three-thanks-blessing." She licked her lips. "Especially since we are here to ask another favor." She looked pointedly at her kitten, who sat with pride and dignity, tail curled around paws and muzzle lifted.

I am being tinted shortly and We would like you to attend. She turned her head farther over her back than a human could manage to look at Trif. *No charge.*

Ilex stared. They hadn't been joking about tinting Greyku. He wondered if they were going for a different color, a pattern, or something incredible he couldn't even imagine. Probably the last.

Lifting her hands in a helpless gesture, Trif said, "The process is expensive. Others must pay Greyku to attend, but I'm a little nervous. It's taking place at D'Ash's and I'd really like you to go with me."

"Who will be there?" asked Ilex.

Trif shifted. "T'Ash and D'Ash, several FamCats, and my cuz Mitchella."

"I thought you considered the Ashes Family, and Mitchella certainly is."

"*Please,* Ilex. They think this is another strange thing for me to be doing, like my quest. I'd like someone who—who respects me." Her face stiffened. "You *do* respect me, don't you?"

"Yes." It came from his heart and his lips before he thought.

"It's not as if those FirstFamilies aren't all a little weird themselves."

"You're calling D'Ash and Mitchella odd?"

"They're HeartMates to important, Flaired FirstFamilies Lords. Of course they must be odd. And they criticize *me.*" She paced back and forth.

"Trif, you're lapsing into emphasized speech again," Ilex said.

She flushed. "I know. Can't you come? I know it's before your shift ends, but don't you have any time off? I took the afternoon off for my Testing and the tinting." Her eyebrows knit as she tried to study the papyrus on his desk. "It looks as if you only have paperwork."

"Thank you," Ilex said drily.

"Sorry." She drew herself up.

At that moment, Chief Sawyr entered Ilex's office. "I heard you had a visitor, Winterberry." He caught sight of Greyku, who'd turned to stare at him, and examined her with disbelief. He'd be even more astonished if she'd been tinted. "A Fam? An animal in my guardhouse!"

"Zanth has visited guardhouses before, I know," Trif said, picking up Greyku.

Sawyr grunted. "Not mine. And a tomcat cleaning out celtaroon nests and bringing the skins for boots is different."

"Huh," Trif said. She lifted her nose. "I'm sorry I bothered you important men. I'll leave." She stalked from the room, and Ilex heard her steps until she reached the teleportation pad, then a slight "pop" as she disappeared.

Sawyr shut the door. "Your HeartMate."

Ilex closed his eyes. "Yes."

"Quite evident when you're together. Even to a medium-Flaired person like me."

"Especially to a trained observer like you." Ilex opened his eyes, but his face felt stiff.

Rubbing his chin, Sawyr said, "Didn't you tell me once you weren't going to claim her?"

"A couple of years ago, yes."

"Because of a foreseeing you had."

"Yes."

"The one where you're dead."

"That's right."

With a grimace, Sawyr said, "I don't like the idea of one of my best guardsmen dying."

"I'm not too pleased with the idea either." He hesitated a moment. "I had the vision again recently." He hesitated, recalling monstrous red eyes, then said in a low tone, "This case is dangerous."

Sawyr glanced at him sharply. "You think the time is coming soon."

Ilex shrugged.

"She's very young, your lady." Sawyr opened the door and marched out. "Give me what you have on your interview with T'Heather, then take the rest of the day off. I'll scry the First-Families Council, who are in charge of this matter and us. They still think they can keep this quiet. They're wanting daily reports—oral."

Dismissing the illusion spell on his work, Ilex gathered his spheres and papyri, went to Sawyr's office, and placed them on his desk. "Thank you, thank you, thank you."

Sawyr gathered the information and grunted. "Keep all your blessings and luck for yourself, Black Ilex. Go."

"After speaking with T'Heather, I think you'll be contacted by more of the FirstFamiles Lords and Ladies."

"I'll send them right to you. In fact, I believe you're going to T'Ash's? You can brief him. Maybe they'll leave me alone." Sawyr showed his teeth.

"I'll do my best to answer any questions."

"Go."

Ilex left, and a few minutes later he alit in a small room of T'Ash Residence designated for teleportation. He stepped off the pad, flicked the safety light back on, was greeted by the butler, and led to one of D'Ash's office rooms where the tinting was taking place.

Greyku stood on a raised, padded table, the center of attention. T'Ash leaned against a wall, arms crossed, and raised a brow when Ilex walked in. On a bench the same height as Greyku's table, other Fams sat fascinated, watching the artist at work. Ilex felt a pained smile cross his face when he noticed his fox, Vertic.

Vertic, did you PAY to watch this?

His Fam kept his gaze on Greyku and the artist, flicked the tip of his tail. *Young dog fox wanted to be a Fam, like me. Brought to D'Ash. She gave me gilt to pay for this. Interesting. Silly, but interesting.*

I hope you don't want tinted.

I change color with the seasons. I am fine.

"Good," Ilex said aloud.

The artist looked up, scowling. "Sshhh! I'm concentrating." She was an angular young woman with an intense expression. She and Greyku seemed the only ones serious about the process.

Trif came up to Ilex and slipped her hand in his, squeezed. Every nerve in Ilex's body went on alert and his focus shifted to her—the scent of her, fresh young woman, the feel of her aura innately expanding to embrace him, warm and sparkling. He swallowed, but left his hand in hers, the skin of his palm sensitized to her touch so he could draw her essence into himself.

Mitchella D'Blackthorn, Danith D'Ash, and several other FirstFamilies Ladies sat on a grouping of stools, murmuring in admiration.

"The artist is Citrula Collinson," Trif whispered. "Once known as Painted Rock."

"Quiet!" Citrula demanded, then stepped back to survey Greyku.

About a fifth of the kitten's hair was irregularly tinted a pale yellow, and the tips of the fur were differently tinted in other, deeper colors, pink, blue, lavender, green. Citrula limbered her arms, then placed her hands gently around Greyku's head, drew in a deep breath, and slowly moved her hands down the kitten's body. Again, some fur turned pale pink, with darker ends.

Breaths sighed out as Ilex and the others recognized that Greyku would be multicolored pastel with highlights of darker colors.

Trif leaned close to him. "She's not going to like this, I don't think. It's not the bold statement she wanted."

Now Ilex squeezed Trif's hand. It wasn't easy living with an unhappy Fam, especially a vain cat. The thought vanished as Trif leaned against him. He wanted her, badly.

And it was definitely time for him to start drawing away from her. They'd gotten too close.

When he looked up, he found T'Ash's narrowed gaze on him. Ilex wondered what the man saw. As much as Sawyr probably. Ilex squared his shoulders and returned T'Ash's scrutiny with a cool stare of his own. T'Ash's lips twitched.

Yes, the FirstFamilies were odd. Ilex had had the idea that T'Ash considered Trif a younger sister, yet he seemed undaunted that Ilex was her HeartMate.

T'Ash sent mentally, *We will talk later.*

Indeed. I have news from Chief Sawyr.

Straightening, T'Ash pushed from the wall.

"Will you people be still!" demanded Citrula as she laid down a color of pale blue.

Fam and human gazes went to T'Ash. He crossed his arms, resumed his stance against the wall, and looked to settle into brooding.

Ilex waited through the process, simply enjoying being with Trif, as the last touches of Flair tinting were done—giving Greyku a four-leaf clover face, with a leaf between her eyes, around each eye, and down to include her nose to the top of her mouth. Finally, Citrula wiped an arm across her beaded brow, then held a mirror angled for Greyku.

No! Greyku screeched. *I don't like!* She hopped up and down on all fours, tail lashing.

Citrula's mouth tightened. "Ungrateful kitten. This is you, young and pretty."

I wanted RED. I wanted GOLD. Black and dark blue and

emerald green. I wanted a tinted collar that looked like jewels, Greyku projected loud enough for everyone, especially the artist, to hear.

T'Ash suppressed a snort. Vertic barked a laugh, and the other cats made noises of everything from disapproval at Greyku's tizzy to agreement.

"You are still a very young cat. Bold colors don't suit your personality at this time," Citrula said.

Greyku growled. *Only good thing is the four-leaf clover.*

Citrula crossed her arms and tapped her foot. "If you feel that way, I *may* be able to do something . . . more. But not now. Perhaps in a couple of eightdays. I'll think on it." She stalked out.

"I take it you paid her in advance," Ilex said to Trif.

"Of course."

Trifffff! Greyku wailed. Since her hair was ruffled and her claws unsheathed, punching holes in the permamoss sponge on the table, Ilex kept Trif's hand in his when she tried to pull away.

Bang! The door hit the wall and Nuin toddled in, grinning. "Noise, noise, noise!" he cried.

T'Ash laughed at his son. "Sure is."

"Pretty kitty!" Nuin was suddenly on the table, staring at Greyku, thumb in his mouth. *Pretty, pretty, pretty kitty!* His mental tone was as loud as Greyku's had been. Greyku glared back at him.

He frowned, pulled out his thumb. "Needs sparkly spell!"

"Wai—" T'Ash lunged forward, too late. Nuin touched his wet thumb to Greyku's nose and garbled a Word.

YOW! Greyku shrieked. All her hair now stood out—except a bunch that fell onto the table.

D'Ash scooped up Greyku, held her close, muttering a few couplets. Greyku sighed and cuddled.

T'Ash picked up his son. Their scowls were similar. "Didn't I tell you that brilliance spells are *not* for Fams or people, just jewels?"

Nuin Ash stuck his thumb back in his mouth and sucked noisily.

D'Ash joined her husband, frowned at her son. She gestured to Vertic, who was the only Fam still sitting on the bench. Zanth sat near T'Ash, the others had bolted. "Fam Vertic brought a young dog fox to us today, ready to be *your* Fam, Nuin. But I can't let you bond with him if you aren't going to be nice to Fams."

The youngster opened his mouth and yelled.

"We'll have a man-to-man talk," T'Ash said above the noise. He looked at Ilex. *Meet you in my ResidenceDen in half-septhour.* Tucking his son under his arm, T'Ash and Zanth strolled out.

"Now, Greyku," D'Ash said. "The shock was rough, but you survived it, and you're back to normal. *Except* your fur. Take a look." She set the kitten back on the table and held up the mirror.

Ilex blinked—he'd been paying attention to the people—but Greyku . . . shimmered. As if every hair on her body had been given a translucent shining coat. The tinting had changed the colors too. They looked bright and glowing.

Greyku turned around and around, admiring herself in the mirror. "Yessss." *Little Ash right. I needed More. I am much More ME.* She sniffed. *But I will want More from Citrula too.*

"Of course," murmured Ilex.

I am very beautiful, FamMan, am I not? She looked smugly at him.

"Very unique, as always."

Trif released a slow breath. "I'm glad you're pleased." She smiled up at Ilex. "Thank you for coming."

He gave a half bow. "You're welcome. But I also needed to speak with T'Ash."

Her face fell.

"If you'll excuse me?"

Waves of hurt flowed from her, but she kept a frozen smile on her face. "Of course."

He went in to his own interrogation.

For Trif, the next morning was a repeat of the previous day.

We have a message. The scrybowl pulses Holly green!

Trif rolled over, opening bleary eyes. When she saw her bright glittering Fam, she flung an arm across her eyes. She hadn't been able to return to MidClass Lodge last evening. There had been a final note in Ilex's voice, and she knew enough about nuance to understand that he wished their association at an end. That was unexpectedly painful.

But she had to face facts. He must prefer more mature, worldly women like himself, not gauche ones who showed up at his *office* bubbling with enthusiasm at passing a Test that he'd done easily and long before. He'd been wonderful, but had grown tired of her.

So she'd taken the brilliant Greyku home to Clover Compound, and her family had oohed and a ahed over the kitten even to Greyku's satisfaction. They'd partied. Trif had toured the section that would become her home, and felt a bit of pleasure as her father and uncles pointed out the space on each of the three stories designated for teleportation, and the addition of cat doors. She had returned late, 'porting to her bedroom and skipping the mainspace altogether.

Come and see. Holly green! Greyku insisted.

There had been talk the night before of the Hollys, and the three Clovers who were training at Tab Holly's Green Knight Fencing and Fighting Salon. They had strict orders to spend as little time as possible in the cursed household.

"All right, all right," Trif grumbled. She rose from her bedsponge, straightened her crumpled sleepshirt imprinted with a saucy saying, and glanced at the scrybowl. It was, indeed, from the Hollys. Tinne Holly. Why would he be calling her? As she ran her fingers through her hair, she realized it was a mess, and her face no doubt had sleep lines. No way was she scrying the HollyHeir back looking this way.

Greyku sat on the scry table, looking expectant.

"Gotta clean up first," Trif mumbled.

Eyeing her, Greyku nodded. "Yessss."

When Trif was dressed and looking her best, she took a few deep breaths, and initiated the scry to T'Holly Residence. "Trif Clover returning HollyHeir's scry."

The man wearing Holly livery who'd answered nodded. The scry was put through to Tinne Holly, who looked a lot more serious than he had at the Maypole. "Greetyou, Trif and Greyku." His smile was perfunctory. "My mamá wishes to audition you as an Apprentice or Journeywoman in the craft of composing. Is Mid-Afternoon Bell acceptable for you?"

Trif opened and closed her mouth. A chill had taken her,

then she flushed. The great D'Holly was interested in *her*? In her twiddle-tunes?

Tinne frowned. "Trif?"

He wasn't accustomed to having to wait. None of the Hollys were. In fact, T'Holly's arrogance had been his downfall and the reason for his household suffering under his broken Vow of Honor.

She cleared her throat, managed a half bow. "I'd be honored."

"Good. See you then." The scrybowl water rippled as he ended the call.

Trif pressed hands to her galloping heart. Her breath came too quickly, unevenly. She could feel the sizzling of her Flair, zooming out of control.

Greyku mewed. Smiled a cat smile. *We go to Holly's today.*

Her knees simply giving way, Trif sat on the floor. Since it was under the scrytable, the area was tiled and cool under her bottom.

"I . . . I am auditioning for *D'Holly,*" Trif squeaked.

We will be purrrfect.

"Uh." She just sat there, dazed, until Greyku began splashing water from the scrybowl on her. "Stop that."

Alarm to catch public carrier ringing and ringing.

She'd been so dazzled she hadn't noticed.

"Yes." She licked her lips. "I wonder what Daddy will say."

He will say great honor. Go and study.

"Yes, he will." She pushed herself to unsteady feet, looked down at one of the ordinary trous suits she wore to work. "I'll have to change for the audition." She went back into her bedroom. Her hands trembled as she undressed.

Greyku smacked a paw on the timer that still rang. *We can teleport to work now. We don't need public carrier reminder. We could teleport home to dress for D'Holly later, then to Holly Residence.*

"Yes, we could. But I don't have the energy and Flair to teleport a lot." She glanced at the timer. If she threw on her nice clothes and grabbed her music case with all her instruments—had she put the silver flute back? yes—they could run and make the public carrier. "Also, I don't want to use all my Flair in 'porting in case I need it for the audition." Fingers scrabbling, she pulled on a fine silk trous suit subtly patterned with leaves in light shades of green. "Hurry! And be careful of my shoulders, this tunic doesn't have pads." She changed her shoes too, then carefully lifted Greyku to her shoulder. The cat's sparkling fur was distracting, but Trif grabbed her instrument case and shot from the apartment.

Sixteen

That afternoon, Trif's triumph at 'porting to the Holly gates was buried under waves of nervousness.

Greyku hooked her claws into Trif's tunic and she felt pinpricks. *We will be purr-fect!* She turned and swiped her tiny tongue up Trif's cheek; then the kitten turned to the scrystone set in the wall and screeched, *We are here! Let Us in!*

A chuckle came from the stone and an older man's wrinkled face appeared. "You must be GentleLady Trif Clover and FamCat Greyku."

The little cat preened.

"Please, enter. A member of the Family will meet you along the glider drive. Or do you need transportation to the Residence?"

Clearing her throat, Trif clutched her instrument case tight. "No, thank you, GentleSir."

With no more than a whisper, the greeniron gates opened. Trif gingerly took a few steps onto the gliderway. She could feel the pebbled white stone through her thin-soled dress shoes.

As soon as she was clear of the gates, they shut behind her. She walked more confidently than she felt up the drive, and when T'Holly Residence came into view she stopped. Trif supposed she'd been thinking it would be an elegant manor house, like cuz Mitchella Blackthorn's Residence. She'd forgotten her grove study lessons that had indicated that this place was a fortress. It loomed tall and gray, only one massive door behind a grille-breaking up the stone of the lower level. There were no windows until the third story.

Then the grille swept up and one half of the iron doors opened and Tinne Holly exited. Again, his expression was serious, though he put on a polite smile when he neared her, then gave her a half bow. "Merry meet, Trif Clover. Greetyou, Greyku."

Greetyou, Tinne Holly, Greyku purred.

Trif smiled back at him. Somehow she wasn't as nervous as she had been. She knew this Holly and he wasn't so formidable. "Merry meet, Tinne."

He offered his arm, and she transferred her instrument case to her other hand and tucked her fingers in the crook of his elbow. These Nobles certainly had much more formal manners.

"My mamá is looking forward to meeting with you."

All her anxiety rushed back. "I don't know that I'm qualified to study—"

"From what I heard at the Maypole, you're very well qualified to study with her. Since she's listened to a couple of informal sphere recordings of your music, she agrees."

The great composer D'Holly had music of *hers*? "How?" Trif asked blankly.

Tinne lifted a shoulder. "We Nobles usually get what we want."

Now that was the simple truth.

But the idea that D'Holly had actually listened to some of her flutings made Trif a little dizzy and she clutched Tinne's arm.

"Don't worry." He patted her hand. "She likes what she's heard. As I said, she's anticipating meeting you. It will be very good for her."

They were approaching the door, and it dwarfed them.

Tinne slowed his pace. "Might I request something of you?" he asked in a low tone.

Trif blinked at him. "What?"

Tension made his arm as iron as the door. "Please, if you have any compassion within you, request that my mamá teach you somewhere else. She doesn't leave the Residence as often as she should." His mouth tightened, then he said, "The place, the broken Vows of Honor, work on her."

Trif caught his sideways glance.

He continued. "If you can possibly think of *any* excuse to get her out of here and to someplace—cheerful, please. I'd be in your debt."

We will ask D'Holly to come to Clover Compound, Greyku said calmly.

What on Celta could they give as a reason for that?

Tinne smiled and appeared more his age. "I'm grateful."

The big door swung open.

Trif goggled as he led her down large corridors filled with weapons—all arranged in decorative patterns.

"Forbidding, isn't it?" Tinne was back to being severe. Trif didn't like it. She'd seen him, briefly, before the events that had made the Holly Family so cursed, and remembered him as someone much like her own self—optimistic and adventurous and cheerful.

"It's not much like T'Ash or T'Blackthorn Residence, and those are the only ones I know," she confessed as they walked up a flight of stairs.

His eyes twinkled at her. "You're not such a Common woman, Trif Clover."

Since she only wanted to wipe her sweaty palms on her tunic, she sincerely doubted that.

They reached a door with the glyph of GreatLady on it, and Trif drew in a shaky breath as Tinne knocked. "Mamá, your new student, Trif Holly, is here."

D'Holly herself opened her door and gestured them into the sitting room. "Please come in."

Trif had seen D'Holly a year before at Straif Blackthorn's Residence Empowering Ritual, but the woman before her looked twice as old and fragile. Through the shock, Trif kept a smile on her face and bobbed the best curtsy she could with Greyku balanced on her shoulder. She warily entered the sitting room.

"I have duties. I'll leave you." Tinne bowed to them, then lifted his mother's thin fingers to his lips and kissed them with real love.

D'Holly shut the door behind him and turned to Trif, who'd been listening to the music wafting through the room with horror. It was hers, all right, one of her improvisations. Oooh, hear that sour note! And that line of melody had gone straight to an inglorious dead end. She could have tweaked it just a bit a few bars earlier and had a real tune.

"Trif Clover?" D'Holly asked.

"Yes." Her trous were wide-legged enough not to show her trembling knees.

"I like your music."

Trif winced. "I don't know how you can!"

The GreatLady's eyes lit and she chuckled. "A little raw perhaps, but such an interesting style."

Trif figured that meant "not good enough."

I am here too, announced Greyku, unlatching her claws and leaping down.

"So you are, FamCat," D'Holly acknowledged. "It's a pleasure to meet you too. . . ." She raised her brows at Trif.

"My kitten's name is Greyku."

"Greetyou, Greyku."

Greyku sat in front of D'Holly, tail curled around her paws. *I have heard of you from My friends, FamCats Meserv and Phyl.*

A flash of pain crossed D'Holly's face, but her voice remained cool and steady. "Ah, the Fams of my son and daughter-in-law."

Surely, D'Holly wasn't supposed to call Holm and Lark her son and daughter-in-law! Hadn't the GreatLady broken her Vow of Honor to accept Lark into the Family? Trif didn't know where to look, so she focused on the small, elegant figure of Greyku.

Meserv and Phyl send their love, Greyku said matter-of-factly.

D'Holly smile was soft. "Thank you."

Greyku lifted a paw and studied her tiny pink pads. *Holm and Lark Apple will be in Druida within the next eightday. T'Heather called them to consult with Healer Lark.*

D'Holly's hand reached out for the solid back of a nearby comfortchair and she sank into it. "Thank you for telling me this," she said, tones husky.

No one said anything, and Trif was painfully aware of the last rattling note of her tin whistle on the music sphere.

Another minute passed; then D'Holly coughed into a softleaf and looked at Trif. "From my own Apprentice days, I do recall that the first thing I did was audition for my teacher."

Trif jerked a nod, raised the instrument case in her death grip.

Gaze sharpening, D'Holly said, "Let's see what you have there."

Trif walked over to a table and opened the case. Made especially for her by her father, it contained enough room for her wooden panpipes in a separate bag, her tin whistle, and her silver flute.

D'Holly joined her at the table; her hand drifted over the fine-grained wood of the top of the box, opened the smaller bag to see the panpipes. "Excellent workmanship. And so are the instruments. Did you make the panpipes yourself?"

Trif flushed. "Yes." She cleared her throat. "The design and where to find the raw material and everything came to me in a dream."

"Don't be so anxious, child, that is often the way. And I don't bite."

But the woman could dash Trif's soaring hope into crystal splinters too small to see but painful in the heart.

"Let's start with this one." D'Holly's fingers hovered over the silver flute, as if feeling the Flair it so often contained. She tilted her head in question.

Trif nodded and D'Holly picked it up. Trif couldn't tell what the Lady felt from her flute, D'Holly was too experienced a musician for that, but knew it had affected the woman in some way.

D'Holly ran her hands up and down the instrument. "Truly, a wonderful flute. Well seasoned with Flair. You have a superior instrument here." Her gaze went past Trif to a collection of her own instruments hanging in a wall case behind a shieldspell. "I haven't played my own flute since . . . I haven't played my flute for a long time." Her voice was soft and her eyes liquid.

All the nerves Trif had felt about the audition faded. In this moment, her own needs were far less important than this melancholy woman's. It didn't matter how Trif performed. It only mattered that she could use her music to comfort. Gently, she took the flute from D'Holly and with great ceremony, led the woman to a soft twoseat. Greyku stopped her exploration of the room to hop onto D'Holly's lap and curl there.

Trif gauged the best spot in the room acoustically and moved to it, finding the carpet worn. Then she lifted her flute to her lips, summoned her Flair and hoped it wouldn't spike, and thought of her good friend Lark Apple, who was married to this woman's son. How well could D'Holly know Lark? Not very well.

So Trif would tell her of Lark. How Lark loved Holm and he cherished her. How joyful their lives were. And she'd start with compositions of D'Holly herself. As she opened with "Holm and Lark's Wedding Theme," D'Holly closed her eyes and leaned against the back of the sofa.

Trif forgot all about the great composer and played for the woman. The music swept her away, she pictured Lark as she'd last seen her, high in the air, solar-sailing with an orange tabby cat—Holm's cat—strapped into a bag on her chest. Trif incorporated the beauty of the flight and the softness of the wind into her tune. Lark landed, laughing, and was enveloped by Holm, who swept his HeartMate off her feet and whirled her around, then dipped her in a passionate kiss.

Desire, longing twined through the melody, then the true love of HeartMates, and Trif was no longer playing for D'Holly, but for herself. Once more, she was drawn to the tune that had haunted her since the night she'd created it in the Maypole, as if she'd known her HeartMate was there, listening, and she called him. Just as T'Willow's HeartGift radiated attraction for his woman.

Finally, the last note faded.

D'Holly opened her eyes and smiled softly at Trif. "Wonderful. You have definite talent." With a final pat, she set Greyku aside, then rose with more energy and vivacity she'd shown so far. "I think we will do very well together. It's past time I had an Apprentice, though you hardly qualify."

Trif's mind spun, her lips felt numb. Her hand holding the flute fell to her side. She'd forgotten she was auditioning before the premiere composer of Celta. "Huh?"

Greyku hopped down from the twoseat and bounced over to strop Trif's legs, purring loudly. *We are getting what We deserve. Good. We are getting MORE.* She sat on Trif's feet, sending off waves of smugness.

The GreatLady shuffled a few papyruses on her desk, moved some music flexistrips around, and held up a sparkling orange sphere. "Yes, I thought I had a recording sphere on. We'll have to work a little on that last song of yours. Obviously a HeartMate call. Not often done anymore, so I'll set you to studying the form and listening to those which were known to be successful." She set the orb carefully on a velvet pad.

Flicking her tail against Trif's leg, Greyku said, *She will show us how to get FamMan.*

Interesting notion.

D'Holly touched the rim of a small scrybowl. "D'Holly to NobleCouncil Clerk."

"Here," said a supercilious male voice.

"Greetyou," said D'Holly. "Please note that I have taken a student. Between Apprentice and Journeywoman status, to be under my tutelage for, um"—she tapped her fingers on her cheek—"four years. Ensure she receives the appropriate NobleGilt for expenses. She'll be bound to the usual public performance schedule to earn it."

"Yes, GreatLady. GreatLady, I need the young person's name."

"Trif Clover."

"Clover! That's a Commoner name."

" 'Talent and Flair have no class boundaries,' " D'Holly said, repeating an old saying that wasn't often true.

Greyku sniffed.

The clerk coughed. "Yes, GreatLady."

"Forward the first installment of her NobleGilt to . . ." D'Holly frowned, then snapped her fingers as if finding the memory. "Clover Compound, care of . . ." She glanced at Trif.

"Pink and Pratty Clover," Trif said weakly.

"Done," said the clerk in officious tones.

"My thanks." D'Holly inclined her head to the scrybowl,

then turned back to Trif, rubbing her hands. "That's done." She looked around the room. "Now where would those HeartMate calls be?"

"Near Journeywoman status?" Trif squeaked.

"No doubt about it. Perhaps in that corner cabinet . . . emotionally Flaired melodies . . ."

Trif's knees weakened and she staggered to a chair and dropped into it. Her flute rapped her knee and made her wince, so she set it aside on a table. Greyku crawled into her lap, making herself comfortable.

All Trif could think of was that she was free of Clover Fine Furnishings at last.

And that her parents would be calling to talk to her soon. Better go to Clover Compound. *Teleport* to Clover Compound, so she could recount the day's extraordinary events and—She remembered her promise to Tinne Holly. Anxiety crept along her nerves, but a promise was a promise.

D'Holly hummed as she set music spheres and flexistrips and history vizes in a bespelled bag; then she walked over to Trif and grinned down at her. "Lady and Lord, Trif, don't look so shocked. You must have known you had talent."

"I made tunes."

"You compose melodies. As I do." A shadow crossed her face. "Did," she said in a lower tone. "I haven't done much creative work lately." She ran a hand through her bronze hair in the first nervous gesture Trif had seen.

Clearing her throat, Trif petted Greyku and looked past D'Holly and said, "I, uh, my, uh. My family is building me a music room in my house in the Clover Compound. Could we possibly work there? So they, we, uh, could test the acoustics?"

D'Holly stared at her. Trif rushed on. "And Clover Compound is built in a square. It would be good to know the acoustics of the inner courtyard too." It was a lame excuse. She'd practiced there for years.

The lady stilled in the act of handing Trif the bag, then slowly nodded. "I would be honored. Tomorrow morning at Mid-Morning Bell?"

Far too soon. Her family would be up all night preparing the Compound for the visit of a FirstFamilies GreatLady. But Trif wasn't about to say no. "Very good." She picked Greyku up and placed the kitten on her shoulder, took her flute, and stood. Curtsying deeply, she said. "I am the one most honored here. I assure you that I will do my very best work for you. I'll try very hard." She had to confess, though. Lifting her chin, she said, "But I have to let you know that my Flair is erratic. It's strongest and best controlled when I play, but still not reliable. And, and, my other gift is envisioning the past. All the way back to ancient Earth sometimes. I sometimes project. You might be caught in those moments too."

D'Holly's brows had raised. "How fascinating." She looked thoughtful. "Unstable Flair." Then she patted Trif 's free shoulder. "Well, you are very young, after all."

Trif wanted to grit her teeth, but made a deep curtsy instead. "Yes, GreatLady."

With a little snort, D'Holly said, "We can't be formal in such a teacher-pupil relationship. Call me Passiflora."

"Yes, Passiflora," Trif said faintly.

Yes, Passiflora, Greyku said.

Passiflora laughed and Trif warmed. She could give this woman something in exchange for her teaching. If anyone could keep Passiflora amused and laughing and strengthen her, it would be the Commoner Clover family.

Seventeen

When she returned to her apartment that evening, there was a strange atmosphere about it, and the slight tang of musk. She frowned and walked through the few rooms, but received nothing but impressions. She thought of asking Ilex to come by—and she'd decided that he was too important to be discouraged by his cold attitude—but she wanted to be *very* prepared before she saw him next. Besides, in her weary exhilaration, she wished to run to him with her fabulous news, but felt it would be one more instance of childish behavior.

Greyku made guttural sounds and stalked around the apartment, sniffing, curling her tongue to the roof of her mouth in that extra sense cats had. *Vertic Fox been here.*

Is that what the scent, the aura, was? Trif hadn't ever noticed Vertic's aura or scent, but she would have expected it to be different.

Time to get ready for bed. Listen to old HeartMate music before We sleep.

Since Trif had just told Greyku that was the plan for the rest of the evening, she smiled. "A good idea."

Too much go, run, bustle at Clover Compound, Greyku grumbled. She'd nearly been stepped on twice.

They'd left her family marshaling everyone to clean and

spruce up the Clover Compound. Some of the furniture in the showrooms would be moved to her music room and any area they thought D'Holly might grace. Trif had been sent off to bed so she'd be fresh and polished—or as polished as she ever got—by the time of her first lesson the next day.

Trif glanced around her apartment and wrinkled her nose. Good fox Familiar or not, the odor needed to be banished, the atmosphere cleansed. Clearing her throat, she chanted two Couplets and all the windows in her chambers thinned to nothingness. There was a brisk breeze that held more than a touch of winter's chill. She shifted her shoulders, placed her instrument bag on a nearby table, and pulled out her tin whistle. A lively tune would stir the breeze and whisk around the apartment with an air blessing.

So she whistled a jig and set a couple of fallen autumn leaves dancing for Greyku to chase. A quarter-septhour later, the temperature of her rooms had fallen a good ten degrees, but her apartment felt cleaner than it had been for days—emotionally and spiritually too. She'd have to remember to do this more often.

She went to stand under the waterfall, put on her nightshirt, joined Greyku on the bedsponge, then ordered the lights off and a flexistrip lecture on HeartMate calls on. This first discussion was demonstrated with only one example—a woman's melody calling to her man, Trif noted with approval. It was ancient, bordering on the visceral, and without listening to any of the other lessons, Trif understood how she could improve her own melody. As sleep beckoned, she grinned. She'd get him.

What was she doing to him? Ilex stood, arms braced against the inside of the door to his apartment, head lowered. Only with great will had he stopped himself at this point. Every muscle in his body was rigid, and his shaft swollen and throbbing with desire.

The melody drifting from Trif's rooms sang in his blood, repeated over and over in his mind. The tune was both better and worse than the one Trif had played at the Maypole, luring him to her. It was better because it wasn't *her* song, wasn't crafted by her solely for him. It was worse because it was a very strong song and just her playing it called to him. Technically better, he supposed.

He gritted his teeth and felt another bead of sweat roll down his spine. How was he going to avoid her in the future? He didn't think he had the willpower. He'd have to leave.

Eventually. Right now, he used every bit of his control to *not* touch the door latch.

Then the music stopped and left him hollowed out, ears rushing with the sound of his own blood.

No, he couldn't go on with this. Pure folly to think that he'd be able to see Trif and not meet her, to meet her and not spend time with her, to spend time with her and not kiss her. All his little rationalizations had led to this slippery path. If he wanted to save her life—if he thought of *her* instead of the demands of his own body and heart—he'd leave.

Even now, the knowledge that he was Trif Clover's HeartMate was nearly an open secret. Chief Sawyr had known. T'Ash had guessed, but had said nothing to Ilex about it. Ilex had sensed that T'Ash had approved.

It would have been a good match.

If he weren't so much older.

If he weren't doomed to die soon.

A few panting minutes later, he was able to relax his muscles enough to push away from the door. He'd need another dip under the waterfall before he went to bed. Icy.

The waterfall didn't help much. When he went to bed, he was still semi-aroused, his body yearning for what his mind refused to allow. He slipped into sleep . . . a moment later, he thought he was in a shared dream.

She reached for him and he drew her into his arms, groaning with relief. She was his and *nothing* would stop him from making love with her. Neither fear nor logic applied. Only sensation ruled this world.

All too real sensation. He was *there* in her bed. In the flesh.

They touched, bare skin to bare skin, all along their bodies. She slid against him, whimpering in desire, and his mind spun, but his body demanded her.

Her breasts plumped against his chest, so soft and warm, increasing his passion. His cock pressed against her soft stomach, cradled so exquisitely, he couldn't bear to move. Finally, his woman in his arms. His HeartMate.

Her hands went to his shoulders, fingers flexing as if she tested him. He heard his ragged breaths and wondered—surely there should be music—but then her hands slid down his arms, curved around his hips, and all thought vanished. Her palms were smooth and warm, and wherever she placed them he felt hot, as if their energy pooled, mingled, *merged.*

He bent his head and caught the scent of the soap she used on her hair and a whiff of woman readying for love. He groaned. Scent was not enough. His hands on her taut butt wasn't enough. Taste might be.

Reluctantly moving his fingers from the upper curve of her bottom to her chin, he tipped her face up. He couldn't see her in the dark shrouded mists, not even the glimmer of her eyes, but he knew where to find her lips.

He set his mouth gently against hers, exquisite softness again, then insinuated his tongue between her lips, raging to explore the secrets of her. Her taste exploded into him, fresh spring-shoots of the lightest citrus. He moaned and opened his mouth wide in invitation, as he set his hands against the smooth skin of back and butt, bringing her close. He needed to feel every bit of her.

Her tongue probed inside his mouth and tangled with his, supple, teasing. She nipped his lower lip and he rolled atop her.

Young, lithe woman. Vital under him, her breath sighing over his collarbone. He groaned in pure pleasure. Energy hummed from her to him, transferred by their skin, by the beat of their hearts, by the press of their hands.

She arched against him, caressing his whole body with hers, and the world narrowed to his shaft and the incredible feel of her under him, the rich fragrance of her calling to him. Her legs parted and his sex slid between them, engorging more as he brushed her plump folds. She whimpered and he *had* to be in her. Now.

He slipped fully inside her moist sheath. Stayed, again wringing all the sensation he could from this one instant. He lifted on his elbows, his pelvis pushing deeper still, and she cried out, clamped her legs around him. He moaned, but pushed his control to the limits. Too beautiful to end too soon.

His hands found her breasts and he filled his palms with sweet womanflesh, nipples prodding the sensitive center of his palms. He was hers. In her. She in him.

Flair flashing between them, his pleasure to her, her spiraling passion flowing to him.

Entwined forever.

Gently, gently, he squeezed her breasts.

She screamed her ecstacy, pumped her hips, pushed him, and they rolled and she straddled him and rode him hard and pleasured herself and him and clenched around him and nothing mattered in the universe but her and he emptied his entire self into her keeping.

She collapsed and he rolled them to their sides, hooking her leg over his hip so he could stay in her long, long. The scent of loving enveloped him, and he knew the moment was pure perfection.

Idly, she stroked his back and the slide of her palm over damp flesh made him shudder, his body flash hard with a last surge of passion.

My man, she whispered in his mind. *My lover. My HeartMate.*

Sluggishly his brain sent a tiny warning. He ignored it. *Yes.*

Love me.

I do.

Now?

Forever, he murmured as sleep drifted closer. The last thing he heard was their blood singing the same song.

Worry was gone. Fulfillment imbued him. He slept long and deeply and didn't dream.

Near dawn, Trif stretched and reached and felt nothing. She was cold. She wanted more.

She wanted him, her HeartMate. Her own calling tune was so innate, so well known, that she needed no flute—could sing the notes in her mind and lure him that way. So she did.

A moment later he was there, with her, and she turned to him, nearly in a dream, but more. He was *here* again, for real!

The hot skin covering solid muscle was there. The textured

roughness of his legs, his chest, the hair around his sex, moved along her, tingling her nerves into sparking awareness.

Her lips that he'd explored so tenderly in the night, as if he'd needed the taste of her deep within him, felt swollen with desire. Heat unfurled from her core to fire pure need.

Her body craved his within her. Her heart needed his touch. Her Flair needed his to steady it.

Blood rushed through her and she let her breath out on a quiet moan. She wanted him, he was here . . . but where was here? Were they—she—just wrapped in an erotic HeartMate dream?

His finger found the point of her nipple and flicked. Lust, for him alone, his touch, speared. She took his hand and trailed it down her body, whimpering as the masculine calluses roused her even more. His fingers went obediently to her swollen sex, stroked, circled, teased until she writhed.

They plunged inside her, fiercely clever. She shattered.

Before she could recover her breath, his shaft was in her and he began a long, slow thrusting. He filled her, withdrew bit by bit, surged again, until the rhythm drove her mad. Her panting mixed with his ragged breath. Their hearts beat fast and hard.

Her hands found purchase, curving over muscular shoulders. She pushed, but this time he didn't relinquish control of the lovemaking. Instead, he went slower still, his body moving in strong, powerful, implacable thrusts—sending her beyond any pleasure she'd ever known, only the drive to ecstasy mattered.

One . . . last . . . stroke and the universe splintered into a cascade of pure, true notes.

He shuddered above her and groaned deep from his chest.

The most beautiful sound she'd ever heard.

The fog of orgasm cleared from her mind, her eyes focused in the dawn light and she stared up into the intense face of Ilex Winterberry.

She blinked and blinked again, mouth dropped open in astonishment. Then all her feelings about him—the guardsman, and *him*, her *HeartMate*—struck her.

"Ilex?" Her voice was a near-squeak.

"Fligger," he cursed and rolled.

She hooked her arms around his neck, her legs around his waist, and they both made a sound of renewed pleasure.

"Don't leave me," she said.

"I must."

Anger surged to the fore. She slapped a palm on his shoulder. "I can't believe you didn't tell me. I can't believe you let me quest for my HeartMate, for you, for, oh, *Lady and Lord*!" Loathed tears of disappointment and frustration that he'd be so uncooperative stung behind her eyes, clogged her throat until her voice was thick. "You *lectured* me."

He hadn't flinched at her halfhearted slap. He did at her words. Reaching for her hands behind his neck, he applied pressure to peel them away. She tightened her legs around his waist.

"I want to know—"

It hit them then—all senses—horrible shrieks, feline, followed by a female's whispered cry. Terror. Chest constricting, breath dying.

Dying!

Mental, emotional trauma flooding them . . . to Ilex, then her.

"Trif, I must go!"

She released him. "Yes, go help!" she gasped.

In an instant, he stood beside the bed. "Whirlwind spell! Cleansing and dressing!" he commanded, snapping his fingers. He shuddered under the onslaught of a scouring wind. Then his clothes flew onto him before her fascinated gaze.

He frowned, swallowed. "My cuz, Dufleur Thyme . . ." He vanished.

Trif gritted her teeth. Just like a man to go without a word. She knew he was shaken at his cuz's circumstances, but surely he could have spared a word for his *HeartMate*. If he had wanted to.

She stumbled from bed, scowling. "Greyku?" she shouted.

I am at T'Blackthorn Residence for breakfast. Mitchella is studying My tinting. She has ideas I can tell to that artist. There was a slight hesitation. *Something is wrong? I felt something bad, but FamMan was there. . . .*

Ilex is my HeartMate!

WHEEE!!! Good, good news!

Something happened to his cuz, Trif said with a frown.

And her FamCat, Fairyfoot? Yesss, I thought I heard a Cat scream through our bond.

You stay there, Trif ordered. Since Mitchella was asking Greyku what was happening and serving furrabeast steak bites, Trif was sure the little cat would stay.

For a few seconds, Trif dithered . . . should she run for the shower or try a whirlwind spell? She knew the spell, but the two times she'd tried it, it had gone horribly awry. Her Flair had spiked as she'd listed what she wanted. But her Flair now felt . . . reliable, quiet and steady. From her lovemaking with Ilex? Probably.

And if she kept the spell simple, maybe it would work. She cleared her throat. "Whirlwind spell, cleansing and dressing!" She snapped her fingers.

The wind came and scrubbed her, and in places that felt too tender to be scoured. She made a noise of distress, but the air was gone before she could form words to banish it.

She looked down to see herself in a dark blue trous suit, appropriate for work, and a light jacket. Good enough. Drawing herself up to her full height, she tested her link with Ilex. It wasn't a HeartBond, but it was a very strong thread—and not too thin either. She could teleport to him from her mainspace. No one she knew would teleport into her apartment. She thought Ilex would avoid her if he could.

Now for another new spell—or a variation on teleporting. She dragged in a deep breath. If this teleportation worked, she'd use up much of her Flair for the day—just have enough to work with D'Holly.

She opened herself in every way to the link between her and her HeartMate. Ilex had squashed his emotions into a corner of his being, though she felt his suppressed horror and anger. For one flashing instant, she *saw* through his eyes and recognized the place, a corner of Landing Park. She knew a smaller park two streets away very well, had attended some grove studies there. She sent a questing spatial probe to that park and found it empty. Blowing out a breath, she took another and muttered, "One my HeartMate, two my HeartMate, *three*!"

Trif landed exactly where she'd visualized, on the edge of the roundpark at right angles to a street leading directly to

Landing Park. She ran until she saw him, stooped between the bodies of two naked women; then she burst into speed. He looked up at her, and even a block away she could se the stark pain in his eyes. "T'Heather!" he called, and the way he did so showed he'd called the highest Celtan Healer before.

She stopped, panting. "What can I do?"

His hands were curled around the fingers of one of the women. A small cat lay curled on her stomach, equally limp. "My cuz is—very ill, I think."

She glanced at the other woman. "And—"

"She's dead. I don't know her, do you?"

Forcing herself to look at the face of the all-too-still person, Trif said. "No." Trif stripped off her jacket and gently placed it over his cuz. Trif shivered, but it wasn't from the cool autumn air. "How can I help?" She squatted and took Dufleur's hand.

"For the third time, and by the Lady and Lord, T'Heather, come!"

A noticeable "pop" sounded behind them. "I'm here! Why call me instead of—" He stopped and joined them, hunkering down. "Oh, Guardsman Winterberry." With one glance he examined the dead woman, put his hand between her breasts. "Dead." He met Ilex's eyes. "The same way as before."

"Do you know who she is?" Ilex asked.

"Yes, Calla Sorrel." His mouth tightened, he looked at Trif from under lowered brows. "She visited Noble HealingHall to be treated for wild bursts of irregular Flair."

Trif froze.

"I'll need to speak with her Healers," Ilex said.

Suddenly, the memory of meeting Ilex at the Gingers' flooded her, tightening her throat so she had to push words out. "What's going on?"

T'Heather ignored her as he examined Dufleur Thyme. "I'm 'porting her to Noble HealingHall transnow. She has heart problems. The cat should go to D'Ash, of course."

The cat opened her eyes. *I will stay with my FamWoman. I am a Hero. I called to Black Ilex through the Family bond. I saved Us. I am a proper Fam. D'Ash can come see Me.*

"Stay then, I'll teleport you both," T'Heather grumbled.

"Will she be all right?" With obvious reluctance, Ilex withdrew his hand from his cuz's.

"Perhaps. When you are done here, send the remains of GentleLady Sorrel to me at Noble HealingHall that I might examine them." His face set in stern lines, T'Heather picked up the cat and put her on his big shoulder, gathered Dufleur close, and they vanished.

Slowly, Trif rose from cramped muscles. "What is going on? And why didn't you tell me?"

Ilex had turned to Sorrel; pulling a sensorball from one of his pockets, he set it going. "If you want to help, take care of that one." He waved and Trif noticed a violently trembling housefluff huddling in the young woman's shadow.

Trif cried out and reached for the small animal—surely it wasn't full grown. "Poor baby," she crooned. The long-eared housefluff burrowed into the crook of her arm, hiding its face in her side. Striving to keep her voice calm, her emotions level, when she wanted to pace back and forth and wave her arms, she said once more, "Ilex. What is happening?"

"Murder." He glanced at her and his eyes were the warmth and shade of ice chips. A muscle jumped in his jaw. "I need to do my job, Trif. Please keep quiet." He raised his hands and sent a warm, quiet breeze around the area, and as he did so, he tranced.

Watching him work almost distracted her from all the other thoughts tumbling in her head—he was her HeartMate. He didn't want her to know they were mated. The Ginger murder and this incident were related. Calla Sorrel had unstable Flair. Trif found herself pacing after all, flattening grass into a path.

Finally, Ilex blinked, shifted his stance, then nodded coolly in her direction.

"Why didn't you tell me!" Trif demanded.

"He was under orders to keep silent," said a man behind her. Trif whirled to see Chief Sawyr.

"What are you doing here, Mistrys Clover?"

She cuddled the housefluff closer.

"She was with me when the cat screamed danger down the Family blood link I have with my cuz," Ilex told him.

Straightening her shoulders, she said, "I thought I could help."

Sawyr blew a gusty sigh. "We couldn't keep it quiet for much longer anyway. I'm sure I'll get cleared by the First-Families Council for a statement to the newssheets later." He sent her a hard stare and stepped between her and the body. "I'll ask you to keep this confidential until Ilex briefs the FirstFamilies."

"Yes," Trif agreed numbly.

"Guardsman Winterberry is still under orders from the FirstFamiles to keep this case quiet. Better learn to accept that if you're going to be his mate. He gave you that retrieval amulet you're wearing, right, at some cost to himself? And has been looking out for you. Isn't that enough?" Sawyr said. He turned and bent down.

Ilex said, "If you want to help, you should take that Fam to D'Ash before it dies of shock."

Startled, she glanced down at the animal she held. Ilex was right. Its life force was fading, something she hadn't sensed. He was so much more mature, in control, than she, and at that moment she nearly hated him for it. "I'll talk to you later," she said, and didn't like that her voice was stilted either, but it was the best she could do.

"Isn't your Family expecting you and D'Holly at Clover Compound this morning?"

He was well informed. A flash of understanding came. It was he who'd given D'Holly some of Trif's music!

"Later." She cleared her throat. "I don't have enough Flair to teleport to D'Ash's."

"There's a guard glider behind you. Can she use it, Chief?"

Sawyr didn't look up from his examination. "We need all the witnesses we have, even if it's a fliggering housefluff." He snorted almost amused laughter. "You can interview it, Ilex."

Ilex didn't react. Not to his Chief. Not to her.

"Mistrys," a voice said at her elbow, and she looked up to see a young female guardsman, not an officer, gesture to the glider.

Trif smiled tightly. "Thank you." Careful of the little animal, she slid onto the bench inside the vehicle. "Chief Sawyr, I need to stop by MidClass Lodge before I go to Clover Compound. Is that all right?"

The man grunted, flapped a hand. "Go, go. You, guardswoman Acacia Bluegum, come back here when you're done."

"Yessir!" She lowered Trif's door.

They shot away, smooth and silent as always, and Trif found her lips trembling, emotions churning. She burned to speak with Ilex now, confront him about being her HeartMate and her quest and the murders and *everything*. But he had work and she needed to get the housefluff to D'Ash, then soothe her anxious Family about D'Holly's visit, *then* master herself enough to *learn* from the GreatLady.

Her life was suddenly too adventurous.

* * *

Ilex watched the glider carrying Trif speed away, and kept his emotions firmly tucked away. Nothing he could do right now.

Sawyr joined him. "Problems in the courtship stage are a very bad omen."

"A great many 'bad' events are happening," Ilex said. They both turned to look at the scene. Bel had risen, but the trees of Landing Park had long, long shadows, and the body lay in one of them.

"You got everything you could?" Sawyr asked.

Stiffening, Ilex said, "I admit I attended to my cuz first."

"Always minister to the injured first."

Ilex eased. "Yes." He handed the sensorball to Sawyr. "But I used this, and also my Flair."

The man grunted and put it in his pocket. "Good. Report."

"There were four people here, three men and one woman—just long enough to dump the bodies. Some panic-sweat tang I can add to my poppets, and I'll need to make another female. I think we'll get enough information to use the dolls. The cult overreached themselves trying for two."

"Good." Sawyr's expression hardened. "One is bad enough. Anything that will delay this fliggering group is good for us. Maybe they'll slow down enough for us to find them."

"I hope so. Also some lingering vibrations of sex amongst them. Unhealthy excitement. T'Heather came."

"What!"

"He insisted I call him if another murder occurred. And I wanted him for my cuz."

"Understand that. Expensive, though."

"Yes." Ilex winced. He'd have to arrange a payment plan with the Noble HealingHall.

"Walk with me and help me spellshield the area. Handle the illusion." They began the low, murmured chant that would mask the area from curiosity seekers, working well together, as usual. When it was done, not even Ilex could discern the bubble that reflected back what was around it. He could *sense* it, but couldn't see it. And a guard warning was attached to anyone who tried to penetrate the spellshield.

Sawyr said, "Would have thought that you'd have warned your cuz about the murders."

"We just met, but I would have, and I wouldn't have given her a Fam, but she told me her Flair was fine. I felt it myself—strong and steady."

"Fam saved her life."

"Yes."

Sawyr rubbed his ear. "Your cuz's Flair was fine?"

"Yes."

"Strange. A break in the pattern. Better talk to her."

"I certainly will."

At that moment, there was a discreet "whoosh" and the Healer, T'Heather, appeared. He nodded to Chief Sawyr. "Greetyou, Chief."

Sawyr bowed. "Greetyou."

"Ilex, you're still here. I thought so." He strode forward through the spellshield.

Ilex and Sawyr looked at each other. Sawyr shrugged. "FirstFamily Lords," he muttered. They both followed the Healer.

T'Heather hunkered down beside the body. "Poor girl. Eighteen her last nameday. Her soul's circling on the Wheel of Stars now, blessings upon her."

"Blessings," Ilex and Sawyr said in unison.

"Heart is definitely gone." A tremor ran through T'Heather. Ilex felt disgust and fury from him. "Pulled from the body alive, I think. I'll know more when I examine her." He bent down and sniffed her skin. "Odd fragrance. That incense you noticed before, Black Ilex?"

"Yes," Ilex said. He still couldn't place it. "Do you know it?"

"No. Hmm." Heather glanced up at them. "As a member of the FirstFamilies Council, I informed her parents, D'Sorrel and T'Sorrel, as well as the rest of the Council. The leader of *all* the Councils, T'Hawthorn, is going to the Sorrels now. He has studied the interviews you've done with the parents of the earlier victims and will question them for you."

Sawyr opened his mouth, then shut it.

"Hawthorn is not a detective," Ilex said mildly.

"He's a keen businessman, and a father to a daughter. He has great Flair. He'll see true and be compassionate. Consider his findings. If you think you can do better, you're authorized to speak with them, Guardsman Black Ilex Winterberry. We thought that this would save you time." T'Heather passed a quick hand down the woman's body. "All her other organs are inviolate. No sexual activity. The girl was a virgin. Pity. My understanding is that the other victims were not virgins."

"Correct," Ilex said when Sawyr didn't speak.

"That is not a factor in their filthy rituals then," T'Heather said. "I'm teleporting the body to my Residence," he said. He cocked his head as if listening, then addressed Ilex. "Winterberry, your cuz is doing well in Noble HealingHall, NobleRoom eight. She's conscious and asking for you."

"Thank you. I'll pay for her care."

"Right." Heather took the dead girl's wrist in his hand and they vanished.

Sawyr let out a breath in one long hiss, glanced around the scene, and tromped back through the spellshield. "FirstFamilies' interference. Have I told you how I *hate* FirstFamilies' fliggering interference in a case?"

"Not since the last time."

"Why can't they just let us do our jobs?" he muttered, then raised a palm when Ilex was about to speak. "Never mind. They're too fliggering arrogant and just plain damn weird with all that great Flair."

"And powerful," Ilex said.

"That too. Think they can do anything. Everything." Sawyr studied Landing Park, tugged at his earlobe. "Think we have all we can get from the scene?"

"I don't know. I'd like to talk to my cuz."

Sawyr nodded. "Go."

Dufleur was pale, but garbed in an embroidered silkeen robe and sitting up on her bedsponge when Ilex entered the luxurious NobleRoom Eight. She smiled, and again he was struck by how lovely that made her. He took a chair and straddled it, smiled. "You're looking better, cuz."

"Thanks to you." She rubbed the furry stomach of her Fam beside her, who lay on her back, four paws curling. "And thanks to Fairyfoot."

"Where's your mother?" Ilex asked.

Dufleur's face went stony. "I asked them not to call her. You didn't, did you?" She stiffened.

"No."

Relaxing, she didn't meet his eyes and said, "My thanks. Mother wouldn't have come anyway. She doesn't like HealingHalls. At least, she never came here the three days my father was dying."

Ilex cleared his throat. "I am sorry for your loss."

She looked away, then back at him with liquid eyes, she said, "I've forgotten, how long has your father been gone? Do you miss him? Were you . . . closer to him than your mother?"

Even if Trif had asked those questions, Ilex wouldn't have answered. But here was a cuz who sat in a HealingHall because he'd given her a Fam and who now wanted to compare notes on their very difficult Family. Their very difficult mothers. "He died when I was ten." It had hurt him, had devastated his fourteen-year-old brother. "He's been gone a long time." Ilex forced the next words out. "I loved him. He was a good man." Ilex hadn't visited his father's memorial in the back of the estate for a long time. His father had left a holojournal too, which Ilex hadn't looked at for far too long. Had his brother taken that when he'd left Druida?

"I'm sorry." Dufleur's whisper brought him back to the present. She lay pale and nearly upright against huge Flaired pillows that conformed to her shape and offered solid support.

"Back to this nasty business," he said. "I knew there were murderers targeting the lower Nobility—"

"Not much lower than me." She made a face.

"—who had Fams, and would never have given Fairyfoot to you if you hadn't told me your Flair was well under control."

She blinked rapidly several times; then a blush crept from the neckline of her robe to her face. She wasn't nearly so attractive when she flushed. "It's true . . . *was* true. Until . . ."

"Until?"

Reaching for a glass of water, she sipped. "I was walking back to D'Winterberry Residence late last night. I'd finished a long, intricate piece of embroidery ordered for GrandLady D'Yew's Nameday. FirstFamily GrandLord T'Yew demanded it today and he's a difficult but well-paying customer." She swallowed some more water, flushed redder, and didn't meet his eyes when she continued. "Anyway, I was walking home when I sens-saw this object."

"Sensed or saw?" he asked.

She wriggled. "Both. It . . . cuz Ilex, it *glowed*." She glanced at him and must have seen his raised eyebrows. "I know that sounds odd, but it glowed golden."

"Where was this?"

"It was in the gutter."

"Where were you located? What is your usual path home? Take me through it, step by step, starting with where you work."

"I work in the shop, Dandelion Silk." She sat straighter and flexed the fingers on both hands. "I am the best embroiderer in Druida."

"Dandelion Silk is in Pomegranate Place." The cul-de-sac held the most expensive shops in the city.

"Yes. Well, I closed the shop . . . I prefer to work there instead of at D'Winterberry's."

"Understandable."

Dufleur drank a bit more. "And I left by the back door."

"That would open onto Manyberries Road."

"Yes."

He shook his head. "Dark and narrow and a blind curve, cuz. I don't like it."

"I'm perfectly capable of looking after myself!"

"Which is why you are here, in Noble HealingHall."

"Noble HealingHall!" She sat up straight, her voice rising high enough to rouse her Fam, who looked at them with glinting eyes.

D'Ash says I am to rest and not be disturbed.

"Sorry, Fairyfoot, but we need to get out of here," Dufleur said.

Fairyfoot sniffed. *I am comfortable.*

"Cuz Ilex," Dufleur whispered. "I can't pay for this."

"I'm taking care of the cost."

"Oh, no!" Her mouth primmed, then she said, "I can only promise to pay you back. I have some savings." She pressed her hands to her chest. "They did some intricate Flair Healing!"

He waved a hand. "I'm sure you could take it out in trade—look at that gown you're wearing, it's top-of-the-pyramid.

T'Heather treated you, and his HeartMate has a fine eye for luxuries. I'd imagine she'd enjoy some embroidery."

Dufleur lay back on the pillows. "That's true." She frowned. "She's a glassmaker, right?"

"Yes."

"Her skills wouldn't be compatible with embroidery then."

"I wouldn't know. Dufleur stop worrying about gilt and help me solve some abominable murders."

"Murders!" Now her voice was a harsh whisper. She paled further, her eyes went flat. "There was another woman there. Where I was . . . the dark room." She gulped, settled herself back in bed, clutching her water glass. "I don't remember much, but . . ." Her eyes filled. "I thought I heard praying . . . from someone else, a younger voice." She touched her temple with shaking fingers. "I was blindfolded."

Ilex was up and brushing her hand away. "If I might touch you? I might gain an impression of the blindfold from your skin." He noted her temples were very faintly abraded.

"Of course."

He grazed his fingers over her temple. "The Healers didn't pay attention to here. . . ." He sent his Flair questing and received information. "A woman tied the blindfold on you. It was bespelled and drugged. Made of black silkeen. Handled by two others—men." He'd know it again if he saw it; more, he finally got a brief impression of personality, someone he'd met lately . . . he couldn't place it. It wasn't the same woman who had dumped Sorrel. Two women. Two men. Another poppet to be made.

He looked down into Dufleur's wide eyes.

"Excellent job," she said. "I hope they pay you well." She looked around the room. "Really well."

"I get by." He sat down near the end of the bedsponge. "Back to your story."

"I'd just reached the end of Manyberries Road when I saw the . . . thing."

"Sensed the golden glowing thing. And you picked it up."

Her eyes flashed. "Just tell me *you* wouldn't have been curious, cuz."

He considered her a few seconds. "I can't."

"Anyone would be." She swallowed. "Then . . . it began."

"What began?"

"The strangeness. It clung to my hand. I went hot, then cold. Felt dizzy and . . . dizzy." She turned away and set the glass on a nearby table. "The instant I touched the soft leather, my Flair went wild—rushing through me as if I hadn't used any at all during the day. A flood. I . . . I fell down, I think." She petted Fairyfoot. "I saw the pulsing blue light of the public carrier coming and managed to stand up and make it to the plinth. People looked at me funny."

"Which people? How many?"

"The plinth is near a couple of private clubs on Aghra Way. There were some people lingering outside the doors." She shrugged. "Both men and women. I stumbled into the public carrier, some other passengers helped me, a . . . a woman, I think; then the next thing I know, the driver—he knows me—was helping me out at my stop, you know where, near D'Winterberry's. I don't remember anything . . . like I was in a fever."

"Or drugged."

She shivered. "Perhaps. I sure was a few minutes later, I'd just turned onto our street when I felt hands on my arms, smelled . . . something dark and heavy . . . and everything went black."

He leaned forward. "May I place you in trance and share your memories?"

Another woman said, "I think not."

Ilex stood and bowed to FirstLevel Healer Lark Hawthorn Apple. "Greetyou, GentleLady Apple. I didn't know you were here in Druida."

"Greetyou, Black Ilex Winterberry. My husband Holm and I come up from Gael City at least once a month. This time, because my best friend's Family wanted me to dissuade her from a HeartQuest." Her smile sharpened.

Everything in him went on alert. He froze. He'd forgotten this woman was nearly a sister to Trif Clover. Had lived in MidClass Lodge once upon a time too. Cave of the Dark Goddess, he didn't need this complication now!

He stepped back from the bedsponge, gestured to Dufleur. "My cuz, Dufleur Thyme."

"Greetyou, GentleLady Thyme," Lark said with an easy smile to Dufleur. The Healer sat down on the bed, staring at

Dufleur with unfocused eyes, then nodded. "You will do very well." She touched Dufleur's chest. "No permanent damage."

"Thank you," Dufleur said. "And T'Heather too. Does D'Heather like embroidery?"

"She does."

Dufleur sighed. "Then I can pay off—"

"No." Lark raised a hand. "The FirstFamilies Council is funding your medical needs."

"But—"

"If you want to protest, I'll be glad to speak to my father, Captain of the Councils, T'Hawthorn."

"Perhaps." Dufleur's voice was stiff with pride.

"The FirstFamilies Council has an obligation in this matter," Lark said. "But if you want to embroider a softleaf for D'Heather, she'd cherish one with bees."

"Bees. I could do that."

"I'd like to examine you more closely—those slight marks on your temples, for instance." Lark smiled not quite nicely at Ilex. "There will be Healing done here, Ilex, you'd best go."

He eyed her. "Have you spoken with Trif Clover today?"

Her smile widened. "Oh, yes. Yes indeed." She gestured to the door.

A feeling of doom slithered down Ilex's spine. Still, he went over to Dufleur and brushed her cheek with a light kiss, then straightened. "You take care." He eyed Fairyfoot, perhaps she'd remember something. . . .

As if sensing his intention, Dufleur picked up the cat and held her close. "No, Ilex. Not today." Her voice broke. "Perhaps tomorrow. Truly, I don't remember much of anything, and Fairyfoot was drugged too. She didn't wake until my . . . my heart was . . ." Her voice broke. "Anyway, that's when she woke and screamed for you and everything went black again until I woke up here." She clutched Fairyfoot even closer.

The ex-feral cat glared at him. *You upset her, go away.*

He looked at Lark. Her arms were crossed.

It seemed as if he'd irritated every woman he'd met that day . . . starting with his HeartMate.

Lark moved back to the bed. He gazed at both women. "Merry meet."

"And merry part," they replied. *Merry part,* echoed Fairyfoot.

"And merry meet again." He bowed formally, then left.

Holm Apple—once Holm Holly—fully armed with blazer on one hip, long sword on the other, pushed away from the wall with a grin. He clapped Ilex on the shoulder. "Rumor is traveling around that you're Trif Clover's HeartMate. What are you going to do about it?"

Nineteen

"*Run away and hide?" Ilex said sardonically.*

Holm snorted. "I don't think so. Not a distant cuz of mine." He sounded more than matter-of-fact, cheerful even, as he alluded to his birth Family—who had disowned him. Ilex observed him. He *looked* good. Healthy and at the top of his form, which had always been formidable and formidably charming—except for those few weeks when he'd bumbled through winning his HeartMate. He was the only Holly that looked healthy.

"Gael City agrees with you."

Teeth flashing, Holm laughed. "I've built something of my own there, with my own hands and brain and heart . . . and only a little bit of funds from my beloved Lark. It's a good feeling, but you know that already, don't you?"

Ilex shrugged, but Holm's hand stayed on his shoulder. He shrugged a little harder and Holm let his hand fall, then rubbed his hands together. "So what *are* you doing about the delightful Trif Clover?"

"Nothing."

"Wrong answer."

Ilex looked Holm up and down. "You can't intimidate me."

Holm laughed. "Maybe not." He caressed the hilt of his sword. "But I can challenge you to a duel and carve you to bits if you make Trif unhappy. Because, you see, when Trif is unhappy, my Lark is distressed, and I don't allow that."

"Do your worst." Ilex took off down the hall to a teleportation pad. The HealingHall was too busy to casually 'port in and out of.

Holm caught up with him after a meter, and matched his pace. Now he appeared puzzled. "You aren't going to make me challenge you, are you?"

"Maybe."

Setting a hand on Ilex's arm, Holm stopped him. Their eyes met. After long heartbeats of quiet, Holm said, "This isn't a laughing matter, Ilex. Trif is disturbed and talked to my lady. Lark has few close friends, so she cherishes Trif. To play with a woman's emotions—and your HeartMate's—that isn't like you, Ilex. Or wasn't when I left Druida. What of your honor?"

That arrow hit its mark. Ilex waited until the red haze of anger faded before he said, "You know nothing of this. Don't interfere. I am doing what is best for us both."

With a few easy steps, Holm blocked his way and fell into a stance that meant business. "You don't claim your HeartMate. You are making your HeartMate suffer. There's nothing you can tell me that will excuse your behavior."

A harsh laugh exploded from Ilex. "That's what you think."

Holm took a step back, a considering look in his eyes. "I think we'd best discuss this outside—in the Healing Grove."

"As you please."

A few minutes later, they sat side by side on a cool bench, and Ilex found the huge trees and ancient spells that lived in the Grove unexpectedly calming. "What would you do knowing your death would claim your HeartMate?" He finally looked at Holm, who had paled. He briefly told Holm about his prophetic visions.

"It's a hideous thought," Holm said finally.

"I've come to live with it. I won't claim her. I won't let her claim me."

"You're hurting her."

Ilex flinched. "I know. But better her emotionally hurt than dead with me. And my time is coming soon. Within the year, I think."

Holm shuddered. "Don't say that." He hesitated. "Did you talk to the prophet Vinni T'Vine?"

"Yes. He told me he couldn't *see*. Matters are too much in flux," Ilex said flatly.

Holm sucked in a breath. "Bad situation."

The door to the HealingHall opened and Lark stepped out. "There you are." She frowned. "You look too serious."

"I'll tell my lady what you said," Holm said.

"As long as she doesn't tell Trif."

"No, I think you'd better tell her yourself."

Lips twisting, Ilex said, "Not something I'm looking forward to."

D'Holly smiled at them all. Her energy seemed to have grown in the few hours they'd played in the Clover Compound, and her skin had taken on a slight flush. Greyku had stuck close to her, openly adoring of the older woman, and that too seemed to please the GreatLady.

Trif felt awkward. Her fingers had stumbled. Her breath had gone ragged now and again and her Flair was all over the place, never in her control. She couldn't stop thinking of Ilex. And the murders. And her Family, who hovered around the courtyard. Every little thing distracted her until she was sure that D'Holly would just stand up and say that she'd made a mistake and that Trif shouldn't study with her after all.

When the GreatLady *did* rise from her seat, dread gripped Trif and her tune squealed to a halt as her breath stopped.

"This morning has been a pleasure, but I have instruments and lessons that would be better for Trif if taken at T'Holly Residence. So we should adjourn there for afternoon study."

Trif's mother, Pratty, bustled forward, curtsied. "We have lunch, GreatLady. Please stay."

D'Holly blinked. "What a lovely offer. Yes." She glanced at her wrist timer. "But we should only take a septhour. I told my household I'd be back one septhour after Midday Bell, and if I don't arrive on time, they worry."

"Of course, of course," Pratty said. "Please, sit."

Subsiding in her seat again, D'Holly seemed amazed as a table was brought before her and Trif and set. She looked at Pratty. "Surely you and your wonderful Family will join us."

Pratty laughed. "Some of us anyway."

Washed and dressed in their best everyday clothes, the women of the family, some of the older children, and a man or two, including Trif 's father, who'd come home from the factory, filled the large table. The awe at having a GreatLady in their midst held only a moment or two before D'Holly charmed them all.

Trif picked at her food. Maybe D'Holly was just waiting until they got to T'Holly Residence to break it to her that she'd never be a real musician, let alone a composer. The lady was kind and wouldn't dismiss Trif in front of her family. And what was Ilex doing? And how was Dufleur?

And what was she going to do about a HeartMate who didn't want her?

"Time, Trif," her mother whispered in her ear. She frowned at Trif 's plate, where even dessert stood untouched, but said nothing more. D'Holly was up and strolling to the teleportation pad—a *new* teleportation pad of the highest quality—and Trif scooped up Greyku and hurried to join D'Holly. Trif wanted to offer to 'port them to T'Holly Residence, but she didn't have the Flair reserves and didn't think she'd been cleared to teleport inside the secure fortress.

D'Holly took her hand. "On three. One Trif Clover, two make music, *three*!"

And they arrived in D'Holly's sitting room.

Zow.

"Please sit, Trif. I'll order caff." She did so, then turned and sat down, gazing at Trif.

Greyku stared at them both. *FamWoman, D'Holly needs Me here more than you,* she mind-whispered to Trif.

Yes, Trif sent back.

Greyku went to settle on D'Holly's lap, and the woman smiled and pet her. "Something troubles you," D'Holly said.

More than one something, but Trif wasn't going to breathe

a word to D'Holly about the murders. She didn't want to think about them herself; they just nibbled at her mind anyway.

The door opened and a young man came in with a tray. As soon as Trif had her cup, and the servant was gone, Trif said, "Man problems. I'm sorry. I'm sorry I was so terrible this morning. I know—"

"Trif, Trif." D'Holly's soft voice stopped her. "When we're disturbed our playing suffers, that's the way of it. And it's harder to focus." She gave a little laugh. "And it's harder still for the young to focus when agitated."

"You're not that old."

D'Holly laughed again, relaxed back in her plush twoseat. "Thank you for that. You have a wonderful Family, and I think it is a good idea that we work a couple of hours in the morning at Clover Compound. It's good for us. They'll settle down once it's an everyday occurrence."

Trif didn't think so, but . . . "You aren't going to tell me I'm not ready?"

Frowning, D'Holly asked, "Not ready for what?"

Waving a hand, Trif replied, "Not ready to be a musician, a composer. That I'll never be ready."

"Trif, you *are* a composer. Naturally. I wouldn't have expected you to be so lacking in confidence." She laughed again. "The artist's fragile ego, I suppose. And so very tender when we are just beginning our career." She shook a finger at Trif. "You'll be playing in public for your Journeywoman Gilt, so you'll have to toughen up."

"I've got a family," Trif muttered. "They'll laugh at every sour note."

"So they will. Now, I've put out papyrus and writestick so you can set down your HeartMate call and we will work on it."

Trif's heart clutched. "I . . . I don't think I can do that today." To her horror, her voice was teary.

D'Holly tilted her head. "No? Man troubles." She sighed. "Men can be *very* trying." D'Holly tapped a finger on the arm of the twoseat. "Perhaps we should stick with something more cheerful and a little easier. I thought I heard a jig or two in your music. Let's see if we can refine them."

Trif stared at her blankly. "I don't recall a jig."

With a flick of her fingers, D'Holly had a music sphere

floating into her raised hand. "Kitten jig," she prompted the ball, and Trif 's tin whistle played a lively melody. Trif chuckled, remembering how Greyku had been tumbling around after a little lightwisp spell-toy. It lightened her heart.

It is a very good tune for Me. All My own, Greyku purred.

"Of course," D'Holly agreed.

The last note ended and D'Holly nodded to Trif. "So set that one down and we can fiddle with it a bit, study the jig form, and perhaps change it for the flute or a band."

Smiling, Trif went to the table and to her task. Later, they discussed the music, and reworked a few bars, then practiced together. Immersed in music and wonderful learning, Trif thought of nothing but that for several septhours. Greyku danced and played and explored and finally settled down to sleep under the twoseat, which had a fringe at the bottom Greyku attacked now and then.

A discreet tap came at the door. "My Lady?" A man's deep voice asked.

D'Holly's face lit up and she hurried to the door and opened it. T'Holly stepped in.

Trif had never seen the GreatLord up close, but he looked much older than she'd expected. This was the man who had refused to sanction the marriage of her friend Lark with his son, Holm. But D'Holly kissed him tenderly, and it was obvious they loved.

Of course. They were HeartMates. No matter how *wrong* the man was, D'Holly would support him. With a stab of envy, Trif watched them together.

Her HeartMate hadn't wanted her.

She swallowed.

"And this is the young Clover?" asked T'Holly. "The musician for you, not the youngsters sent to The Green Knight Fencing and Fighting Salon to learn fighting."

"Yes, GreatLord." Trif curtsied deeply.

"A pleasure to meet you." He strode into the room. His expression eased into a smile when he saw the scattered instruments and papyrus. "Been busy music-making. Good, good." He turned to her and she noted his features weren't as even, his face and form not as handsome, as his sons', yet he was an incredibly vital man. He held a wrapped package under his arm.

"I've something for you, Passiflora," he said, offering the gift.

"Oooh!" she squealed like a girl, smacking a loud kiss on his mouth. "You're wonderful." She sat on the twoseat and placed the package on the table in front of her, unwrapping it carefully and dangling the bow where Greyku could come and bat at it. Then she unfolded the cloth.

She and Trif gasped at the sight of a crystal bowl.

"It's an ancient crystal singing bowl from *Nuada's Sword*. I've modified it for a scrybowl especially for you, my lady." He tapped the rim and a hum resonated clear to Trif 's bones.

"It's incredible!" D'Holly jumped up and threw herself into his arms.

He caught her close and closed his eyes, his expression revealing such tortured love that Trif had to turn away. She went over to her case on the table and replaced her instruments, ignoring D'Holly's sniffling. Then Trif took the ribbon and danced it around for Greyku to chase. Just watching the cat lifted her mood.

"Thank you, dearling," D'Holly said, "but I love my old one . . . also especially made for me, as a composer. What am I going to do with—Trif!" She clapped her hands. "Yes, Trif." She hurried over to the old bowl, said a Couplet, and the water evaporated and the bowl dried. Then she handed the large brass bowl to Trif. "You *must* have this. It's for a composer, you can bespell your very own melodies into it. Most scrybowls only play one tune, but have many light spells to designate the incoming calls. This is different. It has only a few light spells, but holds many tunes. Here, I'll bespell it for that jig you just wrote."

Greyku's jig, the kitten said smugly.

D'Holly's flute flew into her hand, and in a moment the spell was set into the scrybowl. It would have taken Trif, even with control of her Flair, a good septhour to do the spell. But D'Holly was of the FirstFamilies, by birth and by marriage, and had great Flair. No use envying something so far out of her realm, so Trif didn't, just enjoyed watching.

When D'Holly ended and T'Holly handed the gift to Trif with a flourish, beaming all the while, Trif stammered, "But I have a scrybowl. . . ."

"A composer should have this bowl, and that's an end to

it," T'Holly said. He picked up his HeartMate's hand and kissed it. "I'm sure you've both done good and lovely work, but now it's time to play." He glanced at Trif. "The Residence security fields will let you teleport out and in."

"Darling," said D'Holly, "it's been a long day for Trif. She needs a glider to take her home."

T'Holly's gaze met Trif's, blazing with intensity. For a moment, she didn't understand what put that look in his eyes. Then she remembered . . . all the details of the murder came rushing back. He'd know about it, but obviously didn't want her to say anything to his wife of the killings.

Trif tried to keep her face impassive, but didn't think she did a good job of it. In any event, she shook her head slightly to let the powerful Lord know that she had said nothing to of murder.

He smiled at her, but it wasn't as carefree as it had been. "Of course we must ensure Trif gets home. A glider will be waiting at the gates. Tinne?"

Tinne Holly stepped into the room. He kissed his mother's cheek, and there was tenderness there too. He smiled at Trif and held out his arm. "I'll escort you."

"Thank you for the courtesy." She picked up Greyku and put the kitten on her shoulder, took her large bag containing her instrument case, and walked from the room, quietly letting out a sigh.

She loved the chambers and adored Passiflora D'Holly, but being around great Nobles was trying to her middle-class soul. They could be so generous, they could be so self-indulgent. Yes, the FirstFamilies were odd.

The drive from the T'Holly Residence in Noble Country to MidClass Lodge passed in a blur. Trif still struggled with warring emotions—pleasure at her time with D'Holly, humming with music. Then she'd think of telling Ilex about her lesson and it hurt. Rejection, despair swallowed her, even as she felt the echoes of passion, the leaping joy of finally finding her HeartMate.

A limp Greyku was curled on her shoulder, attached by a

spell by an amused Tinne Holly. Both she and the kitten had exhausted their Flair. Walking down her hallway without the usual spring in her step, she hesitated by Ilex's door, but got nothing from it. Her link with him that prickled with shared sensations all day was much more revealing than that door. Lately, she'd never thought to test his place with her charmkey, and now she saw that he'd done his best to mask it from her.

When she entered her own apartment, she detached Greyku and placed the kitten on the twoseat. Instinctively, Greyku stretched, then continued dozing. Trif automatically made dinner for the kitten, but didn't do the same for herself. She wasn't hungry.

She placed her instrument case carefully on the corner table, took the new scrybowl into her bedroom, but left it wrapped. She didn't want to play music either. Even if she could summon the energy to do so, she couldn't bear to fumble around anymore.

So she sat in the mainspace and listened to some of the music flexistrips D'Holly had given her—not HeartMate Calls—halfheartedly paying attention to the lectures while she considered her situation.

Yes, she loved Ilex. A part of her sensed it was the HeartMate bond at work, the attraction, and knowledge of a person complementary to herself. But most of it was simply him. Mature, strong, sophisticated, courteous, respectful, sexy. Every time she thought of him, a new quality came to mind.

But his actions ripped at her. He hadn't wanted her. She could see now that he'd moved into MidClass Lodge after she'd searched the place for her mate, and she hadn't considered doing so again when the rest of Druida beckoned.

Yet when she thought of it, she realized he'd usually been close to her here—even if unseen around a convenient corner. And his being here had strengthened the connection between them that had begun during her Passages.

For a moment, anger washed through her at fate. Why was her Flair so intractable? If she'd had easier Passages, clearer control, could she have found him before this, before he decided he didn't want her? Was that why he didn't he want her? Because of her stupid, unstable Flair?

Why didn't he want her?

She thought of T'Holly and D'Holly. How fragile the GreatLady looked compared to the vibrant woman Trif had occasionally seen in concerts. T'Holly was a HeartMate, yet he was hurting his love with his prideful arrogance in refusing to mend his broken Vow of Honor. He loved her, yet he hurt her.

Trif 's breath caught. Could there possibly be some parallel in her situation with Ilex? He was hurting her for some reason—hopefully not for one as stupid as T'Holly's.

She didn't know. She pressed her hands hard against her heart.

Why do you sit in the dark? asked Vertic. He came and sat in front of her.

She jolted, had to clear her throat before she found her voice. "I didn't realize it was dark." Nor had she noticed when Greyku had jumped onto her lap and settled in for a good petting, which Trif was doing. She looked around, Bel had certainly set. "Why are you here, and how did you get in?"

Good to know where the kit is, where the FamWoman is. You don't usually sit in the dark. You are a light person.

She didn't know whether the fox meant she liked the sunshine, preferred the day to night, or was lighthearted, but all three were true.

"Is Ilex a dark person?"

The fox's plumed tail swept once. *Not necessarily. He goes in night when he must. Lately, his emotions are dark.* He met her eyes and they stared at each other. Then he barked quietly. *This is not good—you dark, he dark. I will go get FamMan.*

Though she watched him, he faded into the shadows near her door, then vanished. A drift of his scent came to her nose. He smelled like autumn leaves. She frowned. There was none of the musky scent from the night before, when she'd thought someone had been in her rooms and Greyku had told her it was Vertic.

She should get up and make dinner, eat. She wasn't hungry and stayed as she was, sitting in the dark, something she hadn't ever done before. She'd always thought she'd be giddy and carefree, blissful, when she'd met and loved her HeartMate. Yet here she sat, enervated, uncertain, self-absorbed. How love changed a person.

Twenty

Ilex trudged down the dim corridor. He was a coward. He didn't want to face Trif and tell her about . . . everything. Discussing the murders and his fear for her would be the *easy* part. He nearly cringed at the thought of "HeartMate" discussions.

He was definitely too old for this . . . and he wondered how excited and passionate she'd get in that discussion and whether he could turn that into lovemak . . . No. That was reprehensible too. Where had his honor gone? His sensitivity? Buried under the tension of trying to solve dreadful murders, keeping his HeartMate safe, and wanting her and avoiding her and loving her . . . He needed a drink.

What he got was Vertic lying in the hallway at the threshold of his door, radiating disapproval. *You must go to FamWoman.*

Everyone was concerned for Trif.

"Yes," he said quietly.

She is sitting in the dark. The cat is useless. It sleeps.

Ilex winced, then straightened his shoulders. He'd go in his guardsman uniform; he didn't know exactly what that symbolized to Trif anymore and it might be good to find out.

Yet his step slowed as he walked to her door. For a few

breaths, he just stood and let a trickle of Flair examine the room. She wasn't crying.

She wasn't playing music either.

He rapped.

"Come," she said. "It's open. Of course, you could fashion a charmkey and enter anytime."

Walking inside, and closing the door, he asked, "Did you try your key on my door?"

"No point in it, is there?" she said, her tones as quiet as his own.

He couldn't see her in the dark, but her voice came from the twoseat. He wondered if he dared sit next to her. His body tightened at the thought—the memories of her scent, the smooth softness of her skin affected him until more than his body yearned for her. He used all his control not to stride to her, sweep her into his embrace.

His HeartMate.

As if the word flowed through their bond, she asked, "Why did you not want me to find you?" Now that he was paying attention to their link, he felt her hurt, heard it behind the coolness of her voice.

"I'm sorry."

"Don't say that. You're not sorry you avoided me . . . or are you sorry we're HeartMates? I'm not the kind of woman you'd be attracted to?"

"You're wrong. I . . ." He couldn't bring himself to say he loved her. If he did it would be all over. They'd make love and HeartBond and *he would not kill her.*

"I'm too old for you, twice your age. Old and worn out." He felt it at the moment.

Her crack of laughter surprised him.

"Ilex, we're *HeartMates.* By definition, we're made for each other. Old? I've never had a more active lover."

Embarrassed heat made his ears burn, then spread to his neck. He shifted. He hadn't *been* that active in bed for some time. "Lights!" he commanded, and the three lamps in the room came on.

Trif blinked, and he saw her attention focused on him. Of course. There were no tear tracks on her face, but he felt a deep melancholy that wasn't natural from her. Had he done that? Taken away her joy? A crime.

She turned her face away, ruffled the fur of her absurd-looking cat.

"She's pretty quiet," he said.

"She's tired."

"How did your lesson with D'Holly go?

"Don't change the subject, I'm wallowing in self-pity. 'Here's Trif Clover confident and optimistic, searching for her HeartMate. He avoids her. Boo-hoo.' "

"Don't say that." He strode over to her.

Frowning up at him, she said, "Don't say what?"

"That your quest was silly. That you were silly to do it."

Her eyes widened. "I didn't."

"You *implied* it."

"You didn't laugh at me and my quest?"

Anger washed through him, he set it aside. "Did I ever seem to laugh at you? It was—touching."

She snorted. "So touching that you evaded me."

He rubbed his temples. "I'm not saying this right. It's been a bad day."

Immediately, her expression changed. "Yes—surprising and upsetting from the start. How is your cuz?"

"She'll be well." He tried a smile. "Figuring out how to thank T'Heather and Lark Apple."

"I'm glad to hear she'll recover."

"Thank you. I think she and I could become close, if we had the time."

Trif tilted her head. "That sounded like a lead-in to something."

"How well you know me already." He drew in a breath, let it out slowly, gestured to the seat beside her. "May I?"

"Of course. You're my HeartMate."

He winced.

Her lips pressed together until they were white; then she said, "It's time to tell me, Ilex."

"I know." He sat beside her and took her hand in his own. Her fingers were warm and soft, yet her blood pulsed with vivid life. Exactly a reflection of her.

He took a deep breath. "Trif, I have a small gift of foreseeing."

Her eyes brightened with interest.

Waving a hand, he said, "I can't *see* much and don't have visions often. I certainly can't foresee anything about these flig—murders." He shifted in his seat. That still rankled. Several times, he'd tried to force a vision, nothing.

"Go on. Did you see . . . see something wrong with me? With us."

"No!" He smiled briefly, kissed her hand. "Nothing could ever be wrong with you."

She pulled her fingers from his grasp and scowled. "It must be. You avoided me. You don't want the bond."

"No, I don't."

She flinched.

"I would give anything to bond with you. But not your life. And I will die soon."

"What!" Her eyes had gone large in her face; her mouth slightly opened in shock.

"Ever since I was a boy . . . since my father's death, I've seen a vision of myself dead as a man." He touched his gray head. "When my hair had gone silver."

"But . . . but . . ."

"I don't get much detail. Lately, I've seen that I have a head wound and wear a brown guardsman's uniform with the rank and insignia I have today. The visions have become more frequent, as if in warning. I sense I'll—pass on—soon."

She just stared at him. "No! You're too young to die!"

"My work can occasionally be dangerous. And I've become accustomed to dying young."

Shooting from the chair, she paced her small mainspace. "That can't be."

He went on inexorably. "And if we HeartBonded, I would rob you of your life. Trif, you are *twenty*! You should have at least another fifteen decades of life!"

She stopped. Her hands went to her throat. "This can't be. I won't let it happen."

"It will happen."

Once more she paced, then turned and stared at him. Frustration pulsed through their bond. "That's it? You're denying us whatever life we might have together because of a stupid dream!"

He couldn't sit either. He stood and strode across the room to halt by the door, as always, keeping his temper in check. "It's Flair, Trif. My Flair, and no more stupid than your quest, and just as powerful as your visions of the past. Do you question them?"

"They occurred!"

"How do you know?"

"I checked some with the Ship . . . those that could be checked."

"And I've had other dreams that come true."

"And some that don't?" She sounded less angry now, more desperate.

"A few," he admitted. "About ten percent."

Trif marched up to him. "I never thought you were one not to *live* life to its fullest." She flung out her arms.

He stiffened. "This just emphasizes our age difference. I *am* more cautious than you. Can't you understand? I *want* you to live life—every moment of your life to the fullest. A long, long life."

She tossed her head, looked him straight in the eyes. "It won't be very full if I don't have my HeartMate."

Impasse. He'd known it would come to this. He turned and crossed to the door, set his hand on the latch, felt her fingers clutch his sleeve.

"No, Ilex, please, don't turn away. You've done that so often. It hurts that you turn away from me!"

The thought of hurting her stabbed at him. He pivoted to see her eyes huge with pleading, and a wave of emotion he couldn't identify shuddered through him. He couldn't deny her.

Her hands slid up his chest, across, as if measuring it, measuring him, and her expression told him that he was all she'd ever dreamed of.

He closed his eyes. He didn't think he could stand being so important to another. He'd gone through life lonely, and now the hugeness of her love—his own—overwhelmed him. As if he'd lived in a sterile empty house whistling with chill drafts and then stepped into a warm, welcoming home with perfumed air, just waiting for him to stay.

But he couldn't stay. To do so would destroy the one who gave him her love. He brushed the back of his fingers against her soft, young cheek. "I want you to live."

She framed his face with her hands. "And I want to live. *With you!*" She pressed her body against his and again he shuddered, this time with desire that filled him until it clogged his throat. He fought to keep his hands at his sides, not to touch, not to cherish, not to love.

A frown line appeared between her brows. "Lady and Lord, Ilex, you are so stubborn. Kiss me!"

"I ca—"

Her tongue was in his mouth and he forgot everything except the taste of her. His hands clamped against her butt, lifted her to settle her sex against his cock straining against his trous. He opened his mouth to moan, scrabbled to hang onto a shred of control.

She drew back, scowling up at him, mouth wet and red and swollen. His breath caught.

"Ilex, *take me.*"

Her demand simply shattered him. He ported them into her bedroom, onto the bed.

"Naked," she whispered, and their clothes disappeared. He lay on her soft body, cradled in her hips, straining for her, needing her, mad for her.

Only this once, and he'd leave after sex. So he lifted himself on his elbows and thrust into her. She was wet and ready and closed tight around him and there was nothing in the world but her.

He plunged again and again, faster, his pleasure spiraling with each little moan from her, each twist of her body increasing the ecstasy for them both.

He climaxed. "Trif!" he cried.

She flung out a sparkling golden link—the HeartBond. He brushed it away. "HeartMate!" she called.

And a strong surge of her Flair washed over them, flashes of bright stars, deep space, tumbling them into darkness.

Minutes passed as he slowly, returned to consciousness. He

wondered if her Flair would always surge at release and if there was any way he could control the aftermath.

"What about the murders?" she said, her voice trembling. He knew she didn't want to talk about her unstable Flair, or the problems between them.

The murders. He stiffened, pulled her tight. He shouldn't stay. Hadn't he promised himself he'd leave after sex? But it hadn't been sex. It had been mating. *HeartMating* . . . his mind said, but he ignored it. He'd refused the HeartBond. It had taken willpower, but he'd done it. If . . . if they continued to love together, would that get easier or harder? A corner of his mouth kicked up. When had things ever gotten easier?

She nudged him with her elbow. "The murders?"

Again, a little shock that she should so easily distract his mind—that just thinking of her should make him forget his other passion—his vocation.

But he was all too afraid for her. He looked down at her, still flushed from lovemaking, and brushed strands of her brown hair back from her face, his fingertips dampening from her perspiration. She'd been wild. So had he—he'd never treated a woman with such lack of finesse, at least not since he'd been full grown . . . and that circled around to the age issue again.

Trif chuckled, touched his face. "You went away on me *again.* You think too much."

"Part of my profession. Which I love."

Nodding, she said, "I understand. I'd never ask you to abandon it . . . but I'd like to know of your cases, particularly the ones that affect you deeply. Is it wrong to ask?"

"I'd like to keep you away from some of the more gruesome aspects. Though since I've been assigned to the Nobles, it hasn't been as—rough—as when I worked Downwind or on the docks, years ago."

"Ilex, I was there this morning. Two women, one dead, one dying."

He didn't want to tell her, to scare her, but he didn't want her ignorant any more either. His fingers traced her collarbone, touched the amulet with his forefinger. "Promise me you won't ever take this off."

She leaned back in surprise, then wariness entered her eyes. "Ilex, you're frightening me."

"Good. There have been four murders—of young people who have unsteady Flair and Fams."

Her body jolted against his and he hated it. She just kept staring into his eyes. "That's why you moved in? Why you've been watching me?"

"No. Yes. I mean, I want you safe, intend to ensure you're protected, but I wanted to be near you too," he said starkly. Just like her to focus on the relationship angle first.

A little of the tension drained from her. She rested back on his arm. "Tell me."

So he did, and when he was finished her eyes were damp. She sniffled. "People like me—except *Noble.*"

"Don't count on that. Don't pretend being middle-class excludes you. Take good care of yourself."

She gave him a watery smile. "Well, I won't be out questing for my HeartMate."

Something in him lightened. Just being in her company, having told her the worst about his fears, relieved the burden of his hiding. They might not agree about how to handle their HeartMate status, but it was out in the open and not a hidden thing anymore.

Her emotions settled, and her gaze intensified. "Your—your manager—"

"Chief Sawyr."

Her fingers curled around the retrieval stone; her body quivered with a fine tension against his, danger-awareness racing, flickering through their connection. "Your Chief said this had cost you."

He glanced away until her fingers stroked his jaw, made him meet her eyes.

She said, "I paid T'Ash for the stone and his work. But that wasn't the half of it. You paid for the retrieval spell. What did that cost you?" Her eyes were jade, unavoidable. He couldn't lie to her. He couldn't evade her anymore.

She let him feel the pressure of her fingernail along his jawline. It didn't have a warning effect; instead, his sex hardened again, his hips thrust instinctively against her. She wriggled closer, making him groan.

"Ilex, I want an answer."

"I want you."

"Pleeease." She batted her eyelids and he laughed. It felt good—until he thought of his mother, sitting like a desiccated spider in her web. All lust drained from him.

"It cost me some gilt. More. I had to . . . request it from my mother. We don't get along."

Her eyes widened and she was silent a long moment. Confusion pulsed through their bond. "You said that before. You don't get along with your mother."

"Not all of us have close, happy families."

Another minute of silence, and he realized his muscles had stiffened with stress and he relaxed them, one by one.

"I'm sorry for you," she said finally.

"I'm sorry for my brother, the Heir," he said, and realized he'd impulsively spoken bitter truth.

She sighed. "Both of you are . . . alienated from your mother and your home?"

"Right."

With a little cough, she said, "There are only two of you?"

"Yes."

"How much did the amulet cost you?"

"It is a *gift* to my HeartMate."

"But not a HeartGift."

His chest constricted. "No. I made that—many—years ago."

"What did the retrieval spell cost you?" she persisted.

"Nothing I wasn't willing to pay."

"Ilex—"

"Darling Trif. The transaction is done. Over. Nothing to dwell on."

She seemed struck silent at his endearment. Her lovely, full breasts rose and fell.

He cast his thoughts away from loving—sex. The amulet was the least he could give her. He touched the stone, warm and slightly damp from her skin, tingling with her Flair. "Let me give you this." It was for his peace of mind as much as a present for her.

"Thank you." She pressed against him and set her lips on his. He thought his bones melted in the kiss.

She drew back until he felt her breath on his lips. "More," she said.

He shouldn't. Her face was so open, as was their connection. She was completely vulnerable to him, and he was—not using her, he'd never do that—but taking advantage of the situation when he had no intention of letting it progress into marriage and HeartBond. He gritted his teeth and pushed away from her, rose, and grabbed his uniform.

"Will you stay?" she whispered, not looking at him, but her yearning for him pulsed down their bond—his touch, his kisses, his form covering hers.

Every muscle in his body went rigid. "I—"

"I want you to stay. Tonight and forever. I want you as long as you will stay. I. Want. You."

Twenty-one

*Ilex couldn't remember the last time he was speechless. Af*ter letting a slow breath out and taking a deep one in, he said, "Yes."

She jumped from the bedsponge and flung herself in his arms, and nothing in his life felt as good as having her there. He dropped his clothes, held her close, and his pulse throbbed heavily. Passion arrowed through him. He never wanted to let her go. Gently he laid her back down on the bedsponge. For a moment he just stood and looked at her, knowing he'd remember her like this for the rest of his life.

His short life. "You are so perfect for me. And I want you too, more than I ever imagined. More than I can ever say." He held up his trembling hands for her to see, let her feel through their connection how tenuous the control on his raging fever for her was. "But I will not HeartBond with you. I will not—"

"Come to me." She lifted her arms. Waiting for him. He shuddered. She smiled slowly, with infinite allure and feminine mysteries in her gleaming eyes. *Come*. The call of her heart to his swept through their link.

He could not resist.

Their mouths met as they savored each other, drank from each other with more than lips.

He had to know her, in every way. First his hands explored her, learning her shape . . . and what pleased her. Then he cherished her with his mouth, discovering the varied tastes of her . . . the throbbing vein in her throat, the exquisite curve of her breasts, the sweetness of her nipples.

She arched and moaned against him, and he let the fire of his need burn him slowly, knowing he'd be consumed by it and never whole without her. He moved upon her tenderly, using hands and tongue and lips until there was nothing they wanted more in the universe than to come together.

Lifting himself, he sought her gaze, found her eyes unfocused. But through the link her soul cried for him.

He slid inside her. Slow, strong, deep. *HeartMate!*

They shattered in ecstasy together.

She sent him the HeartBond, a wave of heart and mind and soul to bind them together.

He blocked it for the second time.

And held her tighter.

*She fell asleep in his arms, and though remorse at his id-*iocy should have eaten at him, he felt nothing but complete contentment and let himself drift into sleep entwined with her in every way.

Sunlight creeping through the windows woke him, and he felt her awaken too. She stretched beside him, and he dared to look at her. She was fully as smug as Greyku at her worst.

Good. He'd loathe it if she had regrets.

He squeezed her a little, then got off the bedsponge and stretched, flushing at her obvious enjoyment of his body. Glancing down at his uniform, he shook his head. "That's got to go straight to the cleanser." He shut his eyes, concentrated on the uniforms in his closet, summoned one. When he opened his lids, his clothes lay across the bottom of the bedsponge.

Greyku pranced in and Ilex stared. "She really does sparkle."

"Yesss . . ." the little cat said, and promptly jumped onto the bed and settled on his uniform.

A crack of laughter escaped him at the same time Trif giggled. A giggle that went straight to his groin. He reached out and yanked his loincloth from his clothes and put it on. Hands on hips, he stared at the cat and just shook his head. "I still have trouble believing the kitten was tinted." With a finger, he stroked Greyku. "It's Flaired tint, not physical."

"Yesss," Greyku said again, craning her head over her back to admire herself. *This will last longer.*

"Lark Apple is back in town and she used to tint the walls of her room. As a friend, she might consider tinting Greyku for fun instead of gilt."

Hopping to her feet, Greyku stalked off Ilex's clothes, leaving wrinkles and multicolored cat hairs. He'd have a hard time explaining that. . . .

Lark Apple is a Healer, not an artist. I wanted an artist.

"And you got one," Trif soothed.

Ilex took his clothes and snapped them; a flurry of hair floated. He dressed, then looked at Trif lounging in the bed. Vibrant and beautiful as always. His heart squeezed. "I happened to meet Holm Apple—fully armed with blood in his eye for me—yesterday."

Trif pursed her lips. "Is that so?"

"So."

She laughed. "Holm's wife, Lark, is my best friend," she said complacently. "So I have connections with one of the best fighters on Celta. And with the rest of the Hollys too. But you know about that, don't you?"

As she ended, her tone had developed a sliver of steel. He studied her. She was maturing. Was he stealing her youth as well as her gaiety? But a mature Trif Clover . . . would be irresistible, unstoppable.

"I did give Tinne Holly recording spheres of your music," he said mildly. "You love music and were wasting your talent in working at your Family's furniture business."

"Oh?" Her eyes narrowed.

He finished dressing. "I love my work . . . my vocation. I wanted you to love your work too."

Her mouth pursed, relaxed. "You're right." She grimaced. "Though I think you could have given her some of my better efforts."

"All your music is wonderful."

She just stared at him, and he had to kiss her. He trusted

himself to bend down and brush her mouth with his—a tender kiss. A loving kiss. A kiss a HeartMate might bestow—he cut the thought off.

"Thank you," she said.

He nodded, picked up his wrist timer from the floor, and strapped it on. "I must report to Chief Sawyr."

Her face went still and through their link he felt her heart pick up its pace, and he cursed himself for reminding her of his wretched case.

"The murders," she whispered.

"Yes. We have some leads. We *will* find these . . . wrong ones. Please promise me that you'll be careful. That you'll teleport as often as you can and don't go out at night." He touched her amulet. "Wear this always."

"I'll promise, if you give me your word you'll be careful too."

He blinked in surprise. "If you insist."

"I do." She rose, not languidly like a tempting lover, but with brisk efficiency. "I'm meeting D'Holly at Clover Compound at Mid-Morning Bell."

"Get her out of T'Holly Residence. Good idea."

"Tinne's," she said.

A tiny spurt of jealousy went through him. Tinne Holly was much more her age, handsome, wealthy, honorable. But perhaps too much like her own temperament. Still, in his mind's eye he could see them together. Ilex knew it was small of him, but thanked the Lady and Lord that Trif Clover wasn't Tinne's HeartMate.

Ilex jerked a nod. "You are keeping quality company."

"Am I? The Hollys are cursed."

"You see that?"

"Easily. I . . . I think that their Family must have been very loving and close until T'Holly and D'Holly broke their Vows of Honor. As close as we Clovers perhaps." She made an abbreviated gesture. "Yet their Family is broken. Suffering. The atmosphere of the Residence is . . . unhealthy." She shivered.

Cocking her head, she said, "But you seem close to the Hollys and are keeping quality company too."

He shrugged. "We're distant cuzes."

A frown line creased between her brows. "But you were with Mitchella's husband, Straif T'Blackthorn, last year and he's a FirstFamily Lord."

"Yes. I've been assigned to handle any cases in which the FirstFamilies are involved."

Her eyes brightened. "Like what?"

"Like T'Ash's HeartGift being stolen. Apprehending the dangerous outlaw Ruis Elder. Monitoring the Hawthorn-Holly duel . . . and accompanying Straif Blackthorn, a man suspected by the FirstFamilies Council of being negligent of his title and his estate, to a mine in the Hard Rock Mountains."

"Zow. Interesting stuff."

"No," he said. "Babysitting." He couldn't stop his lip from curling. "Not good work for a guardsman or a detective. Political work."

At that moment her scrybowl pinged.

She made a face. "I *must* get rid of that bowl."

Greyku bounded in. *It's Mitchella Clover. I think she must want to speak to Me. Get it, get it, get it!*

Ilex snorted.

Trif jumped from the bed, hauled on a slinky pink robe that had his blood humming again. She gave him a smacking kiss on the mouth and ran into the mainspace. "I wonder if Straif is back."

That would be good, Ilex thought. His hopes rose a little. If the best tracker of Celta was back in the city, they'd be able to find the evil group. As far as Ilex could tell, this adult gang had left very few tracks, teleporting to dispose of their victims . . . but Straif had great Flair.

He heard the message cache play Mitchella Clover D'Blackthorn's sultry voice. "Greetyou, cuz Trif. You *must* come by to tell me everything that's going on in your life. The Family is very excited. All they can talk about is your new status. I might be able to give you a few tips about dealing with the Hollys. Come for breakfast." Her voice broke a little. "Straif is still out of town and I'm lonely."

That would definitely ensure Trif went to T'Blackthorn Residence for breakfast.

It was best that they go their own ways. Sensible.

It would have been irresponsible to stay here and make love all day.

It would have been the best day of his life.

Trif returned the call. "I'll be right there. Let me dress!"

Before she reached the bedroom again, Ilex swept by her in the narrow door between mainspace and bedroom. He enjoyed—too much—the brush of her body against his.

"Greyku and I are going to Mitchella's for breakfast." She sounded breathless.

"I heard."

She kissed him again, an absent touch of the lips that had everything inside him clenching. "I'll see you later?" Though her tone was light, the golden thread between them took on a black tinge of anxiety.

"Yes." He couldn't deny her. Couldn't resist temptation.

Her smile was bright and carefree and all the reward he'd ever need for one small assent.

"Good." She hurried to the waterfall and he let himself out of her apartment.

Only as he strode down the hall to the landing pad in the lobby did he realize that she hadn't even noticed the guardsman uniform, she'd only seen the man.

But the uniform he lay dead in was like the one he wore today. Deep inside he might have thought that perhaps . . . somehow . . . he could have her, avoid his fate. He had to stay strong and refuse the HeartBond. She was the most important thing in the world to him. The best person who'd ever come into his life. He had to reject her to keep her safe.

Once in his office at the guardhouse—the familiarity of which soothed his ruffled nerves—Ilex sat behind his desk and looked down at his daily list.

He scried Danith D'Ash and learned that Calla Sorrel's housefluff was unavailable for questioning. The little animal had been sent deep into a Healing coma, and Danith had distanced its memories and emotions. She'd tried to save the memories in a holosphere, but the emotions of the young housefluff had been of overwhelming terror and despair. Those feelings had naturally wiped whatever true memories it might have had.

No help there.

At that moment, a young guardswoman entered carefully holding a spellshielded holosphere. "This just arrived in the guardhouse cache for you. From your cuz, Dufleur Thyme." The guardswoman sighed. "The image on the sphere shows her wearing a spectacular tunic, embroidered in metallic thread . . . I don't suppose you know where . . ." She flushed.

Ilex stared at her and she took a step back. He realized then that he'd never said more than a few words to the woman since she'd been assigned to the guardhouse a couple of months ago. He wasn't usually so unsociable, but he'd obviously been obsessed by Trif.

He tried a warm smile, and the guardswoman smiled back. "My cuz is an embroiderer, so she probably decorated her tunic herself. She works at Dandelion Silk."

The guardswoman grimaced. "Too rich for my blood. Thank you, though." With a little salute, she walked away. The roll of her hips would once have had him riveted. Now he only vaguely appreciated her stride—like fine art. Yes, he was well and truly hooked—on Trif.

Carefully, he dispelled the protection around the fragile holosphere. He noted that it neared the end of its life, the image was dim, and he wished he'd thought to give Dufleur a new one to record her memories. He fisted his fingers in anger. There were plenty of treasures in D'Winterberry Residence that could be sold to provide basic amenities for his cuz. Yet his mother hoarded all the possessions as if they belonged to only her, and not his father's Family. Typical.

When Ilex noticed his knuckles whitening, he relaxed his fingers one by one, closed his eyes, and used his soothing Flair on himself.

After he was sure he'd regained objectivity, he tapped the ball.

"Cuz Ilex. Here are my *best* memories of the events. I tranced and guided my Flair." The little image shrugged her shoulders, pet her Fam faster. "I'm working a half day today and will be home at noon if you need to speak with me." Another hesitation. "Love, Dufleur."

He swallowed. It had been a long time since anyone in his Family had told him they loved him. He rolled his shoulders, dimmed his office light, and settled into the comfortchair behind his desk. Within minutes he was in a trance himself.

Almost lazily, he reached for the ball. And fell into Dufleur's memories.

She closes the door, weary but not as lonely as usual because her new Fam, Fairyfoot, trots beside her, murmuring little comments, amusing Dufleur. She has the satisfaction of knowing that she's done exceptional work and finished a difficult project on time. She hopes for a bonus. If she gets one, she'll be that much closer to moving away from her mother and D'Winterberry and that cold Residence.

She turns and walks down the street, noting the slight, cold breeze. Winter is coming, and the new year. Another year with her mother. No, she isn't going to think of that. She rubs her arms up her light jacket, using a bit of Flair to make it warmer before she leaves the narrow, curving Manyberries Road to step out onto Druida Street, where the wind will be stronger.

Fairyfoot complains of the cold. She is a little cat, and can fit inside Dufleur's coat. The cat wriggles and makes Dufleur laugh.

Something glows—golden. Great, pulsing Flair emanates from it, brushing against her . . . calling her. She hurries to it, picks up the small bag. Heat flashes through her. She wants to drop the object, but she can't. Raw, sexual need batters her and she stumbles, falls. She is only aware of the fine-grained leather that pulses under her fingers.

***What is happening?** Fairyfoot asks mentally.*

Dufleur has no words.

"Here, let me help you." A man offers his hand, but when she puts her fingers in his, he shudders as her Flair spikes. Then it drops away and she has no control of it. She manages to get on the public carrier. Time flickers, wave after wave of heat, then cold, passes through her. She thinks her Flair must be intensifying her aura, then suppressing it. The driver assists her in getting off at her stop.

A man and a woman come near . . . hasn't she seen them

around the neighborhood? The woman touches her in the center of the forehead with a gloved finger. "Sleep!" she orders. Dufleur's forehead burns, turns icy, and everything floats away.

Until the screams. Someone is screaming, screaming, screaming; then it stops abruptly.

There is wild laughter that chills her blood, the patter of footsteps in a strange rhythm. She struggles to move, but can't. All is darkness. She strains to see. Can't. This is WRONG! Terror washes through her. The fever from the object is gone. The little bag gone too. Shouldn't that be a good thing? But she feels a crushing loss.

Hideous slurping noises. Worse, the smell of raw meat, the scent of heavy incense. Garbled speech. She sucks in air to scream herself and giddiness overcomes her. She goes away.

Chanting wakes her, words Dufleur doesn't know. How odd is that? A man's hands touch her bare skin, caresses her breasts, and she flinches. Horrible. Horrible. His palms are joined by others . . . more than two people, all those hands on her. She is like to go mad, yet she fights the drugs, gathers her Flair. She has an affinity with sharp objects like needles, perhaps she can summon a knife. . . .

"Cut the Fam now," one says, female.

***NO!** she screams, but nothing comes from her mouth and if they heard her, they ignore her.*

Fairyfoot whimpers beside her.

Suction. Of her Flair, through Fairyfoot. No!

*Awful pain rips at her chest. Fairyfoot awakes. **What is happening?***

Dufleur can't answer, the pain is too much.

***Guardsman! Guardsman Winterberry!** Fairyfoot shouts loudly, using cat Flair and Dufleur's own. Dufleur sends more Flair to Fairyfoot, amplifies her Fam's mental voice.*

Scrambling noises. Quick, muttered words she can't catch. People grabbing her. Teleporting her! Cold. The pain comes back.

Cuz Ilex is here. Fairyfoot is safe. Darkness is welcome now.

Ilex shuddered from the memories, wiped cold sweat from his face and neck with a softleaf, then made notes of all the impressions he'd gained from Dufleur's experience . . . the sense of space—a medium-sized room, warm and redolent of incense, the texture of the cloth beneath her, the movement of people in the room—the lost Calla Sorrel and her housefluff Fam on another altar beyond Dufleur's head.

Dufleur had been sick and drugged, her observational skills at a minimum. Still, he'd retrieved enough information to update the poppets. He set his four dolls out and sent each bit of data into the appropriate replica. When he was done, one of the replicas of the men had a faint glow about it. Finally, he could use the thing.

Seen them around the neighborhood. That would be near his mother's home. He'd take the poppet there. Maybe he'd get lucky and pick up a trace of the man.

Once again, perspiration beaded his forehead at the work. He used a bespelled cloth to cleanse himself.

Even the impressions of such an ordeal were enough to drive a person mad.

He left his office and gave a short report to Sawyr.

"Slow going on making the poppets. Good that we can use one," Sawyr grunted.

"Yes."

Sawyr grimaced, lifted and dropped broad shoulders. "Better you than me walking through a woman's memories. Never did envy you that."

"They definitely overextended themselves, taking two, and I think my cuz was a crime of opportunity, due to the object on the street."

"Something glowing gold. Tied in with this bunch, you think? Perhaps they made something to skew Flair and was testing it?"

Ilex considered. "I don't know . . . there was something familiar about that portion. . . ."

"You go around seeing glowing objects too?" Sawyr stared at him.

"No." Ilex shrugged. "I think the cult *does* want to step up its ritual murder rate—or perhaps it's only because Samhain—New Year's is in a couple of days."

Sawyr set his brawny forearms on his desk, and leaned on them, crossed his fingers. His eyes burned with righteous fire.

"We'll get them. We'll find them and get them before then. The newssheets Families are already sniffing around this story. If they holo it, we'll have panic."

"There aren't that many younger Nobles with irregular Flair."

"No, not of that age group," Sawyr said, and cold slipped through Ilex's veins as if his blood had turned to ice. "Children," he said hoarsely, "children of seven at First Passage."

Twenty-two

"*Many children experiencing First Passage have unsta-*ble Flair, especially if it's great Flair breaking free, and these killers do like great Flair," Chief Sawyr said, voice rough.

"The Nobles will go crazy. So will upper-middle-class Guildspeople who are more often having children with extraordinary Flair."

"And those FirstFamilies GreatLords and Ladies will descend upon the streets of Druida with flaming swords." Sawyr pounded his fist on the desk. "I *won't* have it." He speared Ilex with a gaze. "So find them. Which reminds me, the FirstFamilies Council have called Straif T'Blackthorn back from tracking that missing botanist." Jaw hardening, Sawyr said, "I want you—us—to get the fliggers first."

"T'Blackthorn is the best."

"I don't want the FirstFamilies to think that only they can save the city." Sawyr snorted. "Though they've made their great mistakes in the past."

"All of which I have been the guardsman to stand by and witness," Ilex said.

Sawyr barked a laugh and waggled a meaty finger at Ilex. "Don't think that you're not continuing your duty assigned to the FirstFamilies, 'cause you are. Always."

Ilex just stared at his Chief. "Until you're no longer Chief, or I make Chief myself and am assigned my own guardhouse here in Druida."

Now Sawyr's laugh rolled through the small building. "You'll always be junior to me, boy."

Taking another moment to try and stare his Chief down, and failing, Ilex turned. "Ah, well, they are usually an interesting bunch."

When he returned to his office, he compared all the witness statements—Fams' and Dufleur's together. He consulted the several thick theses that Sedwy Grove had sent over. Tapping a writestick on his desk, he decided that what he really needed was the number of people in this cult.

He didn't want even one to escape to spread their filthy perversions. Time and again, he immersed himself in Dufleur's memories, but couldn't judge how many there had been in total. He'd picked up tones of five, and that was bad enough, but he was sure there were more foot-patterns than five. If he'd been there—but he hadn't been.

Finally, he knew he'd gone into Dufleur's memorysphere the last time. Any more would warp the ball. He could have stood one or two more immersions, but . . .

All of her impressions had confirmed several things. There were more than four cult members. They used drugs on their victims, but also on themselves—frankincense, myrrh, and something else they saved for the last, after they killed their victim by bringing the heart out of the body.

They chose youngsters who had unsteady Flair because it was easier to drain, to integrate into their own bodies, force the corridors of the brain to expand, perhaps generate more of their own Flair.

Not only criminal. Criminally insane.

They ate the heart, then danced and copulated in a mockery of true spiritual ritual.

He leaned back in his comfortchair, rested his eyes, settled into a light trance that might help him make sense of details. . . .

A knock came on his door. "Guardsman Winterberry?"

"Come."

The young guardswoman, Acacia Bluegum, entered with

his caff mug. "I made caff for the guardhouse. Here's some for you, you've been working hard."

"Thank you." It was as he preferred, of course. She was a guard and noted such things.

She glanced at the memorysphere and the scattered papyruses on his desk, cleared her throat. "I understand that dipping into the memories of the opposite sex can be—difficult. I can help." An undertone of excitement was in her voice. Because of the case?

"Thank you, but Dufleur is my cuz. The Family connection made it easier." Not much, but a little.

She nodded, looked as if she wanted to linger, then faded back to the section of the guardhouse that held her desk—which she shared with three others. Automatically, his Flair followed her, and his nose sent the information that she used slightly musky, but not distasteful, lotions.

Ilex sipped his caff and eyed his work. So much for examining the facts in a trance. The interruption had broken his state of mind. Yet he had figured one thing out.

Fine-grained leather bag. Glowing golden. Strong enough Flair to bring a lesser Noblewoman to her knees and mess with her Flair. Engendered lust.

He initiated his office privacy spell and scried T'Willow. A few minutes later, he was teleporting to T'Willow Residence.

The GreatLord was much as Trif had described him—late twenties, already experienced the Third and final Passage at twenty-seven, and fully in control of his Flair, his title, and his household. He wore a fine white silkeen shirt open at the neck, with large bloused sleeves, but no embroidery around the cuffs denoting his title. His trous were of excellent quality, but comfortably worn.

Under Ilex's narrow gaze, the man looked stressed and as if he was at the end of his rope.

They stood in T'Willow's ResidenceDen and the Lord gestured Ilex to sit down. As soon as Ilex was sure the housekeeper who'd led him to the room had moved far along the corridor, he said, "It's wearing on a man when his HeartGift is circulating in public."

T'Willow stiffened. "How do you know about that?"

"Let's not play games," Ilex said just as sharply, sitting in the closest chair. "You knew the minute you met her that Trif Clover was my HeartMate, and the favor you demanded for a fee was to leave *your HeartGift* in a busy, public place."

As he sat and stretched out his legs, a half smile played over T'Willow's mouth. "And she left it in the Maypole." He glanced at Ilex. "I would not have thought of so good a place."

"Thank you for not telling her about me."

T'Willow shrugged. "Each soul must woo their mate as they wish." A corner of his mouth lifted. "Even if I thought your courtship was inept in the extreme, I would not interfere."

Ilex winced. "I'm not here about matters of the heart. I'm here because of a nasty string of murders. Killings done during a black-magic ritual. I think you experienced something of the sort through your HeartGift.

"You must be intimately and strongly linked to that item. Those of us who make them are. They are a reflection of our very being as experienced in the fugue of our last Passage."

Several heartbeats of silence passed. "Yes. I am. Very linked."

Leaning forward, Ilex said, "I must know what you know. Anything might help me find these people."

T'Willow stared at his hands. "I didn't know what was happening. It was more than a dream . . . I didn't know what to think. My dreams of late . . . since I sent my HeartGift out into the world—" He shuddered, rubbed his head with his hands. "Distorted images, sounds." He stood and went to a cabinet. "Brithe brandy?"

"No, thank you. I still have work to do."

Smile strained, T'Willow said, "I've cut down the amount of consultations I provide for the time being." He splashed expensive liquor into a bell glass. "The ladies universally disapproved—and currently disapprove—of my actions."

"The ladies?"

With a gesture of his glass, T'Willow indicated the sprawling Residence around them. "My G'Aunts, aunts, cuzes . . . Except for me, my Family is female."

A little sound of commiseration escaped Ilex before he knew it.

T'Willow gave him half bow, downed a couple of fingers of brandy.

Ilex considered the man, spoke slowly. "I noticed that you requested a full report of the murders this morning and the Captain of the Councils sent you one."

The GreatLord indicated a small sphere on his desk. A very expensive, very Flaired information orb.

"So you studied it and know about the murders," Ilex said.

"Yes."

"Then you know who your HeartMate is."

"Your cuz, Dufleur Thyme." He lilted her name as if it were the rarest wine to sit upon his tongue.

"Right. I've just come from reviewing a memorysphere of her ordeal. It wasn't pleasant. If you experienced *anything* of that event, I need to know. Now."

A crack came as T'Willow tightened his fingers so his brandy glass fragmented. It, and the liquid it held, vanished at a Word from him . . . a curse word. "You'd best find these murderers or I'll kill them myself for what they did to my lady." His lips curled in a feral smile. "And others will come with me. T'Ash, T'Holly, perhaps even T'Hawthorn."

The Chief had been right. Armed and dangerous First-Families Lords and Ladies prowling the streets of Druida. It wasn't an image Ilex liked. He lifted both hands and sent a wash of calm he didn't entirely feel himself to the GreatLord. But the use of his Flair for that purpose was so standard that it was second nature.

T'Willow settled back into the comfortable leather couch, tipped his head back, and breathed evenly, closed his eyes. "What do you want to know?"

"Everything. Let me lead you through it. Dufleur bent down and picked up your HeartGift. . . ."

"Yes!" Now his smile was pure male triumph. "It had attracted her. I hadn't dared to hope it would fall into her hands so soon." He tensed. "It's somewhere else now, not in the building where she suffered. Oddly enough, it fell away when the fliggers were 'porting her to Landing Park." He turned his head, and his green eyes gleamed curiosity. "Why Landing Park?"

"We believe a couple of them live in that neighborhood. Frequent it anyway."

"Hmmm."

"Please don't investigate on your own. It will only muddle our inquiries." Ilex didn't know if his request was futile or not. "Back to your impressions from your HeartGift . . ." He guided T'Willow through the event, step by step, in excruciating detail. Twice.

Finally, they were both wrung out and they rested in silence.

"Have I helped at all?" asked the young man.

"Yes."

The GreatLord waited, but Ilex said nothing more. Then T'Willow frowned. "Whatever report you file tonight, I *will* get shortly."

Ilex gritted his teeth. Working around—it seemed never *with*—the FirstFamilies was a frustration leading to a major migraine. "Yes," he said. "You provided me with some vital pieces of information."

T'Willow straightened. "Yes?"

"There are six members of the cult."

"I told you that?"

Ilex stood. "You gave me enough detail for me to deduce it."

"What else?"

"I could dimly see the room. I have enough information on one of the men to add to a poppet I'm building that may actually take me to the murder place." He shouldn't have said that. Fierce anger molded T'Willow's features.

"My thanks," said Ilex, then to distract the man: "You now know Dufleur is your HeartMate, and can sense where your HeartGift is. You could retrieve it."

Smiling ironically, T'Willow said, "Then drop it conveniently in her path? Give it to you? No. There are Flair rules for such matters and I will follow every last one. I will not call it back."

"Even if you suffer?"

"Suffering's part of life, and I *will* conduct my courtship right."

"As you wish." Ilex hesitated. "I don't think Dufleur is looking for her mate."

"Certainly not like Trif was looking for you. It seems neither you nor your cuz wants love and marriage."

"Neither of us have seen love in marriage."

T'Willow shrugged. "You had a bad Family life. So did I. It happens. My MotherDam, the former GreatLady D'Willow, loathed that her title and estate would pass to a male for the first time in three centuries. She considered it a personal failure. But I remained open to love. Did you and your cuz?"

Feeling heat around his collar, tinting his cheeks, Ilex said, "There is more to my situation than I prefer to disclose."

The man stared at him for a long moment, nodded. "Very well. I am not in your shoes. Merry meet, cuz."

Ilex flinched a little. "I'm just beginning to know her and already you want to barge in."

T'Willow laughed, slapped Ilex on the shoulder. "My Family is very supportive. I'll look forward to having a stalwart cuz."

"Merry part," Ilex said.

"And we will definitely meet again . . . always merrily, I hope," T'Willow said.

Ilex couldn't resist. "It seems to me that shirt would benefit from some embroidery. I can recommend the shop, Dandelion Silk."

The GreatLord's smile was incandescent. Lady and Lord, what beautiful smiles the children his cuz and this man would have. Smiles powerful in themselves.

Ilex wasn't ready to go home. Trif would be there, and he wasn't sure if they would ignore the enormous chasm about their disagreement on their future together. If she had decided she no longer wanted him. He could delay that pain indefinitely.

The rest of the day had gone well with his investigation. He'd made additions to the poppet of one of the men, had used his Flair to bespell it as strongly as possible—to indicate where the man had been. Then he'd walked the city. He'd been led to the place where Dufleur had been held and the other girl murdered. There guards had gathered even more evidence.

Again, he'd reformed the poppets; again, they'd found another murder scene, a room similar in size and shape to the first. Observation there and from the impressions he'd received from the witnesses had given him enough knowledge to figure out the type of place the cultists preferred for their unholy rituals.

Sawyr had sent guards all over the city to find rectangular rooms of a certain size in old, deserted buildings.

It had been a good day's work.

Leaning back in his chair, Ilex allowed himself to feel the upsurge of hunting anticipation—the strongest and cleanest emotion he'd felt all day. He didn't dare think about Trif.

On the other hand, T'Willow's words about Family and love had prodded a splinter that had been recently embedded in his soul. He needed to reconnect with his brother. And his brother needed to fight for his title of T'Winterberry.

The night guards had gathered in the common room and Ilex's office was dim and quiet. Once again, he leaned back; this time, he focused on the bond with his brother. *Meyar,* he sent down the link. *Scry me. Guardhouse.* He projected the message three times and almost heard the words echoing in his own head.

A few minutes later, his steel scrybowl rang loud. "Here," Ilex said.

"You called?" Meyar's expression had a hint of humor in it. Something Ilex was glad to hear.

"I'd—" He realized he didn't want to talk to his brother through a bowl full of water. "I want to talk to you. To meet." The unadorned walls behind Meyar gave no clue to his whereabouts. "I can't come to Gael City. You haven't left for Brittany yet, have you?"

"I'm closer than you think. I can see you in half a septhour."

Ilex blinked. "Yes?"

"I moved back to Druida a couple of months ago. Our bond was—unsettled. I couldn't go south."

Ilex's throat nearly closed with emotion. He cleared it and said, "I'd like to meet you by Father's memorial."

Meyar looked startled, then his face set in grim lines. "If you insist."

"I'd prefer it."

"See you there." Meyar ended the scry.

* * *

Greyku was dancing with excitement when Trif entered the apartment after her studies with D'Holly ended. The kitten had left mid-afternoon for another tinting session.

Look at Me, look at Me, look at Me now!

Trif studied her. She couldn't see anything different and didn't want to disappoint her Fam. "You look wonderful."

Greyku pranced back and forth, beaming. *It is best when it is dark. I made the windows in the bedroom dark, let's go in there!*

A frisson ran up Trif 's spine as she imagined how Greyku would have made the bedroom dark. She hoped the drapes her aunts had made her didn't have long claw marks or pulled threads. Still, she followed Greyku into the room. The drapes looked fine; the tie-backs lay on the floor, the tassels suspiciously tattered—or chewed. That wasn't too bad.

Shut the door!

Trif looked down indulgently at her young cat, then shut the door.

Eyes!

She shrieked. Fell back against the door, hand to her throat.

Huge eyes *glowed* at her.

Wonderful fun. "Yessss!" said Greyku. *Citrula painted some of the very tips of My coat in a different pattern. Watch this!*

Swallowing hard, Trif stared at the luminescent eyes—whites, bright blue pupils with a touch of red in the center, and black kohl-like lines outlining them. The muscles of Greyku's side tensed and relaxed as she jumped to the bureau, making the eyes ripple.

Trif shuddered.

Greyku lay down atop the chest of drawers and huge eyes stared down at Trif, humanlike, but with no expression. Somehow, they looked three-dimensional too. Layered painting on the fur.

And Citrula said if I moved like this—

The eyes blinked. Opened slowly again. Stared.

Trif pressed hard against the door. The eyes were completely eerie.

Magnificent, aren't I?! Greyku purred.

"Oh, always," Trif said faintly, then, "Lights on!" She

sighed in relief to see her small cat lying on her bureau, tinted much like she had been this morning.

Greyku looked along her side and sniffed. *It doesn't look the same in the light.*

"Amazing," Trif said, and snicked the door latch open.

Wait! It is different on the other side of me!

"The . . . the other side?"

Reversing herself, Greyku demanded, *Turn off the light again.*

Goddess preserve her. Trif gathered her nerve, then banished the light. Round, red, *menacing* eyes glared at her with split silver pupils. She made a stifled noise, then managed. "Lights on!"

I am very beautiful.

Trif cleared her throat. "Is this the last of the tinting?"

Yes, We are done now. I wanted More. I am glad you gave Me More.

"What did the other Fams think of it?"

I scared Zanth-sire. He left in the middle, then came back! He said he was not frightened, but he jumped and his claws extended and tail went fat. She grinned. *Drina said it was unusual and Samba was most impressed. Doggie Primrose piddled on the rug.*

"Sounds like Danith D'Ash had a wonderful time," Trif muttered. "How long is this new tinting going to last?"

Baby Nuin laughed and laughed and clapped his hands and said "Kitty!"

"I'm sure Danith was very proud."

T'Ash was impressed too. Looked Me over top to tail.

"Checking how Citrula tinted you, no doubt."

"Yesss."

"How long is this new tinting going to last?" Trif repeated, a little less casually.

I am bespelled. Three quarters of a year.

"Oh, fun."

"Yesss." *More is very good.*

She'd come to think so, but now doubted. Clearing her throat, she said. "In fact, you are *so* impressive, I'd like to put a dim-fur spell on you." She patted her heart. "So you don't keep scaring me."

Greyku sniffed, considered. *Very well. When I am with you.*

The kitten hopped from the dresser to the bed, then to the floor, bouncing all the way. *Sire Zanth is so struck with my tinting, he is taking Me hunting with him tonight.*

That stopped Trif. "You'll be careful?"

Very careful. And I can teleport too. We learned together and We are good.

"Very well."

Maybe Sire and I will let Vertic fox come too.

Trif considered that, shook her head. "I really can't imagine him appreciating your new tint."

Sometimes he is no fun, Greyku agreed.

And sometimes Ilex was too serious also. Their disagreement wasn't something to be taken lightly, but they'd find a way around it. There must be some way to fight the vision. She wouldn't accept his death, would work hard to prevent it.

As for tonight . . . Trif grinned. She wanted more, and she'd make sure he had fun tonight.

Twenty-three

Ilex reached the overgrown area in the far corner of the Winterberry grassyard before his brother. Twinmoons were almost full, and with their fullness would come the holiday of Samhain and New Year's, the first month of Birch. He knew in his bones the cult would demand a sacrifice, and waited impatiently for Tinne to get back to him with the name of a Noble who might be at risk. Very bad, but thank the Lady and Lord that Trif was too "common" for the cult. They'd want someone of title—and even greater Flair.

He found himself pacing the circular memorial grove, and as he walked, tending it. With ancient spells he scythed the long dead-brown weeds until they lay smooth, revealing the last green color of lower, thicker grass. It was a soothing process that showed immediate and positive results. Something he definitely needed in his life right now.

Meyar appeared and without a word, matched his stride, matched his Flair, and they tidied the memorials together—sending gentle cleansing Flair up the stone plinths, darkening the color of tinted and chiseled letters.

They stopped at their father's cubic stone.

"He was a good man," Meyar said.

"Yes."

"Unlike Mother." There was bitterness in his voice.

"True."

Meyar glanced at the yellow-lit windows of the Residence, then away. "I sensed when you visited her, came back here."

"Did you?"

"Oh, yes. Turmoil due to Family problems is so easy to recognize."

They did another circuit of the grove.

"What do you want of me?" asked Meyar.

"Why did you leave? Give up on the estate?"

"It would have taken a major legal battle to wrest it from her clawed hands."

"You have the name, the Flair."

"The estate didn't have the gilt to survive a fight like that. As for the rest, my other concerns weren't major. I've found that major catastrophes are sometimes easier to deal with than minor, day-to-day life problems that nag you and drag you down. And she was always good at that—belittling us, pecking at us to do as she wanted, never accepting our decisions. Even if I had won, she wouldn't move out, and there's nowhere I could send her. This is it." He spread his arms wide. "The ancestral Winterberry estate—a large grassyard and townhouse near Landing Park."

"Not too shabby a location," Ilex said.

"But all we have. She'd have lived with me and would have nagged at me every day about every fliggering thing and I'd have killed her. One of us had to go." He slanted Ilex a look. "In fact, both you and I had to go. Maybe if we'd been girls . . . but not men she couldn't boss around, manipulate. So I went, and left Druida too."

"You're back."

"So I am. For the moment."

"Don't give up on us."

Meyar whirled, his mouth worked a moment; then he said, "It's too late for me and her."

"And us?"

"I won't give up on you." His lips flattened. "You are . . . not calm and steady as I've sensed for so long." He shrugged. "I know you've met your HeartMate." For a brief moment, their eyes met before Meyar looked away. "I remember that nightmare of death that you had in childhood." He shivered. "I never envied you that touch of Flair you got from Father-Dam's Family. I wanted—to be near," he mumbled.

"Thank you. Do you stay?"

Meyar didn't answer for a long moment, then stated, "I'd like a good wife."

"You had a good wife."

He laughed harshly. "I was too young to know it then and she left me. We had a small Flair bond. I knew when she died several years ago. But she gave me a fine son." Again, his gaze slid in Ilex's direction. "I don't have a HeartMate in this life and whatever you may say, I'd want one. *Everyone* wants a HeartMate. But I'd settle for a good woman, a good marriage, and there's more chance of finding that here in Druida."

Something about his brother's speech didn't ring quite true, but Ilex couldn't discern what it was, and wouldn't probe.

"I do want something of you," Ilex said. "I want you to fight for your heritage. I want you to reclaim the estate and the title. I want it to be respected again."

Meyar just stared at him, hands jammed in Commoner trous pockets. He gazed up at the house. "I don't know if I have the Flair or energy to fight for that. Or the gilt to restore the place."

"I'll help. She recently siphoned off my savings as fee for an amulet for my lady, so there's gilt in the household account."

Shaking his head, Meyar muttered, "More fool you."

In a low tone, Ilex said, "The Residence is barely alive."

His brother flinched.

"I know someone who can help restore it for us. Probably for a minimal fee."

"I don't know," Meyar whispered, but there was yearning in his gaze fixed on the Residence. "What do we do with her?"

They fell silent.

"Her birth Family wouldn't want her back," Ilex said.

Nearly howling with laughter, Meyar gasped between chortles, "Find a solution to that problem, brother, and I'll press my claim."

Ilex shot out an arm. "Thank you for scrying, for coming."

Meyar clasped his wrist. "You are welcome. I'll stay. For a while."

He meant until Ilex's presentiment came true or not.

"And thank you for that. Three thanks . . . a charm."

"Good." Meyar was looking up at the house again. "I think we'll need it." He hesitated, then turned and wrapped Ilex in a bear hug. "I'm glad you called me down our Familial bond. I don't know that I'd have contacted you."

It was good to have his brother back in town, even if it meant a fight.

Yet as he watched Meyar teleport away, Ilex decided to walk to Landing Park one more time.

The poppet in his pocket stirred at the end of the street. He tensed. Though he quartered the area, nothing more happened. He'd missed the man.

Ilex was disrobing and down to his loincloth when Trif came dancing into his bedroom, a wide smile on her face, carrying a bottle of champagne in one hand. Ilex was sure the movement couldn't be good for the wine, but said nothing to dim her pleasure.

"Hmmmm," Trif said, staring at his chest. He was glad she hadn't glanced lower, her presence was having the typical effect on his body. He reached into the wardrobe and took out a robe, slipped it over his head.

"Aww, too bad," she said, a sparkle in her eyes. He didn't trust that look and took a step back, ran into the frame of the bedsponge platform. She laughed.

"You are definitely in a better mood than yesterday," he murmured.

Nodding, she waggled the bottle. "Vinni T'Vine gave it to me." She looked down at it. It was older than she was and she hoped it was still good. Ilex had tensed at the mention of the young prophet's name. Her HeartMate was definitely sensitive about foresight. She'd have to accept that, among his other faults—his overprotectiveness and stubbornness.

He cleared his throat. "Did Vinni say anything?"

She looked at him, exuding limpid innocence. She wasn't going to admit that Vinni told her to keep pursuing Ilex. "He said the future regarding you was still changeable." She frowned. "I got the idea that you're always going to be problematic for him and he doesn't like it."

"Ah," he said, and made to move past her into his mainspace.

She stepped to stand solidly in his way. "We're celebrating."

"What?"

Shrugging, she said, "Many things. Sex with our HeartMates." She sent him a sly glance from under her lashes, let her gaze wander down his body like a caress. When she saw his arousal, she smiled. And daintily licked her lips.

His mouth went dry and he suddenly wanted the champagne. He reached out and snagged the bottle, tested it with his Flair. Definitely explosive. "If you'll let me by, I'll take this to the kitchen."

With widened eyes and raised brows, she backed out of the bedroom and gestured. "Go ahead." When he passed by her, he *knew* she stared at his ass, had a hot image of them moving together on a bedsponge sizzle from her mind to his. His shaft got harder until his loincloth chafed.

He cudgeled his mind for conversation. "You said, 'Many things.' What else?"

"Um . . . Mitchella told me today that Straif Blackthorn is coming home."

"To help with the murders, yes," Ilex said. When she made a sound of surprise, he glanced back at her. "You didn't know."

"Mitchella didn't say."

"Perhaps she doesn't know. I have not been informed exactly to whom the FirstFamilies are disseminating our reports." He sent a variation of the calming spell to the wine inside the bottle, settling it so that the cork would not blow a hole in the ceiling.

"And—and real good news. Mitchella and Straif have reached the top of the list of the Saille House for Orphans to adopt an infant!"

A wave of pure yearning surged through him To have a HeartMate and children, a Family and a future! He had only borrowed time. He focused on gently removing the cork with a touch of Flair. When he thought his smile would be easy instead of a rictus, he turned back to Trif.

"Oh, Ilex!" She rushed to him, held him tightly, and he

could only shut his eyes at the emotion roiling inside him. Not lust, or not simply lust, but the warmth of being loved, of loving. And the hard, twisted ache of anticipated loss. He didn't know how long he could live with the knowledge that what he wanted could never be.

Of course, if his premonition was right, he wouldn't be living long at all—a couple of months perhaps.

He gloried in the press of her body against him, savored every sensation—the scent of her hair, how every centimeter of her felt next to his. He'd stand like this, bathed in her aura, the tingling of her Flair permeating him, forever.

Then she was kissing his neck, laving it with her tongue, nipping, and sexual need banished all else. And he was grateful. Those other hungers he could never satisfy—this . . . He shoved the bottle on the counter with a ringing clatter as it jostled against glasses.

His hands went to her derriere and pulled her close until her mound nestled against his rigid shaft. He opened his eyes to see hers, dark green with desire. He moved until he pressed her against a wall.

"Clothes gone," she breathed, and she lifted herself and plunged down on him, and she was wet and tight and wild in his arms, shivering and crying out his name.

Passion ruled. He tried to slow down, set his hands under her thighs so he could move her more slowly, more deliberately, increasing their pleasure. His muscles trembled and all feeling went to his cock, the lingering withdrawal from her, the sweet slide back. A flood of heated need pulsed from her to him.

"Ilex, Ilex, Ilex!" she screamed, and his name on her lips snapped his control. He plunged again and again, matching his strokes to their panting breaths, faster, faster, until she clamped and shuddered around him and he shattered.

And let the golden rope of the HeartBond caress him one excruciatingly delicious instant before pushing it away.

He held her against the wall, breathing in the scent of her, the scent of them that was the best fragrance of the world.

Her head lay on his shoulder and her tongue licked his neck again so that he surged into her one more time with energy he didn't know he had. Still holding her, her legs wrapped around his waist, he strode to the bedroom and they fell onto the bedsponge.

Trif giggled and again he arched into her.

"Goddess," he groaned.

"Thank you," she said.

He managed a laugh. She was a goddess—the goddess as Maiden. He didn't want to think about that—that he'd never see her as goddess as Matron or Wise Woman—and brushed her tangled hair from her face. She glowed with beauty.

"I love—" she started.

Ilex put a palm over her mouth. "Don't say it."

Her eyes flashed and she pushed his fingers away. Pushed him away until he withdrew from her and was cold.

She was hot. Anger rippled from her. "Why not? I'm not afraid of my feelings. Not afraid of the future, and not afraid of the *now.* I love you." She poked him in the chest. "And you love me. I can feel it, even if you don't give me the words." She rolled off the bed and went into the bathroom. He heard the waterfall whoosh down over the stone ledge, and flung an arm across his eyes so he wouldn't imagine her slick and wet.

A futile hope. With another groan—this one of surrender, he joined her.

Trif had her eyes closed, and was washing her hair with the liquid herbal soap that Ilex usually smelled of, when a pair of masculine hands set around her waist and lifted her with steady solidity. Her lids opened just in time to see his firm jaw, then his soft lips before his mouth took hers.

She melted, opening her mouth for the thrust of his tongue, shivering as his chest hair rasped against her tender nipples. Her sex clenched as need ravaged her, need for this man. Forever.

Her hands slid along his broad shoulders, cupped around his upper arms. She whimpered in delight at the strength of him. He opened his mouth and she explored it, treasuring the intimate taste of Ilex.

When she pushed against him, he lowered her. "Let me wash you," she said, breathless.

He smiled and it stunned her, it was so rare. She set a hand against the rock-sheeted wall and blinked at him.

To her, he was simply beautiful, a man in his prime. She'd

woo him, and tonight she'd touch him—know him better than she had any man, make him more aware of her than he had been of any woman.

She soaped her hands and started with his feet. They were long and narrow, elegant, like the rest of him. He curled his toes at her touch and she chuckled.

Sweeping her hands up, she washed his legs—not too hairy, none of him was too hairy, but just right. Enough hair for texture to tease her palms and the rest of her.

His thighs were long, solid muscle. She soaped and rinsed them, front and back, then stepped closer to cup her hands around his butt. Just as muscular as the rest of him. She glanced up, and found his arms braced against the wall behind her and his eyes closed.

The expression on his face caught her. There was intense concentration, a deep longing . . . and resignation. As if he knew the moments with her would end all too soon and be all too short.

She battered his pessimism with her own joy—and they both tended to live in the moment, though for different reasons. As she sent the bubbling sweet delight she got from just stroking him through their connection, a slight smile formed on his lips.

Good.

Glancing down, she saw he was ready for her and she wanted to tease. So she did. Gently, she stroked him, washed all of him, smiled at the changes in his body, the fine tension in his muscles. She petted him until he groaned and whispered her name.

Once again, she looked up and found his eyes blazing. "Having fun?" he rasped.

She tried an innocent look. "Some. But I want more." She giggled. "That's what Greyku is always saying. 'More.' "

He stared down at her, his gaze lingering on her breasts and her nipples, peaked from the cool air, contracted further. An aching need spread from her core until her breasts felt heavy—and she hungered for his touch. She twined her arms around his neck. "Ilex."

"No." He straightened, put his hands on her waist, and set her gently aside. "Waterfall off. Wind on."

A hot breeze swirled around her, drying her. She scowled. "I don't want wind to caress me. I want your hands. I want more."

He linked fingers with hers. "I am not going to take you against another wall."

She raised her brows. "No? What do you have against walls?"

She thought she heard him grinding his teeth. He stepped over the lip of stone around the waterfall area and tugged at her. The wind followed them through the small room, but with every step he hurried faster. When they reached his bedroom, he picked her up and tossed her on the sponge.

"Ilex!"

But she could say no more because his body was over hers, his tongue in her mouth. With one swift plunge, he was inside her filling her with exquisite pleasure. He stopped. A *very* bad habit of his. It drove her wild.

Arching her hips, rotating them, had him groaning aloud and sending her intimate whispers mentally. *Let me stay inside you, know you. Keep you.*

I want to move!

He withdrew slightly, slid again, prodded one particular spot that sent wicked need to every nerve. *More!*

Yes, more.

Again and again he surged inside her, and she was aware of only him, the muscles of his back flexing under her fingers, his iron thighs spreading her legs, the salty taste of his throat on her tongue.

One . . . last . . . time, he sent to her, and she sensed the explosion of rapture to come, the loosening of his control.

Heady, delicious orgasm hit her. She screamed, loud and long. He did too, and they flew through the universe bursting with stars. She wrapped him with the golden HeartBond and he slipped away from it.

A pulse of tender yearning mixed with suffering came back to her.

"Dark," he said, and the room turned into night. He rolled with her to their sides, then stroked her hair. "Sleep." It wasn't an order, but she found lying in his arms was all she wanted.

"You too."

"Yes."

They fell asleep together, wrapped around each other, heedless of everything else.

Until she walked through his dreams.

Twenty-four

She walked through his dream and his feelings impinged upon her. Fog drifted down a hall that seemed nothing but doors. As Ilex turned to face one, dread filled him until the suspense of being outside was worse than facing what was inside. His hand shook as he set it on the latch. A slight push and the door swung open to a bright, misty place. A place he loved to be.

Noises rushed out, loud cacophony, happening instantaneously. Yowls, a loud metallic ring, then a crash, a horrible bang and thud. Screeching!

Dream Ilex floated through the door. His gaze went to a shadowy area of red clay tiles. Everything focused. Dressed in guardsman brown, his body lay on the floor. The side of his head was broken, face covered with red, sticky blood. Near him was a golden metallic curve he strove to identify and understand. His shoulders twitched with a sensation of being watched by monstrous eyes.

Another scream.

He whipped around and Trif saw herself, hands covering her chest. "HeartMate!" she shrieked, and collapsed. She lay in the sunlight, eyes wide open, unseeing, dead, lengths away from her lover.

Pain shredded Dream Ilex. He covered his eyes, shrank back. "No, no, no!" *I've killed her* echoed in his mind and grief swallowed him.

He shot up straight in bed, sitting beside her, panting.

Wrenched awake, she shuddered where she lay. She could scent his night-panic sweat, but couldn't move. The vision had been too horrible.

She knew it had been a real, Flaired vision like her own of the past. And the quality of it had made it seem all too true. She must have made a noise because Ilex turned to her, his voice calm and steady in the dark. "Trif, darling. What can I do for you?"

Love me.

He shivered. *In a moment.*

Clearing her throat, she said aloud, "In that case, I'd like water."

"Two cylinders of water," he snapped, then held one out to her. She touched it, cold from the no-time, and looked around. His windows faced the garden courtyard and the curtains were open. No shields coated the glass. Moonlight slanted inside, bright enough to see the dampness on his back.

Sitting up, she ran her thumb across the top of the cylinder and it disappeared. The cool water soothed her throat, and she wondered if she'd screamed from the vision, and if that was what had awakened them. She squirmed a little at the idea of being so childish.

Without looking at her, Ilex said, "You were there in my premonition. You *saw* too." He drank.

"Yes. Nothing too detailed." She scooted up to sit beside him, crossed her legs. She'd have touched him, but her hands were cold from the cylinder.

"That's always the way. Not enough to guard against, to avoid. To *fight*. Now you know." His eyes were in shadow, and he'd narrowed the bond between them to a small strand.

"I know what you see." She set the cylinder on the top of the box headboard and rocked to her knees, then wrapped her arms around him. He was warm and substantial and alive, and she found that in trying to comfort him, she received comfort from just hearing his heart beat. "I know what you see," she repeated. "But I don't know that it's true. And neither do you."

After one last swallow, he sent the cylinder away and drew her onto his lap, rubbing his face against her hair. "That was the worst vision I've ever had of my death," he said starkly. "Because you were there. I've never seen you there before."

"Well, I didn't like my part. I can't think I'd just crumple like that."

"Who knows how death claims HeartMates? Some say it is the despair of being cut off from the HeartBond, or the sheer shock of the sudden rendering of the bond kills the other."

She cuddled closer. "I've never seen HeartMates die."

"I saw one die once, but the other didn't follow immediately." His mouth moved against her head and she knew he grimaced. "It took her two more weeks to fade away, I heard. But now you've seen and now you know why I . . . avoid . . . the HeartBond."

She sat in silence for a moment; then she met his steady blue-gray eyes. "I grant you that the dream was more than a dream, but I won't accept that it is a premonition that can't be changed." She lifted her chin.

He closed his eyes, then opened them, and they had turned to stormy gray. "Each time you throw me the HeartBond it gets harder for me to resist—"

"Good."

"—and I think it is harder for you to accept that I won't bond with you."

"Yes." She sat up straight. "But I'm a mature adult. I don't expect my own way all the time. I've experienced rejection before. I don't like it, but I can live with it."

"Can you? Can we?"

"I'm not giving up yet."

He just shook his head.

"You are looking too sober," she said, and jumped him.

He smiled as he toppled over, and then she seduced him and did her best to drive them both mad with passion.

He still refused the HeartBond.

Ilex rose early and dressed, leaving Trif sleeping in his bed. She looked good there, natural, as if she should always be there. But the vision that they'd shared had renewed his determination. He would die, but he would not take her with him.

He would not cut her life short. Yet he sensed that this affair between them would be brief too.

She was young and impatient. He wondered how long she would stay with him, how soon she would tire of his shields against the HeartBond. Even now he sensed the mental and emotional cord that linked them beginning to fray. It seemed their connection wasn't as strong or as pure as it had been even the night before.

He had cherished every moment with her, and would continue to do so until she walked away.

Bespelling a calendar ball to wake Trif in good time for her morning activities, he opened the bedroom door and found a small, absurdly multi-tinted kitten snoozing on the threshold. He scooped her up with one hand. Greyku snuffled and opened one blue eye. *Sire Zanth runs far, hunts hard. I am very tired. Couldn't even 'port through the door.*

He stroked her soft kitten fur—would he be alive to see her grow into a cat? He carried her to the bedsponge and put her near Trif. The kitten's purr followed him back out the door, and he smiled at the simple pleasure of feeling her soft fur and hearing her small rumble of pleasure.

At the guardhouse, he scried Tinne Holly. To his surprise, the young man answered immediately, looking worn. "Here."

"Greetyou, Tinne."

Tinne's face relaxed a little. "Greetyou, Ilex. Can I do something for you?"

Ilex hesitated, then set the ball rolling in the direction he wanted. "As we discussed earlier, all the victims of this cult are young Noble women and men who have unstable Flair and recurring echoes of their Second Passage. Do you know anyone else this applies to?"

Eyes sharpening, Tinne murmured, "You're going to bait a trap?"

"Samhain is just a couple of days away. It's a powerful day in our religion. I can only extrapolate that it would be equally powerful for those who attempt black magic."

"You're right. Offhand, I don't know of anyone else. No one else in my crowd, that's for sure. I'll think about it. Do you want me to make discreet inquiries?"

"Very, very discreet."

Tinne nodded. "I'll do that."

"Blessings."

"And to you too." Tinne ended the scry.

That morning, Ilex visited the various rooms the guards believed to be the best venues for another dark ritual. In every one he left a tiny Flair trip wire, sometimes two—one on the door and one to be triggered when frankincense was burned. The herb was uncommon and expensive.

He returned to his office and recorded his report, gave one to Sawyr, who grumbled as he forwarded it to the FirstFamilies. Both he and Sawyr spent some time roughing out various scenarios to catch the cult members by using Noble bait. Neither of them was happy at the thought.

"Nobles can't be trusted," Sawyr ended. "They think they know everything."

"Then we'll just inform the young person that they must follow our orders . . . advice."

Sawyr snorted. "Good luck."

Restless, Ilex could think of nothing better than to once again visit the places where the bodies had been left, all of them except the last on their Families' estates. The emotional Healers who had worked with the victims' Families had advised them to close their main Residences and move to their country houses, so the estates were deserted.

He stretched his senses and his Flair to the limit, but discovered nothing new.

As was common now, he checked his bond with Trif. Her day was progressing much smoother than his and he was glad of it.

Returning to his office, he leaned back in his chair and entered a light trance, trying to put what he knew together so he could find and stop these fliggers before they struck again. He visualized the list he'd made of all the people he'd brushed against in the time period—after Ginger's death and before Calla's, when he'd recognized the trace of a murderer.

Unfortunately, that included his time at the Maypole, and though he hadn't "met" everyone there, his subconscious Flair had picked up and catalogued every person.

Ilex's scrybowl rang. Loudly, persistently, flashing dark

blue-purple-black. He stared at it. Another FirstFamily Lord about to interfere. There was only one whose heraldry contained those particular colors, young Vinni T'Vine, the prophet.

Ilex wondered if the boy was going to say anything about Ilex's premonition. Whether Vinni had foreshadowings regarding the murders. Like most, perhaps even more than most, Ilex tended to avoid the prophet. He was too uncanny. Which was why his scry was so loud and obnoxious.

Ilex touched the tip of his forefinger nail to the bowl. That was all it took to have Vinni's image materializing in the water mist above the bowl, frowning. He turned his head, taking in Ilex's office. "Close your door. I'll be there transnow." He signed off before Ilex could reply.

Shrugging, Ilex stood and walked from his desk to the door, shut it, and bespelled it for privacy so that even the Chief wouldn't know what was going on.

With a small "pop," Vinni materialized *sitting* in the visitor's chair.

Good Flair. But from all reports and rumors, the young T'Vine was the strongest Flaired person on Celta. Still keeping his hand on the door latch, Ilex asked, "What can I do for you?"

For once, the eleven-year-old had no flip comment. His eyes were deep blue bordering on purple, and pure fear pulsed from him.

Ilex went over and crouched before him. "How can I help?"

The boy gulped and gulped again. With a snap of his wrist, Ilex summoned a cylinder of water for Vinni. He took it in both hands and drank. "I read the reports of the cult killings," he said.

Ilex wanted to swear, but not in front of the child. He straightened and put a hand on the boy's shoulder. "I'm sorry. You shouldn't have."

"I had to know! Find out what was going on." He plunked the cylinder onto Ilex's desk, not noticing the water slopping over the rim. Slipping out from under Ilex's hand, he paced the room—a serious boy with title and Flair and concerns that more befit a mid-aged man. Vinni stopped in a corner and turned, lifting his gaze to Ilex.

"You said that you'd asked Tinne Holly which person was most at risk from the murderers." His voice rose, and Ilex kept an eye on him.

"That's right."

Vinni paced the small office again. "There isn't one. No one struggling with their Second Passage." The boy's hands fisted. "They've already taken them all." Something like a whimper escaped him. "All. And I couldn't stop it."

"Pardon me, GreatLord T'Vine, but your age precludes you from stopping adult murderers."

"I should have been able to *see*! I didn't even know something dreadful was going on until the second murder!" His voice caught on a sob.

"So you didn't foresee the murders?" demanded Ilex.

"No."

"You got no solid visions?"

"No!"

Ilex went over to the boy and picked him up and plunked him to sit on the edge of the desk. "Then why do you think you could have stopped what happened? How can you demand so much of yourself and your Flair?"

"I am *the prophet*." His changeable eyes were hazel now.

Pulling up the visitor's chair, Ilex sat in front of the boy. Vinni was now physically at a higher level than himself. Ilex didn't think Vinni was often in such a position with an adult. At a greater level in Flair, in foresight, but not physically.

"You can only work with what you are given. And in this instance you were given nothing." He handed the boy the water again and watched him sip. "You're very mature for your age, but you aren't a deity. You aren't all-knowing, all-seeing. You're a boy, a human being. You won't *see* events. Or you'll misinterpret what you *see*. It's human nature. So get accustomed to it."

They stared at each other for several breaths and Vinni's eyes stayed the hazel hue. "Thank you." He took a deep breath, then another. "There isn't a good victim for the killers—Noble with great, unstable Flair, having problems during their Second Passage. But there is . . . there is someone. . . ."

"You?" Ilex asked gently.

Drinking, Vinni shook his head. He finished the draught and wiped his hand across his mouth. "No. I won't have Passages.

My Flair will grow, but . . ." He shrugged. "I just won't. Passages are not for me in this lifetime. My Flair will always be under control and stable."

"Who then?"

Vinni licked his lips. "My HeartMate, Avellana Hazel."

Ilex stilled to immobility. "She's only five."

"Yes," Vinni said, and his voice had risen to a squeak again. "She had a head injury when she was three. Her Flair will be unstable until we HeartBond." He waved. "Many years in the future. If she lives through her Passages." He turned now-dark-blue eyes to Ilex. "Her Flair is stronger than mine. She is the perfect victim. Little. Female. Has a Fam. I wish I hadn't convinced her to get a Fam."

"Have you told the Hazels?"

"They won't listen to me. Not me as Vinni. They'll listen to you."

"I'll make sure they take Avellana away from Druida."

Vinni relaxed a little. "Good. You have many links with the FirstFamilies—distant relative of the Hollys, HeartMate of Trif Clover, who is connected to the Blackthorns. You know Straif Blackthorn well, refused to kill Captain Elder, worked with T'Ash." Vinni nodded. "They'll listen to you." He bit his lower lip. "Will you tell the Hazels now? While I'm here?"

"Yes." Ilex went to sit behind his desk and Vinni took the visitor's chair.

"D'Hazel Residence," Ilex said. "Request communication with D'Hazel herself. Guardsman Ilex Winterberry."

The GreatLady appeared above the scrybowl. "Here," she said. She looked strained. Ilex wondered how many of the FirstFamilies were secretly overwhelmed by the case.

"Greetyou, GreatLady."

"What do you want?" It wasn't like her to be rude.

"I have been informed of a threat to your daughter."

"Avellana, our Avellana?" she gasped.

"Yes. And you may have heard that I have certain presentiments."

"Yes! We'll go away. Today."

"Before Samhain."

"At once. We'll leave at once," she said, and the scrybowl water rippled as she ended the spell.

Head tilted, Vinni looked at Ilex. The boy seemed much more in control. "Now for the second reason I came to you."

"Yes?"

"I want to be bait."

"What!"

"That's the best way to stop these killings." His young face set in grim lines. "No one knows the consistency of my Flair. We can spread the word that it's unstable." He tapped the corner of one eye. "My eyes change, so people think my Flair is irregular. It's not. I haven't lost control of it for two years."

"I don't think—"

Vinni went on persuasively. "They'll underestimate me. No one knows the limits of my Flair."

"They'll drug you, and they may *overestimate* the dosage."

"I want to do it. I insist."

Ilex leaned forward. "Do you? And have you had a foreseeing of *this*?"

At his words, Vinni's eyes glazed—and became gold-green. A vision was upon him.

Softly, softly, Ilex said, "And do you see success for this action of using yourself as bait?"

Vinni trembled violently.

Ilex sprang from his desk and caught the boy close.

Colors, shapes, rushed by him—the blackness of the night sky and hurtling stars, twinmoons so bright they hurt his eyes, red of fury, piss-yellow terror.

Both of them shook; then the vision passed and feeling uncommonly weak, Ilex placed Vinni back in the chair, then tossed him a softleaf to wipe his perspiring face, as Ilex did himself. Keeping himself well in hand, Ilex said, "So?"

Rubbing his face with the softleaf, Vinni blew out a breath. "You didn't get that?"

"No, thank the Lady and Lord."

A crafty look came over Vinni's face.

"Don't even think about lying. I've been a guardsman for many years. You can't lie to me."

His shoulders sagged a little. "Guess not." Then he frowned. "I didn't get it all either, but . . . me being bait is *right*." He glanced up, his eyes hazel. "I will come to no harm. *This*

I know." Leaning back, he crossed his arms, as if challenging Ilex to disbelieve him.

The images of Vinni's vision had been couched in the symbolism that specifically spoke to the boy. Yet from what Ilex had felt, nothing in the vision indicated danger to Vinni. The emotions of fury and terror had surrounded the young Lord, but had not been his or threatened him.

"What of your Fam?" Ilex asked. "That housefluff has been traumatized enough."

Vinni licked his lips. "I've thought of that. I found a regular housefluff that looks like my Fam." He glanced away, and Ilex received a clear throb of love between Vinni and his Fam. "It will not be good for the housefluff, but it won't be as terrifying as it would be for my Fam. And people don't always recognize when a housefluff is a Fam."

"You are a minor," Ilex said.

"I *am* a GreatLord." He uncrossed his arms and threw his shoulders back.

"Your Family guards—" Just as Ilex said that, a pounding came on the door.

"Guardsman Winterberry!" Chief Sawyr roared. "There are several guards wearing T'Vine colors here to see you—and the GreatLord."

Vinni sighed. "They found me. They always find me too soon."

Ilex tapped his fingers on his desk. "I think we can work with them." He smiled. "I know a couple. If they weren't your Family, they'd be Druida guardsmen."

"We can do it?"

"We need to do something. Let's see what we can put together."

Twenty-five

As usual these days, Ilex had pushed himself as hard as possible, used up most his Flair, and returned home very late. He was weary, but his step still lightened when he entered MidClass Lodge and knew Trif awaited him. He glanced at his wrist timer and made up his mind. It wasn't too late for a romantic dinner. Hurrying into his apartment, he chanted the verses that would set the stage for him to show Trif how much he cherished her.

When he was finished with a brief stand under the waterfall and dressing in casual trous and tunic, he entered the mainspace. A slight illusion spell had transformed his ordinary furnishings into priceless antiques—a Funchal carved dining table of gleaming reddwood, with a shimmering cloth and napkins of silkeen gold. Pale green celedon china plates and transparent green wineglasses stood on the table, perfect.

At that moment Trif rapped on his door. He smiled at her usual impatience. With a Word, he lit a fat green candle that smelled like clover.

He opened the door and stepped back with a wide gesture for her to come in. "I'll have dinner ready in a moment," he said, enjoying the way her eyes widened and mouth dropped.

He closed the door and took her hand. "My lovely Trif." He kissed her fingers.

"What . . . what is this?"

He stiffened. "I know I haven't shown you much tenderness or romance. It's exactly what it seems, a dinner for two. I don't see Greyku."

"Hmmm? Oh, she and your Fam are exploring the beach. She heard from Zanth last night that if a cat is quick and cunning, she can catch sand burrowers, which are apparently quite tasty. She enjoyed hunting last night and wants more." Slowly, Trif turned around, staring at the windows, which now had glowing murals painted on them in rich hues, then at the set table and candle.

"I didn't want to waste that champagne we never tasted last night," he said, drawing her further into the room and tasting her wrist, the inner skin of her elbow that held her flavor, the curve of her neck.

"Ilex." She sighed his name and she felt her simple pleasure in being romanced—and an undertone of sparkling anticipation that made his body go hot and hard.

"You are so beautiful." So young. So fresh.

"No, I'm n—that is, thank you."

"You're very welcome. And it's the truth."

"I'm not dressed for this." She swept a hand down her body, and Ilex barely noted the old, soft, shapeless robedress. Instead, he saw her high, round breasts, her full hips.

"You're perfect."

She laughed and patted his cheek. He liked how her fingers lingered a bit before she stepped back. "No, I'm not, and you know it."

He took both her hands. "In this moment, there is nothing more perfect to me than you."

Her smile trembled on her lips, her lashes lowered, but he thought he saw the sheen of moisture. "Thank you," she said.

Kissing one of her hands, then the other, he led her to the table and seated her. He went into the kitchen and pulled the champagne bottle from the cooler. It had had time to settle a little and would be all the better for that. He poured the wine in her glass, his own. "To—" Why hadn't he thought of the damn toast before? To love? They loved, but it would not last. To HeartMates? That was true, but a conflict between them. To life? Both of them knew how short he expected his own to be. He kept a smile on his face, clinked her glass gently. "To tonight."

She picked up the wineglass with an unsteady hand. "To tonight," she barely whispered.

He turned back to the no-time and opened the heated-foods section, pulling out a platter with slices of roasted turkey, covered in rich gravy, all of it steaming. Another dish held mixed vegetables. He placed them on the table and sat opposite her, noticed her glass was half empty. "Do you like the wine?"

"It is the best I've ever tasted."

"I think Vinni T'Vine is quite expert already in his field."

Her fork stilled on the way to her mouth. "In prophecy?"

"In knowing wine." He did *not* want to talk about premonitions.

She nodded and finished her bite. "Hmmm. This is wonderful. Did you make it?"

"No, I've had the meal for a while, awaiting a special occasion. Tonight I wanted things to be . . . very special . . . between us." Until he said that, he didn't realize that he was sure he would not live another full month. No need to tell her. He wished he had even better food to serve her.

The evening passed in a dream for Trif—the best night of her life, and she fully intended for the rest of the dark hours to be full of rapture and ecstasy with Ilex.

They loved with tenderness and care, gentle touches and long, quiet sighs, until the last moment, when they held on tight to each other and climaxed together.

Throughout the night he'd turn to her, need in every movement, or she'd lie awake and watching him in the moonslight, stroking him.

Each time she'd crafted the HeartBond and thrown it to him, his shields had gotten taller and stronger . . . and their connection had shrunk. A few more times and they'd be little more than casual lovers.

And each time she became more and more enraptured with him . . . losing herself in him, wanting nothing but him. It was frightening.

By the morning, her heart had filled with tears yet when he reached for her, she couldn't deny him.

The sun rose and the colors of dawn filtered into the room, tinting the white walls with pale pastels of the glow. As the light grew stronger, so did her love. The love that she'd confessed but he had never spoken of. His hands were on her, bringing her mindless joy, arousing her with a few caresses of skillful fingers until she needed, needed, needed. Like he was an addiction.

He thrust into her and flung his head back on an orgasmic cry. He *gave* to her, his seed and his unaddicted love, and the whirlwind of his climax swept her away into her own until she shattered—and flung out the HeartBond.

Once again, he did not grasp it, did not want it. He loved her, and she *felt* that, but he did not accept the whole of her. He would not merge with her in all ways. Even as she gasped out her own transcendental passion, a tiny core of her wept in rejection and withdrew from him.

Ilex rolled and took her with him, holding her tight.

She hurt, a huge ache that filled her, that she couldn't banish any longer. And she knew. Being with Ilex was now more painful than being without him. She couldn't keep offering all of herself and being refused. He had chosen this path for them and despite all the loving between them, he had not changed his mind.

Now she knew what he had been doing the night before with the lovely dinner and the sweet lovemaking. Unconsciously, he'd been saying good-bye. From their bond, she knew he was completely certain that his death drew near—and he'd been conditioned by his visions throughout his life to believe in it. His shields were strong and deep, and she couldn't get through them, no matter how she tried. Had she been a fool to hope, deep in her heart, that he might ever let those shields down for her?

No. She'd brought the pain upon herself, but she'd had to understand that there was no changing him, not with sex, not with loving, not with their growing connection. She would have always wondered if they might have made a HeartMate marriage had she walked away earlier.

He was so strong. He would keep his shield up against her

forever. She had to accept that now, that she couldn't change their circumstances, only he could. It went against her nature, to fail in a fight for what she wanted so desperately, but she had.

And she'd wanted to know what HeartMate loving was—she'd had a touch of that, had experienced sex and affection and closeness with Ilex. She was sure she wouldn't regret that in the future. When this excruciating pain that racked her went away.

They could not be together anymore. She held him, eyes as dry as her heart was empty, storing memories of the heat of him, the texture of his skin, the music of his breathing.

Finally, it was time to rise. She slipped from the bedsponge and stared down at Ilex. He'd thrown the covers off and she had a full view of his prone muscular body. Broad shoulders, tight butt, strong legs. His face was turned toward her, relaxed in sleep. Her heart jolted, then twisted as her hands clenched. She couldn't be his lover anymore, couldn't continue to be rejected. It just hurt too much.

Still, the decision caused a tremor in her nerves that rippled through her whole body.

Ilex awoke with a start, and she knew he'd felt her distress even in his dreams. His blue-gray eyes focused on her and he rolled to sit up. "What's wrong."

"I can't anymore, Ilex."

His jaw flexed and though his pose was still casual, tension delineated his muscles and throbbed through their bond to her. "No?" he said softly.

He'd expected this? Probably, always the pessimist.

Trif moistened her lips. Her voice still emerged raw through a dry throat. "We make love, but we—don't . . ." She lifted helpless hands. "We merge in body, in mind, in emotion, but you keep a shield up, not accepting the HeartBond that flies from my soul to yours." She ended on a whisper. "I can't be with you anymore."

He watched with an impassive gaze that told her nothing, shrank the bond between them to a filament, but his pain equaled hers. She fumbled her clothes on and went to the door of his bedroom. Glancing into the mainspace, she saw the illusion of romantic fantasy was gone.

His hands yanked the linens over his nude body and kept a

fisted hold on the cover. "I told you why I won't accept the HeartBond."

Anger flashed, and she was glad of it. She lifted her chin. "And I didn't like your reasoning, and don't now. But I pushed on anyway. My mistake."

Inclining his head, he took a step backward. "As you say."

The awful devastation vibrated between them, hurting him, hurting her, tearing them apart. Shattering both of them? She wrapped her arms around herself. "Can't you see that I *hurt*? I could hurt no more if you died this instant. Why must we live our lives anticipating a fate which might not come to pass?"

"Because you will *live*. You will not die. I will not be the cause of your death." For a moment, his face showed stark pain; then he swallowed and glanced aside.

She paced forward. "I tell you, I am willing to risk your vision! You think living without you could ever be easy?" Her fist pounded her chest. "What if we HeartBonded and *I* was the one to die first?"

"Then I would welcome death," he stated as fact. "We've had this argument before. I haven't changed my position. I. Will. Not. Be. The. Cause. Of. Your. Death. *Ever.*"

His scent drifted to her, spice and man and sex. She shuddered at all the emotions whipping through her; then the tornado stopped and left her hopeless. Only pain existed. She turned away, setting one foot in front of the other to leave. "You already have killed me inside."

Silence hung heavy in the apartment, but the sharpness of her senses faded, dying as the candle of vitality she'd always treasured flickered and went out.

"You're young. You'll heal," his voice rasped as she hurried to the door.

"I'll move to Clover Compound by the end of the week. Please try and avoid me like you did so well before. Grant me that much. So I can *heal*." She didn't think she ever would. Now, with deft precision, she narrowed the bond between them to a filament. It would always be there, but she'd do her best to ignore it. As he would.

She barely made it into her rooms before a silent scream tore from her.

Her Flair spiked, out of control. She collapsed and let the

vision of the past—and soldiers dying slowly in an ancient Earth war—overtake her.

She gradually emerged from the daze when Greyku started licking her face—salty with perspiration, she supposed. Blinking, she rose to one elbow and stretched, a few minor twinges from falling onto the carpet, but not many.

Greyku increased her purr and the sound innately soothed Trif. Sitting up, she scooted until her back was supported by the twoseat and Greyku hopped onto her lap.

Bad time with FamMan.

"Yes." Her voice was hoarse. From tears? Screams? A combination of both?

Trif hurt. As much as she wanted to, she couldn't run to her family. They'd worm the whole story out of her and she couldn't bear that. What they might do to Ilex, she didn't know—but sensed some of the men, maybe her own father, would be on his side.

She ached as if she'd been hollowed out and no heart remained. She couldn't even think about playing music. How could she handle her lessons today?

Flexing her fingers, she found they reacted well. She snapped them and her tin whistle appeared on her lap next to the kitten, who grinned.

Play My tune.

Trif placed Greyku on the floor so she could dance, and took a chair. After Trif cleared her throat, she played "Greyku's Jig." Her fingers were quick and skilled. The tune sounded well, technically. Only musicians would understand that it had no heart breath behind it. Would this last forever? Had he stolen her music from her?

No. That was wrong. *She* had made the decision. Her head flopped back against the chair. They belonged together, and he had to learn that. She held onto the hope that he would come to her. He had to accept that they were HeartMates. No more lovers or loving until he did. Tears escaped her eyes and leaked down her face. Being alone was too much.

She went over to her scrybowl and fury gripped her. How *dare* he be so *stupid.* So stubborn, so . . . She took the little china bowl and dashed it against the tile floor of the scrybowl area. The smash sounded great, very satisfying. She replayed the noise in her head, smiling. Yes, an excellent sound, and it had relieved her feelings.

Slivers might hurt My paws, Greyku said disapprovingly, eyeing the tile area.

Hands on hips, Trif surveyed the damage as anger drained from her. The scrybowl was shattered beyond repair and she realized that she'd never liked it. Like much of her furniture, it had been passed down from someone else.

Gathering her Flair, she kept a vision of the repairs she wanted in her head. She should be able to do this. Just as she released it, her Flair surged out of her control. She watched, appalled, as carpet ripped back from the main area and the tile, once only under the scrybowl, replicated itself to the wall. The tile area now extended from the threshold of her bedroom door well into her living room, about sixty centimeters.

To avoid the cold tile, she'd have to step over it. She'd have to fix this before she moved out in a week. Or someone would. She'd thought she was getting *better* at managing her Flair.

Greyku rubbed against her ankles. *FamMan will come back.*

Trif could only pray that was so. Well, one good thing, there was no sign of the old scrybowl. The shards and slivers had vanished . . . somewhere.

Into the garden, said Vertic's voice in her mind.

She turned to see him sitting, head cocked at her.

FamMan distraught, he said. He certainly had a good vocabulary.

"He didn't appear that way to me." She jutted her chin.

You lie, he said calmly. *He looked terrible and is all churned up inside. You can feel.*

She didn't want to; it hurt to test her connection with Ilex, that bond that had narrowed to a thread between them due to agony on both sides. She couldn't think about it either.

"Vertic, were you in my apartment a few nights ago?"

I am in your apartment every night. I check on the heedless kitten.

Greyku plopped her rear on one of Trif's feet and lifted her muzzle and sniffed.

You are both very irritating. The fox flowed to his paws and headed toward her door, then simply vanished in the shadows and was gone.

Set up the "Greyku's Jig" scrybowl, prompted the kitten.

To do that, she'd have to enter the bedroom where she'd stashed the scrybowl in the closet.

Greyku unsheathed her claws to prick Trif's foot.

"All right, all right!" She tried to ignore the sight of the bedsponge where she'd made exquisite love with Ilex. A trace of his scent lingered in this room more than the rest of her apartment. Trif chanted the housekeeping spell and put a little extra Flair behind it. Except for the unnatural speed of the spell, it worked well. Her Flair was still slightly out of her control.

She unwrapped the brass bowl and set it on the fancy iron scrystand, filled it with water, and ran her finger around the rim to initiate the spell.

Once again, "Greyku's Jig" filled the room. No faulty Flair this time, not with a bowl that still resonated with D'Holly's Flair.

The song echoed with the joy that Trif had felt when she'd first received her Fam. The tune had substance, was strong and true. Greyku raced around the room, so fast she appeared a multicolored streak, emitting a high cat shriek of glee that didn't accompany her jig very well. The sight and sound of her made Trif's lips twitch up in a smile.

And the scrybowl made her think that she needed someone. Couldn't bear to be alone, even with her kitten. She glanced at a timer on the larger table next to the scrystand. An eightday ago, she'd have been running late for the public carrier going to work. Now, she had more than an hour before her lessons with D'Holly began.

Impulsively, she touched the water in the scrybowl. "T'Blackthorn Residence."

"Here," answered the cheerful voice of the new butler.

"Trif Clover for her cuz, Mitchella."

"I'll alert her. One moment."

It was less than two seconds. "Trif?" Mitchella beamed out at her. The new bowl was larger and Trif could see her whole face—an easy, smiling face. Someone was happier this morning than the one before. Trif licked her lips. "Greetyou."

"Trif, I can see something's wrong. What?"

"Ilex and I—" She swallowed hard. "No longer together. I . . . can I come?" It was more of a plea than a request.

"Of course!"

"I'll be right there. See you shortly." She glanced around the mainspace. The housekeeping spell had whisked through here too, and everything looked clean and tidy. The new tile work on the floor gleamed. Trif wondered if there was any way she could convince the management of MidClass Lodge that the tile was better than carpeting. She frowned. She didn't think so. She wasn't going to enjoy walking from bedroom to mainspace barefoot in the winter . . . but she wouldn't be here in the winter. She was going back to Clover Compound. For a moment, the sense of loss had vanished, and when it flooded back it was worse.

Had she done the right thing? Was this current pain worse than loving Ilex and having him reject her? She'd never been so indecisive in her life. Never felt such grinding hurt for so long. Definitely needed to discuss this whole mess with someone else, and Mitchella would understand best, even better than Lark.

Standing under the warm waterfall, she let it sluice some of her pain away, then dressed in her favorite trous suit. Anything to ease her day.

"We're going to T'Blackthorn Residence," she said to Greyku, lifting the kitten and attaching her to the shoulder pad with a small spell. Again, her Flair worked perfectly.

T'Blackthorn Residence will be good. Drina FamCat will still be asleep and Pinky FamCat is gone with his person to apprenticeship. Neither will pick on Me.

"That's my main consideration, of course."

"Yesss."

She couldn't find her instrument case, and despair threatened to overwhelm her again. Struggling through it, she recalled that D'Holly had said they'd work with panpipes today instead of the whistle or flute. The pipes were separate, in their own bag, so she grabbed it and stood in the middle of her mainspace, ready to teleport. Greyku hummed in her ear.

After a couple of minutes of concentration and breathing, Trif knew she was ready, that the 'porting would be right. She checked the landing light in T'Blackthorn Residence, then on a long exhalation, said, "We go!"

They appeared in a corner of the entry hall and Mitchella hurried up to greet them, hugging Trif hard. Again, sadness welled up, uncertainty. Tears stung her eyes.

Mitchella patted her on the back. "Come into my sitting room and we'll have cocoa with sugarcream."

"Sounds wonderful," Trif said thickly.

A few minutes later, she was cradling a large cup of sweet cocoa in her hands and pouring out the story to Mitchella. When she was done, she drank and let the warm liquid soothe her throat.

"Is this the Trif I know and love? I don't think so," Mitchella said.

Twenty-six

Mitchella tilted her head. "It's true you look more . . . mature, as if you've become a real adult."

Trif shot her a scathing look. "Thanks, something else to be depressed about."

"So you've had a hard knock. Your very first *real* hard blow. I can see that it might slow you down a little. Make you think. And that's all to the good." Mitchella sipped her cocoa. "You've never tended to think things through."

Smoldering anger in the pit of her belly licked out a few flames. "I'm hurting here!"

Mitchella's face softened. "And I'm sorry for that. I'm sorry that your HeartMate courtship is going so badly."

"He doesn't want me." Trif choked back a sob, then saw a flash of lingering pain in Mitchella's eyes. She set her own cup down and rushed over to her cuz, sitting beside her. "I'm sorry now. You're right, I don't think before I act, or I speak. I'm sorry for making you remember."

"Straif didn't want me either. But that was a while back."

"It still shadows your heart."

"The memory can prickle a little, true." Mitchella's lips curved. "But when I think of the loving we had before he left, and my plans for when he returns, it all vanishes." She lifted the cup in a toast. "We're fine now, happy and healthy and building a family." Then she patted Trif on her knee, eyes as green as Trif's own studying her. "The question is, what are you going to do to get *your* HeartMate? Are you going to give up?"

Trif shot to her feet to pace. "Of course not. I'm going to hunt him down. I just feel . . . I feel . . ." She thumped her chest between her breasts. "Angry that I have to do this. That he won't listen."

"That you don't listen."

"I listen! I just don't agree with him."

"Did you ever?"

"I—" Now her head began to ache.

The scrybowl flashed dark green and gray on the pale wall, signifying a call from the Hollys. Mitchella answered it. The voice was too soft for Trif to hear, but she thought she recognized D'Holly's speech pattern and stiffened.

"We understand completely," Mitchella said. "I'll tell her."

Of course the first thing that flashed into Trif's head was that D'Holly had called to end their studies. Surely D'Holly wouldn't dismiss her by a scry to her cuz? Surely not. But Trif murmured a little prayer and petted Greyku, who slept beside her, stomach full of prime furrabeast bites.

Mitchella signed off with the formal "Merry meet again," then glided back to her chair, meeting Trif's eyes.

"D'Holly canceled lessons. There was some upset in the Residence last night."

They stared at each other.

"Something more of the curse?"

Tracing the rim of her cup, Mitchella said, "I don't know. But she appeared over-weary. I got the impression that her daughter-in-law was hysterical, her son furious, and her husband . . . I'm not sure. Upset indeed."

When Ilex reached the office, it was easier to tuck away his devastated feelings. As a young guard, he'd often been screamed at by his mother in the mornings before he left the

Residence to take up his duties. His vocation had been his passion, the guardhouse his sanctuary.

It wasn't quite the same. Because Trif had visited. He could envision her here. Not good. Time to become a professional. He pushed his emotions into a tiny box. He had murders to solve.

Once again, he scried all the herb shops in Druida about incense mixtures, and mentally tested his trip wires, when a mental shriek made him flinch.

Come! I need you! The demand flashed down the Family link, but it wasn't his brother or nephew. The call was from Tinne Holly.

Ilex's heart clutched. *Trif? Is she there? Did something happen to her?*

Not her. I need you as a witness. Ilex sat back, surprised. He'd never felt so close a bond with any of the Hollys. Desperation, worse, a grinding grief struck after the words, coming from Tinne and stirring up his own hurt. He couldn't deny the young man. He stood and walked to the Chief's office.

Sawyr glanced up. "News?"

Ilex shook his head. "Something else. Just got a call"—he tapped his temple—"from Tinne Holly."

With a grunt, Sawyr looked back down at the papyri and spheres spread on his desk. "You're the guard assigned to the FirstFamilies. Go. Come back as soon as their newest brouhaha is over."

"Right." Ilex went to the landing pad and 'ported to the exact spot Tinne had imaged. There would probably be more than one person as witness.

Half-expecting to see bodies on the ground, instead he saw the T'Holly Household, mostly men, clustered in their livery a few meters away. Other GreatLords were there—T'Furze held his daughter, Tinne's wife, close to his side. The older FirstFamily GrandLord glared at T'Holly, who had a sick, gray tinge to his face.

T'Apple, the father of T'Holly's wife, also stood, arms crossed. T'Ash, younger and dressed in a blacksmith apron, stood, hands on hips, expression grim. Tab Holly, Tinne's G'Uncle, stood beside him.

As soon as Ilex appeared, Tinne turned to him. "Good, you're here. You'll be my witness on behalf of all the councils." He was pale, silver-gilt hair ruffling in the cool breeze, eyes dark gray with emotion. What was most unusual was that he wore an ill-fitting bright blue trous suit. He straightened to his full height, set his shoulders, swallowed, then looked straight at T'Holly.

"I disown you, I disown you, I disown you," Tinne rushed out on a breath.

T'Holly staggered back and his fist went to his heart, where the bond between father and son had been cut.

Tinne doubled over, hands on his knees, panting, but still he stared at T'Holly. "My wife, Genista, is a Furze, and they are the most fertile Family of the FirstFamilies, yet we haven't been able to create a child. Both her sisters were pregnant within six months of their marriages and we were two years before she conceived, and not for lack of trying. I think your broken Vows of Honor acted adversely on us in that way too." Slowly, he straightened, looked to his wife sobbing in her father's arms.

"Last night we lost a babe in the womb. We will *not* stay in this cursed house another hour. We will not be associated with a man who breaks his Vow of Honor and is too proud and stubborn to acknowledge his wrong."

Ilex sucked in a breath. His wits spun, and grief slammed into him from all present, most especially from Tinne, and through that bond from Genista. He sank into his balance just to stay on his feet from the pummeling emotions.

T'Furze said creakily, "This marriage was bad business all around. I'd not have granted it if I'd known what would occur."

"Too damn cheap to consult with T'Vine for a prophetic vision," T'Ash muttered.

"I heard that!" T'Furze growled to T'Ash. "Didn't want to talk to a child. Hadn't proven himself—"

Raising his hands, palm out, Ilex said, "Calm," and sent the soothing Flair around the tense group. "I think the miasma of this place affects us." Everyone's auras were dim and muddy.

T'Furze snorted. "We consulted the matchmaker D'Willow, didn't we? Should have been enough." Without another word, he and Genista teleported away.

Tinne licked his lips. His gaze did not go near his father.

"I will take the name—" His voice broke, he coughed, took a deep breath, and his glance went to T'Apple, his MotherSire. That Lord inclined his head.

To Ilex's surprise, Tinne looked at him. Ilex jerked to attention. The boy wanted the Winterberry name? He'd have to face the old besom D'Winterberry, but this could work to Ilex and his brother's advantage. Ilex felt small that he'd had the thought. But his mother would be thrilled at the great addition to the Family. Tinne was rich in his own right. Ilex nodded to Tinne.

"I will take the name Tinne Winterberry." He ended on a cracked note. He blinked rapidly. "I don't know where Genista and I will stay—"

"You're welcome in T'Ash Residence," T'Ash rumbled.

"You can make a home at D'Winterberry's," Ilex said. Lady and Lord help them.

Tinne rubbed his face with his hands. "Right now, I must go to D'Winterberry and pledge my loyalty. Then . . . my cuz Straif Blackthorn's wife has offered me . . . a peaceful place for me to . . . consider our options."

Ilex tested his faint, despised connection with his mother—more a link of distasteful loyalty than a true familial bond. D'Winterberry's lifeforce was sluggish, then awakened with a spurt of excitement. The news of this confrontation was already being spread, by Furze no doubt. Unlike his father, Tinne was the kind of man who'd discuss major decisions with his spouse, so Genista would have known the name he preferred and told her Family.

Yet Ilex must be honorable. "Straif Blackthorn will also accept you into his Family."

"He is not here to take my oath, and though I respect his lady and HeartMate and would give my oath to her in his stead, I am not sure others of the FirstFamilies Council value D'Blackthorn's word. I want all legal matters clear and binding."

"Straif will be back in Druida within a couple of days," Ilex said.

"I prefer not to go nameless, not even for a septhour. Destiny is too uncertain and I have a duty to protect my wife."

T'Holly flinched.

Tinne offered his hand to Ilex. "Shall we go?"

Ilex stepped forward and embraced him. Grief and hurt and anger flowed between them, and Ilex siphoned as much as he could from the young man and sent it into the ground.

"My thanks," Tinne whispered shakily. "This is a hard thing to do, but manageable. Not as bad as enduring my HeartMate wedding another, and certainly not the worst event of my life. That was losing my child last night." His voice grew thick.

"We'll go," Ilex said, and when he stepped away from Tinne, he saw that T'Apple, Tab Holly, and T'Ash had left. "On three." He counted down, and they arrived in the shadowed barren hallway of the D'Winterberry townhouse. At least it looked freshly cleaned, probably Dufleur's doing.

"Why not take the name Apple?" Ilex asked.

Tinne grimaced. "My MotherSire has enough grief. He doesn't need *two* disowned Holly sons in the Family."

"I think you just don't like the name," Ilex said.

"They're artists."

"Artists are prized."

"Not as manly as fighters," Tinne mumbled. "Would be different if I was a bard, but I didn't get my mother's talent. Genista likes Winterberry better too."

"You may very well regret this," Ilex warned him. "There wasn't a lot of time for me to tell you the situation."

Smiling humorlessly, Tinne said, "My Family—" He stopped, gulped. "The Hollys know of your mother's addiction and her unreliability. Every Noble does."

Ilex heard the snick-snick of heels descending the stairs. "I'm SecondSon, as you are. My brother is back in town and will be challenging my mother for the title. Unless you want to do that honor."

"Pledge loyalty, then challenge? I don't think so. I'll leave it to your brother."

"Won't be difficult to prove neglect," Ilex murmured.

Tinne shrugged. "I don't think D'Winterberry's demands will be much. I'll be of a Family, but my own man."

"Good thinking."

D'Thyme appeared, smiling broadly. Carefully, she lowered her heavy body into a curtsy. To Tinne. She ignored Ilex.

"Welcome, Tinne H—welcome. I am D'Thyme, a cuz, D'Winterberry awaits."

"Greetyou," Tinne said politely.

"Please follow me. Everything is ready for the loyalty ceremony."

They went up the stairs and to the Head of Household's suite. To his surprise, Ilex found his steps lagging. He hadn't thought his mother still had that much power over him and his feelings. Wrong.

D'Thyme threw the door open and Ilex's eyes stung with sharp cleaning herbs. He got the idea that his mother, ensconced in her thronelike chair, had been washed where she sat.

Tinne strode forward and bowed to her, outwardly courteous, but a tension around his eyes bespoke a difficult duty. His wife's Family had not offered to make him theirs. That would hurt too. Fliggering shame that Blackthorn was out of the city.

The loyalty ceremony was brief, and only had a little hitch when Tinne said, "My wife is not well enough to vow loyalty in person to you this day," Tinne said. "I have her token, please accept it." He slid a gorgeous golden ring with an equally golden earthsun stone into D'Winterberry's hand.

She goggled at it. D'Thyme's eyes sharpened.

Tinne cleared his throat and with another gesture, a stream of large many-gilt coins poured into D'Winterberry's lap. "I pray for an additional, unusual stipulation in this loyalty oath. I most humbly request that if my former father, GreatLord T'Holly, mends his broken Vow of Honor, that Genista and I are released immediately from our oaths to you and allowed to return to that Family—distant relatives of your own, my lady."

D'Winterberry stared at the gold, then looked up at Tinne. She was shrewd enough to know that granting Tinne any favor would enrich her more than in just gilt. "That stipulation to your loyalty oath to me is granted."

"Food and drink, D'Winterberry," Ilex prompted.

His mother jerked, then motioned to a small plate of cookies that Ilex's nose told him were stale. She drank deeply from the House goblet, passed it to Tinne. Face expressionless, he took a tiny sip. She took a cookie, then offered him the tray.

He chose the smallest, popped it in his mouth, crunched, and swallowed.

"You are now blood of my blood," D'Winterberry intoned.

A thin, but strong link formed between Tinne and Ilex himself and Ilex welcomed it. Welcomed Tinne and Genista *through* it, though Genista's thread was unsteady.

Ilex stepped forward and embraced Tinne again. This time leeching despair from the younger man. It helped them both, since much of Ilex's own depression flowed away, through the house into the ground of their old Family estate below. Ilex couldn't force optimism that he himself didn't feel.

He stepped back, bowed to his mother. That emphasized his distance from her, and in turn echoed the distance he was from his HeartMate. How he longed for Trif's cheerful presence.

His mother spoke, "Our cuz, D'Thyme, has the consort's suite, but you and your wife can have the Heir's rooms."

Tinne stilled. More changes for him. He'd probably always had a suite of his own, and his wife too. He bowed. "Thank you, my lady. Though my oath is to you, my wife and I don't want to impose. I pray you take no offense if we live somewhere closer to her Family." He meant in Noble Country where the great FirstFamilies were.

D'Winterberry's thin mouth twitched in a smile as she nodded, obviously relieved. Ilex deduced she was glad she wouldn't have to pretend to be sober and responsible around this newest member of her Family.

"If you'll excuse us, D'Winterberry," Ilex said carefully. "We must return to our duties." Lives. Not the stagnant existence in this house.

Tinne bowed again. "Unless you have any business for me to attend to?"

She looked blank.

D'Thyme stepped forward, eyes sharp, hands fluttering. "Not at all, not at all. You go to the Green Knight Fencing and Fighting Salon? That's yours, isn't it?" Greed laced her voice.

"It is Tab Holly's for now. I am unsure of the disposition of the business. I do intend to continue with my teaching there."

"Of course."

"I have an appointment with Mitchella D'Blackthorn."

"Yes, you must go," Ilex's mother whispered, her eyes lowering as if she'd fall asleep momentarily.

Ilex bowed to the women, drew Tinne from the room, then took one last look at her. She was his mother, but he felt nothing but disgust. As he walked Tinne back down to the teleportation pad in the entryway, he knew he ached for the Residence, for the estate, more than he cared for his mother. He was glad his brother would wrest it away from her.

He led Tinne to the landing pad and watched him 'port away to the clean, beautiful home of T'Blackthorn Residence. Where Trif might still be. Ilex swallowed hard and ran a hand through his hair. This was a very bad mess.

Before he could 'port away himself, another demand roared down his Family connection with the Hollys. *Black Ilex to me now!* commanded T'Holly.

T'Holly paced on his estate's mown dueling field. If Tinne had been there, Ilex wouldn't have given much for his chances. T'Holly grunted at Ilex in greeting, continued to measure the square with his steps. Ilex joined him and said nothing.

"I won't let that boy dictate to me!" T'Holly insisted.

Ilex whirled on him. "Wrong. If you want the Holly line to flourish instead of die out, you will change your ways."

"I didn't ask you." He eyed Ilex. "And you're more my generation than his."

Inside, Ilex flinched.

T'Holly continued. "You should understand my position more than his."

A crack of laughter came from Ilex. "You're a GreatLord and have never bent your will to anyone else's. Not even to destiny. First an Heir, then the Lord, you don't know what it is to take any orders." Ilex stared into his distant relative's flat pewter eyes. This man could break his career so easily. Perhaps. It was one thing Ilex would fight hard.

"And you lie down for your destiny," T'Holly shot back. "You don't fight for your woman, your HeartMate." A curl twisted his lip.

T'Holly had always been good at delivering crippling blows. Ilex felt the verbal punch straight to his gut. "This isn't about me. This is about you and your Family. Other Families have died out since we colonized Celta. My own brother has walked away from the Winterberry title, considered founding his own Family in Brittany because of my mother's action." Ilex shrugged. "Now your sons are gone. Holm is crafting a good life in Gael City, happy and whole. I saw him a few days ago."

Pain flashed in T'Holly's eyes.

"Tinne will be welcomed wherever he and Genista decide to live. As a SecondSon, his income was provided for by your own mother. They will flourish." Ilex pointed at T'Holly. "You will continue to wither and die." The words reverberated in his own head, but he dismissed them.

"I . . . I . . ." T'Holly sputtered in denial.

Ilex grabbed the man's massive shoulders and shook him. "Look at what your broken Vow of Honor has cost you. Look at yourself. You've aged twenty years since that duel with T'Hawthorn. You've lost the Captaincy of the FirstFamilies Council; they won't vote for you as the leader when you're under a curse. You've lost both sons. You've lost a grandchild.

"And if you don't care for yourself or your children, what of your HeartMate? She has never fully recovered from her wound because she cleaves to you. You harm your woman. Can't you *see* this? Here she comes now." D'Holly had left the Residence and was crossing toward them. "*Look at her.* See how she's aged too. How her Flair and energy have diminished. See how she walks with slow and careful steps."

T'Holly's gaze fixed on his HeartMate. Her expression nearly hid her devastation as she tried to smile at her husband. Her aura was slight, her pace cautious. A fine trembling existed in every muscle.

"Lord and Lady, she doesn't run to me," T'Holly said under his breath. "She doesn't dance. Passiflora has always danced. Music always plays in her mind. Have I driven that music away?" It was a tortured question. Then T'Holly ran to her, scooped her up in his arms.

Ilex saw her frame his face in her hands and her lips move. The whisper of her voice drifted to him. "We'll survive."

The big Lord clamped her to him, rocked them both, sorrow radiating from them.

Scraping up his own energy, Ilex teleported back to the guardhouse.

The rest of the day he spent preparing the trap for the killers.

Twenty-seven

As Ilex was finally preparing to leave the guardhouse to return to the despair that shrouded his apartment, his new brother Tinne scried.

"Yes?" asked Ilex.

"I need some time with you."

"Has something happened to Trif?"

Tinne sighed gustily. "Nothing is wrong with her, though I saw her today after settling in at T'Blackthorn's." He paused. "For once, she didn't look cheerful and optimistic."

Ilex's gut clenched with guilt.

"Though I understand your first thoughts are about her—and your second would be about the murders—I am scrying about myself, and bonding with you as a brother."

"Yes?"

Lines bracketed Tinne's mouth as he stared out at Ilex. "I would be much better for a good fight and some other manly relaxation tonight."

Ilex blinked. He had no idea what Tinne would consider manly relaxation—other than a fight, of course. Ilex could do with a good fight himself; still, he didn't see himself in a tavern brawl. "Fighting where?"

"Sparring at the Green Knight," Tinne said.

A warmth of anticipation suffused Ilex's muscles. He grinned.

"The idea pleases you too. Thought it would. I'll meet you there in quarter-septhour."

"Done!" Ilex broke the scryspell.

The sparring was down and dirty enough to relieve his anger and despair at sending Trif away and Tinne's same emotions at losing his child. He'd even broken one of Tinne's ribs, which had the man disappearing on him—vanishing to Primary HealingHall, since he wore an amulet like Trif's.

When Ilex teleported to the HealingHall to check on Tinne, they both were given a lecture by a Second-Level Healer on the evils of violence as their bruises were efficiently Healed—for an exorbitant price. Ilex paid since Tinne had disowned his Father.

Then they went to T'Mor's Bath House, sat in the steam room, and got a massage.

"I want to go drinking," Tinne said abruptly as they left the place. "Gen's at her parents' Residence, being pampered by her female relatives. I'm sure she'll stay the night. You said once we could drink together. That you have a separate identity for that."

"Yes." Ilex suppressed a sigh.

Tinne wasn't as oblivious as Ilex had thought. "When was the last time you garnered information in lower-to-mid-class taverns about the murders?"

"You have a point," Ilex said. "Let's teleport to my place so I can don my disguise. I'm only glad you don't want to cruise Downwind."

"Downwind isn't that tough since the urban renewal. Most of the real rough folk left Druida and scattered."

"And I'm glad of it," Ilex said. He took Tinne's hand, sent him a minutely detailed vision of his apartment, and they ported.

Once there, he dressed in a shabby commoncloth cotton shirt and trous in a dark blue, tinted his hair black, and grew a beard stubble with a special spell. Finally, he pulled on black boots that were so old they had holes in both the uppers and soles.

Eyeing him, Tinne's expression lightened. "You look like a

different man, all right." He jabbed at Ilex's biceps. "Like one of those rough Downwind ones. Not at all 'Pretty boy Black Ilex,' "

Ilex threw him a scathing glance. "I thought the fighting part of the evening was over and we were going to do the drinking part."

Cocking his head, Tinne said. "What was your original hair color?"

"A little lighter than this. Dark brown."

With a smile, Tinne shook his head. "Different guy, all right. Trif ever see you with your hair tinted?"

"No." Ilex fastened a thick belt composed of many flapped pockets around his waist.

Tinne looked impressed. "That belt is so out of fashion, it makes a statement. Something G'Uncle Tab might have worn in his youth." He poked at one of the bulging pockets. "What do you have in there?"

Ilex smiled back. "A little bit of everything. It's a work belt."

"Holds lots of guards' stuff?"

"Yes." He opened the door and nodded to Tinne to leave.

At that moment, Vertic shot through the door flap in the bedroom, passed them, and turned and sat on the threshold to the corridor, mouth open, tongue lolling. *I wish to go on the adventure too.*

"Is it all right with you if Vertic accompanies us?" asked Ilex.

"Sure. He going to be interested in taverns?"

Mice and rats in taverns, said Vertic. *Warm hunting, good eating.*

"He'll be reducing the rodent population," Ilex said.

"Then I guess we're not going to places where the establishments use anti-vermin spells."

Ilex rubbed his now bristly jaw with a thumb. "I thought we'd start out in the southwest quadrant. In general, that's where most of the murders took place."

Tinne's brows lowered. "The Clover Compound is in the southwest."

"Believe me, I know." He waved Vertic into the hallway. The fox, using some of its natural Flair, stuck to the walls and nearly disappeared into the shadows.

"Is Trif here or in the Compound?" asked Tinne.

"There."

Tinne made a little sound in his throat. "Both our women deserted us."

Ilex squeezed his shoulder. "I sent mine away. I'm sorry Genista left you."

Mouth flat, Tinne said, "She needed to be with Family. Her older sisters will coddle her."

"You're her Family."

Shoulders tense, Tinne just shook his head and gazed aside. His eyes had a liquid sheen. He swallowed. "She'll be back with me tomorrow." One side of his mouth crooked up. "She really can't stand her Family for long." They walked through the lobby of MidClass Lodge and out into the cool night air. Tinne dragged in a breath. His face settled back into easy lines. "Where next?"

Vertic sat next to Tinne, batted the back of his calf with a thick tail, and Tinne relaxed his stance even more.

The street wasn't busy, though there were a few parked gliders belonging to those who were rich enough to own them and liked living in a community such as MidClass Lodge. Ilex started walking to the first cross street. The corner was treeless and wind ruffled his hair.

He lifted his head, but closed his eyes, extending his senses. He scented the beach on the far side of the hollow square that was MidClass Lodge, and the inland fragrances of park and people. Expanding his Flair, he thought vaguely of the taverns in the southwest where he garnered information. Like lights set on a map, the inns glowed yellow, one brighter than the others, his Flair indicating that something interesting might be found there.

Clearing his throat, Ilex said, "What of The Token?"

Vertic barked approval. *Good place to cache food around there.*

Ilex looked down at him in disgust. "You eat well from hunting around here, and I'll always feed you." Even as he said the words, his mind flashed on his body lying on a large area of red tiles and he wished he'd kept his mouth shut.

Vertic's eyes glowed golden, slit pupils enlarging. *I am still a Wild Fox.*

"Granted," Ilex said.

"I don't know that place." Tinne appeared curious. He held out his hand. "You'll have to handle the 'port."

"On three," Ilex said, scooping Vertic up to hold under one arm. Ilex counted down, and they vanished from the corner to appear in a small grassy area ringed with greeniron spikes.

Tinne winced. "You like to live dangerously, eh? We could have landed on one of those spikes."

"No." Ilex let Vertic down, then opened the gate for the fox to trot out. He followed, closed the gate behind Tinne, then flicked the small concealed teleport landing pad light on.

"Huh," said Tinne. "I didn't even notice that. You *are* good."

"Thanks." He deepened his voice slightly, added a rasp.

Tinne's brows went up. "You change your voice too?"

Ilex shrugged. "My disguise is more effective that way. Believe me, most people in this sort of tavern don't want to talk to guards."

Tinne nodded. "I believe it."

"Hmmm." Ilex stepped back and looked at Tinne. "You'll pass. The Token is slightly better than lower-class, shabby middle-class. You look like a younger Lordling down on your luck."

Tinne grimaced. "I am."

Another sentence Ilex would have liked to call back. This evening was turning out to be nearly as miserable as the day. He shifted his shoulders, accepting the burden of tactlessness, and started off to the inn's door. Vertic had already silently disappeared into the dark.

But I am here if you need me, the fox said.

"So, have you and Genista decided where you're going to live?" Ilex asked. He liked Tinne, but there was no place he could offer to the young man.

A wry smile twisted Tinne's lips. "Genista is the ThirdDaughter of a FirstFamily GreatLord, the wife of a FirstFamily GreatLord's Heir. She's used to Residences." He shrugged. "Like I said I would, I asked Mitchella D'Blackthorn if we could stay there, since they have plenty of room and no Family other than the children they've adopted."

"Aren't they about to adopt a baby? Won't that hurt Genista?"

"It was either T'Blackthorn Residence or T'Ash Residence, and T'Ash has a healthy young toddler and fertile wife. Genista knows Mitchella is sterile and will commiserate with her." His voice was brittle. "It was what Genista wanted, and right now, I am endeavoring to give Genista whatever she wants."

"Of course." With an unobtrusive flick of fingertips, Ilex sent Tinne some soothing Flair.

Tinne stopped, shut his eyes, and shuddered as he absorbed the comfort. Then he opened his eyes and walked into the tavern. He strode up to a tall, scarred wooden bar that showed a film of grease and liquor. "Chwisge!" he ordered.

Ilex shuddered, it was a raw form of whiskey.

The barman, a few feet away from them, ignored them to continue with his conversation. Ilex noted that since the last time he'd been in The Token, it had slid a few rungs down into lower-class. He could pass as a patron, Tinne couldn't.

Uncharacteristically, Tinne pounded on the bar. "Did you hear me, I want *chwhis-gee.*"

There was not even a twitch from the barman.

"If I don't get my chwisge, I'll rip your heart out."

Silence fell like a blade.

Ilex wanted to sink his head in his hands, or punch Tinne in the jaw. This was helping him with his case? It was all over town that the bodies were heartless. All the newsheets assumed the chest had been torn open and the hearts removed.

Paling, the barman moved quickly to Tinne, looked him up and down. "You have any gilt, puppy?" His words were less harsh than his tone. Beads of sweat dotted his upper lip.

Narrowing his eyes, Ilex realized the bartender was new, and not too observant. Tinne might be young, and was obviously Noble, but his life hadn't been easy since he'd made the long trek from the Great Washington Boghole to Druida when he was seventeen. His body might not be fully mature, but he had more wisdom than many a man of twenty-two, more than his brother Holm had had at that age. More than Ilex had had at that age too.

Tinne pulled out a coin and set it spinning gold on the bar.

Ilex suppressed an urge to rub his temples and fell into his part. He jostled Tinne. "What you said weren't funny." He smiled with teeth. "Pretty boy."

Shock, then amusement lit Tinne's eyes. He flushed. The barmen snatched up the rotating coin and laughed. So did the other men and two women at the bar.

"Chwisge," Tinne repeated. "Please."

The barman snorted, pocketed the coin, and slapped a bottle and none-too-clean shot glass in front of Tinne. The bottle had a green label. It was probably the best chwisge the inn had, but it could rot the gut.

Tinne poured himself two fingers, slugged it down, and showed no appreciable reaction. Ilex was impressed.

"What you want?" asked the barman of Ilex.

"Ale."

"Draft or cylinder?"

Ilex glanced at the man's dirty hands and the equally begrimed taps. "Cylinder."

"Goddess Brew or Crimson Nut?"

"Nut."

Grunting, the bartender reached down, then pulled a frosty cylinder from a no-time, setting it before Ilex. Ilex made a point of pulling out some coins, carefully counting them, and pushing them at the barman.

Tinne swallowed another finger of chwisge.

A stooped man sidled over to Tinne, nudged him gently in the ribs. "Care to share?"

"Why?"

The man licked his lips, gaze fastened on the bottle as if it was the most expensive brithe brandy. He looked around. "Well, mebbe for a story? Sounded like you was interested in them murders." He leaned over and said confidentially, "You know, I had a friend of a friend who actually saw that Calla Sorrel being discovered in Landing Park. . . ."

"Give the man a glass," Tinne told the barman.

A shot glass slid down to stop before the informer. Tinne poured chwisge to the top.

"Thankee. Yup, my friend of a friend saw that youngster, that other Clover woman—sure have a lotta people in that

Family—find the body and call a guard. She was right broke up about it, but handled herself like a real gentlewoman, they said. The friend of a friend got really close and said the girl-body was all bloody, especially the chest."

Ilex turned away. Perhaps his Flair had been wrong about there being important information here.

The informer swallowed. "An' this friend of a friend said there was a funny odor about that corpse, probably all the corpses—" He coughed.

Ilex stiffened slightly, swearing under his breath. They hadn't wanted that news to get out.

"—like smoke those Cross Folk people use in their rituals."

By now Ilex knew about various ritual incenses. The Cross Folk used frankincense, benzoin, storax, olive, myrrh, sandalwood.

Pylor.

Lady and Lord, why hadn't he thought of pylor incense? It was more a drug to be inhaled in smoke form, but it could be a mixed incense ingredient.

The guy coughed again, wiped his hand across his lips, then on his shirt. "T'only smell like that I ever smelt was when I was workin' on that strange turquoise house a coupla kilometers from here for that woman who became T'Blackthorn's lady." He slid his eyes slyly toward Tinne. "P'raps ya know of her." Smacking his lips, he said, "Mitchella. She who was one a those Clovers. Bright red hair. Body that gives ya thoughts of the best wet dream ya ever had."

An accurate but crude description of Mitchella, Ilex thought dispassionately, then realized that most men would consider Mitchella Clover D'Blackthorn far more attractive than her cuz, Trif. He ached for Trif. A Clover woman surely could stir the passions, bemuse a man.

Tinne stared down his nose at the man. "Perhaps I *do* know GrandLady Mitchella D'Blackthorn."

The man's eyes went wide, he choked on his drink. Covering his glass with his hand as if he thought Tinne would take it away, he scuttled to the end of the bar.

. . . smell like that I ever smelt was when I was workin' on that strange turquoise house a coupla miles here. The words replayed in Ilex's mind. The hair on the back of his neck rose

as connections snapped together. The turquoise house had belonged to GrandLady Kalmi Lobelia. She'd been a pylor-smoke addict, using the drug to amplify her Flair for prophecy. She'd had Straif T'Blackthorn's FamCat on an altar—ready to sacrifice?

Ilex had to investigate. Now.

He plucked at Tinne's sleeve. "Gotta piss, then I'm done here. Don't like the company." He put a little stagger into his step as he headed to the toilet. And on his way there, he overheard even more from a table of men who looked like laborers. "Yuh, I was at that blue-colored house when that Mitchella Clover was workin' on it. That room the other lady used for them Flair consults stank sumthin' awful."

Another man nodded. "That's the truth. I overheard the redheaded decorator say that the smell soaked clear inta the walls and even inta them spelled wooden beams. No way to get 'em completely free of it."

Ilex had the information he came for. The clue he so needed. He used the bathroom, then found a private scry cubicle and set things in motion—asking for guards to find who Lobelia had associated with, particularly younger people; who she had purchased her herbs from, who else bought the same mixture. Excitement of the final stages of the hunt surged inside him.

A rapping came at the closet door. "You, in there, time to go," Tinne said.

Finishing his instructions rapidly, Ilex signed off, then opened the door. He had to force himself into the posture he'd used since he'd entered the tavern.

Tinne frowned at him, whispering. "You should be more careful. You snapped out orders in there like a GreatLord."

Ilex jerked a nod, replying softly. "You're right. My mistake."

Something in his eyes or his voice alerted Tinne and he caught the excitement.

"You think you know—" He broke off as a woman stumbled into the short hallway leading to the toilets and the scry cubby. They moved out of her way, through the tavern, and into the night.

Vertic joined them, swallowed with a large gulp, and smiled at them. *FamMan is hunting!*

"Yes." Ilex wanted to hiss it like a cat. Like Greyku. Yessss.

I see the turquoise house in your mind. The place where the female who now lives in the house near my old den worked. I have been to that blue house often.

"Can you get to the turquoise house from here, Vertic?" Ilex asked aloud for Tinne's benefit.

In response, the fox waved his plumed tail and took off in a ground-eating stride.

"That animal is *fast,*" Tinne remarked.

"Faster than a dog or cat," Ilex agreed.

"Do we run or 'port?"

"I've never ported to the place at night. I don't know the light and shadows. Mitchella D'Blackthorn doesn't have the Flair to teleport and I doubt she hired any workers who could. I sense no landing pad—with or without a light." He began to run, following the fox.

"Just as cautious as I originally thought." Tinne loped beside him.

Ilex briefed him as they ran through the night. The exercise swept more of the cobwebs of depression sticking to his heart away. His mind felt clear and focused, his body strong and tireless. The twinmoons were ripening to full, which would be Samhain, the new year.

Twenty-eight

They arrived at the house that had once belonged to the Lobelia Family, a now defunct line. The courtyard was clean and cobbled. Large skeletal trees were black against the dark blue stars-and-moons-bright sky, hiding a portion of the front aspect. Neat and tidy flower beds ran along each side of the paved courtyard and against the house itself.

The place stood, solid and beautiful with an architecture of times gone by, but the aura from it was young and fresh and cheerful, and reminded Ilex of Trif and Greyku, and he couldn't speak.

Tinne rubbed his hands. "How do we get in?"

Ilex just slanted him a look. "Legally. All building identify spells include access for Druida guards."

"Even deep in the night?"

"Especially deep in the night."

"Ah. Well, I really wouldn't have wanted to mess up D'Blackthorn's work in restoring the place."

"Not to mention that the spellshields will be top-of-the-pyramid. Put in by T'Blackthorn himself at least."

"Not to mention that. Probably would have gotten a shock that bounced me to the Cave of the Dark Goddess and back."

"Probably."

It hears you, Vertic said.

They hadn't kept their voices down and the house began to glow turquoise.

"It's *becoming,*" Tinne said with awe. "Becoming a Residence. A real entity."

"Yes," Ilex said. The house was changing from wood and plaster to a sentient being.

It takes time for a Residence to be born, Vertic said. His mental voice was projected enough for Tinne to hear it. The young man must have passed some internal Vertic-test.

Tinne glanced down at the fox. "So it does. I've never seen it before." He shivered a little. "I've never been in a place that was *becoming*."

It won't eat you. Vertic grinned. *It loves company*.

"Huh," Tinne said.

Standing and flicking his bushy tail, Vertic trotted up to the door. He sniffed around the threshold. *It is a good place now*.

Ilex and Tinne exchanged glances. Tinne shrugged. They walked to the square front door, new and wooden and shining with black tint. Ilex placed his hand in the depression and touched the cold identify. "Guardsman Ilex Winterberry and associates, FamFox Vertic and Tinne . . . Winterberry."

Tinne twitched, but Ilex ignored him. The door opened smoothly and quietly. As they swept over the threshold, pretty spell lamps set in wall brackets lit, glowing gold and picking up the creamy wall color.

"Welcoming," Tinne said.

Thank, said a tiny voice in Ilex's mind. The voice of the house-becoming-Residence.

Vertic's claws snicked down the red tiled corridor and he turned left . . . and the sound disappeared.

"He's doing that on purpose?" asked Tinne, setting his hand on his blazer.

"Yes."

No danger here. Never, never, never . . . again, whispered the house, unhappiness in the sound of its words, and radiating from the walls.

Sighing, Ilex lifted his hands. "Calm." He sent the feeling through the house like a soft, warm breeze.

Thank.

Tinne shifted his shoulders. "Yes, well . . ."

They turned the corner, but there was no sign of the fox.

This way. Vertic sent a map with a fox-red color trail. Ilex was grateful since he was near the end of his Flair energy for the day. Tinne didn't seem much better. Emotional storms played hell with Flair. Finally, they found Vertic sitting at the end of a narrow hall, before a door.

No one goes here. The room is still not ready for a den, not even for humans.

"Ah," Tinne cleared his throat.

Sorry, the house sobbed. The atmosphere in this corner of the house was oppressive.

I will not go in, Vertic said. *Smells are too strong, FamMan.*

Since Ilex was sensitive to odors, he decided to play it safe, and took a bespelled triangle of cloth and put it gently against his nose and mouth. It formed around them and he breathed in sweet pine.

Tinne sniffed. "There's a lingering heavy odor, but nothing too bad." He opened the door.

Emotions poured out, engulfing Ilex. Though they had faded, he still sensed the fight-or-die feelings of the three who'd battled for their lives . . . knew where each had been at the moment death had overcome.

"Lights," Tinne said, and several sconces lit. Strolling in and around, Tinne said, "A nice room." He went to the far end, then paced back, rolled his shoulders. "This part doesn't feel the same, though." He tapped a faded line scarred on the wooden floor. "Used to be a wall here."

"Yes," Ilex forced from his throat. He stepped in, and more layers of people coming and going flowed around him, more recent. Workers. Mitchella Clover. He withdrew a record orb from his belt, went to the middle of the room, and hung it in the air with a spell.

"The guy at the bar was right," Tinne said. "That incense Lobelia used soaked into the walls and floor. Hard to get out, even with a cleansing by a Temple priest and priestess."

"I think there's already been a molecular cleansing."

"You'd have to tear out the walls and floor—"

The house whimpered. Tinne stiffened, bowed. "Sorry, house."

Tinne sighed. "The place is a nice size, but Genista would never live here." A slight drift of air held depression. "Sorry, house, you are quite lovely, but my wife wants something bigger and in a more titled neighborhood."

"I think it is unique, has definite possibilities," Ilex said truthfully.

"Nothing here," Tinne said.

"Yes, there is." Ilex had completed a circuit around the room. He went to a corner where the scent of incense was the heaviest. Gesturing to the right-hand wall, he said, "There was an altar there."

"All houses have altars, though I wouldn't have said this room was a good Ritual room."

"Not an altar dedicated to the Lady and Lord. One to the Negative Force. To Evil."

"Like the current murders?"

"Perhaps," Ilex said. Palms up, he crouched in the corner, running his hands down the walls, sensing energies. "There is an extra shieldspell here, slight, but noticeable, of Lobelia's making. Difficult to unlock."

Tinne joined him and ran his hand where Ilex had. "Maybe you can feel it. I can't."

"Illusion spell to cloak the shieldspell," Ilex muttered, thinking of possible spell-breaking codes.

"Very tricky."

"Yes."

"Ilex . . . the last Lobelia was an oracle, right?"

Ilex stopped concentrating on the corner and looked at Tinne. He'd forgotten that. "Yes."

"You wouldn't want to trigger anything that could, uh, send a blast of that sort of Flair at you, right?"

"No, I wouldn't want any sort of prophetic Flair melding with my own." Ilex stood. "I don't have the time or the Flair to deal with this tonight." He plucked the record sphere from the air, turned it off, and sent it to Chief Sawyr's desk in the guardhouse. Staring at the corner, he narrowed his eyes. "But this is one of the keys to the case, I know it."

•

Tinne nodded. "Good. We might be able to end it before the new year."

"I hope so. I'll come back tomorrow morning and root it out."

Thank, said the house. *Was ordered. Not able to say about hole. Thank.* The air thickened around them as if gathering energy. *I will be clean. Someday.*

Trif woke in her childhood room and was disoriented for a few minutes, then remembered all that had happened. Pain washed over her and she shoved it away, refused to feel it, to think about Ilex. What with the big Holly Family crisis and Tinne Holly . . . Winterberry coming to Mitchella at T'Blackthorn's, all her attention had been focused on helping him and settling him in a guest suite and preparing one for his wife. So she hadn't had time to strategize how to get Ilex to change his mind and come to her.

Going to him would not accomplish what she wanted, but living without him was painful. The bond between them remained the thickness of a fine hair, barely noticeable, and that hurt too.

She slept late, then rose for a late breakfast, leaving Greyku sleeping on a pillow next to hers. Neither her mother nor her aunts scolded her because they were eager for firsthand information about the Holly scandal. Then they had to discuss whether the Clover Compound should remain a venue for D'Holly's lessons with Trif.

"Yes!" Trif said, spitting bread crumbs and hastily covering her mouth with a softleaf and swallowing.

Since no one commented on her manners, she knew they listened. They, the matriarchs of the family, were listening to *her*. She *had* grown up. After another swallow, she said, "D'Holly is a wonderful woman, but she's a HeartMate and supports her husband. Lark told me that D'Holly sent a note blessing the marriage, so her broken Vow of Honor doesn't weigh on her as much. It's T'Holly's that seems to be the curse. He's head of the household, after all. She needs us, needs this place, and I want her to have it."

"Well said," replied one of the aunts. "I agree." There was a murmur around the table and by the time it was done, Trif knew that the Clover women would stand behind D'Holly. Not that she'd thought any differently. The GreatLady had charmed the women.

"To lose a child is ravaging enough, without being ostracized," one of the aunts said. Again, everyone agreed.

Trif 's mother gave a little cough. When Trif looked at her, she'd flushed. "I did want to say that there was a scry from T'Holly Residence canceling your lessons again today, Trif."

"I see," Trif said, though disappointment shimmered through her. What was she going to do to keep her mind off Ilex?

"And there was also a scry from the Noble Council for you!"

"Me? Trif said blankly.

"You are to play for a two-hour set during the New Year Celebrations, in GreatTemple roundpark."

"Me!" This time she squeaked.

"Yes. I saved the scry, the details are in the cache."

"Oh."

But before she could scurry over to the bowl, her mother leaned forward. "What of your HeartMate?" Trif felt like a child again. As she'd expected, they wormed the story from her.

At the end, her mother sighed, frown lines creasing her brow. "I don't like this premonition of his, and if it was anyone other than you, I'd say wait and see." Her voice caught. "But being who you are, you won't wait, will you?"

"No. I'm figuring out what to do next."

"You're right in that if you two are to have a future as equal mates, he must come to you." One of her aunts nodded.

"Thank you."

Picking her words, Trif 's mother said, "What of this man's mother? Could you speak with her?"

"I don't think they get along."

Her own mother folded her hands, nodded. "All the more then. See the mother and you may understand the son better."

"Perhaps. But I don't know that I want to intrude into his life that much."

"He should know you wouldn't give up on him and your

love. You will continue to be in his life, affecting him." This was punctuated with a jabbing finger.

"You may be right."

They all told Trif what to do and she left the dining room with her mind spinning, as well as a list of tunes that she would perform on New Year's according to the scry message. She escaped into her room, but just before she was about to leave the compound, the men clumped home from work for lunch and insisted on a noontime concert.

After that, the women commandeered her efforts for the preparations for Samhain and New Year's; then the children were home from grove study and she had another, more critical audience. The break for afternoon snacks was welcome, and flung her back to her childhood with kids of all sizes jostling for their favorite foods, telling jokes and stories of the day, playing with Greyku. It was impossible not to fall into old habits.

By the time she left in the late afternoon, she'd practiced her pieces and variations on them long and hard enough that she was ready for the performance. She'd taken part in the daily household rituals and the long family traditions in planning for Samhain. All this steadied her, made her think of her connections to her family, and how she wanted to shape her future. With Ilex.

She 'ported from the Compound to MidClass Lodge lobby and stepped out into a puzzling red haze, flicking the safety light on. Then felt a sting like a bitemite.

Greyku gave a startled mew. *Sleepy!*

Blackness swallowed Trif.

That morning, Ilex had spent little time in his apartment, just enough to wash and dress, then went to the turquoise house. It greeted him with a wash of sunlight and warmth, with real pleasure in seeing him again, and Ilex sensed bubbling anticipation—as if it had a deep sliver he would remove.

It took him a morning of straining, delicate Flair work and more patience than he thought he had to unravel the spells that the last GrandLady had layered over the hidey-hole.

Chief Sawyr and a couple of other guards were there when Ilex attacked the final barrier. "You're sure this will lead us to the cult?"

"I'm sure," Ilex said for the twentieth time. He chanted a pair of Couplets and the shieldspell vanished. Scents and emotions like those he'd felt at the murder scene radiated from the small square hole. "Feel that." He moved away.

Sawyr bent down. A shudder rippled through his frame. "It's the same."

"Yes."

"But this safe hasn't been opened for more than a year."

"Right. I think that Lobelia was the originator of the cult."

"She's dead now."

"Yes." Ilex gestured for the Chief to investigate the hole.

"Lightstream," ordered Sawyr, and played a beam of white light over the cavity. "A bag." He picked it up, sniffed. "Pylor. And well, well, well, what do we have here?" He reached in and pulled out a small sheet of folded papyrus, banished the light, and snapped the page open with a flick of the wrist. "Names," he breathed. "Two columns. One with the names of young Nobles who had unsteady Flair and whose Passages might echo and repeat. As they did."

"The other column?" Ilex moved in to look.

" 'Prospective members,' " Sawyr read.

Ilex glanced at it. "I know some of these—and two don't surprise me, but—"

"But?"

"I don't think the leader is listed."

"No?"

"No. I believe she came along later and refined their ceremonies, made them stronger, called forth Evil."

"A few months ago."

"Yes, that would explain why some of the ritual places didn't look or smell or feel the same as the one murder place we found."

Sawyr stared him in the eye. "You have an idea who she is."

"I do, but no proof."

Showing his teeth, Sawyr said, "We'd only have to leak the name to one FirstFamilies lord. . . ."

"You think so? What of the law? You recall what happened when the law was circumvented in the case of Ruis Elder?"

Sighing, Sawyr nodded. "You do have a point. That was a case the FirstFamilies mishandled from the very start." He pummeled Ilex on the shoulder. "Used you too, didn't they."

"Yes. On several occasions. I didn't like it. In the matter of the law, I'll side with SupremeJudge Ailim Elder every time."

"That's a lady we can respect," Sawyr agreed. "Think we could go to her?"

"I think we should follow procedure. Bring in these"—he tapped the column of suspects—"and question them with all the tools we have at hand."

"Truth spells, comparisons of their persons with the poppets you've made from all the data. Scents they wear or their natural fragrance, skin tone, voice timbre. You're close on those, Ilex."

"I think so. That's how I suspect the one I do."

"Right. Let's go! You can 'port me back to the guardhouse."

Guard, whispered the house, anxiety in its tone.

"I need to purify this safe-hole," Ilex said. He took the Temple-blessed smudge-flare that another guardsman had brought for him and put it in the square hole.

They all stepped back.

"Shield your eyes." He waited until he heard everyone say the Words, then did so himself. With a wide gesture, he said, "By the Lady and Lord, may the darkness of this secret place be vanquished by the Lord's bright sunlight and the Lady's twinmoonslight. May this alcove be cleansed and purified!" He snapped his fingers, and an explosion of light took place along with a sizzling and a burst of herbal fragrance that stung his nostrils.

They waited until the spell ended. Examining the sconce, Ilex knew it was now simply an unimpressive feature in the wall. Since it had been shielded from the rest of the room it had little scent or sense of evil. No shadows lingered like dusty black spiderwebs in the corners.

Thank, said the house. Again, the emotion in its voice seemed like a sob—but unlike the night before, this one was of joy.

Sawyr clapped Ilex on the shoulder. "Let's go do our work. If we manage this right, we'll have everything wrapped up to-day and we won't need to risk a hair of that boy GreatLord's head. That will be more than fine with me."

Twenty-nine

"*This time, let's kill the Fam too. Drain it. It can't contain much Flair and we will need it all.*"

The low, malicious voice penetrated the drugged fog in Trif 's mind, followed by a spurt of fear. Her senses sharpened. She lay naked on a soft cloth over hard stone. The dangling fingertips of her right hand twitched enough to contact the dias beneath her and trace the symbols. *Bad* symbols. Black magic.

Ritual Murder.

Inside her head, a little voice began to scream—and stayed inside her mind. The cry didn't connect to the silky-furred form curled above the curve of her right hip—*Greyku!* She actually felt her heart thump hard in her chest. Greyku hadn't heard her. She tested her bond with Ilex. A tiny thread. Inert. No Flair or emotion flowing through it. He wouldn't come.

She didn't feel the warm stone of her amulet on her skin. Had they taken it? Why hadn't she ever asked if it was bespelled to stay with her? If it *was* near, could she get it? Order it to 'port them out of here?

Greyku breathed evenly; the faint trace of her mind that Trif could sense echoed a sleep pattern. Drugged, as she was.

Movement came around her; she struggled to open her eyes and her lashes lifted a crack. Her head was turned to the left and she faced a wall. A straight wall. She was in no round Temple of her faith. The place was nowhere she knew, smelled of incense, echoed like a warehouse. Fear bubbled through her brain, wiping thought away, fighting the drug. When she yanked the terror under control, forced its paralysis away, she was slightly able to think. In this instance, fear was a good thing.

"Shouldn't the rest of us be here?" asked a man.

Another evil chuckle, followed by a melodious voice that Trif strained to hear. "Not yet. I told them to arrive just after sunset, about twenty minutes from now." There was a delicate snort. "I didn't call the whole kurchucx. This sacrifice is not much, a Commoner and a kitten. Look at them—the girl's features can't be called Noble by any standards, and certainly not mine. And a pastel, parti-colored Fam. How preposterous! No, this is just a little tidbit for the most devoted of us. The four."

Now fury sizzled through Trif, and she managed to move her head a few centimeters until she could see the line where a grimy black plaster wall met an even darker black ceiling. Greyku stirred. Trif wanted to spare the kitten, but sensed she'd need all her resources, including her Fam, to escape this horror.

She sent a spurt of energy to Greyku, and the little cat soaked it up like a sponge. The effort exhausted Trif. How could she possibly gather enough Flair to free herself? Drugs weren't the only thing that held her. A spellbond ran below her, immobilizing her wherever her body touched the cloth—back of the head, shoulders, back, butt, legs. Her left arm was imprisoned. But her right was free from the elbow down. And she'd moved her head—that must be the weakest point.

A little hope.

Quiet footsteps came closer and much as she wanted to keep her mind focused and fighting the drugs, she had to shut her eyes. All too easily her lashes drifted down.

A finger traced her torso from the hollow of her throat to her navel. She could imagine a knife following the same path, and her body jerked.

"See that?" The second voice, a man's, pitched high with excitement. "The drug is wearing off. Can we do this sacrifice with the victim conscious? It would be so much more rewarding, I tell you, to feed off the terror. I've studied the texts and I'm sure her Flair would rise stronger, be more powerful if the sacrifice is awake."

"You doubt *my* scholarship?" The first person was close enough for Trif to discover the voice belonged to a woman.

"Let's just try a little experiment. What could it hurt? She's nothing, nobody, a Commoner," the man wheedled.

"All the more reason to follow standard procedure, so we can discover what difference Commoner blood makes in our occult investigations."

The man continued. "Yes, but if the Flair we raise from her, drain from her and the Fam through the Fam's link with her, is greater than usual, we might actually harvest enough for one of us to Acsend." There was a short pause. "Especially if we sacrifice the Fam this time too."

The doze Trif had been sinking into evaporated as the words rang and echoed in her mind. *Especially if we sacrifice the Fam* . . . . Her brain cleared, though her muscles still felt heavy, unresponsive.

Not only she would die. Greyku would die because she was Fam to a woman with unstable Flair. Trif didn't know why the fact that her Flair wasn't under control mattered . . . easier to harvest? Yes! That *felt* right.

Greyku would die because of her. She couldn't bear the thought. Pretty, lively, *kitten* Greyku.

Finally, Trif felt exactly like Ilex had.

Trif felt the shift in air as if the man bowed. "We all agreed that you, as our leader, should Ascend first. Think of it. And perhaps we might not just drain them of Flair, of energy, but of . . . blood. Blood rites have *so* much power." The man made the same line on Trif as he had before, this time firm enough that his fingernail scratched her. "Instead of separating the heart into molecules and drawing it through the body, slash her and we can eat it with *blood* gushing as well as warm and pumping. The kitten is small; there's hardly a good area to slice for us to pull the Flair from the woman through the cat and to ourselves—yourself. Gut the kitten."

The musical voice laughed quietly, raising gooseflesh. "I hadn't thought to play with blood rites so soon. But she *is* a

Commoner, and the kitten trash. I'll consider it as we await the other two. We can compare bloodrites on a Commoner with our bloodless procedure on a Noble.

"And you may be right. With the Flair I receive tonight, I could deceive the great T'Ash and his Testing Stones. I'll be a GrandLady, found my own house."

Shock stabbed Trif. This is what all these murders were about? Despite the unnatural "experiments" and "investigations" the deadly two spoke of, rationalizing their actions, all they wanted was worldly power. Nothing more than wealth and status.

They'd trade her blood and body, and Greyku's, for riches and a higher level of Nobility. Her gorge rose. They were stupid. Gilt mattered little, position even less.

What mattered was *love* and *life*. She was cold. The air was warm enough around her—but the fear in her blood chilled her from the inside out. She and Greyku were bonded closely. Even if she managed to save Greyku and not herself—find the amulet and twine it around her Fam maybe—how would her death scar Greyku? None of the other Fams who'd suffered the loss of their companions had been so young. She was so young, so precious. So beloved.

Like Trif herself was to Ilex.

She had no choice. She had to save them both.

She couldn't teleport—the spell connecting her to the cloth, then through the cloth to the massive altar, would prevent it. But she could send Greyku away perhaps. If Trif could touch her. Her right hand was free. Greyku was on her right side.

More hope.

More.

Her throat tightened. That was what Greyku was always saying. More.

Today Trif would try *everything*. She'd rarely raised her Flair—the only time she used it was in her music and 'porting. She never sought her visions.

Her mouth was dry, tongue coated with a nasty tang. She doubted she could whistle, let alone croak a song, not that her voice was special. She wanted her flute. Again, a slight sting came behind her eyes; again, tears failed to liquefy.

The two people strode away and Trif noted a darkening in

the light beyond her eyelids. Carefully she opened her lashes. Saw nothing but the dark ceiling. She'd moved her head! Straightened it so she could see directly above her. Excitement fizzed inside her, made her breath ragged.

That was the key.

Breathing.

If she could find the right pattern of breathing, she could summon her Flair. Let it rage out of control—yes! A glimmer of an idea flickered in her mind.

FamWoman! Greyku's shrill cry battered Trif. Her pulse increased fractionally.

Calm, beloved kitten, Trif said.

Fur and muscle quivered beside her. *I can't move.*

We were drugged. Breathe with me. I will gather Flair and send it to you. It will be dark soon, and I want you out of here.

You must come too!

You will save me, be a hero.

Sire Zanth is a hero. He has told us kits often. Fairyfoot saved her FamWoman. I can be a hero too.

Yes. Breathe with me a moment.

Instead of forcing her mind and her breath down certain paths, Trif endeavored to relax, to put herself in a mild trance state. Let her Flair collect and pool inside her. Breathe. Keep alert. Breathe. Strengthen the bond with Greyku. Breathe.

The drug's hold seemed to lessen. Though her limbs were weighty, her mind floated, and formed an image.

She was walking the Great Labyrinth.

Ilex.

For a moment, the emotional pain was so sharp, it overpowered all thought, all other feelings, even her love for Greyku. Once again, she *willed* her love for him, disregarded but never vanquished, through their bond. Nothing happened. Weariness dimmed her vision.

Greyku whimpered. A tiny sound.

It strained Trif's nerves, hardened her resolve. *I love you, FamCat.*

The kitten exhaled in a sigh. *I love You, FamWoman.*

I am gathering Flair for you. I think I will have enough for a minor spell and one big burst.

What minor spell? Greyku sounded more curious than afraid. Good.

The evil ones are waiting for night. I will take the fur-dim spell from you.

A kitten chuckle rolled through Trif, comforting her. *My fur eyes!*

Yes.

That will scare them.

Yes. Let me conserve my energy now.

I will collect My Flair too. We will show them!

In her mind, Trif walked the Great Labyrinth remembering the steps and turns, the offerings of the Nobles beside the path. She'd been there for her friend's wedding, and with Ilex. A little spurt of extra Flair came with his name, so she tried it again. *Ilex.* A bit more Flair flowed in her, as if her Flair itself recognized the name of her HeartMate. So she walked and she thought of him, and she trod the path of the Great Labyrinth up the crater walls and let her psi energy rise.

Absently, she heard the door open again, more voices added to the original man's and woman's.

As they talked, an unholy excitement ran around the room, coated her skin, raising gooseflesh.

Focus on the Great Labyrinth.

I will. I see it in your mind, and I looked down from the rim when you were there with FamMan, Greyku replied. Trif had been speaking to herself, but a smidgeon more inner tension relaxed.

People moved around her and she turned her head a few more centimeters, and she saw four naked people holding knives. She recognized Piana Juniper and Cyperus Sedge. The other woman seemed familiar, but the knives gleamed huge and sharp. Her pulse picked up its beat and all calming images vanished. Her small trance burst like a bubble.

The slow pace of the afternoon gnawed at Ilex, though it was all necessary procedure. Two septhours were spent dealing with a FirstFamilies Council, which finally authorized a public manhunt—and issued statements regarding the killings to the newssheets.

Then all the Druida guards met in the main station and Ilex briefed the men and women. The Head of the Guardsmen sent those with enough tracking, hunting, or investigative Flair out to find the people on Lobelia's list. He and Chief Sawyr had already ascertained that two had left Druida, two had died, and several were mysteriously missing.

Finally, Ilex returned to the guardhouse and prepared to hunt the leader down. That one had more Flair than he, and much more viciousness. He donned magical battle gear and protection amulets.

And in the heightened tension of the hunt, thoughts of Trif pummeled him.

She'd been right all along, and he'd been wrong. He had thought that the worst fate that could befall them was death. So wrong. What was the worst was not *living* life to the fullest. Not embracing each moment joyfully, not sharing it with your beloved.

The days without her had been excruciating. He cared for nothing, had no passion. Even with battle-readiness flooding his veins, he felt empty, not alive, but as if he was one of his own poppets, filled with a certain energy but no emotion. Time and again throughout the day, he checked on the tiny fiber that was their bond.

Until late in the afternoon he noticed it was gone.

Sheer panic struck, blinding him, freezing him to the spot in the door to the guardhouse outer office.

One of his poppets flew toward him, the face transforming into Cyperus Sedge's.

One of his trip wires fell. An *inner* wire. He shuddered. He might be too late.

She took one slow, deep breath, exhaled equally gradually, then sucked in air fast and deep and grabbed her Flair and *screamed,* dismissing the dim spell on Greyku's fur.

Other screams as Greyku moved. *I find amulet!*

No— But the kitten ignored her. Trif sensed her speeding around the room. Flexing and leaping so that the painted eyes rippled with horrific strangeness. Trif didn't know how long that would stop the cult.

Only one thing to do. Trif gathered her Flair, flung everything she had into envisioning the past, and as the wave of psi power rushed outward, others were caught in her vision.

The vision of the past—the ancient past of Earth.

The bloodiest one that had haunted her childhood, lingered through her Passages. For once she was glad to see it.

Long lines of men wearing different-colored uniforms, faces twisted in fury and fear, ran at each other, waving swords and holding tubes that shot projectiles—guns. Two armies of soldiers. Huge booms shattered the quiet. Artillery. A clump of men burst into bloody pieces, limbs and heads flying, leaving long arcs of spurting blood.

The scent of death infused the air.

Screams in the here and now ripped from the cultists' throats. A rising screech of horror.

Sounds of people colliding—with each other and bumping against furniture and walls. They gibbered, they swore. Among the cascade of words were some that freed Trif 's head.

A huge wave of Flair exploded through Ilex's link with Trif. He was caught in an awful vision of bloody fighting. Men screaming, clashing, stabbing with bayonets attached to *guns*. Then the guns erupted with sound and men jerked and fell and died. He groaned and fell himself.

"Guardsman Winterberry, attention!" snapped Sawyr, and the vision loosed its hold on him.

Cold water dashed against his face and broke the spell. He staggered to his feet, shaking his head and flinging the droplets away from face and hair. "My HeartMate is on the black altar!" he shouted.

Sawyr's strong finger tightened over Ilex's biceps. "Trace her to the link. We go!" He glanced around, saw the guard who'd dumped water on Ilex. "Come with us, Bluegum." The woman stalked to Ilex, grabbed his arm. Her face was pale, lips compressed.

"One of my trip wires . . . which?" He *had* to think! "Dark," he rasped.

FamMan, here, here, here! A strange perspective tilted in

his mind, some visual, but a *knowing,* completely controlled and grounded location. *That corner. Hurry!*

He knew the place a small warehouse near the docks. "One, we transport. Two teleport. *Now!*"

They landed in a corner. Both Sawyr and Bluegum toppled. Both were steadied by corner walls.

The room was painted black. Flickering candles illuminated three people curled on themselves, whimpering.

The door banged open so hard, it ripped off its hinges and toppled to the floor, trapping one of the females. Piana Juniper moaned.

"Guards!" gasped a man—Cyperus Sedge then: "I will not be taken!" His eyes were more mad than sane. He plunged a dagger into his own chest. Died.

Screams from the other two.

A black velvet hooded robe draped the only one standing, the leader. The cowl shadowed her face. She flung out an arm and sent a sizzling stream of Flair toward Trif.

Thirty

Ilex flung himself in front of the black altar and took the Flair against his bespelled chestplate. He swept his blazer from his holster, but the room was full of moving people.

The leader hissed an impotent scream. "I'm not finished with you, Trif Clover," and ran out the door.

Sawyr boomed a powerful chant that vanquished the dark spells shrouding the room.

"Go!" Trif ordered. It was more of a mental cry, a mere whisper from her voice, but Ilex heard, saw her arm jerk and point at the door opening. "Catch . . ."

He drank in the sight of her, hesitated.

Go, she repeated.

"You were right," he said. He had to tell her. "Right about everything."

Her eyes went wide.

Guardswoman Bluegum held up Trif 's amulet. "We'll activate this transnow!" She place a panting Greyku in Trif 's arms, wrapped an arm around Trif, flicked her thumbnail against the stone, and they vanished.

Sawyr spellbound the remaining two. "There should be two more."

Fury shook Ilex. He burned to find the person who'd

harmed his HeartMate. A red haze rose before his eyes and he shot from the room and onto the street.

Behind him he heard Sawyr demanding names of the missing.

No one to be seen. He longed for T'Blackthorn's tracking ability, then dismissed the futile wish. The leader would not escape. Ilex extended all his senses, used his own Flair and some from Vertic, to *sense* the murderer.

And he did. The faint stench of incense had him turning to his left, running down the street to a maze of narrow streets near the docks. His feet pounded the cobblestones, and soon scent was the least of his senses in hunting the leader. He should have lost the trail, but his Flair was greater than he'd ever known, preternatural for him. The effect of loving his HeartMate? Would it diminish?

He brushed the stray notion aside as the blood pumped through him, his Flair sang of the hunt. There! A dark movement against the night—a last swirl of robe as the wearer whisked around a corner . . . bolting.

Why didn't the murderer teleport?

With the next footfall, as he turned the corner and saw the running figure and closed the distance, he knew.

She was pressed against a brick wall, gathering her Flair. That shot of evil psi at him had nearly drained her.

"I'll . . . pay . . . you . . . back . . . for this," she panted.

"Wrong, Zinga Turmeric," Ilex said.

She shuddered at her name.

"Yes, I know you and will hunt you until I find you. All of Celta has turned against you. You will find no refuge."

"I will triumph!" Her image thinned, wavered, then she vanished.

He sent his Flair questing, but she hadn't 'ported a short distance. Striding to the place where she'd stood, he crouched and set his hand against the ground her bare feet had touched. His body jerked as he felt her vile power. Strong, stronger than he'd expected. Dark slime seemed to coat his hand. He knew her now, but didn't think she'd be found in any of her haunts.

Ilex pulled an evidence-collecting cloth from a pouch of his belt and wiped his hand clean, capturing everything that had been transferred from the killer to him. Even the black magic soaked into the cloth, a great relief. He stood and went back to report to Sawyr.

The Clover Family descended en masse on MidClass HealingHall, crowding into Trif 's room. First her mother and father plunged into Intake, her mother loudly demanding Lark Apple—who showed up a moment later. They hovered as Lark examined Trif behind a modesty spell, Healed minor scrapes and scratches, including the long mark down the center of her body that made Trif sick to look at.

Danith D'Ash rushed in too. And the Clovers nodded in approval. She glanced at Trif and her scared expression eased; then she went to Greyku and examined the kitten, who stretched and purred under her stroking hands. "She's all right. Even mentally." Danith frowned at Trif, turned to Lark. "I think Trif should see a mind-Healer."

"No!"

"She objects too loudly." Lark nodded. "I'll schedule her with my cuz." She brushed back hair from Trif 's face and the gesture was sheer comfort, soothing Flair.

Ilex had soothing Flair too. "Ilex!" Trif cried.

"He's fine." Danith held Greyku close and from her distracted expression, Trif knew Greyku was describing their experience in minute detail.

"You can tell through your bond," Lark said gently.

Trif 's mouth trembled. "It hurts to access our bond."

"What did that man do to you?" boomed her father.

With a desperate look to her mother, Trif said, "Just a . . . difference of opinion."

Her father snorted. "I'll see about that."

Lark said, "I think there are too many people in this room." She glanced through the half-open doorway. "And too many people in this HealingHall. Trif is cleared to leave. She has no remaining physical hurts, but I'll want a mind-Healer to examine her."

A whimper came from Trif 's lips. Lark smiled gently. "Tomorrow." She handed Trif a soft, thin pouch. "A sleep pillow, lavender, hops, and a gentle spell. Its efficacy will minimize over the next eightday, so I suggest you make that appointment with my cuz."

"We'll make sure she does." Trif 's mother nodded.

"May I *please* have some clothes?" Trif 's voice was plaintive, but she didn't care. "And I really, really want to spend some time under a hot, cleansing waterfall."

"I have a good robe for you," Mitchella said, sweeping in. Narrowing her eyes, she swept a stare around the room. "Leave her to me. I've ordered gliders to take the lot of you back to Clover Compound. Trif will stay behind strong FirstFamily Residence spellshields tonight!"

Reluctantly, her mother and father retreated. When they reached the hall, the raised voices were a cacophony that made Trif 's head ache. She looked up to see Lark studying her with Healer eyes. Then Lark covered Trif 's head with the spread fingers of both hands. A little zing buzzed in her mind and head and the pain was gone. "Good job," Trif managed.

Lark nodded. "You'll do. I'll make rounds here, I haven't been her for some months, then Holm and I will join you at T'Blackthorn's Residence."

"And Tinne too," Trif said, remembering the latest disaster of the Hollys.

With a sober expression, Lark said, "Yes, Holm looks forward to being with his brother, but . . ."

"This is not a good situation," Mitchella said, shaking her head. "D'Holly . . ."

"The Holly Family is truly broken," Lark whispered.

There were a few breaths of silence. Then Mitchella thrust her arm holding a plush green robe through the modesty spell.

Trif accepted it gratefully and slipped it on. Then Danith gave her Greyku and she held the kitten close. Trif glanced around at the three women—two of whom were powerful in their Flair, all of whom were of the FirstFamilies one way or the other. She licked her lips. "It's not entirely over. The—the leader threatened me and, uh, escaped."

The other three stiffened; their faces went from sympathetic to fierce.

"You're coming home with me," Mitchella said. "With Holm and Tinne in the Residence, and ready to act as bodyguards, we'll make sure that you're safe until the killer is caught. Straif should arrive tonight or tomorrow. He'll track down and find that evil one."

"But my instruments—other things in my apartment. I need them—"

"Surely, you won't need them before morning," Lark interrupted. "You must rest." She helped Trif down from the Healing dias.

Danith D'Ash picked up Greyku and shoved the kitten at Trif. "You aren't the only one who had a horrific experience. Take care of your kitten. She needs sleep and comfort too."

"All right." Trif grimaced. "Try and break this news to the family gently."

"I will," Mitchella said. She nodded to Lark. "It's a blessing that the men will be with us. They'll strengthen the spellshields of the Residence too. See you later, Lark."

"Blessed be," Lark murmured.

Mitchella linked arms with Trif and they walked from the room, down a corridor, and out into the cool night, where a glider awaited to take them to T'Blackthorn's.

The night was long and busy. Time and again the thought of Trif in danger sped Ilex's heart—and kept him focused.

He spent most of his time scouting out places where Zinga Turmeric might hide. D'Grove and Sedwy Grove had been shocked at the revelation of how Zinga had used Sedwy and her knowledge.

Others looked for the two missing members of the kurchucx—Piana Juniper had revealed their names. One they captured. The other, a son of a GrandLord high in the airship guild and a pilot, had killed a couple of men and stolen a small airship. Neither *Nuada's Sword*'s sensors nor the newly arrived Straif Blackthorn had any luck tracking him.

A FirstFamilies Council was called, and Ilex had to take time out from his searches to report every couple of septhours, which had him irritable and fighting impatience. The Nobles seemed to think T'Blackthorn would find Tumeric and she was as good as caught, so they moved on to planning the upcoming rituals. It was enough to make Ilex grind his teeth.

The Council, Sawyr, and the rest of the guards put evidence together against the cult members. Though the trial was set for a few weeks later, with truth testing and the spheres the killers had made of their rituals, Ilex didn't think the trial would take long or the judgment would be in question. The FirstFamilies had already consulted with SupremeJudge Ailim Elder, and determined what punishment would be appropriate for the unusual, horrific crimes. Cyperus Sedge indeed had been the lucky one, escaping into death, though what sort of life he'd live next with such sins on his soul was something for hard thinking.

Ilex finally was able to bow out as the Council was discussing trial procedures. He had something more urgent to do. He knew Trif was safe in every way, but he longed for her. He'd accepted that they had to be together and tried not to think of his past visions. Trif had been adamant that life with him was what she wanted, and they would enjoy every moment together.

No matter that dawn was a septhour away, he wanted to see her and ask her to HeartBond with him.

As he walked down the large hallway of the Guildhall, he heard his name.

"Black Ilex Winterberry," a husky voice said.

Whipping around, he saw young Vinni T'Vine standing behind him. He'd left the FirstFamilies Council deliberations.

The boy glowed. A rainbow aura shot with gold surrounded him.

"Yes, Vinni?"

"I will not be needed as bait."

"No. She'll go after Trif and me now."

"T'Blackthorn has returned to Druida."

Ilex stiffened. "This is my case. He can help, but I will find—"

"No. It is too late. Events have been set in motion so there are only two outcomes."

Sheer horror curled in Ilex's gut.

Vinni cocked his head as if listening; different colors came and went in his eyes. Emerald, blue-gray, hazel. "I heard you say to your HeartMate that she was right in wanting to Heart Bond." The boy prophet's voice had an odd, echoing quality to it. "Do you still believe that?"

"Yes."

"Then give her your HeartGift. Now. It is the only thing that will save you both."

Vinni opened the door to the council room and went back in.

Blood pounded in Ilex's ears, still rushing with adrenaline, fear for Trif. He believed completely that Vinni's vision was strong and true.

He had to get his HeartGift.

Glad he was already in CityCenter, Ilex went through the three levels of security at the deserted bank vault where he kept his HeartGift. Finally, he was alone in a privacy cubicle, ready to open the large no-time which held the gift for his HeartMate that he'd created during his last Passage so many years before.

He muffed the Couplet opening the safe three times before he steadied his voice and said the rhyme correctly. The door to the box slid up and Ilex was hit with the power of his HeartGift—a blast of lust that doubled him over. All he saw were visions of Trif as she pulled him to her, felt himself slip inside her tight sheath, heard her pant his name as she reached release. He groaned and braced himself against the table, sweat pouring down him, arms shaking, fighting off an embarrassing climax.

When he'd stashed the HeartGift, he'd never thought he'd open it again. He'd intended it to rest in the vault until after his death. Waves of passion, sensuality poured from it. He fumbled for the small scrap of papyrus with a shielding spell on it that he'd put next to the safe. His fingers touched the note, trembled so much it flicked away, and he realized his eyes were shut tight. Forcing his eyelids open, he saw the papyrus, snatched at it, got it, and touched it to the small tray that was the bottom of his gift. The papyrus stuck as it was supposed to; then came sweet relief from the pounding lust.

He lifted shaking hands to wipe his face on his arm . . . the softleaf in his pocket was as soaked as his clothes. With a minute of determined thought about the murders, his body subsided enough for him to stand straight.

His gift was beautiful. He'd loved making it. Loved the wistful, futile dream of giving it to his HeartMate.

For a moment he just stared at it, a lacquered tray filled with sand raked in tiny patterns, particularly around the three smooth stones and two rough rocks.

The small zen meditation garden was of a tradition more ancient and of a different root religion than that of the colonists of Celta, but they'd brought many crafts and records of other cultures to their new world.

Just looking at it gave him hope. He smiled, then his optimism faded. Could Trif actually like this simple, serene piece of art? She tended to the overblown. . . .

Stop.

Stop doubting himself. Was that the true reason he hadn't claimed her, because he didn't think he was good enough for her? Too rational, too staid, too old. Perhaps, though the very thought of her dying made his bowels go to water.

In any event, he'd decided to go to her, to apologize, to beg for another chance. He hoped giving her the HeartGift would show her how much he cared.

He picked the tray up carefully, though a spell held the sand and rocks in place until he gave it to his lady. Then *she* would find it pleasing, or make her own patterns—or they could create one together.

Perfect.

Trif slept well, with no dreams of evil murderers ready to slice her open during a bloodrite, and no tossing and turning from anxiety about her relationship with Ilex.

She'd gone to bed early, taking one of the luxurious guest suites that Mitchella had redecorated. Yet she woke at a commotion in the early hours of the morning.

Straif T'Blackthorn had returned.

She dressed and went down. Greyku accompanied her, and Trif was surprised to see that Vertic the fox sat in the parlor along with Straif and Mitchella. She was firmly ensconced on Straif's lap.

Frowning, Trif noticed that Mitchella still wore the robe she'd had on when she'd come to the HealingHall. She didn't look as if she'd slept. But whatever sadness and tension had been in her before was gone now she was in the arms of her beloved HeartMate.

"I've been awaiting Straif, and I didn't want to leave you, and I couldn't sleep, and the Residence said that there was a FirstFamilies Council meeting going on, so I participated by scry." She waved an arm at a huge hologram that took up much of the parlor. "They're still at it."

Trif matched her little shiver. No Clover family meeting had taken more than a couple of septhours.

"Greetyou, cuz Trif," Straif said. His gaze was grim. "One member escaped besides Zinga."

Trif flinched.

He raised a hand. "He's gone from Druida—and wasn't at your ritual." Straif's jaw flexed. "We traced him to an airship field, then lost him. The mind Healers we've consulted think he'll never come after you. As for Zinga, I'll rest for a few minutes, then start on the trail of this heinous bitch." His mouth thinned. "I must work with Ilex Winterberry. He knows Druida better than I ever will." Straif's eyelids lowered briefly. "I understand you are his HeartMate, so you'll be able to locate him for me through your bond."

Trif hesitated.

Time for Fams to take a paw in this matter, Vertic projected.

Straif Blackthorn stared at the fox. "What matter?"

The mating matter.

Trif flushed, shifted from foot to foot, then said, "Very well, see what you can do. I'm not giving up on Ilex."

Vertic laughed in short barks, eyes closed, tongue lolling. *We will hunt first, then you.*

"Sounds good to me," Mitchella said.

"I will strategize and wait for my prey," Trif corrected.

"Right." Straif rolled his shoulders, waved the Fams away. "Go."

Greyku pranced over to Trif and stropped her ankles. *I love you.*

Eyes stinging as she looked down at her Fam, Trif said, "I love you too."

Straif squeezed Mitchella and made her laugh. "I love Mitchella and Trif. Mitchella loves everyone here, Trif loves everyone here. Now can we get on with the day? Let's wake up the cook."

Vertic flowed to his feet, then cocked his head. *FamMan returns home.*

Trif blinked. "Just now?"

"A guardsman's work is never done," Straif murmured.

We go. See if you can keep up, kit. Vertic sped from the room, and Greyku followed.

The Blackthorns were kissing deeply. Trif cleared her throat. She coughed. Finally, she said in a loud voice, "I'd like some answers here!"

Slowly, Straif ended the kiss and pulled away to look at her. His eyes were glazed. "You say something?"

"What has the FirstFamilies Council decided to do with the cult members?" asked Trif.

Mitchella scowled. "If Zinga Turmeric—she's the leader of the cult who's missing, Ilex discovered that—is smart, she'll take her own life too. There will be a trial in a couple of eightdays, but the Council is already preparing a special judgment ritual for when the culprits are found guilty." Her eyes fired. "There's plenty of evidence to convict them."

Straif toyed with his HeartMate's fingers. "There was a lot of discussion." He looked up and his expression was feral. "Most of us just wanted to rip them to shreds. And Turmeric better pray I don't find her."

Trif didn't think he was joking. Her knees felt weak and she took a chair.

"But the rule of law prevailed. Something to be said for civilization." He shrugged. "Though I'll bet there will be a mob of Nobles and Commoners too who'd like to do the same."

Not wanting to visualize that—she'd seen mobs in her visions of the past and they hadn't been pretty—Trif hurried into speech. "What sort of special punishment ritual?"

Mitchella lowered her voice. "They will be banished, of course, and not anywhere near civilization. Ruis Elder, the Captain of *Nuada's Sword,* will take them to an uninhabited, wild, and isolated island in the middle of Great Platte Ocean."

Straif took up the explanation. "During the Ritual, a suppress Flair chain will be embedded under the skin around their necks. They won't be able to use any Flair to support themselves, and if they tinker with the chains their heads will blow off."

"Yech," said Trif. She thought of the night before and trembled. She'd have bad dreams for sure, and her visions might be more violent and disturbing too. No way around it, she'd have to visit a mind-Healer. It wasn't something Clovers did.

"They have sensors on them that report to *Nuada's Sword.* No one expects them to live very long," Straif said.

Trif's hands shook so, she twisted them together in her lap. "Terrible."

"Better than letting the Families of those they killed punish them. They'd be tortured to death."

Nodding, Trif said, "Yes. Deservedly so, but that is not our way."

"No." Mitchella studied her. Once Trif would have shifted under such an intense gaze, but not now. "You've matured. HeartMate love will do that. Have you talked to Ilex?"

Trif compressed her lips, then forced them into a wry smile. "He must come to me."

"I agree."

"Oh, I got you a present, Trif," Straif said. "Catch!" With his Flair, he shot a crystal sphere straight at her chest.

She stopped it several inches away from her. Set it spinning. It was an orb of white quartz with striations that she knew would perfectly hold tunes for several generations.

Straif grinned. "That was a test. Your Flair is fully under your control. Congratulations, Trif. I think your last Passage will be quick and easy."

Trif just blinked, still trembling with surprise. She closed unsteady fingers over the sphere. Instead of being cool, it was warm. "I suppose I should thank you."

Waving a hand, Straif said, "Think nothing of it." Then he bent to kiss his wife again, and Trif just couldn't take being anywhere but home anymore. She went upstairs to get her bag and panpipes—which had been taken with her by the cult, and returned to her in the HealingHall.

The past days had been outrageously shocking to her nerves. She wanted home. She wanted music.

She wanted Ilex. She ached with the need to play her flute. If she felt the cool silver in her hands, she'd know everything would turn out fine.

Straif T'Blackthorn caught her sneaking out one of the side doors. He smiled genially, rocking back on his heels and shaking his head. "You can't creep out of a Residence, or escape a tracker's notice."

Thirty-one

*Ilex returned to his rooms to bathe and don his dress uni-*form. He wanted to look his best when he proposed to Trif.

He'd also decided to drop by Trif's apartment before he went to her. He knew her. Despite all warnings, she would want to return to her home, and he intended to ensure it was safe and as shielded with strong spells as he could make it.

After a short stint under the waterfall, and dressed in clean clothes that didn't stink of incense, he felt much better.

He picked up the HeartGift and went to check Trif's place. The spell on the HeartGift was wearing off. Heated lust radiated from the zen garden, tempting him to think of Trif and bed.

Opening her door, he walked into the apartment to set the zen garden onto the table next to Trif's scrybowl. Here he could renew the protective spells. He didn't want to present the HeartGift to her and have them both rolling on the floor, mating, in a parlor of the T'Blackthorn Residence.

Everything happened at once.

Fun sandbox! shrieked someone inside his head. Greyku? Where had she come from?

NO! roared Vertic.

Both animals whirled toward him, he jerked aside. There

was a clang, a crash, and droplets of cold water hit him. Huge, spinning monstrous red eyes made him reel.

Greyku screeched again. Vertic barked loudly.

"How amusing," Zinga Turmeric said, entering the apartment and closing the door. She smiled, and her beautiful features twisted until she was ugly.

In her hand she held a blazer. She sent a stream toward the animals, then ordered, "Halt!" Her spell was as strong as his own. The Fams fell to the ground.

Even with Flair, Ilex couldn't unsheathe his sword or blazer fast enough to save himself. He no longer wore the Flaired body armor.

"Why don't we wait. That child-bride of yours will be along soon, I'm sure. Then I'll take care of you both and be on my way to bigger and better rituals in one of the smaller cities." She smiled, showing teeth that appeared to be bloody—an illusion of his own Flair, showing that she'd eaten human hearts.

"No. I won't let you."

"You can't stop *me.*"

She sounded like an evil cat. He glanced down at Greyku, who was frozen in a pitiful huddle between him and Zinga. Vertic was sprawled near Zinga's side.

Vertic can you hear me? whispered Ilex mentally.

Yes.

I think I can release you. When I do, attack!

Yes.

Ilex had nothing to lose. He cursed himself for delaying too long. He should have gone directly to T'Blackthorn's and given Trif his HeartGift, filthy, sweaty, and all.

"Sit down." Zinga gestured with the blazer. It wobbled a little in her hand and Ilex realized it was too large for her—and she wasn't used to it.

Now he smiled. "No."

Surprise flashed in her eyes.

"You can't understand," he said. "You want power and great Flair. You steal life from others because you're afraid to die. I've lived with visions of my death all my life." *Now!* He flung all his Flair to Vertic, formed it into a whirlwind shooting across room.

He lunged at her, but she pulled the trigger of the blazer, and the ray caught him in the left shoulder and he jerked backward. Pain seared him and he smelled the burning of his own flesh. He fumbled for his own blazer, couldn't reach it. His sword seemed to heavy for his hands.

Vertic attacked, biting into her calf. She screeched high and long and fell toward him, fire from the blazer flashing again and again.

Ilex dodged to miss the streams. She was within reach. He grabbed her blazer, twisted it, and sent the ray pulsing into her body, emptying the charge.

Her eyes went wide. She flinched, shuddered several times, then fell against him.

He staggered, slipped on the spilled scrybowl water, twisted, but his head cracked hard against the corner of the scrytable. The last thing he saw was a curve of brass—a new scrybowl—that had haunted his visions for so long.

Trif was shakier on her feet than she'd anticipated, though 'porting from T'Blackthorn's to MidClass Lodge had been easy. Straif had given her the courtesy of letting her 'port them.

She knew Ilex was here in the Lodge. Her steps dragged as she walked down the hall to her door.

They were halfway down the hallway when she heard screaming and barking and smashing sounds. A fearful mental shout from Greyku blew into Trif's mind.

Evil one here! FamMan hurt! Come, come, come NOW!

Trif and Straif sped down the hallway.

Hideous pain snapped her head back. "Ilex!"

Straif jostled her aside and flung the door open with Flair, rushing in. Trif followed.

Zinga Turmeric lay on the floor, twitching in death throes, a blazer on her chest. Straif went to her.

Trif scanned the room for Ilex. He lay still, the side of his head was bloody—as was the corner of the iron scry table.

Her heart gave one great leap, then settled in her throat.

She ran to him, fell to her knees. The faint pulse in his throat fluttered and stopped.

"No!" she screamed. Leaning down, she hooked an arm around his waist, then grabbed her protective amulet. "Primary HealingHall!" She yanked at it and the chain cut the back of her neck, but they teleported.

And lit on the soft permamoss of Emergency Intake. "Lark!" Trif screamed at the top of her lungs.

Healers surrounded her. "His body has died. His soul is almost gone."

"No!" Trif cried. Grabbing Ilex's hand, she *reached* mentally for him. *Ilex don't leave me. Stay. I love you! We're HEARTMATES!*

GreatLord T'Heather himself, the best Healer in Celta, placed his hands around Ilex's skull. "Keep calling to him, Trif. Keep him here."

Ilex, beloved, stay. Stay, stay, stay. It became a chant, from her lips and her heart. She barely noticed when Lark came and put her hands on Ilex's chest.

Trif could barely sense his essence. She closed her eyes and followed the thinning thread of their link. For the first time, she realized that it had strengthened in the last hour or two; otherwise he would have been gone.

HeartMate, she called into blackness to the twinkling light of him, and she didn't know if they were inside his mind or out in the vastness of space or on the way to reincarnation on the Wheel of Stars.

Stretching her limits, she brushed him, but still he sped away. *Stay!* But he wasn't listening to her mind-voice. She had to pull him back with something stronger. With HeartMate Flair.

With music.

Forcing back fear, she sought the melody that had once drawn him, the echoing, calling song that she'd first sent at the Maypole, and had since refined. The HeartMate call formed in her mind and she broadcast it far with her thoughts, and hummed it under her breath.

The whirling rainbow of sparkles that was Ilex paused in his flight away from her. She boosted the volume, more, she lured him with her own love, her own need of him. She recalled all the times she'd pushed the HeartBond at him, and instead of sending, she *summoned,* lured, tempted. She *offered* the HeartBond, a shining rope of pure gold issuing from the heart of her etheric body. *Come to me, bond with me.* She let her melody encompass her, draw him.

He too was shadowy, more the remembrance of a body than an actual form, but transparent gray fingers touched the HeartBond.

Trif quivered and all her love for him poured forth.

HeartMate. It was the merest mental whisper. *Trif.*

Yes! BLACK ILEX WINTERBERRY!

His love merged with hers, his strong emotion roared through her. *MINE!* His fingers gripped hers.

Then others were with her, adding their Flair to hold him tight, bond them all together, kitten and fox and woman and man. Love cycled through them in unbreakable links.

"Trif, it's all right. He's alive and will Heal." The patient voice repeated the words over and over until Trif opened her eyes to find Lark beside her, wiping tears from her face with a softleaf. Trif found she was rocking and the melody she'd thought she'd been singing was a low, harsh moaning.

Lark smiled at her. "Ssshh. He'll be fine. But it would be best if we could move him now."

Clearing her throat, Trif sniffed. "Yes, of course."

"We'll put him in a private room. T'Holly insisted."

Trif wet her lips. "Ilex is Healing?"

"Yes. The head wound was bad, I won't deny it."

"Fatal." Trif gulped back more tears.

"Yes. But you got him here within minutes after he 'died,' and both T'Heather and I were here and able to Heal him—T'Heather his skull and I restarted his heart and kept it pumping. The blazer injury in his shoulder has been mended too." She stood and offered a hand to Trif, nodding to where she'd intertwined her fingers with Ilex's. "And you called his soul back." Lark smiled. "Good teamwork by all three of us."

Trif really didn't want to let go of Ilex's hand.

"He'll be fine," Lark assured her. "You're HeartBonded and you both have enough Flair and strength and energy to keep each other grounded here in the physical world. Now he only needs to sleep through the rest of the day and the night."

"I won't release his hand. He's mine."

Lark rolled her eyes, then gestured to several people surrounding the large permamoss sponge. "Lift that and Trif Winterberry will accompany her HeartMate."

"Thank you." Smile watery, Trif matched standing and moving with the others as they used Flair to float the pad from the floor and down a hallway. "Trif Winterberry," she whispered, half to herself.

"It's pretty evident you are." Lark's tones were back to businesslike. She gestured to a red-plumed tail in the corridor in front of them. "Follow the fox."

"I want to stay with Ilex."

"Of course you do."

They reached a huge room and the pad Ilex rested on was settled on an equally large bed. "Patient NobleRoom One," Lark said drily. The luxurious room was the equal of any in a FirstFamily Residence.

Not letting go of Ilex's hand, Trif pulled a chair next to the stacked bedsponges. When everyone else had left, she crawled onto the bed and drew an exquisite llamawoolweave cover over them. Then she threw an arm around him, clutched a handful of softleaves, and wept into the pillows.

Greyku jumped onto the bed. *Very tired. Much work to get him back and keep him safe.*

Vertic grunted and settled himself on Ilex's other side.

Late that evening, she woke to gentle fingers stroking her hair back from her face and met Ilex's gray-blue eyes. His expression was one of wonder.

"You called me back. I heard you playing and I came back." He touched between her breasts. "We're HeartBonded."

"Yes." Her insides quivered. It was a big step, one she hadn't carefully considered. She'd always thrown him the HeartBond during sex, then offered it when he was dying.

His jaw firmed. "And my vision was true."

"In general," she said. "I didn't fall down dead. I came running to save *you.*"

"If we'd been HeartBonded then . . ."

She put her hands over his lips and gazed at him fiercely.

"I'd have done the same. But that's *past.* Whatever our lives may bring, now we are together."

Vertic barked. *And me.*

And Me! said Greyku.

Ilex rolled onto his back. "A happy Family." He looked at Trif. "Did you like it?"

"Like what?"

"My HeartGift."

She blinked rapidly. "What HeartGift?"

"You didn't see it? That's why I was there." His smile turned rueful; he gestured like a fencer conceding a match. "You won our bout of hearts. I was delivering my HeartGift. Once you accepted that . . . ."

"I'd be legally bound to you. Not just having an affair with my HeartMate, but essentially your wife."

He picked up her hand and kissed her fingers. The bond between them flowed with tender emotion. "My HeartMate. I couldn't deny it. I was ready to accept the HeartBond."

"You *did* accept the HeartBond." She studied him. "How do you feel?"

With his free hand, he probed his temple. "Fine. I hit my head on the corner of that iron scrytable of yours."

"You'll have a scar there, something that looks like a white starburst."

"That seems appropriate for the time I spent in the space between life and death and rebirth." He sat up. "I was dodging racing animals. My Fam chased yours away from my HeartGift."

Greyku stared at them with huge, innocent eyes. *Just looking.*

"Hell you were," Ilex said. "You were going to rearrange it."

The kitten huddled to make herself appear even smaller and more helpless.

Vertic barked. *Meddling cat.*

"Yes, a happy Family," Ilex repeated. "I take it Zinga Turmeric is out of our lives."

"Yes. She died."

"I would have wished she'd suffered more."

Trif remembered the twitching body, the scent of the

woman who'd soiled herself. But Ilex's expression was hard and cold—the fighter, the guardsman, the man—all aspects of him had wanted punishment for Zinga. Had yearned to destroy the one who'd hurt his HeartMate. That Trif knew from their bond.

But she wanted to change the subject, and curiosity burned. "What is it?"

"What?"

"My HeartGift, *what is it*?"

Ilex raised his brows. "Perhaps we should go and see." He gestured to papyrus resting on a table. "Lark was here and dismissed me. I was only waiting for you to wake." He sighed. "The Fams have been noisy."

Greyku sniffed.

He slid from bed, and tugged on her hand. "I've had enough of HealingHalls lately."

"It's a nice place," she said, finally noticing the expensive and exquisite furnishings.

"It's not our place." He lifted her fingers to his lips. "We will never live apart again, thank the Lady and Lord."

She cleared her throat. "I had hoped that we could live in my house in Clover Compound."

"Yes."

Some inner tension she didn't know she carried relaxed.

Greyku and Vertic sat waiting for them on the landing pad. Ilex pulled her against him and it was like the first time they'd kissed.

He was aroused and ready.

Her heart pounded in her ears.

"Why don't you take us hom—back to your rooms at MidClass Lodge." His voice was husky, she felt his lips brush her hair.

"One," her voice shook with yearning. "Two."

His arms caught her tight.

"Three!"

Overwhelming passion inundated her, loosened her muscles, sent warmth flooding into her core, preparing her for his penetration.

"HeartGift Flair," he rasped. His arms dropped from her

and he lurched to the table, found a scrap of papyrus, and stuck it on a small tray. "This must have come off."

Stiffening her buckling knees, Trif caught her breath. The place had been cleansed—very soon after the events, she sensed, and by several GreatLords and Ladies. Nothing of evil or death remained.

The HeartGift was shielded so the atmosphere was no longer hot and heavy, pulsing with desire—though Ilex made no attempt to hide his erection. He stood next to the table in a soldierly stance. Her gaze went to the tray she'd noticed years before—yesterday—and she walked to the table to study it.

"Ohhh." Her breath went out on a long sigh.

"Oh?" He tensed.

"It's lovely." She touched a fingertip to a irregularly shaped red sandstone rock, looked up at him. "It's a—a special garden. I don't know what they're called." She glanced aside.

He touched her cheek, gently persuading her to meet his gaze. "We're HeartMates now. There is and never will be any reason for you to think you are less than perfect for me—that you are—"

"—stupid and gauche?"

"No! You are fresh and delightful."

She wrapped her arms around him. "And you are sophisticated and fascinating." She heard a little thump and saw a small paw reach toward the patterned sand in the box. "Don't you do that!"

"What?" Ilex raised a brow.

"Behind you."

He turned and took her with him and they stared at Greyku, who was licking a forepaw. He chuckled. "Ah, a temptation for the kitten." His gaze laughed down at Trif. "Young ones have problems resisting temptation."

She snuggled against him and liked how his breath caught. "And it's a good thing I do, isn't it, HeartMate."

"Oh, yes . . . and I don't have any willpower in resisting temptation when it comes to you either." He bent his head.

She stepped back. "We'd better take care of the . . ."

"Zen garden."

"Zen garden." She grinned. "Exotic words for a fabulous HeartGift. Exotic and fabulous, just like you." Trif stared at it. Somehow, the arrangement of sand and stones seemed familiar. Then she laughed. "You know what this looks like, don't you?"

Ilex stared, blinked. "No. I made it when I was twenty-seven, didn't much look at it since."

She pointed at a square-looking rock, the uneven edge of sand that looked like it had been lapped by water. "It's the beach beyond MidClass Lodge. The rock is where the fish vendor usually stands."

"Lady and Lord, you're right."

Tenderness clogged her throat as she gazed up at him. "Where we first kissed."

He took her hands, eyes locked on hers, and pulled her slowly to him. The warmth between them spiraled into heat until her nipples peaked and every inch of her wanted to be pressed against him, feeling the hardness of his muscles.

This time when he kissed her, she melted into him, opening her mouth, moaning when his tongue swept against hers, sending pure, sizzling delight down every nerve.

Greyku yowled.

Their kiss broke and they saw her glaring at the garden and holding her forepaw gingerly.

Ilex laughed. "Just a small shock, FamCat. There are several spells in that papyrus; one is to keep the garden the same unless Trif or I wish to change it."

The kitten flicked her tail and hopped off the table, not deigning to answer.

Vertic chuckled. Trif looked at him. "Oh! That's the first time he's curled on my twoseat."

I am Family now, Vertic said. *I like the Clover Compound, but my den will be in Clover Grove or the park.*

She smiled, then her gaze caught on the zen garden again. "Lovely gift, thank you."

"Let's have our HeartMate marriage on the beach."

She could only sigh. "Yes."

"Soon, within a couple of eightdays, before it gets too cold."

"Yes."

Now he let out a deep breath, kissed her mouth, her eyelids. "I love you, Trif. Always. To death and beyond."

She swallowed hard. "I couldn't have lived without you Ilex." She stroked his cheek. "I might have survived, but I wouldn't have lived. I love you, to death and beyond."

Greyku purred. *And We all get More.*

Epilogue

*Ilex stood hand in hand with Trif, their wrists lightly teth-*ered together with a meter length of ribbon, watching the tide come in and listening to the final notes of their HeartMate song. They were in the middle of a Ritual Circle, surrounded by their friends and families who sang the tune composed by D'Holly—the last formality of their HeartMate wedding.

"We pronounce these two individuals legally bound!" said the Birches, who officiated as Goddess and God. "The Circle is now open, let the merriment begin."

A cheer went up; then the large circle broke into small clumps of people, talking.

"This is perfect. *Perfect.*" Trif spun around, her gauzy dress whirling. Ilex quick-stepped with her, then caught her close, savoring the fast beat of her heart against his chest. She'd never looked so beautiful.

He'd never been so happy.

"Perfect," she said once more before she brushed her lips against his.

She was almost right. Everyone sent blessings toward them, as was expected in a wedding. He was especially pleased his brother, nephew, and nephew's pregnant wife attended. Family.

But Ilex didn't need any Flair to notice the roiling emotions of all the Hollys—and former Hollys—present. No hope for it, they'd had to invite them.

D'Holly was Trif 's teacher, and had just formally notified the guildhall that Trif had mastered Journeywoman status. Naturally, they'd had to invite D'Holly's HeartMate, GreatLord T'Holly.

Lark Apple, HeartMate of the former Holm Holly, son of T'Holly and D'Holly, was Trif 's best friend.

The former Tinne Holly was now Tinne Winterberry and Ilex's brother, as Genista Winterberry was Ilex's sister.

It was enough to make his head ache—and his heart, if he hadn't been so happy.

Trif was his.

Bound together in every way, and now by long, formal, legally witnessed HeartMate Ritual.

"Let's dance!" demanded Trif. She waved at some of her musician friends, who picked up instruments and mixed lively music with the sound of wind and wave. She began a traipsing line dance down the beach, then grabbed D'Holly's hand. "You first!" she ordered Ilex, and with complete joy he led them down the beach.

D'Holly clasped her husband's hand and the chain lengthened. Trif 's eyes sparkled up at him in a glance. *Circle round Lark and Holm now, like we planned.*

Ilex took the revelers to Lark and Holm Apple, slightly slowing. The atmosphere leadened around them, charged with electricity.

T'Holly hesitated, then grabbed Lark's hand—the woman he'd disowned his son over. He brought her fingers to his lips, and after he kissed her hand, his voice boomed, "Blessings upon you and my son Holm, daughter-in-law, Lark Holly!"

A visceral shout tore from everyone. Ilex felt it rise from his gut at the lifting of the curse, the mending of the Broken Vows of Honor.

Tears rolled down Lark's cheeks.

Ilex stopped, and so did everyone else.

Holm Holly stepped forward and embraced T'Holly. "Father," he said. He turned to his mother. "Mamá."

"Blessings upon your marriage and your HeartMating, beloved Holm," D'Holly said.

Tinne and Genista Winterberry approached the Hollys. T'Holly stiffened.

"I made it a stipulation of my loyalty oath to D'Winterberry that should this moment come to pass, both Genista and I would no longer be Winterberrys, but Hollys."

T'Holly closed his eyes, opened them, and his arms. Tinne hugged his father. Genista air-kissed T'Holly's cheek, her manner cool. The actions were repeated with D'Holly.

D'Holly raised her voice. "Music! Let's dance."

This is a perfect complement to our wedding, Trif said along their link. *What a blessing we have been given, that we have mended such a rift on our day.*

The musicians started "Greyku's Jig," and the kitten ran in front to lead the dance. Ilex followed her, smiling at the sight of her multicolored pastel fur gleaming in the sunlight. He wound around others, gathering them into the chain, into the joyous celebration of his marriage.

The air sparkled with the additional benediction of a Family made whole.

Raucous Clover children played with Fams and raced up and down the beach. Vinni T'Vine spun off to join the adult dancers. He took Ilex's hand and led the dance in a gleeful caper. *That was very well done, Trif and Ilex Winterberry.*

Trif answered, *It came to us both, in a vision.*

Then you are both blessed.

We know, Ilex projected at the same time Trif did.

And they laughed together.

Her bright eyes and radiant face raised to his, and his breath stopped at the beauty of her, and his future. "I will love you always, to death and beyond."

"To death and beyond," she said, and their words echoed around them in a song.

Now for a preview of
Robin D. Owens's next novel,

Heart Match

Coming soon from Berkley Sensation!

DRUIDA CITY, CELTA,
405 years after Colonization, winter, morning before Workbell

Dufleur watched the fresh pinecone wither before her eyes and fall into dust. This experiment with time was not going at all well.

"No, not good." She wished she had her father's notes.

You want to reverse time.

She knew what she wanted to do and didn't need a cat to point it out, but managed to keep her comment between her teeth.

With a Word she dismissed the clear force field around the tube. The cylinder exploded, sparks flying. Dufleur flung her arms in front of her face, shoved back her chair. What had happened? And why now and never before?

A yowl came from her left, along with a nasty singeing odor. Fairyfoot was hopping around, the ends of her whiskers glowing red. "That was interesting," Dufleur said.

Noooo, moaned Fairyfoot, racing through the only door of the secret room into Dufleur's bedroom. *My whiskers are ugly! Horrible, horrible, horrible! How am I to judge distances with damage to my whiskers?* She jumped up and down and spat at her reflection in the spotted mirror on Dufleur's bedroom closet door.

"I'm sorry," Dufleur said. Her stomach clenched. Is this what had happened to her father's lab that fatal night? She shoved the thought aside; that would lead to emotion, and emotion had no place in touchy scientific experiments. "Want me to—"

You have done enough. Fairyfoot plopped down and began meticulously stroking each whisker with a licked paw.

Dufleur gulped and braced herself on the battered table set in the middle of the large stone room on the lowest level of Winterberry House. With a writestick, she noted down the failed results. She hadn't slowed time but had done the complete opposite—sped it up to such a rapid rate that the fresh spruce pinecone had disintegrated. There might be a use for this spell someday, if she could standardize it and incorporate it into an object people could use. But right now it was just a failure of what she really wanted to do.

A knock came at the door of her bedroom, beyond this hidden room she used for her illegal, secret experiments.

Damn, her cuz, *Guardsman* Ilex Winterberry, was here a little early to collect the gift she'd made for him and his wife.

Using a voice-projection spell she called, "One moment!" Shrugging from her lab coat at a run, she flung it onto the chair, shot into her bedroom. Then she muttered a couplet to slide the stone door of the concealed room shut and grabbed her outdoor cloak.

She opened the hall door to her cuz. "Greetyou," she said, only a little out of breath.

"Greetyou, cuz," Ilex said, smiling. He was always smiling now, his serious nature lightened by his HeartBonding to the vivacious and optimistic Trif Clover and with a baby on the way. "Trif sent me for the baby robe. Still six months before the child comes and she's wild to have the gown. And when she's anxious she gives me no peace." He sniffed and a puzzled look crossed his face.

Oh, no! She'd forgotten he was sensitive to smells. With less care than she should have, she picked up the small gown she'd finished the night before and handed it to him.

"Exquisite. Simply exquisite." He met her eyes. "This will be a treasured Family heirloom for us."

The kindness in his eyes, the affection emanating from him for her, closed her throat. She smiled back. "Thank you."

"You're ready for work? Why don't I walk you to the public carrier plinth?" He set the gown back in the box she'd pulled it from, put the lid on the box, and sealed it with a tap of his finger.

Was she acting suspicious? Guilty? He'd notice that, too.

Fairyfoot hissed. He glanced down. "My apologies for rudeness, Fairyfoot. Greetyou."

Dufleur looked down at her Fam. Her whiskers looked fine. *One word about the experiments and you find yourself a new FamWoman,* she sent privately to the cat.

Tail high, Fairyfoot left the bedroom for the basement hallway. Dufleur exited the chamber and let Ilex shut the door behind her. He sent a glance around the bedroom. He might very well know of the secret room. She hurried to the stairs that led up to the main level entryway.

"Dufleur?"

Tensing, she turned back with a strained smile that froze on her face when she saw his fingers curve over the door latch. "Yes?"

He said a short spell. "You forgot to spellshield your rooms." Now his gaze was blank. "You might want to keep your personal things . . . personal."

Her heart thumped hard. Did he have any idea she was carrying on her father's work? She wished she could do it openly, but that bitch D'Willow had made a mockery of her father's name and experiments. If anyone knew she was as fascinated with time as he had been, she'd lose all credibility and perhaps even her job. Perhaps this place where she lived and worked. Hot rage sizzled deep inside.

Ilex cleared his throat. "Our mothers can . . . pry."

She forced herself to present a calm front, to pull her mind to this lesser concern and answer him. "They're snoops, you mean."

His lips curved. "Yes." The smile didn't reach his eyes. Neither of them had good relationships with their mothers, who lived upstairs. Of course that was because neither of their mothers was a reasonable person. She spared him the knowledge that his mother, D'Winterberry, was too deep into the yar-duan liquor addiction to leave her rooms anymore.

"Your mother has paid little attention to me. As for mine," Dufleur shrugged. "Fairyfoot has been a blessing in many ways, not the least because my mother is allergic to cats. If she pries, she pays." Her smile was just as bleak as his.

He nodded.

They were out the front door and into the winter cold before Ilex spoke again. They had reached the corner and turned left. Four carrier lines stopped here, in the once noble neighborhood that was slowly disintegrating. Dufleur rode straight into CityCenter.

"Sure you don't want to teleport?" Ilex asked.

It would take too much of her psi energy, her Flair, that she would need for her daily work, as well as more experiments this evening. "I prefer not to."

He held out his hand and she put her fingers in his. "Thank you again for the lovely gift."

"You're welcome."

"Dufleur . . ."

"Yes?"

"Be careful." He dropped her hand. As she watched, he disappeared from view, teleporting back to his beloved wife and her large, optimistic family.

Dufleur had never felt so lonely.

Saille T'Willow, GreatLord T'Willow, stood with his hands clasped behind him as he stared at the cryogenics tube holding his not-quite-late MotherDam, struggling to keep his bitterness from showing.

Ruis Elder, Captain of the ancient colonist ship, *Nuada's Sword,* stood beside him. "As you can see, her life indicators are still doing well. When the Healers find a cure for her debilitating disease, we will be able to awaken her for treatment."

"I thank you for all you have done," Saille said evenly. He hadn't made any of the arrangements. *She* had, the former GreatLady T'Willow, also named Saille, who had despised him. Unlike most Celtans, she hadn't accepted death like a reasonable person, but had fought its coming . . . because she loathed him, hated the fact that he was her Heir and would take the title.

For generations the strongest Flaired person in the Willow Family had been female. Until him. His grandmother took it as a personal blow that he, a man, would be the foremost matchmaker on Celta.

Now she lay in the cryogenics tube, and deep in the fissures of her brain where a neuron still sparked with life she no doubt hoped that she would be revived. When she was, she'd reclaim everything he had . . . or struggle for power with a descendent of his. It was lowering to understand that he'd prefer that.

"Want to pull the plug?" Ruis whispered.

The phrase meant nothing to Saille. "What?"

Ruis bent down and opened a panel in the stand on which the tube rested, pointed at a thick cable. "This is her life support." Leaving the door open he stood and looked at the large woman. "I can't think this will ever work. I know it doesn't seem right to me."

Saille stared at the cable. Now it seemed to throb like a mutant gray slug. Temptation beckoned. Yes, he *yearned* to "pull the plug." But he couldn't. "She contracted with you." Paid the Captain an extortionate amount of gilt to refurbish the tube and be placed in it, kept alive before the last, fatal stage of her disease began.

Ruis tapped a forefinger on the clear material of the tube. "Sometimes rules—and contracts—must be bent to ensure justice. She'd die in, what, two weeks, if she weren't inside here?"

"That's the amount of time the Healers gave her." Saille found the laugh coming from himself sounding far too harsh. "I wouldn't be surprised if she proved them wrong." She ever was contrary.

"Arrogant," Ruis said. "I've never cared for arrogant people. She didn't negotiate with me, you know." His mouth twisted. "She knew better than that. She was one of the people who voted for my execution. Instead she caught my wife in a soft moment." He shrugged. "Or my wife's telempathy assured her that D'Willow should be spared." He looked around the gleaming metal walls of the ship. "Still, it's a drain upon Ship's power and systems, even though Ship considers this an interesting experiment."

"Spare me interesting experiments," Saille said.

"My feelings exactly." Ruis scratched his chin. "I believe in accepting death, in the soul's circling the wheel of stars into reincarnation." He waved at the tube. "This is unnatural. Our ancestors used these tubes while they traveled from one planet to a new one, not simply for life extension. Unnatural."

Saille could only agree. But he couldn't say so. "This is what she wants, and I will obey her instructions."

Ruis slanted a look at him, lifted and dropped a shoulder. "I hear your Family has welcomed you as the new head."

Now Saille could smile with real feeling. "Yes, the ladies are an affectionate bunch." He spared one last look at the mound of his MotherDam. "She was a difficult woman to live with as the disease took its toll." And for about a hundred years before that, too.

"Well, then, you have some blessings in your life."

"Many." That was the truth.

A high, giggling shriek echoed down the hallway outside the room and Ruis laughed as the metal door slid open and his year-old daughter toddled into the chamber.

Saille's smile froze. The little girl only reminded him that he had no beloved HeartMate. Yet.

Once more he glanced at his predecessor. She'd deliberately hidden his HeartMate from him. It had taken extraordinary measures—sending his barely spellshielded HeartGift out into the world—to find his HeartMate.

Now he knew who she was. Time to act.